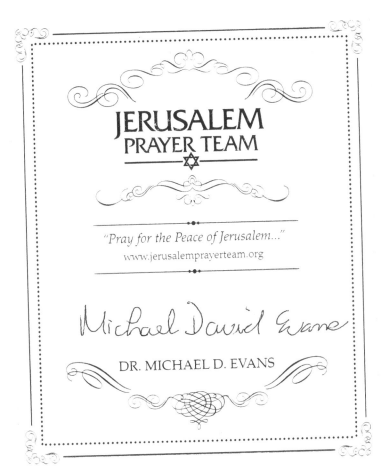

JERUSALEM
PRAYER TEAM
✡

"Pray for the Peace of Jerusalem..."
www.jerusalemprayerteam.org

Michael David Evans

DR. MICHAEL D. EVANS

HiTLER

THE MUSLiM BROTHERHOOD

AND 9/11

A NOVEL

HiTLER

THE MUSLiM BROTHERHOOD

AND 9/11

#1 *NEW YORK TIMES* BESTSELLING AUTHOR

MIKE EVANS

TIMEWORTHY
BOOKS

P.O. BOX 30000, PHOENIX, AZ 85046

Hitler, The Muslim Brotherhood, and 9/11
(a novel)

Copyright 2020 by Time Worthy Books
P. O. Box 30000
Phoenix, AZ 85046

Hardcover: 978-1-62961-225-6
Paperback: 978-1-62961-224-9
Canada: 978-1-62961-226-3

This book is a work of historical reconstruction.
The appearance of certain major historical figures was
unavoidable. All other characters, however,
are products of the author's imagination.
Any resemblance to actual persons (living or dead)
as well as their conversations is purely coincidental.

I dedicate this book to
the first responders of 9/11

who selflessly gave their lives
to save those in need.
"Greater love has no one than this,
than to lay down one's life for his friends"
(John 5:13).

List of Characters

Amin al-Husseini—Grand Mufti of Jerusalem

Kemal Hadad—Amin al-Husseini's secretary

Rashid Ali al-Kaylani—temporary prime minister of Iraq

Hasan Salama—native of the Palestinian village Qula and veteran of guerilla warfare near Nablus during the revolt

Abdul Latif—native of Jerusalem, Berlin editor of Amin al-Husseini's radio addresses

Karimeh—Amin al-Husseini's wife

Herbert Samuel—British High Commissioner and supreme authority in Palestine under the British Mandate

Joachim von Ribbentrop—Nazi Germany's foreign minister

Hassan al-Banna—an imam from Ismailia, Egypt, and founder of the Muslim Brotherhood

PRELUDE

LOGAN AIRPORT,
BOSTON, MASSACHUSETTS, USA

MOHAMMED ATTA hurried down the corridor toward the gate, checking his watch with a glance every few steps. They were late. The flight from Portland had been delayed—something about a crew change—and now they were in Boston but behind schedule. To his left was Abdulaziz al-Omari, a Saudi Arabian whom he knew from school. They had traveled together that morning, but the others—Wail al-Shehri, his brother, Waleed al-Shehri, and Satam al-Suqami—were nowhere in sight. If they weren't already on the plane, the plan was in trouble.

As the gate came into view, Atta saw that the area was empty. A wave of panic swept through the pit of his stomach, but he ignored it. Out the window he saw the airliner—a Boeing 767—still with the Jetway at its door. But there was no way to know if the others were aboard.

Atta's mind whirred. Should he cancel? Should he abandon the plan? No. His heart told him all was well. And anyway, the tickets were purchased. If the others were not onboard, he would enjoy the flight to Los Angeles and regroup from there.

He mumbled in Arabic, "I will shoot them myself if they turned coward."

Nervous and tense, Atta tried to remain calm and did his best to appear relaxed, hoping to avoid calling attention to himself. He gave his ticket to the gate attendant who printed a boarding pass, tore off the receipt portion, and handed him the rest. "Hurry! They've been waiting for you."

"It is not my fault that we are behind," Atta retorted. He hated it when women spoke to him that way.

The gate attendant ignored the comment and hustled him up the Jetway and into the plane. As Atta moved toward his assigned seat, he glanced around the passenger compartment and noted with relief that the others were present. Wail al-Shehri and his brother, Waleed al-Shehri were seated near the bulkhead, just behind first class. Satam al-Suqami was a little farther back. To his right, however, he caught sight of a man he was certain was Jewish. But something about him made Atta nervous. Before taking his seat, he caught Waleed's eye, then glanced in the man's direction. Waleed seemed to understand the gesture.

Atta squeezed into his seat and placed the seat belt across his lap. Moments later, the aircraft pushed back from the gate and rolled down the taxiway. Atta was nervous. Almost jittery. The veins in his neck throbbed and his skin felt clammy. He flexed his fingers a few times, balling them into a fist and tensing the muscles in his forearm. *Nothing to worry about,* he told himself. The others would take care of the rough stuff. He and Omari would fly the plane. That's all he needed to think about. Flying the plane.

After a pause at the end of the runway, the aircraft moved forward, picked up speed, and leapt into the air. Atta felt his back pressed against the seat and he gripped the armrest with both hands. He hated flying.

As the plane gained altitude, it banked to the right. Out the window, Atta caught sight of the coastline as it moved away. They were turning westward, he surmised. Steering to a heading that would take them toward California. He glanced around at the passengers seated near him. A smile tightened the muscles in his cheeks. They had no idea they would never reach their destination. At least, not the destination they planned.

Fifteen minutes into the flight, the seat belt sign went off and the pilot announced that beverage service would begin soon. Atta unfastened his seat belt and stood, then glanced in Waleed's direction. Of the three men brought onboard for muscle, Waleed was his favorite and the one in whom he had the most confidence. A look, a gesture, a nod was all it took to communicate with him and he never hesitated. He acted.

Without lingering, Atta stepped into the aisle and started toward the cockpit door. He reached it just as two attendants appeared in first class with a beverage cart. One moved toward him, a look of concern on her face, but before she could act or speak, Waleed grabbed her arms and pinned them behind her back while Wail secured her wrists with a zip tie.

Atta heard a commotion behind him, then a scream, and knew that Waleed had taken care of the Jew. Nothing would stop them now. He grasped the knob for the cockpit door with his right hand, gave it a twist, and pushed. The door opened into the cockpit and the four of them rushed inside. Wail slit the pilot's throat with a box cutter. Satam did the same to the copilot. Blood gushed from the gaping wounds in their necks, spilled down their clothes, and dripped onto the deck. Waleed unbuckled the pilot's harness and dragged his body from the seat, then threw it on the flight deck to block the door. Satam did the same with the copilot. And while they did that, Atta climbed into the pilot's seat.

Settled in the seat, Atta grasped the wheel with both hands and felt the weight of the plane pull against his arms as the autopilot disengaged and the flight controls came alive. A smile turned up the corners of his mouth as he banked the plane sharply to the left.

While the aircraft slowly moved in that direction, Atta glanced across the instrument panel and found it a bewildering set of screens, gauges, and panels. He'd trained for months on a simulator at the school in Florida and was certain he understood what they all meant. One for the navigation system. Another for the engine controls. A dozen more he'd determined were unnecessary and had quickly forgotten. But now, in the moment when it all counted, he felt confused. Atta closed his eyes, took a deep breath, and forced his body to relax. He knew this. He had read the manuals. He could figure it out.

Atta opened his eyes and glanced once more across the indicators on the panel. The navigation display appeared to be in map mode and there was a button to press to change it. Somewhere. Somehow. The adrenaline coursing through his body caused his thoughts to bounce from one to the next, to the next.

"Compass," he snarled. "Where's the compass?" The flight instructor had told him in an offhanded, almost joking manner that if all else failed he could use the magnetic compass. But where was it? His palms were sweaty, and he felt the fabric of his shirt stick to the skin of his back. Everyone had performed as planned. They were in control. Now the entire operation rested on him and—

Just then he caught sight of the compass—a round black ball with white letters and numbers—mounted at the top of the windshield, near the center. Atta breathed a sigh of relief and hoped the others hadn't noticed how desperate he'd been.

Using the compass as his guide, he set the plane on a course to the south. Off to the left, far in the distance, the water of the Atlantic Ocean was barely visible. He turned the craft farther in that direction, pointing it more southeasterly on a path toward the coastline.

Minutes later, as the ocean drew nearer, Atta banked the plane to the right and followed the water, keeping it just off his left shoulder and hoping not to fly past the city. It all looked much smaller from twenty thousand feet.

Fifteen minutes later, New York City came into view. Satam pointed over Atta's shoulder. "Look. That is the city."

Atta smiled and pushed the wheel forward, causing the plane to gradually descend. "Not too much," Omari cautioned. "Not yet. We must get all the way there."

"I know," Atta growled. "I've done this many times in practice."

Over Yonkers, the Twin Towers of the World Trade Center came into view, standing stark and angular against the clear blue sky.

"There it is!" Omari exclaimed. "There it is!"

"Allahu Akbar!" Atta shouted and the others picked it up as a chant. "Allahu Akbar! Allahu Akbar! God is great! God is great!" All the while, the Trade Center loomed larger and larger in the airplane's windshield.

ONE

JERUSALEM 1908

THE GRAY LIGHT OF DAWN filtered through a window to the left as Mohammed Amin al-Husseini, eleven years old, stood at the door to his father's bedroom. The light cast a soft glow over his father, Mohammed Tahir al-Husseini, who was lying in bed. According to his mother, his father had not long to live and the young boy found it difficult to see him like this. He'd been so powerful, so determined, and now he was reduced to a feeble shell of himself, unable to do more than lift his head to eat.

For as long as Amin could remember, his father had been the ranking qadi and the chief justice of the Sharia court in Jerusalem. The Hanafi Mufti of Jerusalem. A powerful man. Qualified to render binding opinions regarding the application of Sharia law to daily life. The one who told others how the Quran applied to events of the day.

Not only that, he sat on the Committee of A'ayan, which, among other things, scrutinized sales of land in Jerusalem to foreigners. Since 1897, when he first joined the committee, he had effectively stopped the sale of Ottoman land to Jews wanting to emigrate to Palestine. But that year, with his illness growing steadily more severe, his influence seemed to wane. More Jews than ever before found their way into Palestine, sponsored and coordinated by the World Zionist Organization. That year, also, the Jews established the Jewish Agency to oversee their effort. Housed in a ramshackle red building on the outskirts of Jaffa, the Agency was operated by Arthur Ruppin and paid for by someone named Rothschild who, based on comments from his father, Amin thought must have lots of money.

"The Jews are always looking for one more Arab willing to sell his soul to the infidels," Amin's father explained. "One more Arab willing to give up his land to the Jews." It had been a constant battle and right then, staring at his father as he lay in bed, Amin wondered if the struggle against the Jews was to blame for his father's condition. The Jews stole Arab land. Now they were stealing his father.

As the young Amin al-Husseini stared at his father, he remembered stories the old man told him. Of an Arab kingdom from the past ruled by daring men who vanquished every foe, even the apostate Europeans who dared to come near Arab lands. Stories of Islamic scholars whose work created the foundations of mathematics, science, and astronomy. All of it a gift from Allah to his people. A gesture of blessing for their obedience in conquering the land, imposing Sharia law as far as their reach allowed, establishing a human order according to Allah's divine word, worshipping him in righteousness and truth. That was the way Allah intended it to be, his people ruling and reigning over—

Just then, the old man's eyes popped open and he looked over at Amin, then motioned for him to come closer. With fear and trepidation Amin approached the bed, but halted a few steps away. Still the old man urged him closer and, when Amin was within arm's reach, took the boy by the forearm and drew him even closer. Standing against the edge of the bed, the old man's body brushing against his hip, Amin smelled the musky scent of his father and the stale bedclothes wrapped around him.

The old man looked up at him with a smile. "You must be strong in the days that are to come."

Amin nodded. "I will do my best to look after Mother."

"I am sure you will," the old man replied. "But I am thinking far beyond the immediacy of the moment."

Amin frowned. "I do not understand."

The old man nodded. "I know. But someday, when you are a man, you will take my place. When that time comes, you must not be afraid. You must discharge the duties of our office with knowledge, wisdom, and discipline, but never with fear."

"Yes, Father," Amin replied.

"And above all, you must not allow the Jews to take the land."

"But shouldn't Kamil do this? He is the oldest."

The old man sighed. "Kamil will hold the seat, but only until you are old enough to accept it. He is a good man, but he lacks the vision for what must be done."

"And what is it that must be done?"

The old man gestured for him to lean closer and tugged at his arm. Amin leaned down, his head turned to the side to avoid the old man's hot, stale breath. His ear, though, was pressed near the old man's lips. "We must kill them all," the old man urged in an angry, coarse whisper.

Amin shrank back, startled by what he just heard, but the old man gripped Amin's forearm tighter and focused his gaze with intensity. "All of them," he insisted, using his finger in a pointed gesture. "Every last Jew must die. Or they will kill us all." He stared at the young boy intently, as if to emphasize his point, and held his gaze for what seemed like a long time, and only when Amin nodded in approval did he let go.

With his point made, the old man seemed to relax and a smile returned to his face. "When you are older, you will remember this moment and know I am right. And when that day comes, you will take courage. Allah is well pleased with you, Amin. He is very well pleased."

The old man rested his hands on his chest and closed his eyes. Moments later, Amin heard the rhythmic sound of his father's breathing as he drifted off to sleep. He stood there watching, not understanding anything his father had said except the last of it. That Allah was very pleased with him. That part left him feeling warm and comfortable inside. Knowing that Allah was pleased made the mystery of his father's words seem like a future filled with hope. And right then, young Amin al-Husseini very much needed hope.

A few nights later, Amin was awakened by the sound of his mother's mournful wail. Terrified by it, he slid farther down in bed, the covers pulled over his head, and knew that his father had died.

✦ ✦ ✦ ✦ ✦

The death of Amin's father did little to change his daily routine. He still awakened before dawn, just as always, and prepared himself for the day. As the sun rose above Jerusalem, he faced toward the Qibla—the Kaaba mosque in Mecca—as required by the Quran. He knew the direction to face by the location of a mark his father had made for him on the bedroom wall; a mark determined by using an astrolabe.

Oriented toward the Qibla, Amin raised his hands to shoulder height with his palms turned out and said the intention, the first act of Morning Prayer. That was followed by the Salah, also prayed while standing, then the Ruku, and on through the morning ritual. When his religious duty was complete, he ate breakfast and departed for school.

That was the same morning routine Amin had followed for as long as he could remember. None of that changed with his father's death except that he no longer felt the old man's presence in the house or heard the rumble of his voice as he prayed in the next room. But one thing—one very important thing—had changed.

When Mohammed Tahir al-Husseini was a young man, he married and had a family that included seven daughters and one son, Kamil. By the time Tahir was sixty years old, his children from that marriage were adults with families of their own. But the year Tahir turned sixty, his first wife died. Not long after she was buried, he married again to a woman named Mahbuba, who was almost forty years younger than he. With Mahbuba, Tahir produced one child each year for the next eight years, one of whom was Amin, the oldest of the second group.

Life was good for Amin and, owing to his father's position and the many generations his family had lived in Jerusalem, he and his siblings enjoyed many privileges. But now, with his father no longer alive, Amin knew he would come under the influence of Kamil, his father's oldest son by his first wife, who was almost certain to inherit his father's position as Mufti.

Many years separated Amin from Kamil. They saw each other on family occasions and got along well, but they had a different mother and did not grow up together. Amin was concerned about what that might mean for his future and especially how he, his mother, and his siblings would fare. At his father's death, his father's business interests fell to Kamil, and much of what might happen to Amin would depend on just how honorable Kamil proved to be. Amin had heard many stories of older brothers brutalizing younger siblings in just such a situation and he worried the same might happen to him.

Amin attended the Rashidiya School located near Herod's Gate. A center of learning for Muslim boys in East Jerusalem, the school taught a version of Salafi Islam promoted by Rashid Rida, an Egyptian cleric. Salafism promoted a return to the Islamic faith of the Salaf—the first three generations of Muslim leaders, which the Salafists viewed as the true and correct form of Islam. Begun in the eighteenth century by Muhammad ibn Abd al-Wahhab, the Salafi movement was primarily a reaction to innovation among Islamic groups and the encroachment of Western lifestyle on popular Islamic culture. In response, Salafists sought a return to strict adherence to Sharia law and the practice of regular worship.

Teachers at the Rashidiya School did their best to impress upon their students the necessity of following a strict view of Islam while not squelching the youthful enthusiasm of their pupils. Their demand for rigorous study, devoted worship, and a life of contemplation struck some of Amin's fellow students as more than necessary. Amin, however, found it liberating and invigorating. He also enjoyed the social interaction the school afforded.

Two months after the family's mourning ended, Amin and his friend, Nafez Musallam, sat outside the school during an afternoon break. As they enjoyed the warm sunshine, Amin broached the subject of his worries regarding his homelife and future. Nafez listened patiently, then said, "Do not to worry. Your brother is smart. He will do the right thing."

"I am not so sure of that," Amin replied.

Nafez shrugged. "Even if he does not, you are smart and you pay attention to the smallest detail. Allah will easily take you to your destiny."

Amin frowned. "You say that as if you know it to be true."

"Yes," Nafez nodded. "I do. Because it *is* true."

"But how do you know it is true? How do you know I even have a destiny? And if I do, how do you know that Allah will take me to it?"

Nafez smiled. "My father tells me this every day."

"And what does it mean?"

Nafez folded his arms across his chest. "My father tells me that I should do the next thing and not worry about the question of life and purpose and meaning. He says those questions are too big for me now. That I have not lived long enough for Allah to reveal things easily. Only just the next thing. If I do the next thing, Allah will combine all of the 'next things' into a path. But it will only become visible to me when I have lived long enough to look back and see how he has led me."

The words seemed to find a place in Amin's soul. He was about to ask another question when one of their classmates, Saleem Namir, appeared. Saleem was from a minor branch of the Nashashibi clan, a prominent Arab family of merchants and landowners. Some of Namir's relatives were the ones who wanted to sell their land to Jews and were blocked by Amin's father. "It is worthless land," they argued. "It is only right that we charge the Jews twice what it is worth and watch them die trying to make a living from it." Amin's father had been unpersuaded by that argument and adamant in his opposition to the Nashashibi sales, for which Namir's family, and many members of the extended clan, resented him deeply.

Namir caught Amin's eyes. "I hear your brother is among those being considered for the position of mufti."

"Yes," Amin replied. He did not like the look on Namir's face and was certain Namir was looking for trouble. "What of it?"

"He is too young and inexperienced for a position like that," Namir said.

"He has been a qadi for many years."

"Yes, but everyone knows only the Nashashibi have the intellect for responsibility of the mufti's position."

Namir's words burned deep inside Amin. An insult to Kamil was bad enough, but the comment about intelligence was a slap at Amin's father. He had been the Mufti of Jerusalem for a long time and now one of the Nashashibi—perhaps all of them—was saying his father was not intelligent enough to hold that position in his own right and had gained it by nefarious means.

Amin's neck stiffened. The veins in his neck throbbed and he clinched his fist. "You insult my father," he growled.

"Your father is dead." Namir smirked. "And it is long past time for the Nashashibi to take back what is rightfully theirs."

Surely, Namir was repeating words he had heard from his kinsmen. Baseless, slanderous accusations born of envy and greed. But one who repeats the words of another makes himself liable for the import of them just the same as if they came from his own mind, and as the last phrase slipped from Namir's lips, Amin lunged for him. He grabbed Namir by the hair, pulled his head down to his side, and in rapid succession punched him three times in the face. He was about to add a fourth when Nafez stepped between them.

"It is enough, Amin," Nafez shouted. "It is enough!"

Amin let go and Namir took a step back. "You will pay for this," he snarled.

"Insult my family again," Amin replied, "and you will pay with your life."

They were but juveniles. Mere boys on the school ground. But everyone who heard Amin that day knew he meant every word of what he said. The look on Nafez's face said he did, too.

✦ ✦ ✦ ✦ ✦

A few months later, the Jerusalem Hanafi Ulama, a group of scholars in the Hanafi school of Quran tradition, who sat as Sharia judges in Jerusalem, gathered to consider a successor to Mohammed Tahir al-Husseini. The two leading contenders were Tahir's oldest son, Kamil al-Husseini, and Raghib al-Nashashibi, a member of the rival Nashashibi clan. After two days of deliberation, the Ulama chose Tahir's oldest son, Kamil. He was designated Hanafi Mufti and took his father's seat on the Sharia court.

The next day, after the Ulama made its decision, Amin confronted Namir at school, taunting him about his brother's appointment as mufti. "It was only because of sympathy and a bribe," Namir sneered.

"A bribe?" Amin exclaimed.

"Yes," Namir replied coldly. "Everyone knows the Husseini have no hope of success without corrupting those in power."

As before, a fight quickly followed. This time, however, Nafez stood back and let the two go at it. But when Amin had Namir pinned to the ground, pummeling him repeatedly with blows to the head, Nafez became worried that Amin might actually follow through on the earlier threat and beat Namir to death. With the ease and self-assurance only a friend could show, he grabbed Amin with both arms around his chest and lifted him off Namir. "That's enough."

"I'll kill him!" Amin shouted.

"I know," Nafez replied. "That is why you must stop."

Reluctantly, Amin allowed his body to relax and stood watching from a safe distance while Namir scrambled to his feet and started in the opposite direction.

"Let him go," Nafez advised. "Pay no attention to what he says."

"He's an idiot," Amin retorted. "Just like everyone in his family."

"I don't think he will ever like you," Nafez said.

"Yes," Amin replied. "And I don't care. I just don't care."

TWO

THE FOLLOWING YEAR, Hussein al-Husseini, Kamil and Amin's uncle, was chosen as mayor of Jerusalem. By tradition, the post had been held by a member of the Husseini family for many generations, and Hussein's election to the office was viewed by the family as a foregone conclusion. After all, they had enjoyed a longstanding tradition of influence in Jerusalem affairs and, indeed, in the affairs of Palestine and the region they knew as Greater Syria—an area comprised of Syria, Lebanon, Palestine, and Transjordan. As might be expected, members of the Nashashibi clan held a different view and ran candidates against the Husseini, but to no avail. Hussein al-Husseini won the position by a wide margin.

With family members holding the positions of mufti and mayor, two of the most important in Jerusalem religion and politics, Amin's life followed the predictably stable pattern he had known before. Moreover, Kamil was nice to him, even if distant, and, as Nafez had suggested, the relationship between the two brothers proved to be not as difficult as Amin thought it might be.

His father still was gone but living in his brother's shadow had its advantages, at least at first.

Kamil received the reproach of the Nashashibi, not Amin, and Kamil bore the brunt of criticism from other scholars who sometimes disagreed with his rulings. But it was Kamil who received the approbation and praise from the men of the city, something in which he seemed to take great pleasure.

As the days passed, however, the weakness Amin's father had pointed out on his deathbed became evident. Kamil was a good man, but he was not as decisive as their father, and when difficult things had to be done, he wasted time searching for a way around it rather than simply doing it.

None of that situation, or of Amin's growing frustration, was lost on Mahbuba, Amin's mother. One evening, as she sat at the table with him while he prepared for the next day's school lesson, she said, "You must learn all you can and become a scholar. Like your father."

"But that would require attending university," Amin replied.

Mahbuba nodded. "And you think that is a problem?"

"It costs money."

"I will find a way to pay," she assured.

"And I would have to leave Jerusalem."

She glanced away. "We all must leave from time to time."

"You left Jerusalem?"

"For a time. Before I knew your father, I went to live in Damascus."

"Were you afraid?"

Mahbuba frowned. "Why would I be afraid?"

"Isn't Damascus a large city?"

"No larger than Jerusalem. And besides, I lived with my uncle."

"You think I should go away, too?"

Mahbuba reached across the table and took his hand, then

looked him in the eye. "I think you have not much of a future living here in Jerusalem in the shadow of your father's family."

"I love my family."

"Yes, but there are too many of them here. And too many who are ahead of you in line."

"Where would I go?"

"You should study in Cairo," Mahbuba answered firmly. "At Al-Azhar University."

"You know of this school?"

"I have made inquiries, and I think it is best for you."

Amin shook his head. "I have never heard of it."

"Ask your teachers," she suggested. "I am certain they will tell you just as I have. It is a good school."

The next day, Amin did as his mother suggested and asked his teachers about Al-Azhar University. All of them told him what a great school it was and how all the classes were taught by the best minds of Egypt.

Later that day, Amin told Nafez about his mother's wish for him to attend the university in Cairo. To his surprise, Nafez knew about the school, too. "My uncle studied at Al-Azhar University."

"Your uncle?"

"You sound surprised."

"Your uncle is a carpenter."

Nafez was amused. "Not that uncle. The one who studied in Egypt is Emile. My father's brother."

"I have never heard of him."

"He does not live here now."

"Where does he live?"

"In Syria."

"Why did he go to Cairo to school?"

"His father sent him there because of some trouble he faced, but that is where the Rida teach and he met them."

"Rashid Rida?"

"Yes. He taught my uncle."

Amin's eyes opened wider. Rida was a Salafi cleric and a member of the clan for whom their school in Jerusalem was named. "He studied under the Rida?"

"Yes. Why do you keep asking me?"

"You never told me this before."

"The subject never came up and he is still under suspicion for the trouble, so we do not talk about it much."

"So, going to Cairo is not a bad thing."

"No, it could be a very good thing for you. Perhaps you could learn from Rashid Rida, too." Nafez smiled at Amin. "Perhaps this is your destiny opening up for you." The comment seemed to find a place in Amin's soul.

The following year, Amin turned fifteen. A month after his birthday, a cousin went with him from Jerusalem to Cairo and helped him enroll at Al-Azhar University. The process was not difficult, but his mother insisted that someone older should accompany him.

Amin found lodging in the home of a family who lived near the school. Two classmates, Kemal Hadad and Hasan Salama, lived there, too. Hadad was acquainted with Nafez's older brother and Salama was someone Amin had seen from time to time in Jerusalem but never really met. The three got along well and quickly grew to be friends.

Salama attended the university for a short time the previous year, but not long after arriving in Cairo he had been introduced to Rashid Rida. He attended several of Rida's open lectures and remained behind a few times to ask questions. Rida was impressed and invited him to join their school as a student. Salama dropped out of the university in the spring of that year and began attending class with Rida.

"Perhaps you would like to hear one of Rida's lectures," Salama suggested. Amin was eager to give it a try.

Rida's public presentation was designed as a general overview of his thoughts and presented as a way of enticing potential students to express their interest. Salama and Amin attended it together. At the conclusion of that lecture, Salama introduced Amin to him. That introduction led to an extended conversation about Amin's ideas on the effects of Jewish immigration to Palestine. "No one invited them," he said. "And yet, the Ottomans, who claim to be our friends, continue to sell them their land."

"You are interested in Palestinian politics?"

"I am interested in Arab politics and the propagation of Islam."

Rida smiled. "The only way to accomplish that goal—the spread of Islam and the establishment of an Arab state—is to combine Islam with Arab nationalism. To do that, we need a modernization of Islam."

Amin shook his head. "I am not in favor of changing our beliefs."

"No, no," Rida responded. "Not our beliefs. And not our practices. Only in the way we view those who disagree with us."

"The infidels?"

Rida placed his hand on Amin's shoulder. "You misunderstand. Our quarrel is not with the outside world. Our contention is among ourselves. Islam contains a wide variety of beliefs and practices. If we are to prevail in the struggle of peoples, we must find a way to accommodate the breadth of Islamic theological perspective, but always within a framework of devotion to Allah."

Amin was intrigued by the idea—Islam with broad appeal and tolerance for differences of opinion regarding the Quran, in a framework of true belief and actual observance, combined with political expression in the form of an Islamic kingdom. Personal belief and corporate expression in Islamic revivalism, stressing regular prayer and fasting, and an end to Muslim participation in the corruption of the West.

Over the next several weeks, Amin returned again and again to hear Rida's lectures. As he did, an arrangement of ideas formed in his mind. Of piety and an Arabic state but one that could get along with the Ottomans, perhaps as a way of coaxing them into keeping the Jews out of Palestine. A way of strengthening Arabs and uniting them, as well as a way of halting the Jews without the need for open conflict. Just convince the Ottomans to stop allowing them entry. To stop giving the Jews a place.

Amin talked about his views with his fellow students. "We must make the Arab position unassailably righteous and politically unavoidable." Not many seemed to understand but he kept repeating himself at every opportunity. Suggesting to those who would listen that they could reestablish the Arab kingdom of old. The way it used to be. The way it appeared in the stories his father told him.

As Amin's ideas took shape, Rida mentioned a man named Izz ad-Din al-Qassam. "He is from Jableh, Syria. Qassam was a student of mine a few years ago. He has ideas about Palestine and the Jews, also. Perhaps you will find a way to discuss your ideas with him."

✦ ✦ ✦ ✦ ✦

A few months later, during a break at the university, Amin visited Jerusalem. While there, he took a few days away and traveled to Jableh to meet Qassam. During Friday prayers, he listened while Qassam told about an invasion of Libya being carried on at that moment by the Italians. This was the sort of Western intervention that Amin sought to oppose, and as Qassam railed against it, Amin felt his entire being energized and empowered. "Infidels," Qassam said, "are attempting to impose their will on land given to us by Allah. We need volunteers to wage jihad against the invading Italians in Libya. Volunteers to become the mujahideen—those who engage in jihad."

Afterward, they talked most of the afternoon and Qassam, though older and far more experienced, gave Amin his time and full attention. For the remainder of his stay in Jableh, Amin thought of nothing but joining the mujahideen. Of following Qassam to Libya. Of cleansing the land of Western corruption.

When he returned to Jerusalem, Amin continued to talk of the things he had learned from Rida in Egypt and experienced in Syria while visiting with Qassam. He talked to Nafez at length about the need to join the fight against the West. When Nafez tired of hearing it he spoke with Salama, who also had come to Jerusalem during the break. Amin was energized with purpose and meaning in a way he had not felt before and it filled him with a sense of wonder and excitement. Mahbuba, his mother, however, was filled with the opposite and worried that he might not live long if he pursued that path.

To address her fears, Mahbuba sent for Kamil and invited him to her home for tea. They met a few days later. "You must speak with your brother Amin," she began.

"Why?" Kamil frowned. "What is the matter?"

"Those ideas of his. They are leading him in the wrong direction."

Kamil appeared perplexed. "Who is leading him?"

"The ideas in his head. About fighting in Libya against the Italians. About waging war against Western corruption. About stopping the Jews by force."

A relaxed expression swept over Kamil and he smiled. "He has always thought of those things. He got them from our father."

"Yes," she acknowledged, "but now he has found others who agree with him, and the things they say to him only encourages him."

"What people?"

"In Cairo, he met a boy named Salama who introduced Amin to Rashid Rida."

"Ahh," Kamil nodded thoughtfully. "The Salafi."

"The Wahabi," Mahbuba said with disdain.

"Yes."

Mahbuba shook her head with disgust. "They make themselves out to be so righteous, but Amin is young and does not know what they really are like."

"I understand they can be quite brutal in the imposition of Sharia."

"Will you talk to him?"

"What would you like for me to say?"

"Convince him that the true path to change is through changing minds, not through war."

"You wish for him to follow the life of a cleric?"

"Preferably, a scholar."

"He already attends university."

"He needs to attend school somewhere else."

"I think the best option for him is to follow the path of our father and become a cleric."

"Perhaps," Mahbuba conceded. "Whatever it takes to divert him from the direction he is going."

The following day, Kamil returned to the house and found Amin studying at the kitchen table. As casually as possible, he struck up a conversation with him about school and life in Cairo, then turned the conversation toward the topic foremost on his mind. "I understand you have been to Syria."

"Yes."

"And you visited with Qassam."

"You know Qassam?"

"Only a few have not heard of him."

"You have heard his call for the mujahideen to join him in fighting the Italians?"

Kamil nodded. "Yes, but there is something you must know."

"Mother does not want me to go."

"No. She does not. But you already know that."

"She has managed to convey that message."

"Look. I know you want to be involved, but Qassam has military experience you do not have. And he is looking for men who are similarly trained."

"He did not say that in his address."

"No. But did you notice the ones who volunteered?"

"Yes."

"And I'm sure they were older."

"Most of them."

"He is looking for men who have military experience."

"I spoke with Qassam."

"You met him?"

"I met him and then we talked for almost an entire afternoon."

"And in that time, did he invite you to join him?"

"No."

"That is because he could see you are young, and even he knows the best place for you is in the university."

"I suppose."

"You have not yet experienced a Hajj, either."

"Many have not taken the traditional pilgrimage to Mecca."

"That is true. But that is something you can do to help yourself. Attend university and make the pilgrimage."

"And that would make me more useful to Allah?"

"Yes."

"Perhaps you are right."

"I know I am. And if you will do these things, I will pay your expenses for the Hajj."

The Hajj was a religious pilgrimage to the Kaaba—the house of Allah—in Mecca, a city on the Arabian coast near the Red Sea. Making that trek at least once is required of all Muslims. Once at the Kaaba, pilgrims participate in a week-long rite held in the final week of the Islamic year.

When Amin turned sixteen, he completed the pilgrimage to Mecca and received the title Hajj. Kamil paid for the trip. As his mother hoped, the experience turned Amin's mind from fighting alongside Qassam to the life of a theological scholar. Shortly after completing the Hajj, Amin transferred his educational pursuits from Cairo to Istanbul, where he studied at Istanbul University. Saleem Namir, from the rival Nashashibi clan, also was a student there.

In order to make money, Amin advertised as a language tutor willing to help students of any race or country. Students came to Istanbul from far and wide, but not many of them understood the Arabic-Turkic language used in class. One person who responded to his advertisements was David Grün, a Jewish law student from Poland. Like many others, Grün came to Istanbul intending to study law but his lack of language preparation made class difficult. When he responded to Amin's advertisement, he brought a friend, Yitzhak Ben-Zvi, who also needed help in learning the Arabic-Turkic language used in class.

For a moment, Amin was confronted by a moral dilemma. Grün and Ben-Zvi were Jews. They were in Istanbul, an Ottoman city, to gain an education. And Amin had more than a suspicion that they intended to reside in Palestine once their studies were finished. Still, both men offered to pay cash for Amin's services and he sorely needed the money. Principle or food. Principle or a place to live.

In the end, making a choice did not take long and the lessons began that very day. Besides which practicality presented itself to both sides. The Arab had to accept the Jew's money to reach his goal, and the Jew had to accept the Arab's assistance to reach his. Neither could gain anything by denying the other what he had to offer. And besides, he was not selling them land in Palestine, merely the ability to communicate. Moreover, an amicable acquaintance across ethnic lines might prove valuable in the future.

Usually Amin gave tutorial lessons in his room, but one day he met Grün and Ben-Zvi at a café. While they sipped coffee and reviewed the daily language lesson, Saleem Namir arrived. Namir did not know Grün but he noticed that Grün was a Jew. "You talk about them all day as if they are swine, and then you drink coffee with them as if they are your friends? Is that what the Husseini do?"

"Saleem," Amin replied, "this is none of your business."

"He is giving us language lessons," Grün explained.

Namir glared at him. "I didn't ask you, Jew."

Grün stood and Namir stepped closer, as if to strike him, but Amin rose from his chair and came between them. "As I said," Amin stared directly into Namir's eyes, "this is none of your business."

"We will see what they say about this when they learn the Mufti of Jerusalem's brother is helping Jews." In a huff, Namir turned away and soon left the café.

Amin returned to his seat. "Pay no attention to him."

"Who is he?" Ben-Zvi asked.

"He is Saleem Namir, a member of the Nashashibi clan."

"I have heard of them," Grün nodded. "Merchants in Jerusalem."

"Yes. And they think that their success in selling goods qualifies them for any position they desire."

"Was he correct?" Grün asked. "Is your brother the Mufti of Jerusalem?"

"Yes," Amin said. "But that is my brother's job. Mine is the position of tutor." Amin gestured to the notepads on the table. "Let us return to our lesson."

Ben-Zvi took a sip from his cup. "And to our coffee."

Amin smiled. "Yes. And to our coffee. It is very good here, which is why I wanted us to meet here."

The dustup with Namir unsettled Amin and he wondered whether the Nashashibi would use it in an attempt to make trouble for Kamil. It all proved academic, though. Before any of them concluded their studies in Istanbul, war broke out between Germany, France, Russia, England, and the Ottoman Empire—the Great War, as they would call it: a war to end all wars.

With the world choosing sides, Amin found his desire to defend the Arab cause with arms re-ignited. "The Ottomans may not be perfect, but at least they are not European. And the Europeans will never embrace Islam or Arabs. They saw in the past what we are capable of and they will never allow us to achieve that greatness again. Certainly not without opposing it." Now the situation was compounded even further by the discovery of oil in the region.

Without asking his mother or consulting his brother, Amin enlisted in the Ottoman army. When it was learned he'd attended university in Cairo and Istanbul—and when it was known that he was brother to the current Mufti of Jerusalem—he was commissioned as an artillery officer.

THREE

AS THE GREAT WAR intensified, the British War Office sought an increased military presence in Egypt as a means of hemming in Ottoman expansion and creating a front from which they could first contain, then gradually destroy, the Axis presence in the East. Doing that required the approval of Egypt's King Fuad. After several rounds of negotiations, Fuad agreed to permit a British military presence in exchange for the payment of a sizeable subsidy. As was its practice, British authorities readily accepted Fuad's terms, and appropriate sums were transferred on a regular and continual basis.

Once arrangements with King Fuad were concluded, British troops and naval vessels began arriving in great numbers. Soon, Cairo, Alexandria, and all Egypt's major cities and towns were crawling with British soldiers, sailors, and the required civilian support staff.

With the buildup of troops underway in North Africa, the British turned to the second prong of their Middle Eastern strategy: finding Arab allies willing to seize upon the war as an opportunity to revolt against the Ottoman Empire. It seemed like a perfectly sound approach at the time. After all, for centuries the Ottomans, who were not Arab but Turk, had imposed their will on Arabs living in the region. Surely the native population would jump at the chance to throw off the yoke of domination and assert their independence.

To that end, British General Gilbert Clayton was dispatched to Cairo to establish a military intelligence unit. He placed Stewart Newcombe in charge of recruiting personnel. Newcombe prevailed on a friend, T. E. Lawrence, then serving at the rank of second lieutenant, to join him.

Lawrence was a graduate of Oxford University, where he studied archaeology, primarily pertaining to Syria. In pursuit of his education, he'd spent considerable time trekking through the region and working on archeological digs. He was familiar with the people and got along well with them. In fact, he very much admired the Arabs of the Middle East and developed a proficiency in Arabic and several tribal dialects used by the Bedouins that plied the desert trade routes between Damascus and the Red Sea.

Prior to being assigned to Clayton and Newcombe, Lawrence had worked in the War Cabinet's mapping department in London. Consequently, when he arrived in Egypt, he was placed in charge of the intelligence unit's mapping room. His expertise, however, reached far beyond mere geography, a fact that quickly became obvious. Within a matter of weeks, he was acknowledged as the intelligence unit's foremost authority on the region.

While working in the mapping room, Lawrence learned of the British interest in obtaining the cooperation of the Arabs in the fight against the Ottoman Empire. He also learned that Ibn Saud, leader of the Saudi tribe that controlled the Najd and about a third of the Arab population of Arabia, had recently defeated their primary rival, the Rashid, a tribe loyal to the Ottomans. With that victory, Saud gained control over Riyadh, one of the principal cities of the peninsula. Now he was attempting to exert authority over the entire northern section.

To Lawrence, Ibn Saud and the Saudi clan seemed like a perfect match for the British Middle Eastern strategy. The Saudi were organized, intentional, and led by proven, battle-tested commanders. In addition, they controlled a portion of the peninsula known to hold vast oil reserves, a commodity the British sorely lacked.

When Lawrence approached Newcombe with the suggestion that they attempt to win the Saudis to the British cause, Newcombe readily agreed. He took the suggestion to General Clayton, who immediately understood the benefits the Saudis could provide and approved an operation to explore the matter with Ibn Saud in person. Owing to his Middle Eastern expertise and language skills, Lawrence was assigned that task and soon found himself on the way to Riyadh to meet the Saudis.

The meeting took place in a tent at a camp outside Riyahd. Ibn Saud was reclining against a pillow on the carpeted flight deck. Lawrence joined him and, after tea and dates, outlined the reason for his visit. Saud listened politely, then spoke, "It is true, we are committed to establishing control of the entire peninsula, as is our right as native peoples. And we would not be opposed to reestablishing a Muslim kingdom throughout all of Palestine and Mesopotamia. But we do not wish to be involved with Western powers."

"They can offer you support," Lawrence suggested. "Money. Weapons. Information about your enemies that would be of great advantage to you."

Saud nodded. "All of what you say is true. But what you have not said is what the Western powers would want in return."

"They wish to defeat the Ottomans. That is all."

"And they wish to have our oil."

That was an unavoidable fact and Lawrence knew it. "The British, whom I represent, would like access to your oil, but they do not wish to steal it from you." He wasn't sure that was correct but there was nothing else he could say. "They want merely the opportunity to negotiate a fair price under acceptable terms."

A smile spread across Saud's face. "That is what they always say at the beginning, but once they are here they will never leave. This is how it has been throughout all of Africa. India too. They come and they do not leave. We will not recognize European control over Muslim lands."

They continued to discuss the matter, but the longer they talked the more Lawrence realized he was not dealing with the typical Arab. Most would argue awhile, then tell you what they thought you wanted to hear. They wouldn't follow through, necessarily, but they would end the conversation politely by giving in to your side of the argument. Ibn Saud was not like that. "We wish you no personal ill will," he said finally. "But we are not interested in British promises or British actions. European powers are only interested in their own pursuits, which, in this instance, do not coincide with our own. You want Arab support for British purposes, not for Arab purposes. We are not interested in that arrangement."

With Ibn Saud avoiding the war, General Clayton and his team of strategists turned their attention to the Arab peninsula's other major power, the Sharif of Mecca. Traditionally a member of the Hashemite family, the Sharif ruled a narrow strip of Arabia that lay along the Red Sea known as the Hejaz. He also served as caretaker of Mecca and Medina, Islam's most holy sites. The current Sharif was Hussein Hashemi. As before, Clayton assigned Lawrence to broach the subject of an alliance with the Sharif.

In preparation for that meeting, Lawrence learned that the Sharif had three sons—Abdullah, Ali, and Faisal—who had been attempting to organize an army to assert the Sharif's dominance over the Arabian Peninsula. The Sharif's interests, however, were in direct conflict with those of Ibn Saud, and in the few confrontations between the two sides, the Saudis had proved superior.

Lawrence thought that the British might be able to exploit the Sharif's competitive nature and use his followers to create a force capable of inflicting damage on the Ottomans. The arrangement would not be as advantageous as the one he had proposed to Ibn Saud, but workable nonetheless. The British would help the Sharif; he would help the British. Lawrence was encouraged in that regard when he discovered a series of secret messages that had passed between the Sharif's second-oldest son, Abdullah, and Lord Kitchener, the British consul general to Egypt.

Lawrence began his attempted rapprochement with the Hashemi clan by arranging a meeting with Abdullah. That meeting took place on a hot, dusty afternoon at a hotel in Jeddah. As they talked, Lawrence learned that the Sharif was, indeed, interested in working with the British. He suspected that enthusiasm for outsider support stemmed from the Hashemi clan's need of assistance in resisting the Saudi threat. He wondered also how serious Abdullah and his father's clan were about joining the war against the Ottomans, or whether they were merely going along with the British plan thinking they could use British support to strengthen their own position in the region. And he wondered if Abdullah really was the man for the job.

None of these questions seemed particularly critical to Lawrence. Not even the very real possibility that he was correct in his assessment of the Sharif's motivations. The British, after all, were attempting to exploit the Arabs for solely British goals. He was under no illusion that the British would ever follow through on any promises they might make. That being the case, why should he care if the Arabs used the same approach in dealing with the British?

A few days later, Lawrence traveled from Jeddah into the desert and met with Faisal, the Sharif's oldest son. Faisal appeared more organized than his brother and he possessed something that immediately caught Lawrence's attention—a fighting force that appeared capable of actually going to war.

Upon arrival at Faisal's camp, Lawrence was ushered to a tent where, like he had with Ibn Saud, he found the man he sought reclining on a carpet and propped against a large pillow. Lawrence was offered the same seating arrangement and they sat across from each other. When he was comfortable, Faisal began, "I understand you have been talking with my brother."

Lawrence was impressed that Faisal knew already where he had been. "Yes. I had a rather lengthy meeting with him."

"And what did he tell you?"

"That your father is interested in supporting the British."

"My father is interested in supporting the British. I am interested in supporting the British. My brother Abdullah is interested in supporting Abdullah."

Already in only the first few minutes of their conversation Lawrence was certain he had found the man the British needed to lead an Arab revolt. As he and Faisal talked further that day and into the evening, he became even more convinced and laid out the plan in detail. Faisal would lead an uprising that would include as many of his fellow Arabs as could be recruited. "Not just members of the Hashemi clan," Lawrence stressed. The British would supply weapons, ammunition, and provisions for that effort. This uprising would be specifically directed against Ottoman interests in the region.

"And what do we get?" Faisal asked.

"You get freedom from the Ottoman yoke."

Faisal smiled. "We are already free of that. They do not bother us."

"They own you."

"We are not slaves," Faisal retorted. "Look around." He made a sweeping gesture with his arm. "Do you see an Ottoman army?

They do not come to the desert." He took a deep breath and steadied himself. "So, I ask again, if we do these things that you desire and help you defeat the Ottomans, what do we get?"

"What do you want?"

"A kingdom," Faisal replied immediately. "We want a kingdom. Devoid of Western control and free of harassment from the Saudis."

As they talked further, Lawrence and Faisal outlined a plan. Faisal and his men would recruit other Arab clans to join them in revolting against the Ottomans, with British support. After the war was successfully concluded—and only then—the British would guarantee the Hashemi clan a kingdom that stretched from the Egyptian border northward to Palestine, and east through Mesopotamia.

✦ ✦ ✦ ✦ ✦

A week later, Lawrence returned to Cairo and reported the result of the meeting to General Clayton. "So," Clayton began, after hearing the report, "an Arab uprising seems possible?"

"Yes. But there is the matter of the Hashemi rivalry with the Saudis."

"We can manage that, can't we?"

"We'll have to promise the Sharif and his sons something the Saudis can't get."

Clayton arched one eyebrow in a skeptical look. "And what is that?"

"A kingdom."

Clayton frowned. "What kind of kingdom would that be?"

"An Arab kingdom," Lawrence explained. "Covering the entire region. Palestine north of Egypt and all of Mesopotamia. Not just a fiefdom on the Arab Peninsula."

Clayton appeared intrigued. "We could do that," he replied with an arrogant tone. "We could promise them a kingdom."

"You would have to deliver, too," Lawrence rejoined.

"Or what?" Clayton scoffed. "Will they send their camels to nip us in the hind parts?" He laughed. "Or have them spit at us?" That made him howl with laughter.

"No, sir," Lawrence replied, certain then that Clayton was only willing to promise something the British would never deliver. "Far worse."

"Such as?"

"Centuries of war and animosity."

"Ah," Clayton gave a dismissive gesture. "That will never happen. Tell Abdullah and the Sharif that we will gladly supply them with all of the support they require, just as long as they agree to side with us against the Ottomans."

"And openly revolt," Lawrence added.

"Yes, yes." Clayton seemed still amused at his earlier remarks. "And openly revolt. Tell them that."

"I thought that was the point of our effort."

Clayton nodded. "That is our point. We want them to revolt and help us oppose the Ottomans. If they will help us, we will help them."

Using Lawrence, his affinity for the Arabs, and his contacts among Arab groups, General Clayton, Lord Kitchener, the British War Cabinet, and a host of other officials led the Sharif to believe that the British would support and facilitate the establishment of an independent Arab kingdom at the end of the war. A kingdom ruled by the Sharif and his three sons. Lawrence suspected the British were being disingenuous, but he liked the Arabs and wanted them to revolt, to have their own kingdom. He had no qualms about using the British as a means of obtaining arms and munitions for that cause, even if it meant betraying his own country to do so.

This arrangement was codified in an exchange of letters between Sir Henry McMahon and Abdullah's father, the Sharif. Those letters were transmitted by Lawrence, and in them British officials promised the Sharif a kingdom in exchange for his help against the Ottomans.

Each time he brought the Sharif a letter, the Sharif had Lawrence read it to him, a fact that convinced Lawrence the Sharif could not read English for himself. Not only that, but the correspondence from Clayton was couched in the language of British diplomacy, which was ambiguous at best and often obscure. Lawrence was convinced that the Sharif had no understanding of the actual content of the letters, the importance assigned to key words and phrases by the British, or any of the diplomatic context in which the letters were prepared. Lawrence remained quiet about it, though, and let the relationship develop in hopes that things would sort themselves out in the end.

✦ ✦ ✦ ✦ ✦

While Lawrence worked with Faisal to encourage Arabs to side with the British and revolt against the Ottomans, British officials in the War Cabinet received a cable from the Oriental desk in Cairo alerting them to a potential conflict between British overtures to the Arabs and the British alliance with France: "French diplomats have heard of our meetings with Abdullah and Faisal and of our previous correspondence with them regarding an alliance with Arabs willing to oppose the Ottoman Empire. They have raised concern that we mean to hand over French interests in Lebanon and Syria to the Arabs. They are not averse to a diplomatic arrangement necessary for the war's successful prosecution but are keen to retain as much of their colonial empire as possible."

The cable touched off fresh concerns about the strength of the alliance—the Triple Entente of England, France, and Russia—to wage war without French support, and the tenuous nature of the effort in the Middle East. "Do we even need this strategy?" one minister asked. "Do we care about the Middle East?"

"We need the oil," another replied.

"And it provides a potential back door into the Ottoman Empire."

After several days of discussion, officials determined that Mark Sykes—officially, Sir Tatton Benvenuto Sykes, the 6th Baronet—was available in Cairo to assist in resolving the matter. Sykes was an eclectically educated aristocratic who served as a diplomatic advisor to Lord Kitchener, General Clayton, and other members of British leadership operating from Cairo. Loathed by some, lightly regarded by others, he was, nevertheless, tasked with the responsibility of smoothing out differences with a suitable French representative.

Operating from a desk at the office of the British consul general, Sykes contacted French diplomat François Georges-Picot. Unlike Sykes, Picot was trained as a lawyer and had enjoyed a long career as a professional diplomat. Well before Sykes contacted him, he had been tipped off by an informant that the future of the Middle East was a pending issue between his government and the British, and that Sykes would be appointed to represent British interests in an attempt to reach an amicable arrangement. He'd been studying the matter in detail and knew precisely what his superiors expected to obtain.

The two met in a room at Cairo's Savoy Hotel and, from an inauspicious beginning, proceeded to conduct a week of daily sessions at which they discussed a plan by which the two countries—England and France—might divide the Middle East once the war was successfully concluded and the Ottoman Empire banished from the region—an outcome which neither man ever once doubted would occur.

As indicated in the earlier British cables regarding the issue, Sykes learned quickly that France intended to keep as much of its empire as possible. "We regard our influence in Syria and Lebanon as matters of top priority," Picot warned. "And we do not wish to see our position threatened by a strengthened and organized Arab presence on our eastern flank."

Sykes cared little for asserting British dominion over either of those countries and knew the ministers in London shared his opinion. Syria was a quagmire of contentious tribesmen with little to offer in natural resources or business opportunity, and Lebanon, as popular opinion went, was not much better. "You have no need to worry," Sykes assured. "We have no desire to create an effective Arab presence on either of our flanks. And no interest in diminishing your sphere of responsibility."

Still, Picot pressed the matter. "But what of your purported promises to the Arabs? Surely, they will be offended if you do not honor what you have said."

"Our arrangement with them is ambiguous enough to accommodate our interests," Sykes stressed. "Both our present interests and those that may emerge in the future. In any regard, although we did make certain promises to the Arabs, there are no hard-and-fast boundaries as of yet regarding any interest they may obtain and no timetable for when those interests might take effect."

"So," Picot pressed, "there is plenty of time for you to revoke those promises?"

Sykes found the comment offensive but mustered a tight-lipped smile. "Plenty of latitude to settle this matter between us and to accommodate our own interests, however those interests may come to be as the war progresses."

After a week of intense negations, Sykes and Picot reached an agreement to divide Ottoman holdings in the Middle East into spheres of influence. France would retain influence over Syria and

Lebanon. England would retain its hold over Mesopotamia, Palestine, Transjordan, and areas that included Persia and Iraq. When the agreement was reduced to writing, boundaries of geographic distinction were specified in detail.

While in Cairo to organize a shipment of supplies for Faisal, Lawrence learned of the discussions between Sykes and Picot and obtained a summary of the terms of the final arrangement. Before he'd finished reading the document, he realized, as he had suspected earlier, that the British had no intention of honoring their agreements with the Hashemi and, in fact, were prepared to negate their promises altogether.

As he trekked back to the desert with a string of camels and mules bearing supplies, Lawrence's anger grew at the audacity of the British, the arrogance of their attitude, and the lack of integrity that now appeared to be characteristic of the men to whom he was accountable. He considered throwing aside his British citizenship and aligning permanently with the Arabs. Considered it—but only for a moment.

Sometime in the night he calmed himself enough to consider the matter rationally and came to the conclusion he could force the British to honor their agreement with the Hashemi in spite of the agreement they'd apparently reached with the French. All he had to do was help Faisal and his men assert their authority on the ground. Go on the offensive. Seize as much of the proposed Arab kingdom as possible and do so now, rather than wait for it to be given to them after the war. If they did that, the British would be unable to take it away without an armed confrontation, something he was certain they would never do.

By the time Lawrence reached Faisal's camp, he'd made up his mind to do just that. The Arabs, with his help, would take by force the kingdom they were promised rather than wait to receive it from the whim of British benevolence. A benevolence he now knew would never be directed toward the Hashemi.

FOUR

IN NOVEMBER 1916, while serving as an officer in the Ottoman army, Amin al-Husseini became ill with influenza. He languished in a medical tent for a week, doctors hoping he would recover enough to return to the front. When his condition failed to improve, he was loaded aboard a railcar fitted for hospital stretchers and sent home on leave to recuperate.

All the way from Istanbul to Aleppo, Amin did little but sleep. However, on the second day, as the rail line turned south toward Damascus, he felt a surge of energy and lay awake staring out the window most of the afternoon. As his strength allowed, he propped himself up on one elbow to catch a glimpse of the countryside as it moved past the window.

When the train arrived at the station in Jerusalem, corpsmen carried Amin to the platform. He was met there by his cousin Abd al-Qadir, and after an argument about whether he should walk or not, Amin and Qadir made their way to the street where a friend with a delivery truck waited to take them to the home of Amin's mother.

The short drive from the station to Amin's family home was cramped in the cab of the truck, but Amin did not mind. The sights and sounds of Jerusalem were more than enough to compensate for any physical discomfort he might experience. The sights, the sounds, and the smell. He loved the smell of the city and breathed deeply, filling his lungs with as much of the city's aroma as he could hold.

Amin and Qadir arrived at home to find his mother waiting at the door. Qadir helped him from the truck and carried his bags the short distance. He was about to leave when Amin's mother took him by the sleeve. "Stay," she insisted. "You shall eat with us."

"I should go," Qadir replied. "You need time with your son."

"I have plenty of time with my son." She smiled at him. "We have Mandi." Meat cooked with a special blend of spices and served over rice, Mandi was Qadir's favorite food. Amin's too.

Qadir was obviously tempted and Amin chided, "He cannot resist Mandi."

"You like it too," Qadir quipped.

"Yes," Amin admitted. "It is my favorite." He gestured for Qadir to enter and then ushered him inside. Soon they were dining together.

After they finished eating, Qadir departed and Amin retired to his room, where a bed was made ready for him. His mother followed close behind, guiding him as if to make certain he rested. "You must take care of yourself. Good food and plenty of rest. That will make you well."

"And then I must return to the front," Amin added.

She looked worried. "We will see what happens."

"Are you angry with me?"

She had a puzzled expression. "Why would I be angry with you?"

"I joined the army without asking you. Or Kamil."

"You are a man. You must do what you have to do."

"This is the kind of life you hoped I would avoid."

"You must find the life Allah has destined you to live. I have done my best to guide you in the way I thought you should go. Now you must find the way for yourself."

Amin had a playful smile. "You are abandoning me to it?"

"No. I am releasing you to it." She glanced in his direction. "This is the way of all men. They must one day find their path on their own. You have reached that day. But do not worry. Allah will show you." She pointed to the bed. "Now you must rest. There will be plenty of time to discuss this when you are well."

A moment later, his mother was gone from the room. Amin removed his clothes and laid them across a chair in the corner, then put on a nightshirt and lay down on the bed. It felt good to be at home, in his own room, lying on his own bed, and he smiled again as he pulled the blanket up to his neck. Soon he was fast asleep.

✦   ✦   ✦   ✦   ✦

Gradually, over the next several weeks Amin regained much of his strength and was able to sit for long periods to read and study. While at home, he also renewed his friendship with Nafez Musallam, his childhood friend, who came to see him every day despite the concern that he might become sick with Amin's illness, too.

During one of their visits, Kamil joined them. He was unusually excited. "We have learned," Kamil answered, "that Hussein Hashemi is calling for an uprising against the Ottomans."

Amin was surprised. "The Sharif of Mecca and Medina?"

"Yes, and he has the support of the British army."

Nafez had a skeptical look. "They are backing the Sharif over the Saudis?"

Kamil nodded. "British officials approached the Saudis about joining them in the war, but the Saudis refused. Ibn Saud felt it would be a trap."

Amin spoke up. "Ibn Saud is wise to think that."

Kamil seemed amused by the comment. "And why do you think that?"

"The Sharif, in all his glory, will never defeat the Ottomans."

Kamil seemed unconvinced. "Not even with the support of the British?"

"Not even," Amin added flatly.

"They are offering him weapons and the support of their expertise."

Amin had a disapproving look. "The British think we need their help to fight in the desert?"

"We need their weapons," Kamil noted. "And we need access to their sources of accurate information about the enemy."

"We?"

"The Sharif may be a troublesome old man, but he is the Sharif. He is Arab. As are we."

Amin had a quizzical look. "You think the Ottoman are our enemy?"

"They are now," Kamil said. "If the Sharif is fighting *against* them, we should not fight *for* them."

The point of Kamil's comment made Amin angry. Kamil was always talking down to him, as if Amin could not think for himself, but Amin chose to ignore it and instead asked, "But what would be the point of this revolution?"

"To defeat the Ottoman Empire," Kamil answered. The tone of his voice was even more condescending.

"And then what would we have?"

"Ahh," Kamil beamed. "The British have promised Hussein Hashemi and his sons a kingdom."

Amin had a puzzled expression. "A kingdom?"

"Yes." Kamil grinned. "An Arab kingdom, stretching from the Arabian Peninsula to Mesopotamia."

"Including Palestine?"

"Including the ground on which this house is constructed."

Amin was sure that this suggestion of an Arab kingdom was too good to be true, but he refused to argue about it any further and for another hour that afternoon the three sat in Amin's room and reminded themselves of the things they'd learned in school and the stories they'd heard of a magnificent Islamic kingdom of old. Of gold and silver and costly jewels. Horses and swords and gallant men to ride and wield them. But as they talked further their conversation turned from brave men fighting mortal enemies to brave men fighting the enemies of their soul. Men who knew the men of old. Men devoted to Allah.

Hearing those stories, something stirred within Amin, and he remembered his earlier interest in calling Arabs back to a renewed commitment to Islam. Something he felt was fundamentally lacking among the men he knew and lacking in those who spoke of an Arab future. An Arab cause.

Finally, though, as the afternoon grew late, Kamil left to tend to other business. When he was gone, Amin lay on the bed, starring at the ceiling, and a melancholy expression came over him. Nafez, still with him, noticed the change in Amin's mood. "What's the matter? Are you not excited by what you have heard from Kamil?"

"I am excited. But I am suspicious, too."

"Suspicious?" Nafez frowned. "Of Kamil?"

"No." Amin shook his head. "Of the Europeans."

"Why are you suspicious of them?"

"We have a history with them."

Once again, Nafez seemed puzzled. "Your family has a history with them?"

"No." Amin sighed in frustration. "We Arabs. Islam. Arabs and Islam. Our ancestors very nearly conquered all of Europe."

"Oh." Nafez seemed to understand. "That was a long time ago."

"But they still remember."

"How do you know they remember?"

"Because *we* remember."

"And you think that will be a problem for us?"

Amin looked over at him. "We are a threat to them, and they know it. They have seen what we can do. Our armies conquered everything, all the way to Spain. The Europeans know the power of Islam and they know Allah is with us. When we assert ourselves, they will do everything in their power to oppose us."

Nafez nodded. "But they are promising Faisal a kingdom."

Amin shook his head. "It is a kingdom they cannot give."

"Perhaps," Nafez conceded with a shrug. "But perhaps we could use them for our purposes as they wish to use us for theirs."

Amin's eyes opened wider. "You mean lead them to believe we are naïve enough to take them at their word, but all the while we use their strength to prepare ourselves to take the kingdom on our own?"

"That is exactly what I mean."

Amin grinned. "I like that idea."

✦ ✦ ✦ ✦ ✦

As Amin's health returned to normal, he became less content with the prospect of returning to the Ottoman front. Especially since learning for certain the Sharif had obtained British support for the establishment of an Arab kingdom. But he became even more reluctant when he learned that the Sharif's son, Faisal, was actually in the field, leading an armed revolt against the Ottomans.

While wrestling with what to do, Amin ventured from the

house a few hours each day and strolled through the Jerusalem neighborhood near where he lived. One day he ventured as far as the home of Nafez's parents. He and Nafez sat outside in the pleasant sunshine, sipping from cups of tea.

As they sipped and talked, a young woman came from the house and started up the street away from them. Amin noticed her and was immediately taken by her beauty. "Who is that?"

"That is Karimeh."

Amin's mouth fell open. "Karimeh?"

Nafez grinned. "Yes."

"Your sister?"

Nafez nodded in response. "That is her."

"She isn't a little girl anymore."

"No." Nafez shook his head slowly. "She isn't a little girl."

Half an hour later, Karimeh returned carrying a basket filled with groceries. This time Amin interrupted his conversation with Nafez and rushed to her side. "Let me help you."

Karimeh smiled in response and handed him the basket. "You didn't know who I was when I came out a while ago, did you?"

"You've changed."

"As have you."

Karimeh was several years younger than Amin and Nafez; when they were boys in school, Amin had never paid her much attention. Now, however, she was grown up and quite beautiful. Amin couldn't keep his eyes off her as he followed her into the house with the basket. Soon they were deep in conversation and Amin forgot all about Nafez, who still was seated outside. Not long after that, Amin began making regular trips to the home of Nafez's parents, ostensibly to talk with Nafez, but everyone knew the real reason he came there. And Karimeh welcomed him gladly.

✦ ✦ ✦ ✦ ✦

The following month, the Sharif of Mecca and Medina, Hussein Hashemi, proclaimed himself King of the Hejaz. Amin still was living at his mother's home when news of that proclamation reached Jerusalem. Inspired by the Sharif's action, he decided to remain in Jerusalem and avoid returning to his post with the Ottoman army. "Too much is happening here now," he explained. "I don't want to miss any of it."

✦ ✦ ✦ ✦ ✦

A few days later, Amin and Nafez joined the Sharifian Army, also known as the Arab Unit—a unit of Arabs being assembled with British assistance to serve under Faisal. They were Arabs, training on Arab soil, but primarily controlled by C. D. Brunton, a captain in the British army.

Shortly after their induction into the unit, Brunton learned of Amin's family associations. Aware now of the extent of Amin's connections, Brunton offered him a position recruiting Arabs to join the unit. Amin accepted on one condition: "Nafez must serve with me." Brunton readily agreed and soon the two were traveling through Palestine urging Arab males to join the revolt.

✦ ✦ ✦ ✦ ✦

A few weeks later, Saleem Namir, Amin's old rival from the Nashashibi clan, volunteered for the unit as well. Saleem, always ready with a flattering comment when necessary, readily ingratiated himself to the British and to Faisal. Amin watched as he rose quickly to a position of prominence among the troops.

Namir's apparent success perturbed Nafez no end. "Saleem is such a dog. Shamelessly promoting himself far beyond his ability. If I didn't know his family, I would think he was really a Jew."

Amin laughed. "He does find ways to promote himself."

"He has always been that way, even when we were little."

"Don't worry." Amin patted his friend on the shoulder. "Namir only promotes himself because he has nothing else to offer."

"Yeah," Nafez groused. "But it's guys like that who cause trouble for those of us who actually have something of substance to contribute."

Despite being distracted by Namir, Amin and Nafez concentrated on recruiting people for Faisal's army. They had little trouble obtaining volunteers, a response that convinced Amin an Arab revolt could succeed, and expanded their recruiting effort beyond Jerusalem to Damascus.

As men from Jerusalem and the surrounding countryside joined the Arab Unit, Amin made sure to select the best of the recruits not only for the army but also for his own purposes. He didn't know what those purposes were, exactly, but he knew circumstances in Palestine were changing and he wanted to be ready for whatever opportunity might present itself.

Among the most promising men were Abdul Latif and Abd al-Qadir, the cousin who met Amin at the train station when he arrived from Istanbul so many months ago. Kemal Hadad and Hasan Salama, Amin's classmates at the university in Cairo, joined them, too. Amin kept Salama and Qadir close and had them assigned to his recruitment effort.

Hadad, however, was assigned to a part of Faisal's army that was under the control of Saleem Namir. Every morning they went out to train, and every evening he came back to Amin with the same response. "I hate that Namir."

"Is he cruel?"

"No. But he always leaves me feeling like he's up to something. A plot. A plan. Something that benefits him, not all of us. And certainly not the cause."

Nafez had a sudden look of realization. "That's it!" he exclaimed.

Amin frowned. "What's *it*?"

"Namir. That's the thing about him. Always up to something that benefits only Namir. Never anyone else."

Amin gave a dismissive shake of his head. "I'm telling you, he is of no consequence and his callous disregard of others will show him out to be exactly what he is."

"Perhaps so," Hadad conceded, "but he is far too close to the British. And too close to Faisal's brother Abdullah."

Amin looked concerned. "Abdullah has joined them?"

"Yes."

"What is he like?"

"Brunton pays him no attention, but I think Abdullah is the most decisive one of them all. Faisal is well-spoken, and the British gravitate toward him as the one for us to follow. But Abdullah has the look of a king in his eyes."

Amin listened, but could think of little that Namir might do, other than cut him out of the decision-making process. He could do that. He could get so close to Faisal that Faisal came to rely on him, and then Namir would be the one planning strategy and handing out assignments. If that happened, Amin knew which assignments he would receive—the worst, most dangerous, most difficult. But that was the extent of what Namir could accomplish.

"I have even bigger questions than Namir," Hadad added.

"And what is that?" Amin asked.

"Why are we cooperating with the British?"

"What do you mean?"

"They are not Muslim. They are not Arab. Why do we help them?"

"The Ottomans aren't Arabs, either," Amin countered. "And no one raised that question with them."

"That is because the Ottomans at least are Muslim," Qadir offered. "The British aren't much of anything."

"Christian," Nafez noted. "The British are Christian."

"Not really," Hadad responded. "They might attend Christian church services. They might read from their books and sing their songs on Sunday, but they do not live the Christian way."

"We are only cooperating for a time," Amin said finally. "Creating a corps of Arabs that will one day throw off the Ottoman yoke and then throw off British domination, too. And we will—"

"I'm not so sure," Salama interrupted. "The British are here under the *guise* of fighting the Ottomans, but they intend never to leave."

Nafez shot him a look. "How do you know this?"

"I sense it," Salama answered. "It is the way Europeans act."

"It's certainly the way the British think," Hadad agreed. "They have colonies throughout the world. I fear their presence here is but one more attempt to expand their empire to include us."

"Precisely my point," Salama argued. "And if we cooperate with them, we are cooperating in the colonization of ourselves."

"We can overcome them," Amin assured. "When the time is right."

Hadad had a skeptical frown. "You really believe that?"

Amin nodded. "When the time is right, we will be prepared and ready and then we will do it. Today we are not ready. Today we are not prepared. But one day we will send the British back to England and they will gladly go." He flashed a broad smile. "But first, they must teach us how to do that."

Nafez and the others laughed in response.

FIVE

WHILE BRITISH MILITARY officials in Egypt and Palestine sought Arab support for England's war effort against the Ottoman Empire, officials in London sought the support of Palestinian Jews. It was a double-sided affair—one group promised the Arabs a kingdom that included Palestine, while another faction promised the Jews a homeland in the same region. Making matters potentially worse, neither the Jews nor the Palestinians knew of the conflicting nature of the promises being made.

To be fair, negotiations between British officials and Jewish representatives were nothing new. They had been ongoing for more than two years, but the process had been protracted due in part to electoral changes in the makeup of England's government. Opposition to the policy from various British political factions also had contributed to the delay. As might be expected, those who were privy to the discussions conducted by General Clayton and his staff with the Sharif of Mecca and Medina were especially opposed to it.

Nevertheless, by the summer of 1917, the war in the Middle East had ground to a stalemate. The hoped-for Arab revolt had yet to produce tangible results, and an overt alliance with Jews who resided in Palestine seemed like the best option to get the war moving again.

To help things along, the War Cabinet turned to Mark Sykes, the architect of the as-yet-still-secret Sykes-Picot Agreement. Jewish interests were handled by Chaim Weizmann, a prominent chemist and ardent Zionist who had initiated the effort in conjunction with his work for the World Zionist Congress. Neither Weizmann nor the public knew of Sykes' negotiations with Picot or the agreement they had reached regarding France and England's post-war division and partition of the Middle East.

For most of the summer, discussions between Sykes and Weizmann focused on the language of a proposed declaration of support to be issued by the British government. Weizmann argued for terms explicitly denoting British approval of a *Jewish state—* a strong term with political, legal, and diplomatic implications already defined by precedence. Sykes could only obtain support from the prime minister's government for the more ambiguous *Jewish homeland—*a term lacking immediate definition of any kind.

As the language of the pending policy announcement developed, opposition emerged among the British prime minister's advisors to the issuance of a formal governmental declaration at all. Especially one issued over the prime minister's signature. After considerable discussion, Prime Minister David Lloyd George conceded that whatever statement was issued, it should not come from him or his office. Consequently, the matter was handed off to the foreign secretary, Arthur Balfour, for final resolution.

Two weeks later, Balfour convened a meeting of advisors to consider the matter. They gathered at a conference table in

Balfour's office. After explaining the situation in detail, Balfour opened the matter for comment.

Kenneth Murray, an assistant undersecretary from the Colonial Office, was the first to speak. "This will only cause trouble among the Arabs and gain us nothing in return."

"Nonsense," Peter Whittle retorted. "Nearly a hundred thousand Jews live there now." Whittle had visited Palestine twice while serving Balfour during his recent stint as prime minister.

"Gentlemen," Balfour interrupted, "the matter of whether or not to issue a statement of policy is not up for discussion. The current prime minister has decided a statement should be issued and that this office should issue it." There was a note of disdain in his voice and not a little condescension. "The question before us today is not *whether*, but *how*."

John Beaumont, a specialist on intergovernmental affairs, spoke up. "Mr. Secretary, I suggest you do this in the form of a letter."

Balfour looked puzzled. "A letter?"

"Yes, sir."

Whittle, seated down the table, nodded. "That is an excellent suggestion, Mr. Secretary. And precisely what we need. A statement, but not a statement."

The perplexed look on Balfour's face deepened. "But a letter to whom? Where would we send it?"

Percy Mellors suggested they send it to the Jewish Agency. Murray shook his head. "That would be too strong."

Whittle turned to him with a grin. "I thought you were opposed to this altogether?"

"I am," Murray answered. "But if it's going to happen, we need to do it in a way that gives us lots of room. And in a manner that gives the least offense to our other interests in the area."

"You mean the Arabs."

"Yes."

Again, Balfour had a quizzical expression. "What do you mean by *room*?"

"Diplomatic room," Whittle clarified. "That is what Mr. Murray means." He shot a look in Murray's direction. "This is what you meant, isn't it?"

"Yes," Murray acknowledged. "This situation is going to require lots of diplomacy before it's over and the more we can accommodate that reality *now*, the better we shall be *then*."

Mellors spoke up again, "What about addressing the letter to Chaim Weizmann? He's the one with whom we've dealt the most."

Sykes, who was seated next to Balfour, disagreed. "I don't think he'll go for it."

"Why not?" someone asked. "He's been going for it for years."

"I don't think he will see a letter addressed to himself as having the force he intended," Sykes explained. "He has insisted all along that we voice our support as an official statement of official policy. Weizmann is an important figure, but he is not the political peer of a British foreign secretary."

"Then, who else is there?" someone asked.

"What about some other prominent Jew?" Mellors offered. "A rich one with a broad reputation."

This time Sykes looked perplexed. "I'm not sure how that is any different from issuing it to Weizmann."

Mellors tried again. "A letter from the prime minister to a Jew of note. Someone the world *and* the Jews respect."

"Not the prime minister," Balfour corrected. "As I've already stated, he must not have his name attached to it. That's the whole purpose for our involvement."

Whittle leaned away. "Who would issue it?"

Murray pointed in Balfour's direction. "How about you?"

Balfour sighed. "I suppose—"

Whittle interrupted. "Are you certain that's a good idea?"

"I think it's our only option," Balfour replied. "I will sign the letter, but we still must determine whom to send it to."

Sykes spoke up. "If we're going with a prominent Jew, I suggest you send it to Lionel Rothschild."

"You mean Baron Rothschild," Balfour corrected again.

"Yes." Sykes nodded. "One and the same."

"But," Beaumont interjected, "will that be direct enough for Weizmann?"

"He can take what he gets and like it," Whittle retorted.

"I think I can get him to like it," Sykes offered with a note of resignation. "The point of the thing is to get a statement of our position in the public record. A letter from the foreign secretary will do that, and Baron Rothschild is a rank or two above Weizmann."

"A pound or two above him, also," someone quipped. It was meant to be funny, but no one laughed at the remark.

"A letter to the likes of him will give us plenty of diplomatic room," Whittle added.

"Yes. Room," Balfour sighed. "By all means, give us *room*."

"Then it's settled?" Sykes asked.

"Yes," Balfour answered. "A letter from me to Baron Rothschild. You have the proposed language, I assume."

"Yes, Mr. Secretary." Sykes took a page from a folder and slid it across the table for Balfour to see.

✦ ✦ ✦ ✦ ✦

Early in November, the letter from Arthur Balfour was delivered to Rothschild. As previously agreed among government ministers, the letter expressed British support for the establishment of a Jewish homeland in Palestine. It became public shortly after it was signed and conveyed. Newspapers picked up the story about it almost immediately.

Amin was seated in his room, studying, when Nafez arrived with a special issue of *Falastin*, an Arab-language newspaper published in Jaffa but widely circulated throughout Palestine. The paper was devoted to articles about the Balfour letter, referring to it as the Balfour Declaration. A copy of the document was included. Nafez dropped the paper on the open book from which Amin was reading.

"What is this?" Amin asked, startled by the interruption.

"Read it," Nafez insisted. The paper was folded open to a copy of the Balfour Declaration. He jabbed the page with his index finger for emphasis.

Amin read it quickly, the look in his eyes growing more intense by the moment. "This is what my father knew would happen," he replied at last.

Nafez nodded in agreement. "And your father was right to worry. Not just about land sales to the Jews but also about Jews taking control of the British and making them their servants."

Amin pointed to the notice. "Lionel Rothschild was the one who funded most of those purchases."

"Rich Jews like to flaunt their wealth. But you notice Rothschild did not move here."

"That's because he is British," Amin said.

"He's a Jew," Nafez retorted.

"Yes, but he is also a British citizen, and the British are committed to their lavish lifestyle. Men like him would gladly pay for others to come, but he would not give up a single sip of the champagne that is served at his table."

A frown wrinkled Nafez's forehead. "He drinks champagne?"

"You know what I mean." Amin returned the paper to Nafez. "I suppose Namir will be glad for this."

Nafez grimaced. "Why would he be happy for this?" He gestured with the paper. "Is he not at least enough of an Arab to be incensed by what the British do to us?"

"Namir is a Nashashibi," Amin said. "And the Nashashibi were in favor of selling land to the Jews merely for the sake of getting Jewish money. No doubt they had plans to sell more land to the Jews, too, which is why they were upset when Kamil was named mufti and not one of their own. Now the British are dealing with those who supply the money. Everyone will want to sell, and the Nashashibi will be first in line."

"But won't they see," Nafez implored, "the British are promising them a Jewish state in the same place where they have promised us a kingdom."

"It does not say a Jewish state," Amin noted. "It says a Jewish homeland."

"And there is a difference?"

"I think the British think so."

"But whatever they give the Jews, won't it diminish the kingdom they promised to us?"

Amin smiled. "Let us wait and see. Anyway, there is nothing we can do about it right now."

Within days of the letter from Balfour and its subsequent publication, the Russian government released the full text of the Sykes-Picot Agreement. As it did with the Balfour Declaration, *Falastin* reprinted the agreement in its entirety. This time, Amin needed no one to show him a copy. He found it for himself and read it while having coffee with Salama. When Amin finished, he turned the paper for Salama to see. "Did you read this?"

Salama took the paper from him and scanned the article. "This makes no sense. The British made promises to us. The Sharif declared himself King of the Hejaz in reliance on those promises."

"And yet here they are," Amin sighed, "dividing the land between the French and the Jews."

"The same land they promised to us."

"Promised to us as an inducement," Amin noted. "In exchange for our help with their war."

Salama looked over at him. "What can we do about it?"

Amin shrugged. "I don't know, but I intend to ask them about it."

"About what to do?"

Amin shook his head. "No. About why they did this."

"You'll ask Captain Brunton?"

"He is our point of contact."

"I don't think he'll know."

"Neither do I. At least, nothing to which he will admit."

Later that day, Amin found Captain Brunton in his office, a makeshift arrangement in a warehouse near a British supply depot. He strode into the office and laid a copy of the newspaper on Brunton's desk. "You have seen this?"

Brunton glanced at the article. "I read it earlier." He sounded unconcerned. "What about it?"

Amin glared at him. "You were aware of this agreement? You were aware of the agreement all this time?"

"No, but it does not surprise me."

"This is an agreement to divide Palestine, Lebanon, Syria, Mesopotamia, the entire region, between England and France. The very same area you promised to the Sharif of Mecca as a kingdom."

"I didn't promise anything to anyone. And the agreement only creates spheres of influence."

"That is not what you told the Sharif." Amin felt himself getting angrier as they talked. "That is not what you told Faisal." He reached over the desk and tapped the paper loudly with his finger. "This is not what you led them to believe. And it's not what you led all of us to believe."

Brunton looked up at him with a look of incredulity, which Amin knew was manufactured. "What do you mean?"

"You promised us a kingdom covering all of Palestine and Mesopotamia. You said that to all of us. 'Come and join us in the fight against the Ottomans. Win your freedom from them and establish an Arab kingdom in their place.' That is what you said, is it not?"

Brunton leaned back in his chair. "Something like that."

"Now we learn that while you were making those promises, you already had given much of that territory to the French. And just days ago, you promised a portion of the land where we are standing to the Jews."

Brunton had a faint smile. "It's a big area."

"It's a big lie!" Amin shouted.

Brunton sat up straight. "That's strong language. And I would remind you, I am a captain in the British army."

"People who have been deceived usually respond with strong words!" Amin shouted. "And with strong actions."

Brunton scooted back his chair and stood. "I had nothing to do with any of this. Not the promise to the Sharif. Not the agreement with the French. And not the declaration about the Jews. I had nothing to do with any of that. I am simply an army captain trying to help you win independence from the Ottoman Empire and get out of here alive. Once we have accomplished that, I am certain all of this will get worked out."

"You mean once the British have achieved their goal of defeating the Ottomans, the region will become a colony in the British Empire."

"I don't know anything about that, either."

"But you don't deny it."

"The only thing I know is this: None of these things matter at all unless you break free of Ottoman control. So I suggest you continue to work in support of the Arab revolt and recruit enough able-bodied men to do the job." Brunton took his seat. "Now, if there isn't anything more, I think we both have a job to do and I suggest we get to it."

Amin was certain Brunton was lying when he said he didn't

know about the agreement with the French. And as he turned to leave the office, he was convinced more than ever that the British were merely Jewish pawns and could not be relied upon to keep their promises. However, he knew better than to press the matter further. Instead, Amin left the office and went to find Nafez.

In the months that followed, Amin and Nafez continued to recruit Arabs for the Arab unit, acting as if they did so in cooperation with the British. However, the men they disclosed to the British were only a fraction of those who agreed to serve. The bulk of their recruits were diverted from the Arab unit to a separate organization controlled exclusively by Amin.

At the same time, Amin used his access to British weapons and munitions to create a stockpile for his own purposes. He met daily with his men to educate and train them. And for additional work, he assigned Abdul Latif to see that they were formed into a corps of men capable of whatever action they might be called to undertake.

SIX

BY EARLY SUMMER 1918, Faisal's Arab unit was trained, armed, and prepared to join the British in a final offensive against Ottoman forces remaining in Palestine. Amin and Nafez were with them as they mustered the men before leaving Jerusalem to begin the conquest of what they hoped would become a strategic part of an Arab kingdom.

Late one evening, Amin gathered with his men to review operational details. "As we have discussed many times already, we will begin in the Negev, then sweep north along the western side of Palestine before pressing into Galilee."

Yousef, who came from a village near Gaza, said, "I hear the Ottomans have many strongholds yet remaining."

"Especially around Tiberias," another noted.

"They do indeed hold many advantageous positions," Amin conceded. "Which is why we will approach with Captain Brunton from the south, moving up the Jordan Valley. General Allenby will cover our left flank."

Walid, one of the youngest men, had an ironic smile. "Will we actually see fighting?"

"Yes," Amin chuckled. "We will see plenty of fighting."

"Good," Walid replied. "We've been training for this and I would hate to see all of that effort go to waste." All of the men laughed in response, and the tension suddenly evaporated.

"Remember," Amin cautioned, "no matter what happens, do your best to appear as if we are in full support of the British. For now, they must not know our true heart."

Someone else spoke up. "Should we really wish to see the British succeed? I mean, is it in our best interests for them to win?"

"I wish for *us* to succeed," Amin replied. "That is what we are fighting for. We are fighting for ourselves and for the Arab kingdom we are establishing."

"Then shouldn't we be fighting *against* the British instead of with them?"

"Right now the Ottomans are our first enemy," Amin answered. "We cannot defeat them on our own. As I have said many times, we need British help to do that."

"But aren't the British merely a European version of the Ottomans?"

Amin looked around at his men. "Would any of you prefer a continuation of the experience we have had with the Ottomans? We and our forebears?"

"No!" they shouted in unison.

Amin nodded. "Good! At least we agree on that."

"But what about—"

Amin cut him off. "Were the decision up to me, I would prefer we rule ourselves now and that all others be gone from this land." Shouts of support went up from the men. Amin gestured for silence. "But that is not possible for us at the moment. We must take what we can get from the situation and keep our eyes on the future."

"But the British have given our land to the French," someone said.

"And taken the rest for themselves," another chimed in.

"Except for what they gave to the Jews," someone else groused.

Again, Amin cut them off with a wave of his hand. "This is the path we chose from the beginning." His voice was stern but calm. "And it is the path Faisal has agreed to follow. We will stick to the plan we made earlier—use the British to make ourselves strong, and once we are strong enough, we will vanquish *all* of our foes."

"And you still think the British will one day leave?"

"The British are far from home," Amin explained. "They are not capable of living as we live. They can only live as the British live. When they are away from it, they long for nothing more than to return to it. We will bleed them for support and use it to equip ourselves with all that we need to achieve victory. Then, when we confront them with our full force, they will flee to their comfortable lives in England."

"And how will we bleed them?"

"As we are doing now. By accepting as much of their training as they will allow, and by stockpiling as many of their weapons and as much of their munitions as possible."

✦ ✦ ✦ ✦ ✦

Clearing the Negev took only a few days, but fighting in Gaza proved difficult. Still, by the end of the following month, the Arab unit had maneuvered its way to the Jordan Valley. From there, they slogged northward. Fighting was intense but with the help of British regular troops, Faisal and his men prevailed. By midsummer they were encamped on the Syrian side of Lake Tiberias.

Late one afternoon as the men rested before the final push to the border, Nafez looked over at Amin. "What is next?"

"We will fight our way to Lebanon and then they will send us home soon."

"I know," Nafez agreed. "But with the Ottomans gone, what will we do next?"

Amin had a playful smile. "I was thinking of Karimeh."

"What of her?"

"Is she promised to anyone?"

"No."

Amin waited a moment. "Would you object if I called on her?"

"No. I don't suppose."

"Would your parents?"

"No." Nafez turned in Amin's direction. "But isn't she a bit young for you?"

Amin grinned. "Not anymore."

The expression on Nafez's face turned cold. "What does that mean?"

"Nothing improper, I assure you of that."

"Then, what?"

"She's different now. I know she's young, but when we were ten, the age difference mattered. Now that we both are older, the difference is not so great a thing."

✦ ✦ ✦ ✦ ✦

With the Great War over in Palestine, a sense of normalcy returned to everyday life. As he suggested that day on the battlefield, Amin returned to Jerusalem and visited Karimeh at her parents' home. Most days, they sat together behind the house, sipping tea under the watchful eye of Karimeh's mother. Sometimes, in the afternoon, they went for a long walk with Nafez as a chaperone. And on Sundays they strolled the streets of Jerusalem surrounded by Karimeh's extended family. It was a traditional courtship with traditional boundaries and after a few months, Amin and Karimeh were married. Not long after that, she became pregnant with their first child.

With the war drawing to a close everywhere, the British and French governments solidified their control of the Levantine by establishing separate Occupied Enemy Territory Administrations over each country's portion of the region. As envisioned in the Sykes-Picot Agreement, the French took an area of influence over Syria and Lebanon. The British asserted influence over Mesopotamia and Palestine.

Daily control of the British zone was administered by Ronald Storrs, who was appointed governor of Jerusalem. The announcement of Storrs's appointment sparked a new level of tension among Arabs, many of whom had fought alongside the British army thinking they were working to establish an Arab kingdom, only to learn that the British had already divided the region with others. Still, most Arabs thought the British would eventually honor their pledge and the much-anticipated kingdom would become reality. With the arrival of Storrs, the hoped-for end no longer seemed possible.

In an attempt to ease Arab animosity, Storrs decided to elevate Amin's brother

Kamil to the position of Grand Mufti of Jerusalem. Not actually an elevation, it was more the thoroughly British act of bestowing a title. Storrs adopted the moniker from earlier practice in Egypt, where creating a Grand Mufti in Cairo had seemed helpful.

Most members of the British delegation knew the title was meaningless. Merely a token like so many other titles bestowed by the government. Nothing more than a phrase that sprang from the imagination of a British diplomat. They did, however, view Storrs's action as a shrewd diplomatic gesture, sure to placate any Arab animosity over England's continued presence in the area. After all, it was a *British* title.

For most Arabs, the title was seen as an acknowledgement of Arab significance and authority. An act of respect from a world power that indicated the legitimacy of the Arab cause. Kamil saw it that way, as did many of his fellow Qadi on the Sharia court in Jerusalem. Others, however, were not so favorably impressed.

Amin was glad for his brother to receive an accolade, but he had experienced enough British machinations to know Storrs's new title was a hollow gesture. When the subject came up over lunch at his mother's house, he did his best to hold his tongue. Then a cousin glanced in his direction. "You are unusually quiet, Amin. What do you think of your brother's new title?"

Amin shook his head. "I should not say."

Kamil, who was seated at the head of the table, looked perplexed. "You do not approve of it?"

"The British are laughing at us," Amin huffed.

Kamil pushed back from his place. "Why do you say such a thing?"

"Because it is true." Amin focused his gaze on his brother. "Have you not considered the arrogance of what they have done?"

Kamil responded in a sharp tone. "How is it arrogant?"

"We are Muslim. They are Christian."

"And?"

"The title of Mufti is a matter for *us* to determine. Not them."

"They did not create the title of Mufti," Kamil noted. "But of Grand Mufti."

"Does it make you any grander than you were before? Do they have the power to say that you are supreme above all the other judges? Have the others not already set you at the head of the court?"

"Amin." Kamil shook his head. "You are always—"

Amin interrupted. Others at the table gasped at the affront, but he kept going. "Does the Quran grant additional authority to one bearing that title?"

Kamil scowled. "Everyone knows the title is not mentioned in the Quran."

"Exactly," Amin snapped. "The title of Mufti is a title created by practice and custom among Muslims. How do British Christians now have the authority to tell us who we are?"

Kamil shrugged. "I'm not sure I know."

"Exactly," Amin snapped again. "Do we get our purpose from the British?"

"No." Kamil had a thin, tight smile. "Of course not."

"Then, why do we accept this kind of treatment from them?"

"I do not consider it as anything more than what it is," Kamil answered flatly.

"And what is that?"

"A gesture."

Amin glared at him. "But a gesture of what? A gesture of British dominance over us? A gesture of their superiority? We are the child; they are the parent? They give us gifts; we bow and curtsy in response?"

Kamil was clearly angry now. "I do not appreciate the tone of your voice. Nor do I care for the way you are addressing me."

"Look . . ." Amin paused a moment, as if to relax, before continuing. "If Storrs read a passage from the Quran and said that it meant all Arabs should worship according to the Christian practice and recite the Christian creeds, what would you say?"

"Enough of this." Kamil gave a dismissive wave of his hand. "This line of argument is ridiculous."

"No. It's not ridiculous," Amin insisted. "Because that is exactly what he has done."

"He has done no such thing."

"Where in our tradition does it say that there is such a position as the Grand Mufti?"

Amin's mother spoke up. "They have such a person in Egypt."

"Because the British created that title," Amin reminded.

"So, it is *their* title, not ours," she responded. "Is it such a big thing to argue over?"

"They think we are mere children," Amin explained. "And they are amused by our apparent naiveté when we grovel at their feet."

Kamil glanced at the others seated at the table with a genuine smile. "I suppose they can amuse themselves as they wish."

"Well," Amin sighed angrily. "They will not be amused with us forever."

✦ ✦ ✦ ✦ ✦

After multiple rounds of intense negotiation, the Paris Peace Conference produced a treaty, known as the Treaty of Versailles, that formally concluded the Great War. Several regional issues, however, proved intractable. Rather than delaying resolution of the major issues, the conference relegated those matters to the affected parties for further consideration at ancillary conferences. One of those unresolved matters was that of the Middle East. The treaty acknowledged French control of Syria and Lebanon, and British control of Palestine and Mesopotamia, but final terms of the scope, extent, and duration of that control were to be determined at a conference scheduled to convene in San Remo, Italy.

When news of this arrangement was made public, Arabs in the Middle East reacted negatively. Many of the groups that had joined the Arab Unit and fought with Faisal alongside British troops for Palestinian liberation from the Ottomans now called for open revolt against British and French domination, which was viewed widely as an oppressive extension of Western colonialism. As calls for open revolt and armed opposition grew, Amin gathered with key people from his unit to discuss the matter. Hadad, Salama, Latif, and Qadir attended. His friend and now brother-in-law, Nafez, brought Aref al-Aref, someone who previously had not been a part of Amin's inner circle but was known to all of them by reputation.

Aref was a former member of the Ottoman army but had been captured during fighting in the Caucasus and spent the latter part of the war in a prisoner-of-war camp. After being released at the conclusion of the war, he returned to Jerusalem and went to work as editor of *Suriyya al-Janubiyya*, an Arabic-language newspaper devoted to the unification of Palestine with Syria, a cause to which Aref devoted most of his time.

The gathering took place at Amin's home and when everyone was seated, he spoke. "As you all are now well aware, contrary to their promises, the British are digging in for a long stay in Palestine. They have convinced their European allies to codify that arrangement in the treaty. All of which will make our position more difficult but must not alter our ultimate goal."

Salama spoke up. "You still are committed to the idea of using them to make us strong so we can send them home?"

"Yes," Amin replied.

Hadad looked concerned. "But why? Why should we continue to support them?"

"Because we don't have a choice," Amin answered.

"Our ancestors did not give in to European domination," someone noted. "You have said so many times. The men of old dominated *them*."

"Almost."

Aref interjected. "The British see us as a threat but also the potential source of great wealth. They want us for our natural riches and to keep us under control, but that is all. They want to use us for their purposes. And the only way they can do that is to keep us divided, which is exactly what the current arrangement does. We should be part of Syria. A unified country. Syria, Lebanon, Palestine. One country. One government."

"We will never be united unless we fight to be united," someone added.

Amin interrupted. "The prospect of continued European

dominance is now a grave reality. I don't like it, but we must not give in to the temptation to strike back. We must, instead, view this as a long-term effort."

Latif shook his head. "I think we must fight."

"Not yet," Amin responded. "If we fight, they will only come against us with force. A force we cannot overcome. The only way to prevail is to use the British for our own purposes."

"But this is a fight for our future. For our life."

Hadad said, "I hear there is a man in Syria—Qassam. He is calling for war and is assembling an army."

"I know Qassam," Amin said. "He is a good man and a capable leader, but I do not think revolution now is a good idea."

"But the British promises of an Arab kingdom are now meaningless," Aref noted. "European powers intend to carve up the Middle East and spread control among themselves that keep us divided, pitted against each other, and leaves no room for an Arab kingdom."

"They're already doing it now," someone added.

"They've already done it," another said.

"And on top of that," Aref continued, "the British are moving forward under the terms of the Balfour Declaration. Honoring their intention to create a Jewish state right here in Palestine."

The meeting continued until late into the night, but Amin was unable to convince many of them that his plan was correct. Even some of his closest associates thought it might be time to stand and fight.

After everyone else was gone, Aref lingered. "You have something to say?" Amin asked.

"I understand your strategy," Aref began. "But it seems like we should hold the British accountable for the things they promised."

"And how would we do that?"

"Protest. Fight. Revolt."

"Many of our people would die," Amin observed.

"Yes, but our message would get through."

Amin shook his head. "I'm not so sure."

"If we don't fight, if we don't push back, they will think we accept the way they are treating us."

"We have ways of letting them know that, without fighting."

"Amin"—Aref adopted a professorial tone—"we have been deliberately deceived by the British. Anyone who acts like that cannot be reasoned with or trusted. They will not understand subtle gestures and they will not change their actions until they are confronted by the consequences of their decisions."

"And how do you propose to make them understand?"

Aref gestured with a clinched fist. "A hard shot to the jaw. Force is the only thing they understand."

Amin took him by the hand. "There will be time for that, I assure you. There will be plenty of time for fighting. But for now I need you with me. If our people fight, the British army will crush them and there will be nothing left from which to create anything, much less a kingdom. We cannot allow them to follow their passion on this. We must do this without getting into a war with England. Will you help me?"

Aref sighed. "I have worked day and night to promote a unified Syria."

"I know. And we will get to that. But first we must survive this British occupation."

SEVEN

IN THE WEEK FOLLOWING his meeting with his closest advisors, and after the subsequent discussion with Aref, Amin used his brother's contacts and arranged a meeting with Faisal, who then was living in Damascus. A few days later, Amin traveled there by car and met with Faisal in the home where he was staying.

"They tell me you wish to discuss the matter of Palestinian unification," Faisal noted. "And the promises of a kingdom made to us by the British. What did you wish to say to me about those things?"

"Many of our people in Jerusalem are calling for revolution."

"But you do not agree with them."

"No, I do not."

"And why do you hold a different view?"

"We face two major problems—the Jews and our own people who wish to revolt against the British."

Faisal seemed troubled. "Our own people are a problem?"

"Yes."

"How so?"

"They threaten our unity."

"But the British are not a problem, too? After all, they lied to us. Surely that must be addressed."

"Yes," Amin acknowledged. "They lied to us. But the British will one day leave. They will not stay in Palestine. The Jews will stay. They will remain until the last Jew is dead. They are our biggest problem."

"My father tells me your father opposed Jewish immigration," Faisal noted. "I understand he tried with all of his might to keep them from buying Arab land."

"And he was effective at that until late in life. But now Jews are everywhere, and the British cower at their appearing."

Faisal nodded. "They are attempting to form their own state."

"If we don't form our own state, the Jews will dominate the region and kill all of us."

"So, what do you advise that we do?"

"I think you must resist further cooperation with the British that impinges upon the integrity of your kingdom. And you must become the voice of opposition."

Faisal frowned. "But you have said many times that we cannot fight the British."

"Not in open warfare," Amin conceded. "But many of our people think we should. Their voices threaten our unity. To save them, you must become their leader."

Faisal seemed intrigued. "By calling for a revolution against the British?"

"No. By becoming the voice of those who call for it. And by you becoming the leader you aspire to be."

"I aspire to be head of an Islamic kingdom."

"You can do that only by using the British as your foil. The British are not our ally. They have lied to you. To all of us. You must make that known. But we have to convince our people to look past the British to the Jews. The Jews are our real enemy."

"They think we will only have an Arab kingdom when we take one for ourselves."

"They are correct," Amin said. "But there are many ways to take a kingdom. First, however, we need a king who will step into his role with authority and integrity." Amin pointed to Faisal. "You are that king."

✦ ✦ ✦ ✦ ✦

A month after the meeting between Amin and Faisal, the British Foreign Office summoned George, the Duke of Marbury and Marley Green to London for a meeting with Kenneth Murray, an assistant under-secretary from the Colonial Office. Murray got right to the point. "You are being asked by the prime minister to procure the signature of the Sharif of Mecca to a copy of the Treaty of Versailles."

George arched an eyebrow. "I was not aware that the Sharif was a party to that agreement."

"No," Murray acknowledged. "He was not, but that is none of your concern."

"Then, why am I being asked to do this?"

"Rumblings from Arab constituencies in the Middle East have set everyone here on edge," Murray explained. "The prime minister is demanding that the Sharif or someone from his family sign the treaty as an acknowledgment of the authority of its terms."

"You mean acknowledging our authority under the treaty."

"Yes."

"Very well."

"Your mission," Murray continued, "is to get one of them to sign the document and do it straightaway."

George smiled. "Any family member in particular?"

Murray shrugged. "The Sharif would be best, I suppose. But any of them will do."

George stood to leave. "If the prime minister requires a signature, then a signature he shall have." He started toward the door but as he reached it, Murray called after him, "And tell them to put an end to this nonsense about revolting against us." George acknowledged him with a nod, then disappeared into the hallway.

After receiving a copy of the treaty and consulting with Foreign Office advisors, the decision was made for George to approach Faisal Hussein. He was the Sharif's son but, more importantly in the eyes of Foreign Office staff, the family member most amenable to Western standards. With due haste, Faisal's location in Damascus was confirmed and cables were exchanged procuring his agreement to meet with a representative of the British government.

George departed London accompanied by an assistant, and two days later they arrived in Damascus, expecting to meet with Faisal that day. "With any luck," he said to his assistant, "we shall be on our way back to London by tomorrow."

Instead, the duke was forced to wait in his hotel three days before he and his assistant were summoned to Faisal's residence on the opposite side of the city. They found him seated on a throne-like dais wearing what appeared to be royal garments.

George approached Faisal without waiting to be invited or announced. "Thank you for seeing me." Faisal did not respond. George continued anyway. "As we mentioned in our cables, the prime minister would like you to sign the recently concluded Treaty of Versailles indicating your ratification of its terms."

Faisal appeared unfazed. "And why would I do that?"

George seemed taken aback. "Because . . . the prime minister has asked you to do it."

Faisal wagged his finger. "You mean the prime minister of England has instructed you to tell me to sign it."

"We don't need to make this difficult," George replied.

"*We* are not making it difficult," Faisal responded. "*You* are making it difficult." He pointed with his finger for emphasis. "Your government is making it difficult. Your prime minister is making it difficult. I have done nothing in this regard."

George appeared tense. "I'm afraid I must insist."

Faisal rested his hands in his lap. "Your government promised us its full support for an Arab kingdom including Palestine, Lebanon, Syria, and all of Mesopotamia." The last part he emphasized with a sweeping gesture.

George had an arrogant smile. "I was not a party to those discussions."

Faisal let his gaze bore in on George. "I was," he said emphatically. "I was a party to those discussions, and the object of those promises."

George tried again. "Sir, if we could just get your signature—"

Faisal continued. "Your government promised us a kingdom, and yet now we have learned that while you were making those promises to us, you were also making similar promises to others. Promises regarding the same land supposedly reserved to us."

George kept trying. "Sir, if I—"

"And now you present us with a treaty that institutionalizes your control over the region. British control and French control over the same areas promised to our kingdom. And in addition to that, you have issued a proclamation supporting the establishment of a Jewish state here as well. Promises from your government to us, to the French, and to the Jews. As well as reservations of interest for itself. All regarding the same area. How do you think this is going to turn out for you today? Or for your government?"

"All of that will be—"

"A proclamation in favor of a Jewish homeland—which we all know is English for *political state*—and yet there is no proclamation in support of an Islamic kingdom. Why is that? Why has there been no public proclamation affirming your promises to us? Why have you not issued a declaration in favor of the kingdom you promised to establish?"

"I am sure all of that will be addressed in good time."

"You did not say that to the Jews," Faisal rejoined. "Or to the French."

"We need you to sign the treaty."

"If you need my signature, then now would be a good time for your government to acknowledge its promises to us. Promises to join us in establishing the kingdom that is rightfully ours. Now would be a good time for your government to publicly state its undying support for us."

George shook his head. "I am not authorized to make such a declaration."

"Very well." Faisal stood and gathered his robe around him. "Tell your ministers that when they give us your government's support for our kingdom, we will talk of their treaties."

Without saying more, Faisal crossed the room and disappeared through a door on the far wall. George, the Duke of Marbury and of Marley Green, was left alone in the room with only his assistant for company. When Faisal was safely down the hall, a member of his staff returned and escorted them from the building.

✦ ✦ ✦ ✦ ✦

When George, the Duke of Marbury and Marley Green, requested a meeting with Faisal, one of Faisal's advisors contacted Amin and asked if he knew the reason for the visit. Amin asked his contacts among the British in Jerusalem and soon determined that George's mission had something to do with London's apprehension about Arab sentiment toward a continued British and French presence in the Middle East. Amin relayed this information to

Faisal's associates and asked that they inform him of the meeting's results as soon as possible.

Within hours of Faisal's refusal to sign the treaty, Amin received a telegram informing him of George's request and of Faisal's response. "At last," Amin muttered to himself, "Faisal is stepping into his role as king." That role, and Faisal's position in it, was tenuous at best. Amin feared that any further move toward an open revolt by Palestinian Arabs, however well intentioned, would bring a negative response from the British. One that might crush the fledgling king and kingdom before they got going.

In an effort to curtail further threats of violence, and to focus Arab attention on a collective effort to reach attainable goals, Amin traveled to Syria and met with Izz ad-Din al-Qassam. He hoped a reasoned discussion would restrain Qassam from instigating action against the British. It was a delicate task, but one Amin felt held the key to a productive Arab future.

Amin and Qassam met at Qassam's home, a modest courtyard house made of sundried bricks near the center of Jableh. Qassam recalled their earlier meetings and was aware of Amin's growing influence in Jerusalem. Amin reminded him they'd been instructed by a mutual teacher, Rashid Rida. The two found they were in agreement with much of Rida's teachings—that Islam needed a revival.

"Our theology and, indeed, all of Arab life, has been too heavily influenced by European thought. And the current dominance of the region by the British and French armies is inconsistent with the teachings of Islam."

"I agree. But I wonder if the call for armed resistance isn't misplaced."

"Perhaps. You have some thoughts on the matter?"

"I fought alongside the British in the Great War," Amin answered. "They have a powerful army. As do the French."

"This is true."

"It seems that armed resistance does not have much hope against them."

"You have a different plan?"

"I have been instructing my people that we should wait," Amin informed. "Gain as much knowledge, training, and equipment from the British as possible. Later, when we have developed a cadre of capable men, we will be able to drive the British away."

"You think we are capable of driving them away?"

Amin shook his head. "Not now. But in the future. And even then we will not be able to overwhelm. But we can make their life difficult enough that they will long for home. Then they will leave and return to the life they knew in England."

"You are asking me to join you in this effort?"

"There have been reports that you are one of the promoters of revolution. I'm asking you to give Faisal a chance."

Qassam seemed doubtful. "Faisal has not the wisdom or temerity to be king."

"You think a king must be audacious?"

"He must be bold. Bolder than anyone he has ever known. Especially now. Especially Faisal."

"This is what we have been given. Faisal. The promise of British assistance. We should use both to our advantage."

"I'm not sure Faisal can do this alone," Qassam responded.

"Which is why we need a coordinated response. From the entire region."

"Of all Palestine?"

"Of all Syria—including Lebanon and Palestine—and all of Mesopotamia."

Qassam smiled. "You have spoken rightly. Everything from here to Egypt is Syria. And all of it, including Mesopotamia, is rightfully ours as Arabs."

Amin gave him a winsome smile. "Will you help bring everyone together?"

"I will do what I can, but another would be better to act on our behalf."

"And who would that be?"

"Are you acquainted with Hashim al-Atassi?"

Indeed, Amin had heard many stories about Atassi—most Arab-speaking people had. He was a man of great political stature and operated on a level to which Amin aspired but had not yet attained.

Born to a landowning family, Atassi had lived a life of opportunity, studying government at the University of Ankara before returning to his native Homs, where he served as a representative to the provincial assembly and, later, as governor of Homs. Since the end of the war, he had been involved in promoting Syrian nationalism and traveled the region, giving speeches and organizing groups to promote the Arab cause.

"I know that he is a Syrian politician," Amin replied. "And a man of great respect. But I have not been introduced to him."

Qassam nodded. "Would you like to meet him?"

"Yes. But how long will it take to arrange that?"

Qassam shrugged. "Not long. He is in town. We can walk there this afternoon."

Later that day, Qassam introduced Amin to Atassi. After a brief conversation, Atassi agreed that something must be done in response to the continued British and French presence, and that armed resistance was futile. "A unified regional political response would be best," he said.

"But how do we make that happen?" Amin asked.

"I suggest we convene a meeting of Arab leaders to discuss the matter. Perhaps a gathering of that nature could formulate a united Arab policy toward establishing our independence."

"We need someone of influence and stature to call such a meeting," Qassam added. "Would you be willing to do that?"

"I would be happy to issue the call," Atassi assured him.

✦ ✦ ✦ ✦ ✦

In May 1919, at the behest of Atassi, a Syrian National Congress was convened in Damascus, Syria, to consider the future of Greater Syria—Syria, Lebanon, Palestine, and Mesopotamia. Representatives came from across the area. As expected, the initial session elected Atassi to the office of congressional president. Jamal al-Husseini, Amin's cousin, was elected secretary. Both were included in the congressional executive committee.

Amin attended the congress also but spent much of his time at the general sessions listening to others speak. Gradually, he came to sense that he had been attempting the impossible, trying to placate the British while maneuvering toward their own political state. The British would never allow that, no matter how much trouble Arabs might make for them. But the prospect of armed revolt left him feeling heavy inside, as if it were the wrong thing to do. Yet, from the congressional discussions and deliberations, it seemed inevitable. There seemed to be no way to stop the momentum of the day, which appeared destined for conflict, no matter how devastating the result might be.

After each of the general sessions, the congress divided into working committees and in each of them the talk was the same—the British had lied; they only understood force. For most delegates, even given time for sober reflection, there was no other way forward but to fight and die and hope that sooner or later, they could achieve the expected result.

Late in the afternoon of the second day, as Amin listened to delegates of a committee discuss the elements necessary for a functioning government, an image flashed through his mind. In an instant, he saw a young Arab man dressed in Western garb with pants and shirts and shoes that seemed to be made of rubber and canvas. His shirt was open, and through the opening Amin saw something like a vest strapped to the man's chest.

The man's face was covered but Amin had the sense that he was happy and perhaps chanting a verse from the Quran as he walked toward a café. The café door was open, and the man disappeared through it. Moments later, an explosion erupted, sending fire, smoke, and debris flying through the windows and onto the street.

Just as quickly as they appeared, the images vanished, and Amin came to himself to find he was sweating profusely. He rose from his seat and walked out to the corridor for a breath of fresh air. Aref and Nafez were there and, seeing that he was not himself, came to his side. "Are you all right?" Nafez asked.

"Just needed a break," Amin replied.

"You don't look so good. What happened?"

Amin shook his head. "I'm not sure."

Aref looked concerned. "Someone said something that upset you?"

"No, it's just that everyone wants to fight, and I am sure that fighting will take us to a bad result. A terrible result. We will be choosing a life of struggle and conflict not merely for ourselves but for our children."

"That is the life we have now," Aref said. "And it was the life of our ancestors for many generations before us."

"Perhaps. But no one sees any other way." Amin shook his head. "This is not what I wanted from this meeting."

Nafez spoke as he touched Amin on the shoulder. "If you see another way, you should tell them."

"And what way is that?" Amin was unsure of what Nafez meant.

"The way you have been telling us. Use the British to make us strong, and then we will be able to drive them away."

"Yes, but now I do not think the people have the patience for that."

"You could show them the way of patience."

"No." Amin shook his head. "It has gone too far now."

"Perhaps there is a middle way," Aref suggested.

Amin looked perplexed. "A middle way?"

"Not too much of one and not too much of the other."

Amin smiled as a sense of realization came over him. "Maybe you are correct. Maybe the middle way will work."

In the committee room once again, Amin asked for permission to speak. The meeting was chaired by his cousin Jamal, who readily agreed. "As many of you know," Amin began, "I was an officer in the Ottoman army during the Great War. While serving in that capacity I was sent home to Jerusalem to recover from an illness. While there, I learned of the British desire to foment rebellion of our people against the Ottomans. At first, I was against such an idea, but then I learned that the British had promised the Sharif of Mecca and Medina a kingdom if he would assist in this regard. A kingdom covering all of Palestine, Syria, Lebanon, and Mesopotamia. Upon learning of this, I decided to remain in Jerusalem and join with my brethren in seeking to establish such a wonderful thing.

"We were led by the Sharif's son Faisal, whom many of you know and whom many of you served as well. We were accompanied and facilitated in our efforts by British soldiers and officers who supplied us with every weapon imaginable. And we were successful in vanquishing the Ottoman army from Palestine.

"Now it appears the British have made conflicting promises. Promises to the French and promises to the Jews involving the division of the land they promised to us. But the kingdom of the Sharif, the kingdom of Faisal, the Arab kingdom we all have longed to see, is a kingdom no one can promise, and no one can take away. No one can divide it. And no one can withhold it from us. It is our kingdom and ours alone. A gift from Allah to his people."

Shouts of encouragement and support went up from across

the room, but Amin waved for silence. "Yet our kingdom is now dominated by outsiders—non-Arabs who wish to impose their will on us for their own purposes. To appropriate the gift of Allah and keep it from his people. Many of you think we should resist their presence by force. That we should fight and die no matter how remote the prospect of success might be. But I think there is a better way."

For the next fifteen minutes, Amin repeated to the committee the things he had been saying to his men in the Arab Unit about using the British to train and equip themselves to be ready for the day when fighting might produce the desired result. "I have seen the power of the British army," he concluded. "And it is a power against which we cannot win today."

Someone stood. "What do you propose we do?"

"I suggest we engage the British on a political level," Amin replied.

"What does that mean?"

"Declare our kingdom," Amin explained. "And maneuver politically for its recognition and establishment. On our own terms, but in a way that avoids armed conflict."

Qassam was in the committee meeting and afterward he urged Amin to address the entire Congress. Amin agreed and the following day appeared before the assembly. He repeated many of the things he'd already said, but his appeal for a political solution rather than an armed one seemed to strike a receptive note with those in attendance. Others joined in voicing their support for a strategy that included declaring a kingdom and choosing a king, but as a way of forcing the British to admit their promises and give their support, not as a precursor to war.

At its last session, the Syrian Congress took up the matter in debate over a formal resolution. Final language, however, declared support for an Arab kingdom with Faisal as its king but stopped short of denouncing armed conflict.

Amin was glad the meeting had not resulted in a call for war but was disquieted by the result. "My attempt at finding a middle way has produced a mediocre result," he lamented.

Nafez seemed not to grasp what he meant. "How is that so? They agreed to support the kingdom and to support Faisal as its king."

"Yes. But in failing to disclaim the use of force, they have set us adrift the easiest path. And that is the path of war."

EiGHT

SHORTLY AFTER RETURNING from the Syrian
Congress, Amin began hearing rumors of Jews arming themselves
and training as military units. Some said there were dozens of
these units preparing for war against the Arabs of Palestine.
Others said they were being assisted by special British instructors.
"The best the United Kingdom has to offer," someone reported.
"And the best of their weapons, too."

Amin was skeptical that any of it was true, but the rumors
persisted and after a while he asked Nafez about them. Nafez had
heard the rumors but nothing more, and offered to ask around.
A few days later he came to Amin's house, and while they sipped
tea in the kitchen, he told Amin, "Credible witnesses say the Jews
are using a site near Kefar Sava, a village not far from the coast at
Jaffa, as a training site."

"Are the British involved?"

"No one knows for certain. But everyone is convinced the
Jews could not be doing this without British knowledge and
approval."

"Are there any other reports like that? Of confirmed sites?"

"Not that I could find."

Merely hearing rumors of Jews training for conflict had left Amin suspicious, but reports of a location carried a note of alarm and raised his level of concern. "Tell Hadad and Salama to investigate the matter."

"I can go myself," Nafez insisted.

"No, I need you with me. You are family; they are not. Tell them to investigate the matter and find out whether the rumors are true. Ask them to actually go to this place and see what the Jews are doing."

Unstated, but implied in the conversation, was Amin's desire to impose order to his relationships. Since his experience at the Syrian Congress, he'd come to see himself as a man of influence and to appreciate the need for a hierarchy of those whom he trusted. He wasn't sure how the circumstances of his life might unfold, but he wanted to position himself for greater leadership should things move in that direction. Always in his mind were the words of his father from his deathbed, about how he would one day step into the role of mufti. Amin wanted to be prepared when that time arrived.

The following day, Nafez did as Amin said and asked Kemal Hadad and Hasan Salama to spy on the Jews at the location where they'd been reported to be training. Hadad and Salama were glad for the assignment and arranged to use a car that belonged to Hadad's cousin for transportation. Setting out early the next morning, they reached Jaffa in a matter of hours and had little trouble locating the site where the Jews were conducting training exercises.

Hadad parked the car out of sight behind a hill, then he and Salama climbed to the top. From just below the crest, they watched through binoculars as a group of men marched in formation across a flat plain three hundred meters away. To the right, another group practiced with rifles, shooting at wooden boards for targets.

"These are Jews," Hadad observed.

Salama, who was watching the target practice, shook his head. "There is one over here who is not." He pointed as he spoke.

Hadad turned in that direction and through the binoculars saw a Caucasian male dressed in civilian clothing, giving direction to the men. "Is he British?"

"I don't think so."

"How can you tell from such a distance?"

"I don't know." Salama shrugged. "It just seems like someone else."

"But who?"

"Russian, maybe."

"Maybe."

"What kind of rifle are they using?"

"They have three," Hadad noted. "Italian rifles, I would say. Mannlicher–Carcano, I think."

"I'm guessing some of them have done this before. They seem to shoot rather well."

"Probably served with the British army during the Great War."

"Jewish Legion members," Salama added.

A moment later, Hadad said, "Hey, I know that guy."

"Who?"

"The one with the hat, standing beside the truck."

Salam turned in that direction. "You actually know him?"

"Sort of."

"Who is he?"

"Ze'ev Jabotinsky. I met him once when he lived in Turkey."

"Really?"

"Pretty sure."

"That guy is crazy."

"Yes. And he is seriously committed to moving us out."

They watched awhile longer, then Salama spoke. "Come on. We need to tell Nafez about this."

Late that afternoon, Hadad and Salama reported to Nafez, who, in turn, told Amin about what they learned. "The Jewish group is, indeed, training. Hadad and Salama said they were marching and taking target practice."

"Just like a military unit."

"Yes. They're being led by Ze'ev Jabotinsky, a Russian Jew and an ardent Zionist. A leader from the Jewish Legion."

Amin shook his head. "I know of him. He's been agitating for a Jewish state since before the war. Thinks the Jews must fight to establish their freedom and safety."

"Hadad met him when he lived in Turkey," Nafez offered.

"Yes, and he worked as a representative of the World Zionist Organization. What about the British? Any sign of them at this site?"

"No, but they did see someone helping."

"Who was it?"

"They weren't sure. Thought it might be another Russian." Nafez waited a moment before asking, "What does this mean for us?"

"I'm not sure," Amin answered. "But this is how the Jews intend to have their state. They will arm themselves and take it by killing us all. And the British will help them."

Nafez smiled. "Then we must kill them first."

Amin looked away. "I had hoped to avoid this." There was sadness in his voice and a distant look in his eyes.

"As I have told you," Nafez reminded, "this is the life of our ancestors. A life of struggle. A life of conflict. It is who we are."

✦ ✦ ✦ ✦ ✦

By the spring of 1920, tensions were running high in Palestine, although open confrontation between Arabs, Jews, and British troops was limited to sporadic incidents. Jews were energized by the Balfour Declaration and apparent British support for working within its framework to establish a Jewish state. Arabs were energized by the same thing, though in the opposite direction and were deeply offended by British betrayal regarding promises of an independent Arab kingdom.

After the Syrian Congress adjourned, Amin took a position in Jerusalem as teacher at the Rashidiya School, a respected school for Muslim boys that met in a building near Herod's Gate. As an established institution, the school afforded Amin an opportunity to teach an approach to understanding the Quran and Islam that he adopted from his education under Rashid Rida—that Palestine belonged to the Arabs as a gift from Allah, that Jews were interlopers and should never have been allowed to reside there, and that one day Allah would return the region to its rightful caretakers as part of an Arab kingdom.

Most important to Amin, his position at the school elevated his stature from merely being Kamil's younger brother to that of a rising young Islamic scholar. At first, he'd resisted the notion of following that path, but after working with Faisal and the Syrian Congress, he saw that having a distinction all his own could be a useful way to add heft to his opinions. That spring, as the annual Nabi Musa Festival approached, Amin hoped to continue his rise in the public eye by combining his position at the school with his family's influence to garner an opportunity to deliver one of the many public speeches presented during the festivities.

Each spring, Palestinian Arabs celebrated the festival of Nabi Musa, a series of events that honored the life of Moses. The center of the event was a weekend of worship, entertainment, and religious devotion that coincided with Easter and concluded with a pilgrimage from Jerusalem to the site of Moses' tomb, which was located near Jericho. However, events at key sites in Jerusalem were scheduled each Friday in the month preceding the final weekend. Being invited to address the crowd was an honor. Speakers included many of the well-known figures in Palestinian politics but also included one or two people of promise, usually young men who had distinguished themselves in some way. Amin worked hard for an opportunity to be included in at least one of those events.

✦ ✦ ✦ ✦ ✦

That same spring, the San Remo Conference was set to convene. Triple Entente members were slated to determine the final disposition of Palestine, and the news of it only added to the tension of the region. In the run-up to the conference, Ronald Storrs, the governor of Jerusalem, met with Arab leaders in an effort to convince them to ease tensions among Arab residents. After meeting with Kamil, other Sharia judges, and prominent members of the Nashashibi clan, Storrs summoned Amin to his office. They sat at his desk, Storrs on one side, Amin on the other.

"As you no doubt are aware," Storrs began, "British delegates are scheduled to attend a conference next month to resolve the remaining issues pertaining to Palestine."

Amin nodded. "And this is when you will publicly declare your support for an Arab kingdom?" He knew better than to expect such a response, but he wanted to make a statement and, having Storrs's ear for the moment, he intended to make the most of it.

Storrs smiled politely. "No, the *Allies* will be working these details out among ourselves."

The arrogance of Storrs's statement angered Amin and it became obvious in the tone of his voice. "You mean you intend to hold a conference to determine the future of Palestine, without including Palestinian Arabs in that discussion?"

"I'm afraid that isn't possible." There was a hint of condescension in the tone of Storrs's voice. "We simply cannot—"

Amin interrupted. "You do realize, Arabs are the largest group of people living in the region."

"Yes." Storrs rested his hands in his lap. "I'm sure we are quite aware of that fact."

"Then, why are Arabs not included in the discussion?"

"The Allies have won the region from the Ottoman Empire." Storrs was growing increasingly perturbed. "We defeated them. We were victorious. The fate of this region is ours to decide."

"You defeated the Ottomans. You were victorious. But you did it with Arab help," Amin argued. "Help you solicited from us with a promise of support for an Arab kingdom once the Ottomans were gone. You are aware of that promise, are you not?"

Storrs nodded his head slowly. "Yes. We are aware. But these things—"

Amin was even angrier than before and cut off Storrs again. "Your government has no intention of honoring its promises to us, does it?"

Storrs was indignant. "Young man, that is *not* the subject of this meeting."

Amin leaned forward. He hated being talked down to even more than being deceived. "Then, what *is* the subject of this meeting?" His voice was loud and his tone intense.

Storrs seemed to sense their discussion had gotten away from him and that he had ventured onto indefensible ground. He took a deep breath and tried to reset. "We would like your assistance in curtailing animosity between Arabs and Jews." He spoke in a careful, even tone without actually looking at Amin. "Things have been tense lately and, with the conference coming, they are likely to get even more tense."

"Has there been any animosity between Arabs and Jews?" Amin pressed.

"Only a few incidents," Storrs replied. "But we are concerned that with the conference and the spring festivals, things might . . . get out of hand."

"And what are you willing to promise this time in exchange for our assistance?"

Storrs frowned. "I'm afraid I don't like the tone of your voice."

Amin leaned closer. "And I don't like the fact that your government promised to assist us in establishing an Arab kingdom—one that extended throughout all of Palestine and Mesopotamia. Yet all the while you were promising us that kingdom, you were agreeing with the French to divide the same territory between yourselves."

Storrs turned sideways in his chair. "As I said, that is not—"

"And as if that weren't enough—promising us something and giving it away to the French—you promised the Jews a homeland from the same area."

Storrs pushed back from his desk and stood. "I would remind you that the British army controls the Middle East. You and your fellow Arabs would do well to remember that."

Amin stood as well. "And I would suggest that you and your European colleagues would do well to remember the power that Islam has demonstrated in the past. And that we are fully capable of demonstrating again."

Storrs was beside himself. "How dare you threaten me like that!"

"And how dare you threaten me!" Amin retorted.

"I am an officer of His Majesty's army."

"And I am a messenger of Allah."

✦　✦　✦　✦　✦

Using family connections and his brother's influence, Amin was successful in gaining a spot on the dais at an event held near Al-Aqsa Mosque on the second Friday of the month. He appeared with his cousin Musa Kazim al-Husseini, who was mayor of Jerusalem. Both men presented a message similar to the one Amin had given to the Syrian Congress—that Palestine was part of an ancient Arabic kingdom, that the Jews were trying to steal it away from them, and that the British had been blinded by Jewish sorcery into applying their considerable military power against Arab-speaking peoples.

Unable to avoid the opportunity presented by the festival, Ze'ev Jabotinsky learned the location of Arab events and organized coinciding events near the same sites. When Arab speakers finished their presentation, Jabotinsky gave his, which included a hardline Zionist message. "The land of Palestine once had been the land of Abraham. Jews are Abraham's direct descendants and the descendants of blessing. As the true descendants of Abraham, we are rightfully entitled to control the region. The land of Palestine is the land of the Jews and we intend to make it so!"

When Amin heard that Jabotinsky was giving speeches in direct opposition to those presented by Arab dignitaries, he was indignant. "The arrogance of this man astounds me," he fumed.

Salama and Hadad were with him when they learned of Jabotinsky's actions. Salama seemed at a loss. "What can we do to stop him? The British authorities seem to welcome him."

Amin shook his head. "I do not know, but we must do something."

"We could gather a crowd to oppose him," Hadad suggested.

"Yes," Salama agreed. "Shout him down."

"Drag him down," Hadad added.

"No," Amin insisted. A sense of realization came over him and he smiled. "We will organize speeches to counter his speeches."

Hadad looked perplexed. "What do you mean?"

"Our people speak to our people. Then Jabotinsky appears across the street with a message for *his* people. Both crowds are there."

Salama seemed to sense something. "And?" he asked expectantly.

"When he finishes with his speech, I will rise from the opposite side and give a speech to counter his."

"With both sides present," Salama observed, "there is sure to be trouble."

Amin grinned. "And trouble is just what Jabotinsky needs."

With the help of Salama and Hadad, Amin organized counter events that followed Jabotinsky's speeches. However, unlike the message he presented when he appeared with his cousin the mayor, these were angry denunciations of Jewish and British collusion against the Arabs. Filled with vitriol, they were intended to raise the ire of an Arab crowd and incite them to action.

"The Jews are raising an army to fight against us!" he shouted. "They intend to wipe us out and take Palestine by force. We have seen them and observed them with our own eyes. They are training in the desert near Jaffa. Arming themselves with British weapons. Using the assistance of European advisors. Preparing to make war against us. Soon they will be powerful enough to drive you from your home."

Swept up in the moment, he added, "If we do not oppose them now, they will grow too powerful for us to resist. The time to act is now!"

Those who heard his speeches were whipped into a frenzy and very nearly on the verge of rioting. Only the intervention of armed British troops kept them contained.

Through the remainder of the month, meetings, gatherings, and speeches continued. Jabotinsky argued the Jewish message. Amin, his cousin Musa Kazim, and Aref al-Aref argued the Arab perspective. Each one taking turns trailing the official speakers and seizing on the crowd they gathered to deliver an increasingly bombastic and confrontational message.

Incited by the various speeches, a riot broke out on Easter weekend. Four Jews were killed in the fracas. Musa Kazim, Amin, and Aref al-Aref were arrested on charges that they incited Arabs to riot. All three were held at Acre Prison.

Two days after their arrest, all three were allowed to post bail and were released pending trial. After being released, however, Amin and Aref left their family and friends behind and fled to Damascus.

With Amin gone, Nafez assumed leadership of the group he'd formed in Jerusalem. Hadad, Salama, Latif, and Qadir stepped up to help. Together, they organized Palestinian Arabs to protest against British action in arresting only Arabs but not Jews after the Nabi Musa riot. With little effort, they filled the streets with angry mobs. Day after day they marched and shouted and closed down Jerusalem to commercial traffic. When that produced only defiance from the British, they threatened a general strike.

Finally, Storrs sent British troops to search the homes and offices of prominent Jews. Among them was the office of Chaim Weizmann, who now lived near Jaffa and served as the head of the Jewish Agency for Palestine, and the home of Ze'ev Jabotinsky.

Soldiers found nothing at Weizmann's office, but a check of Jabotinsky's home yielded a cache of weapons and ammunition. As a result, Jabotinsky was arrested. At a subsequent trial, he was found guilty of violating British weapons law and sentenced to fifteen years. Amin was tried in absentia for his alleged role in promoting the Nabi Musa riot. He, too, was convicted and sentenced to ten years in prison.

In the aftermath of the riot, Weizmann and other Jewish leaders brought great pressure on the British to remove Musa Kazim from his position as mayor of Jerusalem. They argued that he was an instigator of the riots, too.

After some debate, Storrs dismissed Kazim and appointed Raghib al-Nashashibi, from the rival Nashashibi clan, to take his place. Amin, still living in Damascus, learned of Kazim's fate during a visit from Salama. He was incensed. "This proves once and for all that the British are mere pawns of the Zionists."

NINE

IN THE SPRING OF 1920, the much-anticipated San Remo Conference was finally gaveled into session. After a week of discussion, delegates reached a resolution of issues regarding administration of the Middle East that had carried over from the Paris Peace Conference. The agreement, appended to the Treaty of Versailles, granted a Palestinian Mandate to England and a Mandate of Syria to France, giving each country the authority and influence they'd previously agreed to in the Sykes-Picot Agreement. In effect, conferees merely ratified Sykes-Picot and did nothing about resolving tensions in the region.

In response to the San Remo Conference, a call went out from Atassi, president of the Syrian Congress, to convene a second congressional session to discuss the results of the San Remo Conference. The congress was scheduled to meet in May. However, when British authorities learned of the planned gathering, they issued orders forbidding the meeting to be held.

Despite the British prohibition, Amin invited congressional delegates to Damascus to discuss the situation. On May 31, delegates gathered at the Arab Club. Most of the attendees came prepared to take action against the British.

Aref al-Aref was among those at the Damascus meeting, as was Nafez, who traveled from Jerusalem to attend, and Salama, who accompanied him. In the course of their discussion, the group established an organization known as the Palestine Arab Workers' Society. Amin and Aref were elected as officers. The society was designed to be a permanent body that would seek to establish groups in each of the areas represented by the Congress. Amin hoped it would become a way of maintaining a cadre of people like the one he'd formed in Jerusalem with Nafez and the others, but with congressional approval and support.

After the general session ended, Amin met privately with Nafez to review events in Jerusalem. Nafez recounted their experiences with the protest. "I hope you do not mind that we did this without seeking your approval first," Nafez offered. "There was no way to get word to you, and we thought we should act quickly."

"That was good," Amin replied. "We need more action like this."

"It runs counter to your position that we should not confront the British directly."

"I may have been wrong about that."

"Oh?" Nafez looked surprised.

"I have listened to our people and I have seen how the British acted toward us and toward me. I do not think our people can wait to express their disdain. They have been lied to and they know it. We who have been attempting to lead them have been deceived, and the people know that, too. If we do not act now, with force, our own people will perceive us as gullible. Or worse, as weak."

"What would you have us do?"

"More protests," Amin insisted. "And do it in a way that provokes the Jews, just as we did with the riots during Nabi Musa."

"And the Congress will approve these things?"

Amin's look hardened. "The Congress will approve them or lose all credibility."

"And should we confront the British troops also?"

Amin shook his head. "Not yet. Not with the British. They are militarily too strong. We are not yet equal to the task of engaging them in combat. We must organize, prepare. And that is something you can do very well. Organize our people. Recruit them to small, interconnected organizations. Use the protests to do that." He looked over at Nafez. "But work around the edges with the British. Always remember, our primary enemy is the Jews. Them we can attack."

"So," Nafez recounted, "protest. Organize. And harass the Jews."

"Yes." Amin smiled. "Harass the Jews."

"How far should we go with that?"

Amin looked him in the eye. "Kill as many Jews as possible."

"Won't the British come to their defense?"

"That is a risk we must take. We need trouble with the Jews as a way of making their political ambitions untenable with the British. If they see that a Jewish state will cause conflict with us, they might at least slow down the processes long enough for us to organize a permanent response."

"And when the British take their side?"

"If they do that, it will only make our case. The world will see that they are puppets to the Jewish puppeteers."

✦ ✦ ✦ ✦ ✦

Two months later, the British government named Sir Herbert Louis Samuel, a Jew, as the first High Commissioner of Palestine. From that position, Samuel had charge of the day-to-day administration of the British Mandate. As soon as the appointment was made known to the public, Nafez sent Salama to Damascus to make certain Amin knew.

"They are saying this makes Samuel the first Jew to rule Palestine in almost two thousand years."

Amin was livid. "I have tried to work with them!" he shouted. "I have tried to confine our efforts to something that fits within the British framework. Faisal has attempted to do the same thing. And every time we do, the British run to take the Jewish side. Never have they shown the slightest regard for their promises to us. But always they do the bidding of the Jews."

"What shall I tell Nafez?"

"Tell him to wait," Amin advised. "I want to discuss the situation with Faisal."

✦ ✦ ✦ ✦ ✦

A few days later, Amin arranged a meeting with Faisal at his residence in Damascus.

"You are aware of the decisions reached by the British at their conference in San Remo?"

"Yes."

"And you are aware that they have appointed a High Commissioner for Palestine?"

"A Jew."

"The Jews sense that they now have the upper hand in Palestine. First with British support for their idea of a political state and now with the appointment of a Jew as their agent for Palestine."

"And you think we must do something."

"Yes," Amin replied. "If you truly want to be king, you must assert yourself."

"And what do you propose that I do to assert myself?"

"Assemble an army and attack."

"We have an army," Faisal replied. "The one you helped recruit."

"Then you must begin now to train them."

"Will you help us?"

"Yes. I will be glad to help."

"I thought you were against armed confrontation with European powers."

"It will not come to that," Amin insisted. "If you gather your army and move forward, the British and the French will concede the kingdom you were promised."

✦ ✦ ✦ ✦ ✦

Later that month, Faisal assembled an army—tribal members he'd gathered while working with Lawrence and those he'd commanded in the Arab Unit of the British army—and began training them for organized warfare. At the news of Faisal's actions, Qassam, still living in Syria, assembled the force he had tried to use against the Italians in Libya and marched them to Damascus, where they joined Faisal. Shaykh Saleh al-Ali, an Alawi commander from the Jabal Ansariyah Mountains near the coast, also joined forces with Faisal.

After several weeks of training, and after protracted discussions with Amin, Qassam, and Ali, Faisal decided to divide his forces. He sent Ali with Qassam to occupy the Jabal Ansariyah Mountains near his home along the coast. "Both of you know the region and your men are from there. They will be fighting for family and friends. With the other half of the force," Faisal announced, "I will travel north and attack at Aleppo."

Ali shook his head in disagreement. "That is too far to travel. Surely the French will learn of your intentions and they will cut you off before you arrive."

"Perhaps they will," Faisal replied. "But I believe this is the will of Allah."

"Do you have enough men?" Qassam asked. "Aleppo is no small village."

"I have men who are trained and experienced," Faisal said proudly. "And I expect to gain additional forces as we go."

Ali tried again to dissuade Faisal, but when Faisal persisted, Ali gave up. Instead of arguing the point further, he prepared his men for the trek to the coast. "At least we will be going home. They will be glad for that."

With little opposition, the combined forces of Ali and Qassam easily took control of the mountains. Faisal likewise made the trip from Damascus to the outskirts of Aleppo with no opposition. And he acquired enough men along the way to double the size of his force. However, when they reached Aleppo, they encountered French regular troops holding well-fortified positions. Faisal and his men dug in for what they thought would be a long siege.

After two weeks of heavy fighting, however, the French army flanked Faisal's position and surrounded him. A messenger delivered a simple but effective ultimatum. "Surrender or die." Faisal surrendered, and the Syrian Hashemite Kingdom dissolved.

With Faisal no longer in power and the kingdom no longer in existence, French forces cut off access to the mountains where Ali and Qassam were encamped. Ali and his men dispersed. Making use of little-known mountain trails, they returned home or simply disappeared. Qassam and his men did likewise and made their way south into Lebanon.

Nafez, who had been traveling with Faisal, returned to Damascus a few days after Faisal's surrender. He found Amin sitting alone in a darkened room, depressed and despondent. "This is why we cannot yet confront the British. We are not ready."

"If armies and equipment are the measure, will we ever be ready?"

"We do not need to become an imperial power to shape our own destiny. We only have to wait until time and circumstance make the imperial powers vulnerable."

"What does that mean?"

"As I have said many times. They are British. They are used to a luxurious European lifestyle. They will grow tired of life in Palestine and then they will leave. We must be ready when that day comes."

✦ ✦ ✦ ✦ ✦

On his run from the French authorities, Qassam arrived in Haifa where he found a teaching position with Madrasa Islamiya, an Islamic educational institution with many schools in Haifa and the surrounding area. Funded by the Jamiat Islamiya, a *waqf*, the school had no lack of funding. Equally important, Madrasa Islamiya was administered by prominent Muslims from the city, many of whom were wealthy landowners and successful business-men. Through them, Qassam located a residence large enough for his family, and he sent for them to join him.

Unlike other Muslim scholars, Qassam made himself easily accessible to the public, often finding himself hailed on the street by passersby looking for advice. In the classroom, he promoted the same Islamic revivalist message he learned from Rashid Rida, the Salafi cleric under whom he studied in Egypt. As part of his Islamic revivalist teaching, he denounced and discouraged sev-eral local Palestinian traditions, including unorthodox funeral rituals, visitation to the al-Khidr shrine near Mount Carmel to give thanks for their children's well-being or achievements, and Syrian tribal dances that were held at religious sites. "These are nothing more than superstitious innovations to Islam," Qassam stated. "They are an offense to Allah and to the teachings of the Prophet Muhammad."

After a few months in town, dispensing advice on the street and knowledge in the classroom, he came to feel that Allah was opening new avenues to him. With access to the lower classes, he established a night school for casual laborers and preached to them as an imam, first in the Jerini Mosque and later in the Istiqlal Mosque. Rather than resisting Muslims on the street, he sought them out in brothels and hashish dens. His greatest following came from the landless ex-tenant farmers drifting into Haifa from the Upper Galilee where purchases of agricultural land by Jews had disposed them of their farms and exclusionary practices denied them an opportunity to work on the Jewish collective farms.

As a result, Qassam became increasingly popular among poorer Muslims living in the northern part of Palestine and was frequently invited to preach at Muslim festivals and on other special occasions. Through those events, news of Qassam's activities eventually reached Amin in Damascus. He made a note of Qassam's location and filed it away for future reference.

TEN

FACED WITH FRENCH and British occupation of the Middle East, and with the collapse of Faisal's kingdom, Amin grew increasingly concerned about the future of the region and about the role he might play in it. Damascus was a large city, but it was not Jerusalem. Stuck in Syria, he might easily be pushed aside or, worse, forgotten and ignored.

Rather than quietly sit by and watch his prestige and influence diminish, Amin searched for a way to keep his hand in events, to keep himself relevant to the cause, and to find a way forward for Arabs. To that end, he began agitating for yet another meeting of the Arab Congress. Aref, who was with him daily, agreed. "Even if the British try to stop us, we still will make our point and get our message out to other Arabs. And to the world."

"Whatever the British do," Amin clarified, "we must make sure our people see it as proof of their real intentions. They are interested only in supporting the Jews. That has been their aim all along, even when they were recruiting Faisal and the Sharif. Jews have money. The British will always yield to the money."

"That does seem to be the case." Aref glanced away as he spoke and there was a hint of uncertainty in his voice. Amin noticed it immediately. "Whether I am correct or not, that is our message."

"If we do this . . ." Aref cautioned, "if we call for another Congress, I think we will incite our people to acts of violence. They're moving in that direction on their own."

"If the people do that, then that is what they will do." Amin spoke with a sense of detached emotion. "But the meeting we are calling is not one to instigate violence. We are attempting to motivate and organize Arab leaders to put political pressure on the occupying European powers. And, perhaps, to draw the world into our fight."

"The world?"

"Yes." Amin had a look of realization. "That is what we really are doing, and I did not think of it that way until just now. We are trying to gain public support among Arabs and among the world at large. The British might not listen to us, but they will listen to the United States. To Russia, maybe. And to people from other countries. Public opinion matters to them—not as much as Jewish money, but it matters nonetheless."

"But we do not want them turning to war?"

"No. If we wage war, we will be seen as the aggressors. We need *political* action," Amin stressed. "Not military action. And for that, we need a meeting on the order of the Syrian Congress. To show the world that it's not just you and me talking about this topic."

"I agree that we need to meet, but the last time we tried to do that the British refused to allow it," Aref reminded him.

"We are not British subjects," Amin rejoined.

"They certainly think we are."

"We are Arabs," Amin insisted. "We are subject only to an Islamic king."

"So we call for another congress. What else can we do?"

"We need to get the word out to the world about what has happened to us."

Aref smiled. "*That* we can certainly do. I know a little something about publicity." As a newspaper editor, he had numerous media contacts with influential publications throughout the Middle East.

After discussing the matter further, Amin and Aref decided to produce a series of articles addressing the current situation. Occupation by foreign powers. Jewish efforts to establish a political state. Refusal to support a corresponding Arab state. As ideas for the articles took shape, Amin summoned Abdul Latif to Damascus to assist them.

After a week of intense writing and revision, Amin and Latif produced six articles that were ready for publication. Using his position as an officer of the Arab Society and his contacts in the newspaper business, Aref convinced six major Arabic journals to publish the articles. They appeared over the following six weeks as a series and attracted wide attention in Palestine. Two were reprinted by a newspaper in Istanbul, the editor of which was a friend of Aref. Not long after that, people all across the Middle East took notice of Amin's message.

Having gained attention to their cause, Amin and Latif produced follow-up articles. More pointed and bombastic than the first series, they accused the British of desecrating Islamic holy sites in Jerusalem. Subsequent articles argued that merely by their presence in the region, European troops were an affront to Allah, Islam, and Arabs everywhere.

Even more than the first, the second series of articles struck a chord with Palestinian Arabs and were reprinted by newspapers from Egypt to Mesopotamia. A few weeks later, they appeared in London newspapers, too, including the *Times*. Most citizens of London read the articles but gave them little attention, counting them as little more than Arab screed. Officials of the British government, however, took quite a different view and were highly offended.

Incensed by what he viewed as an affront to British integrity and a smear of his own character, Corbyn Barrowman, the new foreign secretary, contacted his counterpart in Paris and demanded that the French government arrest Amin immediately.

Authorities in Damascus sent soldiers to find him, but, tipped off to Barrowman's demand, Amin and Aref fled to the desert where they were given sanctuary by a clan of Bedouin tribesmen. It fell to Georges Leygues, the French secretary of state for foreign affairs, to explain to Barrowman that, although France held a mandate for administering Syria, taking Amin and Aref from the Bedouins by force was a political and logistical impossibility. Barrowman was not pleased.

✦   ✦   ✦   ✦   ✦

Living as they were in the desert with the Bedouins, under sanctuary from the tribal warlords, Amin and Aref were untouchable by French or British authorities. From the safety of the desert, they continued to issue articles attacking the British and French presence in the Middle East. Aref kept a steady stream of messengers flowing from the desert to the editorial staff of Arab-language newspapers, all of whom were sympathetic to the cause and glad for the increased readership the articles produced.

Amin employed his own messengers, who kept him up-to-date on the latest events and served as his spokesmen in delivering the call for an Arab gathering. Convincing others to join him in a concerted effort against the British proved difficult, however, primarily due to the remoteness of Amin's location. As weeks went by and there still was no movement to convene a congress, Amin began to feel he really was losing his position as leader of the Arab cause.

Frustrated by the cumbersome nature of the situation, Amin raised the issue with Aref, who offered a suggestion. "You need an emissary. A person who can speak for you on his own. Someone who could advocate for the things you believe in, without having to check with you every time. Someone who could speak as if you were speaking yourself."

Amin liked the idea, but the thought of being bound by someone else's opinion of his opinion left him nervous and unsettled. "I'm not sure there is such a person. Even Nafez requires supervision."

"There is one," Aref noted.

"Who is that?"

"Qassam."

Amin's eyes opened wide at the mention of his name. "I had forgotten about him."

By then Amin's newspaper articles were a regular feature in many publications. Keeping up with the demand for weekly installments kept him busy. Still, there was time in the schedule for other things, and when they took a break from writing, he asked Latif to find Qassam and bring him to the desert.

Two days later, Latif located Qassam in Haifa and delivered Amin's message. Qassam responded immediately and returned with Latif to the desert camp. Amin and he sat together in Amin's tent and talked.

"I need your assistance," Amin began.

"How may I help?" Qassam asked.

"As you can see, I am confined here in the desert, free to wander the sand as I please, but unable to enter even the smallest village for fear the French will arrest me."

Qassam looked puzzled. "I am not certain I can help with that."

"I need an official emissary," Amin continued. "Someone who can speak for me and on my behalf."

"Someone who could speak as you would speak."

"Yes, without needing to consult with me first."

Qassam nodded. "Someone with authority to decide as you would decide."

"Exactly." Amin smiled politely. "Would you serve me in that capacity?"

Qassam was older than Amin by several years and, no doubt, had once seen himself as rising to a level of leadership that would command the service of others. That, however, had not occurred and now he was being asked to assume the role of servant. Still, this was the life he had chosen to live. A life of scholarship and service. Whatever Allah wanted, that was what he wanted, too. "I would be honored to serve you," he responded.

"Very good. We have much work to do."

For the next hour, Amin outlined his desire for another Syrian Congress at which he hoped delegates could be convinced to hammer out a united approach against the continued European presence in the Middle East. "Others are breaking free of European domination," Amin noted. "The Turks have asserted their independence and are pushing to remove all Allied troops from their territory. We need to do likewise."

"I agree. But many of our people cannot agree on borders. Already, competing interests are emerging among Arabs. Egypt would like to control Palestine. The people east of the Jordan are begging for a king. Syrians and Lebanese demand respect for their traditional borders."

Amin frowned. "Syria's traditional borders would subsume the entire Levant."

"Yes." Qassam nodded. "And that is what I mean. The region is on the verge of fracturing into nationalism and nothing more. Everyone is zealous for their own interests."

"That is why we must meet and work these things out as one. For the sake of resisting the occupation and for the sake of our own identity."

"Won't the British and French oppose such a gathering, as they did before?"

It was the same question Aref had asked, and Amin was in no mood to argue the point again. "We can't let that stop us," he urged. "I don't care what you call it or how you promote it. Just get everyone there and get them to work on a united opposition to the British and the French."

"And you do not plan to attend such a meeting?"

"No. I cannot. French and British authorities will be looking for me and would arrest me the moment they saw me, but I will not be there. You will attend in my place. You will answer for me. Whatever you decided will be my decision.'"

"Very well," Qassam responded. "I will do my best to serve you in every respect."

Using Qassam as his representative, Amin finally succeeded in organizing a meeting of Arab representatives at Haifa on December 4, 1920. Almost immediately, the gathering became known as the Haifa Conference, but to add credibility to the event, Qassam promoted it as an extension of the Syrian Congress. Attendees came from throughout the region. Nafez, thinking someone needed to keep an eye on Qassam, attended, too, as did Latif and Salama.

At the meeting, delegates established the geographical parameters of a Palestinian state based on details from the earlier McMahon-Husseini correspondence that memorialized the Sharif's cooperation during the Great War. The resolution that defined the geography of the kingdom also declared the British administration of Palestine unwarranted and illegal. They objected to the creation of a Jewish homeland in Palestine and opposed further Jewish immigration to the region. Consistent with Amin's concern about direct armed confrontation with the British, the conference stopped short of calling for military action. Syrian delegates, already sensing the French would withdraw, lobbied to exclude Syrian territory from the resolution. Before adjourning, the conference appointed an executive committee that included Qassam and Nafez. Qassam made sure the committee was dominated by Palestinian delegates.

After the conference, Qassam and Nafez traveled with the executive committee to Jerusalem, where they met with Herbert Samuel, the British High Commissioner and supreme authority in Palestine under the British Mandate. At that meeting, the executive committee raised the issue of Jewish immigration and the expanding Jewish population in Palestine. It was an awkward conversation—Arabs talking to a Jew about the threat Jews posed to Arab control of the region—but Qassam and the others did their best to address the issues in a thoughtful and substantive manner.

After outing the historic nature of the struggles, Qassam said, "The Jews mean to form a political state here in our homeland and they mean to kill us to do it."

Samuel gave a dismissive gesture. "That is preposterous," he scoffed.

"They have been recruiting and training military units," Nafez retorted. "We have seen them with our own eyes."

"Those are merely for defensive purposes. Jewish farming collectives are located at remote sites. If there was trouble, our troops could never reach them in time to respond."

"What need is there to response?" Qassam asked. "We have no army."

"I assure you," Samuel repeated, "they mean you no harm."

Someone else from the committee spoke up. "*Now* who sounds preposterous?"

Qassam was insistent. "You do not understand these people."

Samuel bristled. "These people?"

Qassam ignored Samuel's bluster and continued. "Jews from the Jewish Agency present a good face to the public. And many of them are capable leaders. But they are not representative of all Jews. Some of them are ruthless and, I assure you, they want to kill us to take our land."

The discussion continued, at times veering into heated argument, but participants failed to resolve any of the central issues. Finally, Samuel indicated he'd heard enough and stood, indicating the meeting had ended.

Qassam and the committee presented a written memorandum that summarized the decisions reached at the Haifa Conference. Samuel glanced at it, then laid it on his desk. "I appreciate your time and effort in presenting your concerns. But I want to make clear to you that, while I am not unsympathetic to your situation, the Balfour Declaration is settled British policy. You would do well to accept it."

"I assure you," Qassam stressed, "that is something we will never do."

Samuel appeared taken aback. "And why not?"

"Because we would be accepting our own death. And that is something we cannot possibly do."

✦ ✦ ✦ ✦ ✦

After meeting with Samuel, members of the executive committee who were from other regions departed for the return trip home. Members who were from Palestine, however, gathered at Nafez's apartment to discuss the situation further. "I think our approach is unworkable," Nafez began.

Qassam had a questioning look. "What do you mean? Surely we have only demanded what the conference approved."

"We are Palestinian," Nafez explained. "That is all. We cannot solve all problems facing all Arab people everywhere."

"We have only made demands regarding Palestine. And not the part of Palestine that includes Syria or Lebanon. So, what are you saying?"

"The Syrians showed us how weak their resolve is when they were offered a kingdom under Faisal. They should have risen up as one to drive out the occupiers. Instead, they sat by and watched as Faisal and his men were crushed."

Qassam was offended by the slight against his fellow Syrians, but he felt vindicated in the opinion he had expressed to Amin earlier that the region was fracturing along national lines. "We were not well prepared"—he did little to conceal the defensive tone in his voice—"but perhaps this is for the better."

"How so?" someone asked.

"A response to the situation we face requires planning, organization, and time. That would be better accomplished in working with a smaller area where there would be fewer conflicting interests."

"Whatever we do," someone urged, "we must be patient."

"And we must be focused," another added.

"But how long must we wait?"

"As long as it takes," Nafez answered. "And we must focus our efforts on Palestine. Let the others solve their own problems. Our problem is Palestine. We cannot hold out for a global solution at the expense of our own people."

"Is that what Amin says?"

"That's what he would say if he were here," Qassam noted. "If we wait to act until we have a solution for all Arab problems in every region, nothing will get done and the Jews will end up with the entire area under their control. And remember, the Jews are our principal enemy."

"Yes," Nafez agreed. "Our real enemy is the Jews."

Without realizing the momentous decision they'd made, Nafez, Qassam, and the others who'd gathered that day with the executive committee had reached an historic turning point in the Arab struggle. Prior to that day, their efforts had been dominated by a Damascus-oriented Pan-Arabism. One that sought to solve the greater Arab question as it manifested throughout the entire Middle East. As Nafez noted, the situation now was too complex for a single solution. A Palestinian-focused attempt to secure an Arab state solely in Palestine was the only workable solution for Palestinian Arabs. Anything else risked relegating Arabs in Palestine to exclusively Jewish control.

ELEVEN

IN THE MONTHS that followed, tensions remained high among Arabs as they continued to wrestle with the consequences of British deception regarding the promised Arab kingdom and with the continued influx of Jewish immigrants. Many also were angry with their fellow Arabs who continued to sell land to Jewish organizations, which made ongoing immigration possible. As if that was not enough, reports continued to appear in Arab newspapers about Jewish paramilitary units training for action against Arab villages. To those Arabs who knew the truth about the situation, the facts regarding the armed Jewish units were not as salacious as the rumors, but they were unsettling, nonetheless.

As Samuel indicated in his earlier discussion with Qassam and the Haifa Conference executive committee, leaders within the Jewish Agency—the principle facilitator of Jewish immigration and the establishment of Jewish farming settlements—were no longer confident the British government could maintain the security of the settlements, particularly those established in remote locations. To address that concern, they formed a paramilitary group called Haganah. Comprised primarily of armed settlers, Haganah's duty was to provide armed protection for the settlements. Although members continued to work their assigned duties on the farm, they also trained like organized militia and were increasingly well armed. News of their activity spread quickly among Arabs and served to fuel a growing sense of impending conflict.

Samuel knew full well what was happening with the Jewish militias and the Arab displeasure about it, being informed with daily reports concerning these developments. And he regularly met with Jewish and Arab leaders in an attempt to diffuse the situation. But nothing he did seemed to make much difference, and he began to wonder if British attitude and policy weren't at the heart of the trouble.

In an attempt to find a new approach, Samuel convened a meeting of his staff at which he hoped to create a plan that would restore peace and harmony among all residents of the Levant. After considerable discussion over a wide range of topics, which seemed not to move the meeting even a small step toward resolution of the underlying issues, Samuel related, "I am considering issuing a pardon to everyone involved in the Nabi Musa riots. Both Jew and Arab alike."

A gasp went up from those in the room, followed by an awkward silence, before someone said, "I'm not so sure that's a good idea."

"Why not?"

"Because it would only validate Arab actions."

"It might validate their concerns," Samuel replied. "Aren't we obligated to address their concerns?"

"They started a riot," someone groused. "Aren't we supposed to address that, too?"

"Has anyone proved who started this riot?"

"We don't have to prove what we already know," someone answered. "Arabs are responsible. That's why they're in jail."

"This isn't merely an issue of Arab conduct," Samuel countered. "It's a matter of Jewish conduct, too. And of our own."

"Our own?" The tone was indignant.

"British troops were present that day. *We* were present, and whatever happened, we were part of it. We need to take ourselves out of the equation in order to remove us as an excuse for unproductive attitudes on both sides of the situation. As a means of prodding Jews and Arabs to define their issues in Jewish and Arabic terms, not with regard to anger toward the British government."

"That is commendable," someone noted. "But you simply cannot pardon all who were involved."

"Why not?"

"Some of them are criminals."

"Especially Amin al-Husseini and Aref al-Aref," someone chimed in.

Samuel was offended by the comments. He was surprised by that reaction in himself, too, but it was the way he felt—a sense of righteous indignation at the injustice that lay behind the attribution of blame made solely on the basis of ethnic identity. He did nothing to hide his feelings from the tone of his voice. "You would have me pardon the Jews and not the Arabs?" It was more an accusation than a question.

"I would have you pardon none of them," someone argued. "But certainly not those two. They were the primary instigators."

"What about Jabotinsky and the Jews who were involved?" Samuel asked. "They are not criminals, also?"

"The riot started with the Arabs," someone spoke up sullenly. "Not with the Jews."

Samuel shot him a look. "You were there in attendance?"

"No, but—"

Samuel cut him off. "Then you are merely repeating what you have heard from others."

"If it hadn't been for Husseini and Aref," someone argued, "there might still have been a confrontation, but there never would have been any violence."

"You were there also?" Samuel asked.

"None of us were there, but that doesn't invalidate our opinions."

Samuel took issue. "You do not think Jabotinsky knew what he was doing when he arranged his speeches to coincide with the ones given by Husseini?"

"I'm not—"

"He was there on the same day." Samuel took an imperious tone. "And at the same location. Delivering speeches designed to counter, point by point, those presented by Husseini and other Arab speakers."

The group was silent a moment, then someone reminded, "You can't pardon Husseini."

"But as I said before," Samuel countered, "if I pardon the others and not him, I would be pardoning all Jews without pardoning all Arabs. Won't that be a problem?"

"Perhaps," someone reasoned calmly. "Which makes it a good thing not to pardon anyone at all."

They discussed the matter further, and gradually, though he thought it a mistake, Samuel acceded to the request of his staff. Even though he had misgivings about what the Arab reaction might be, a few days after the staff meeting, he pardoned everyone involved except Amin and Aref. It seemed like a cowardly thing, letting his staff push him to a policy he did not think was correct, but he needed their support on other matters and he couldn't dismiss them all. Still, as he affixed his name to the last of the documents, the thought came to him, *Let them have their way now and when this all falls apart they will know I was right all along.*

Two days after Samuel signed the pardons, news of the action was announced to the public. As he suggested, Arabs throughout Palestine saw the terms of the pardon as an example of favoritism—a Jewish administrator treating Jews favorably while disregarding the interests of Arabs. Within hours of the announcement, Nafez began organizing a response. That evening, Arabs took to the streets of Jerusalem, clogging them with protestors and bringing all other activity in the city to an abrupt halt.

From his office window the following morning, Samuel watched and listened as the noise from outside grew to a roar. He mumbled, "This could all have been avoided if I had done what I wanted to do and pardon everyone."

Albert Lemon, an office assistant, stood nearby and heard the remark. "The Arabs are weak."

Samuel gestured toward the scene outside. "You think this is a sign of weakness?"

"They are like children throwing a tantrum. They will shout and scream, but in the end, it will all blow over."

Samuel shook his head but said nothing. In his mind, though, he was certain the confrontation between Jews, Arabs, and anyone who involved themselves in the region would never end well.

✦ ✦ ✦ ✦ ✦

In March 1921, Arabs learned that the British government planned to convene a conference to discuss the future of Palestine. Nafez approached Herbert Samuel about attending. Samuel refused his request. "This is an internal matter," Samuel explained.

"But how can you discuss the future of Palestine without consulting Arabs who live here?"

"We have talked with you many times."

"And each time, you have ignored our concerns."

"We cannot dispossess residents from land they legally purchased."

"We did not want you to permit them here at all."

"I understand your concerns," Samuel reiterated. "But you cannot attend the conference."

"You mean the British are deciding our fate for us. Without our involvement in the process."

"Not exactly."

"Then, what?"

"A representative will meet with you after the conference."

"Will the Jews have representatives in attendance?"

"This is an internal British matter," Samuel repeated.

✦ ✦ ✦ ✦ ✦

Later that month, Winston Churchill, the new Colonial Secretary, convened a conference in Cairo to explore British policy in Palestine. As indicated by Samuel and others, the conference was indeed an internal British convocation. It was called by Churchill to facilitate an easier means for British officials in the region to discuss and resolve internal British policy issues that remained from the Great War without the need for protracted correspondence. The primary issue attendees faced was that of reconciling the conflict between promises of a kingdom to Arabs, as reflected in the McMahon correspondence with Faisal, and the promise of a Jewish homeland, as reflected in the Balfour Declaration.

After almost a month of discussion and negotiations, the conference agreed to implement a policy, known as the Sharifian Solution, named after the Sharif, that gave Abdullah bin Hussein administration of the territory east of the Jordan River, known as Transjordan. Faisal, his brother, was granted the newly created Kingdom of Iraq. Financial support would be supplied to both by Great Britain. The Sharif of Mecca would be recognized as King of the Hejaz, and Abdul Aziz ibn Saud would remain in control of the Nejd, an area he now controlled anyway and was not likely to surrender to anyone, much less the British army.

On a note less favorable to Arabs, attendees concluded that both the French and British governments should continue to administer their respective mandates over Syria and Palestine. And they were adamant that British support for the creation of a Jewish homeland was the United Kingdom's immutable policy.

A week after the Cairo Conference ended, Churchill came to Jerusalem and met with Qassam, Amin's cousin Musa Kazim, and the Haifa Conference executive committee. Churchill provided the group with a summary of the conference's decisions. Most were glad for the declaration of an Arab kingdom, though they had hoped for a united political entity that would control all of the Middle East.

"That is not possible," Churchill explained. "Political realities will not permit the inclusion of everyone under a single entity."

When Churchill had fully explained the decisions reached in Cairo, Qassam, as he had done many times before, provided an overview of the circumstances Arabs faced in Palestine—Jews immigrating every day, buying land, forming settlements, recruiting and training armed units to assert themselves against their Arab neighbors, and an administration that favored Jews over Arabs.

"We are certain," Qassam insisted, "that the Jews intend to kill all of us and take our land by force."

Churchill shook his head. "That is the most preposterous thing I've ever heard."

"Of course you have not heard of these things," Musa Kazim responded. "You do not live here, and the representatives of your

MIKE EVANS

government who *do* reside here are completely on the side of the Jews."

Churchill was indignant. "You impugn the integrity of the British government?"

Qassam spoke up. "You have a Jewish administrator overseeing all of Palestine who recently pardoned all Jews involved in the Nabi Musa riots but refused to pardon all Arabs. A Jew, lording it over Arabs, in an unfair and inequitable manner. What are we supposed to think?"

Churchill lit a cigar and took a long puff from it. "And what, in your estimation, would be required to correct the situation, as you think it exists?"

"End further Jewish immigration," Musa offered. "Withdraw support for the creation of a Jewish state in Palestine, at least until the matter of an Arab kingdom is resolved. And allow us to establish an Arab government in Palestine."

"As to an Arab government for Palestine," Churchill replied, "we have not addressed that issue. However, I can tell you this much. The Balfour Declaration is settled British policy. You have no choice but to accept it."

Nafez spoke up. "You reached a decision regarding the Balfour Declaration without consulting us. Did you consult your Jewish friends before declaring it?"

"It is a matter of British prerogative to discuss governmental matters with anyone we like."

"So you consulted with the Jews."

"Discussions were had with their representatives."

"So it is true," Qassam rejoined. "It is the policy of the British government to prefer the Jew over the Arab."

Churchill again shook his head. "That is not what happened."

"But your policy favors the Jew over the Arab. You talked to them but did not talk to us before reaching your decision. You support creation of their political state but deny ours, even though we are the largest single group of people living in Palestine. You arrest us but pardon them. You tell us we must accept them, yet you do nothing to see that they accept us."

Churchill stood. "Gentlemen, I believe this meeting is concluded."

With that, Churchill abruptly crossed the room to the door and disappeared. When he was gone, Albert Lemon appeared. "The High Commissioner would like a word with you."

Qassam stood. "I believe the time for discussion has passed." He gestured toward the door.

Lemon moved as if to block his way. "You would refuse an audience with the High Commissioner?"

"We must be on our way," Qassam asserted. "We have much to do now."

They stood facing each other—Qassam staring into Lemon's eyes, Lemon staring into his—and some in the room thought they might come to blows. But after what seemed like a long time, Lemon stepped aside and the executive committee departed.

When they were gone, Lemon reported the matter to Samuel. Churchill was seated on a sofa at the far side of the room. "They have a point," Churchill noted.

Samuel turned to face him. "And what is that?"

"You are a Jew, who administers Palestine for Her Majesty's government. Arabs constitute the single largest race of people living here. You pardoned all Jews who were arrested after that riot but did not pardon all Arabs."

"It smacks of favoritism?"

Churchill nodded. "It was a mistake. If you couldn't pardon all, you should have pardoned none."

Samuel shrugged. "Perhaps so."

"London agrees with you," Churchill added.

"What do you mean?"

"They see Jewish nationalism as an asset, and Arab

nationalism as a problem. I don't agree with them, but they take your side in the matter."

"What would you have done?"

"I would have fired you on the spot."

"Yet you did not."

"They convinced me that firing a Jew from the single most important job in the ancient land of Israel would create far more problems than it solved."

Samuel smiled. "For once, I am glad for British bureaucracy." He took a seat near Churchill. "We need to find a way to accommodate Arab nationalism."

"We have just announced support for a kingdom on the Arabian Peninsula, a kingdom in Transjordan, and a kingdom in Iraq. What more is there to do?"

"There is the matter of Palestine."

"I'm not sure we can resolve that."

"Why not?"

"No matter how it is couched, Jews see the entire region as their historic homeland. One to which they assert an unqualified right of control. Arabs see it the same way but without a Jewish presence. The two views are mutually exclusive."

"But this is a situation of our own creation. This modern version, at least. We encouraged Arabs to think of a kingdom. And we encouraged Jews to live somewhere else besides the British Isles."

Churchill shrugged. "Perhaps we did. And perhaps we shall yet find a way to keep all of our promises. We never said what form a Jewish homeland might take and we never said precisely when we would lend our support to such an endeavor."

"I wouldn't—"

Churchill cut him off. "Now is not the time, Herbert."

"The Arabs are growing increasingly tense and restless."

"They are Arabs. This is what they do. They make a loud noise, and when they see they cannot get their way by making a scene, they slink off to their rooms and wait for supper. Besides, once they have considered the matter thoroughly, they will realize we have just given them as much of what they wanted as they are ever likely to receive."

TWELVE

A MONTH AFTER Churchill's visit to Jerusalem, Kamil al-Husseini, Amin's brother, died. He'd been ill but had not been in poor health, and his death was unexpected. News of his passing spread quickly among Arabs. Rumors about the cause of his death did also.

When Qassam heard that Kamil had died, he thought of Amin, forced to live in the seclusion of the desert, and of his wife, left alone in Jerusalem to grieve with her young children. In an attempt to help, he traveled to Jerusalem, thinking he might be of assistance in some way. Much to his surprise, he arrived to find Karimeh, Amin's wife, preparing to leave. Qassam was taken aback. "Where are you going? Will you not attend the funeral?"

"I am going to the desert to find my husband." Her voice was stern but not angry.

Qassam shook his head. "Can you not send someone to do that for you?"

Karimeh glared at him. "You are suggesting that I send

someone to tell my husband that his brother is dead? Would you prefer to hear news like that from a stranger?"

Qassam conceded the point with a shrug. "Do you even know where he is located?"

"I have sent for Nafez. He will help me."

"He has agreed to go?"

"I have not asked him yet, but I am his sister and he will not refuse me."

"I will take you," Qassam offered. The thought of them going into the desert, just the two of them, was more than he could bear.

Karimeh looked over at him with a hopeful expression. "You know where to find Amin?"

Qassam nodded. "I will take you to him."

"And Nafez?"

"He can come, too."

A short time later, Nafez arrived at the house, and when he heard that Qassam and Karimeh wanted to find Amin, he insisted on going. The following day, as mourners gathered to bury Kamil, they set out for Damascus.

✦ ✦ ✦ ✦ ✦

Three days later, they came to the Bedouin camp where Amin and Aref lived. Amin was standing near his tent when they came into view and knew immediately Karimeh was with them. He rushed to her and took her in his arms.

"I have missed you," he whispered.

"And I have missed you."

They embraced and after a long kiss, he leaned away. It was then that he noticed the look on her face. "Something has troubled you. You have bad news for me?"

Tears filled Karimeh's eyes. She nodded. "I have very bad news."

"What is it?"

"Kamil has died."

Amin's countenance dropped and he pulled her close once more. They stood together, locked in each other's arms until Nafez came to Amin's side. "It was from an illness," he explained. "Not from the acts of another, so far as we can tell."

Amin sighed. "I suppose there is some consolation in that."

For the next two days, they visited in Amin's tent. Amin asked about his mother and other family members, then about whether he might be granted permission to come to Jerusalem. "Just for a day or two. To make sure all is well."

Qassam shook his head. "I do not think that will be possible."

"Herbert Samuel would have to agree," Nafez said, then quickly added, "but I will ask."

"You do not think he will agree?" Karimeh added.

"It is not likely," Nafez answered. "Even for a time such as this."

After talking further about the circumstances of Kamil's death, arrangements for his funeral, and the attitude of the British toward his demise, the conversation moved on to other topics. The Cairo Conference, the grant of support for Arab kingdoms in Arabia, Transjordan, and Iraq. Amin was glad for that result but remained unpersuaded that he should give up the struggle for Arab independence that he'd begun years before. "The British are attempting to coerce us into accepting their Jewish friends," he noted. "And if we do, we will all soon be dead. They mean to take control of Palestine completely and they see no place for us."

Qassam replied, "The British insist that will not happen."

"The British will leave one day," Amin responded. "And when they do, the slaughter of Arabs will begin. This grant of a kingdom in various places is good, but do you see how they have done it? They have given part to this one and part to that one and—"

"They have divided us," Qassam interrupted.

"Precisely." Amin nodded. "You understand the situation well." For a moment he was jealous and sensed that Qassam might be a threat to his position, but he let the thought pass and continued. "We must never forget. The British are allies and servants of the Jews. Whatever they offer us, it is always tainted with the corruption of the Jews. And it is offered for only one purpose: to strengthen the Jews and eliminate us. Not just from Palestine—though that is their concern for the moment—but from the entire world. The Jews mean to wipe us from the face of the earth."

✦ ✦ ✦ ✦ ✦

When Nafez and the others left the desert, they traveled together as far as Tiberius. From there, Qassam journeyed west to his home to Haifa while Nafez and Karimeh continued south to Jerusalem. The day after they arrived at home, Nafez arranged a meeting with Herbert Samuel. They met in Samuel's office and sat opposite each other at Samuel's desk.

After an exchange of greetings, Nafez began, "Amin has been informed of his brother's death."

Samuel raised an eyebrow. "You have visited him?"

"I have . . . made certain that he knows of this tragic news."

Samuel had a somber expression. "I'm sure he was saddened by his brother's passing."

"Very much so. As we all were."

"I noticed the funeral was conducted shortly after Kamil died. I did not attend, of course, though I meant no disrespect by my absence. It just seemed that if I were there, I would be a focal point of attention and that would be inappropriate."

"His family is appreciative of your respect."

"Was there something specific you wanted to see me about?"

"Yes." Nafez shifted positions in his chair. "Amin would like to come to Jerusalem to visit with his family. A brief visit, only to console them in their grief. Would you grant him safe passage for that purpose?"

Samuel shook his head. "I'm afraid that would not be possible."

Nafez pressed the point. "Surely you can understand his interest in being with his family."

"I understand it very well. But his return, even for a day or two, would be as disruptive to the city as my presence at Kamil's funeral would disrupt his family. Even more so."

They talked awhile longer, but Nafez could see that Samuel was firm in his resolve to deny Amin the right to return home. Instead of being asked to leave, he rose from his chair and started toward the door. As he did, Samuel called after him, "Do you think he would ever return?"

"Amin?"

"Yes. Do you think he still wants to return here? To live."

"I am certain of it," Nafez replied.

✦ ✦ ✦ ✦ ✦

After Nafez was gone, Samuel sat at his desk, thinking of the present situation and rolling it around in his mind, considering each party's viewpoint. The Jewish desire for the safety of a political homeland. The Arab desire for the same. The need of the empire for Middle Eastern natural resources and the stability required to exploit them. His mind went far and wide through topic after topic, but as the afternoon moved toward sunset, he came back to the present situation and the dilemma it posed for him.

With the death of Kamil al-Husseini, the position of Grand Mufti of Jerusalem became vacant. By law and practice, an election would be held among the *ulema*—a body of only twenty-one Islamic leaders who were both scholars of Islam and judges of

Sharia law—to fill the post, but the results of the election would produce only a list of three top candidates. Under rules imposed by the British Mandatory Authority, the election was only advisory, not determinative. The final choice was left to the High Commissioner. Samuel alone would choose the mufti, albeit from the list determined by the electoral process. *This might provide an opportunity to move the region toward a better social and political footing,* he thought to himself. *To shift Arab opinion of the Crown from antagonistic to that of partner. And if not partner, at least to assuage some of the angst associated with the British presence.*

Samuel considered the matter of Kamil's replacement as he rode home from the office and as he enjoyed the evening with his family. He thought of it as he lay in his bed to sleep and as he awakened the next morning to face the new day. When he arrived at the office, he convened yet another staff meeting to discuss the matter.

Several names were put forward as potential mufti replacements. "If we can get them to enter the election," someone noted.

Samuel had a questioning frown. "Are we having difficulty finding candidates?"

"We can find plenty of candidates," someone answered. "Just not the kind we want."

Another explained. "Of the sympathetic Arabs, those who could actually do the job are not well versed in the nuances of Sharia law. Those who fully understand Sharia law are not attuned to British expectations."

Samuel nodded his head. "So we face a dearth of qualified candidates."

Someone spoke up. "The position has been filled in recent decades by a member of the Husseini family. Is there not one among them who is up to the task?"

"I think we should avoid the Husseini at all cost."

"Oh?" Samuel looked perplexed. "And why is that?"

"This is an opportunity to break their hold on the office, just as we did with their grip on the mayor's office."

"Yes," someone added. "The Husseini are powerful. We can use this appointment to diminish their influence."

"If that's the case, we should appoint a member of the Nashashibi family. They are bitter rivals of the Husseini. We could pit the two against each other and create internal strife."

"We have plenty of Arab strife as it is."

"Having already removed the Husseini from their position in the Jerusalem government, adding the mufti position to their tally would risk creating a new dynastic family. Making the Nashashibi potentially as much a problem for us as the Husseini."

From the discussion, which rambled on until almost noon, Samuel realized that choosing the new mufti from the Nashashibi clan not only risked turning that clan into a new dynasty but the even greater threat of further offending the Husseini family and turning them into a permanent enemy. That would only compound the situation the British government faced, not improve it. Furthermore, appointing a member of the Nashashibi family to the mufti position gained him nothing he didn't already have from giving them the mayoral office.

Indeed, many Arabs other than the Husseini family already were angry with the Mandatory government over the removal of the mayor. A move they regarded as solely in response to Jewish protests over the riots, making the removal of Musa Kazim yet one more buttress to the Arab claim that the British were merely Jewish pawns. Appointing a member of the Husseini clan as mufti would go a long way toward countering that opinion, which might greatly benefit the Mandatory government's ability to administer the region. And perhaps provide a British success in Palestine that might, in turn, improve Samuel's own career options with the office in London.

Having heard from his staff, Samuel was convinced Amin al-Husseini was the obvious and only choice to fill the mufti position. Husseini, however, was a convicted criminal and a fugitive. Appointing him as Grand Mufti would be complicated. Members of his staff would adamantly oppose the decision. Some of them might resign, and London would hear about it straightaway. The Foreign Office might even send someone to investigate.

Still, Samuel decided it was the right thing to do—to pardon Amin al-Husseini and work to appoint him as Grand Mufti. This would be an opportunity to show that he was a fair-minded administrator capable of seeing beyond racial division to make a good decision, even when that decision was contrary to popular opinion among his peers. An opportunity to calm the Arab community and a way to win back some goodwill with Arabs in general and the Husseini family in particular.

Accomplishing that task, however, required several steps, all of which posed a daunting challenge. The first was to issue a pardon for Amin al-Husseini. Rather than follow normal procedure and ask his staff to work up a file on Amin that could be subjected to review, Samuel decided to issue the pardon on his own. To cut through the procedure and simply *do it*. Before he left the office that day, he ordered a staff secretary to prepare the necessary documents.

A few days later, with pardon documents in hand, Samuel asked an advisor if he knew where to find Husseini. An hour later, Alan Mayhew, one of the military intelligence officers working from the basement of the building, appeared at Samuel's office and told him that Husseini and Aref al-Aref were living with a Bedouin tribe that had given them sanctuary in the desert.

"Do you know where this tribe is located?" Samuel asked.

"Yes, they are in the desert of Transjordan, but if you mean to seize Amin al-Husseini and remove him by force, I must say, confronting the Bedouin to take him would incite great trouble among the Arab community."

"I do not mean to take him by force," Samuel responded. "I only want to talk to him."

Mayhew frowned. "Face-to-face?"

"Yes."

"Shall we assemble a force to accompany you?"

"No, you and I shall do this alone."

Mayhew was astounded. "Alone? Just the two of us?"

"We shall need no others." Samuel leaned over the desk toward Mayhew and lowered his voice. "And not a word of this to anyone until we return."

"But—"

"Not a word!" Samuel snapped. "That's a direct order."

Mayhew braced to reply. "Yes, sir."

✦ ✦ ✦ ✦ ✦

The following day, Samuel and Mayhew traveled from Jerusalem, across the Jordan River, and into the desert. A day later, they located Amin at an oasis east of Petra. Amin and, indeed, the entire tribe, was surprised to see the High Commissioner and even more surprised to see him in the company of only a single companion.

As might easily have been possible, some of the Bedouin wanted to take the men hostage and demand payment for their return, but Amin prevailed upon them to do no harm. Sensing that Samuel came for a purpose other than his pending legal case, Amin invited them to his tent and sent for Aref, who soon joined them.

Seated together, they sipped tea and munched on flatbread until the sun went down, talking only of family and friends. Then, in the cool of the evening, they finally got down to business.

"First," Samuel began, "let me express my sympathy at the loss of your brother."

"Thank you."

"He was a great man and served his people well."

"You knew him?"

"I met with him on several occasions. And he always proved to be very accommodating."

"I am certain he was."

"Now," Samuel continued, "we must choose his successor."

Amin's eyes brightened. "You would like my help in naming someone?"

Samuel smiled. "Yes, I would. But before we get to that, I would like to know if you would accept a grant of amnesty."

"Amnesty from the British government?"

"Yes."

"Covering all the crimes alleged against me, or that could be laid against me?"

"Yes. Up to this day," Samuel added. "Not crimes yet to be committed."

"Amnesty that would give me the right to return to Jerusalem without fear of arrest?"

"Yes. Certainly."

Amin thought a moment. "I could only accept your offer if it extends to Aref also."

"Very well," Samuel replied. "I will grant amnesty to you both. But only under one condition."

"What is that?"

Samuel looked Amin in the eye. "You must return to Jerusalem and stand for election to your brother's position as mufti."

Amin grinned. "I would be honored."

✦ ✦ ✦ ✦ ✦

Amin returned to Jerusalem, where he was greeted by his wife and family. Friends and relatives gathered for a celebration that lasted into the night. But when the party was over and everyone was gone, he lay in his bed and thought of all that had happened. The riot. His arrest. Fleeing to Damascus. Then to the desert. And then Kamil's death, and the pardon from Samuel.

As he thought of those things, he remembered the words of his father. *"Kamil will hold the seat but only until you are old enough to accept it. He is a good man, but he lacks the vision for what must be done."*

"And what is it that must be done?" Amin had asked. The words of his father's reply still rang clear in his mind. *"We must kill them all."* He was referring to the Jews and back then, when his father had said those things to him, Amin had been frightened by them. Now he saw the wisdom of the old man's words.

"He was right," Amin whispered.

Karimeh, who lay beside him, turned to face him. "Did you say something?"

"No. I was simply remembering."

She slipped an arm around him and drew him close. "We do not have to only remember now." She nuzzled his neck. "We can experience the wonder of our lives again."

✦ ✦ ✦ ✦ ✦

Amin found being at home with his wife and children a great relief, but there was much to be done if he was to have a chance at winning the mufti election. Despite the reputation of his family name, Amin had little personal relationship with the ulema. He was widely known, but that was all. If he were to have a chance at being named mufti, he needed to capitalize on the name and emphasize the lineage from his father, to his brother, to him. And he needed to remind them that his family's tradition of service had greatly benefited the court. The trick, however, was to spread that message to ulema members without seeming to boast or coerce.

To help with that, Amin enlisted the aid of Nafez, who brought with him Hadad, Salama, Qadir, and Latif. None of them had Amin's family lineage with the ulema, but Hadad's family had deep ties to the Jerusalem commercial sector. He prevailed on those connections to exert as much influence as possible, but reports coming back from the effort were not encouraging.

"You are popular with the people and they know who you are, but the ulema has its own requirements."

Amin was disappointed. "Whom do they favor?"

"Hussam ad-Din Jarallah is the front runner."

"A member of the Nashashibi clan."

"Yes," Hadad said. "And his support appears to be solid."

Nafez spoke up. "Should we do something to derail him?"

"No, I think we should work hard to convince the members to choose me but allow the election to play out however it occurs. We don't need to give the Jews an excuse to create trouble just yet. And I think Samuel has his own ideas about how this should turn out."

✦ ✦ ✦ ✦ ✦

After the votes were counted on election day, Amin stood in fourth place. Even making the list was a feat in itself, and many were impressed to see his name so near the top three. Still, he was not one of the three and that meant that, by law, Samuel was prohibited from choosing him to fill the post.

As he reviewed the results, Samuel still was determined to name Amin as mufti, and he searched for a way to do that. To put Amin in a position from which he could be chosen.

"All we need is to move him into the third position," Samuel told an aide. "That's all. Just nudge him up one spot on the list."

"The votes have been counted," the aide replied. "There is nothing else we can do."

Samuel sighed. "There is always a way."

"We can't falsify the vote," the aide protested.

"No." Samuel nodded in agreement. "But we can influence the candidates."

The aide frowned. "What do you mean?"

"If we can find a way to move one of the top three candidates out of the way, Amin al-Husseini would move up to third."

"But how are you going to do that?"

"I'm not sure," Samuel responded. "But ask Raghib al-Nashashibi to come for a visit."

The following day, Raghib arrived at Samuel's office. The two men spoke while seated around Samuel's desk, sipping tea and eating slices of sweet cake.

"I have seen the election results," Samuel began.

Raghib smiled. "It is a well-known fact that you wanted Amin al-Husseini to place in the top three."

"Yes," Samuel conceded. "I did."

"And now you want me to help you do something about that."

Samuel grinned. "You are a perceptive man."

"I keep my eye on the things that matter to me."

"And what do you think it would take to move him up?"

"I suppose you are speaking of Jarallah, my kinsman."

"Yes."

"Jarallah is a man of reason." Raghib gave a nonchalant shrug. "I am sure we can reach an accommodation."

"It occurs to me," Samuel suggested, "that Jarallah would make a fine chief qadi and inspector of the Muslim religious courts."

"Yes." Raghib nodded. "Chief inspector for *all* of Palestine."

"I am certain he would do a great job. A position like that

would allow him to travel the country at his own schedule. And it would give him time to pursue other matters."

"Of course," Raghib noted, "he would need sufficient funds to do that."

"Certainly. A stipend would be in order for that position."

"A good stipend," Raghib added.

"A very good stipend," Samuel agreed.

Samuel and Raghib discussed the amount of stipend that would be sufficient to permit Jarallah to accept the position and then Raghib assured him the matter would be concluded without delay and without controversy. The following day, Jarallah announced that he was withdrawing from the election and would not accept the position of mufti.

With Jarallah no longer in the running, Amin moved up to third place on the candidate list. Two days later, Samuel appointed him as Grand Mufti of Jerusalem. Shortly after that, Samuel's office announced that Raghib had accepted the post of chief qadi and inspector of the Sharia courts for all of Palestine.

A week later, Amin and Samuel met in Samuel's office. As they sat across from each other at the desk, Samuel asked, "How did our situation go so far astray?"

"Your predecessors promised us a Hashemite Kingdom," Amin offered. "One that would govern all our traditional lands. From the Arab peninsula to Persia and all of Mesopotamia. But at the same time, members of your government agreed with the French to divide the area among yourselves. And then you agreed to give the Jews a homeland in the same region." He had a thin, tight smile. "With a beginning like that, nothing could go right."

"But we have straightened all of that out with the Cairo Conference."

"You said so. But you still have not implemented those decisions. And the deception regarding the kingdom and the French has cost you dearly with the people."

"They do not trust us?"

"Worse," Amin replied. "They do not believe you. You asked us to revolt against the Ottomans and help you win the war. Which we did. Then you stabbed us in the back not once but twice."

Samuel frowned. "Twice?"

"Once with the French," Amin explained. "And once with the Jews."

"But that was then," Samuel argued. "Can't we get past that?"

Amin had a stoic expression. "Such a thing will not be easy for our people to forget. Especially since more Jews continue to arrive every day. Arrival that has the full support of your government."

THIRTEEN

DESPITE THE PROGRESS that seemed to be made at the Cairo Conference, British officials in London were slow to approve details of the plan. A few months after Amin was appointed Grand Mufti, Winston Churchill returned to Jerusalem to discuss the matter with Samuel and other British Mandatory officials. "As you know," Churchill began, "we have yet to implement the decisions we thought we reached at the Cairo Conference."

"Yes," Samuel replied with a wry tone. "I noticed. The Arabs have noticed, too."

"There has been resistance to the notion of an Arab kingdom."

"They mean to maintain a permanent presence here?"

Churchill shrugged. "Oil is a primary concern."

"We need stability in the region in order to exploit the oil."

Churchill nodded. "Many in the government think our presence will give us that."

"Our presence will lead to complete disruption," Samuel

argued. "The only way to bring the kind of stability to the Middle East that we, and the world, need is for us to give the residents who live here control of their own affairs."

"Well." Churchill sighed. "London is having a difficult time believing that."

"They think the Arabs will lock them out?"

"They think that giving the Arabs a kingdom would be foolish."

"The situation here *is* complicated," Samuel noted. "That much is true."

"Yes, and not just with Jews and Arabs."

"You mean the French?"

"They aren't too happy with our proposal, either."

"They moved Faisal out of Syria and now we want him back in place?"

"Yes," Churchill nodded. "And things aren't going so well for Hashemite control of the Hejaz, either."

"I understand they are under serious pressure from the Saudi clan."

Churchill shook his head. "I never thought the Sharif could hold on to the area."

"We could make Faisal king of Iraq without bothering the French," Samuel suggested. "Or the Saudis."

"I suppose."

"And we could put Faisal's brother, Ali, in position to succeed their father in the Hejaz."

"As I said," Churchill repeated, "I don't think they will control the Hejaz for much longer."

"But we could ignore that fact," Samuel suggested. "Deal with them as if they *are* in control. And who knows, perhaps placing Ali in a strong position would help them against the Saudis."

Churchill shook his head. "I have met Ali. He wouldn't last very long against the Saudis."

"Perhaps not." Samuel shrugged. "But the results of the Cairo Conference have been announced. If we do not do as we said we would do, we will lose all hope of ever controlling the Arabs. Our credibility was seriously damaged with the way things were handled at the end of the Great War. If we back out again, we'll never be able to influence them. We will lose even the moderates."

"But if they can't handle a kingdom," Churchill rejoined, "why should we give them one?"

"Because we said we would. And if they lose their kingdom, then it is they who lost it. Not we who refused to abide by our promises. And besides, if the Saudis take over, we can always work with them. They are not antagonistic to us."

That point seemed to strike a chord with Churchill. "And the third son—Abdullah—what would become of him?"

"We can make him a regent or something in Iraq," Samuel suggested.

Churchill seemed interested. "I'll take this up with the cabinet when I return to London, but I would note that we already are suppling Ibn Saud with arms, intelligence, and money. He is the strongest of any of the pretenders. If he decides to take the Hejaz, no one can stop him. And I don't think anyone in London would want to try."

✦ ✦ ✦ ✦ ✦

Late that summer, while ministers in London continued to deliberate British policy towards Palestine, the matter was brought to a head when, to everyone's surprise, Abdullah Hashemi seized Amman and took control of the Transjordan region. Within weeks of declaring himself king, Abdullah named Saleem Namir, one of Amin's chief rivals, as his closest advisor.

Following Abdullah's seizure of power, British officials moved quickly to acknowledge his authority and position. And, as suggested by the Cairo Conference, they readily agreed to supply arms, munitions, and financial support. They were playing both ends against the middle, but no one seemed to think that strategy presented a problem.

In an effort to contain Abdullah's ambition, and in an attempt to stay ahead of the developing situation, the British foreign secretary's office announced implementation of the accords reached at the Cairo Conference and declared the establishment of a Hashemite Kingdom of Iraq with Faisal as king. At the same time, rule over the Hejaz was acknowledged to remain in the hands of the Sharif, with British subsidies supporting both Faisal and the Sharif.

Privately, however, continued British support for the Sharif was made contingent on his signature to the Treaty of Versailles. Like Faisal, the Sharif refused to sign the treaty, citing British support for the Jewish presence in Palestine. "Signing the treaty," he reasoned, "would be tantamount to conceding the point of a Jewish state, which I will never do."

As might be expected, such a flurry of activity legitimizing Arab interests in the region left Jewish leadership in Palestine quite nervous. In an effort to calm their fears, Samuel moved forward with establishing the Mandatory governing apparatus. Within days of the announcements from the foreign secretary's office, he issued an order acknowledging the Jewish Agency for Palestine as the entity responsible for administering details of the British Mandate for Palestine as they pertained to Jews. The Zionist Commission, a nonprofit organization previously created by the World Zionist Organization, acceded to that role. Chaim Weizmann served as president.

✦ ✦ ✦ ✦ ✦

Not long after Weizmann's role was announced, King Abdullah dispatched Saleem Namir as his emissary from Amman to pay a visit on Weizmann. Namir and Weizmann met at Weizmann's office and, after an exchange of pleasantries, got down to business.

"King Abdullah would like to invite you to Amman," Namir began.

"And what would be the purpose of this visit?"

"I think," Namir suggested, "you might find talks with Abdullah beneficial."

"What does he wish to discuss?"

"He would like to talk with you about the future of Palestine."

Weizmann's eyes opened wider. "He has something in mind?"

"He is aware of your interest in establishing a Jewish homeland in the region and, as everyone is aware, what you really want is a Jewish state."

"He is opposed to that, I presume."

"To the contrary. He thinks your presence here can be stabilizing, and he would like to assist you in that regard."

"You mean he thinks we will prevent rival Arab groups from establishing a presence here."

"The arrangement would be mutually beneficial."

When Namir was gone, Weizmann met with the Jewish Agency executive committee and briefed them on the meeting. Many were against any discussion with Abdullah and thought the proposed talks were a trap. Weizmann, however, saw himself as a diplomat of considerable ability and was enticed by the possibility of reaching a rapprochement with Abdullah. Despite objections from the committee, he agreed to the meeting.

Later that month, Weizmann traveled to Amman and met in secret with King Abdullah. As Namir had suggested, they discussed at length the future of Palestine. Abdullah was insistent that Jews hold their political independence in Palestine subject to his ultimate authority over the entire region. "An autonomous region," he underlined, "but always within our ultimate control. That will be to your benefit in preventing other nations from attempting to conquer you."

Weizmann was equally adamant that Jews should have a genuinely independent political state. "We have seen what happens when we live in less than absolute Jewish control. For centuries, our people lived in Eastern Europe under just such an arrangement as you propose. And each time our people were forced to submit to all manner of degrading conditions and political uncertainty."

As the discussion continued, it became evident that the one thing Abdullah was concerned most about wasn't a Jewish state, but a situation in which Amin gained control of Palestine. "Now that he has been named Grand Mufti, there will be no limit to what he will do to assert his influence."

"I assure you, we would never let that happen."

"And I assure you," Abdullah replied, "you have no idea the nature of the man you are dealing with in Amin al-Husseini. I would prefer any of the Jews to Husseini."

Throughout their meetings and Weizmann's stay in Amman, Abdullah, and Weizmann were assisted by Namir and a small group of advisors. Meals were catered by an array of servants who saw to their personal needs as well. All of the servants were Arab and no one gave any thought to their presence. Both Weizmann and Abdullah spoke freely at all times.

One of the servants was Abu Munif, a member of the Salafi movement and a follower of Rashid Rida. Munif was deeply offended by comments he heard regarding Amin in particular and Muslims in general. That night, after everyone was asleep, he slipped away from the residence and traveled across town to the home of his brother, who was a friend of Hasan Salama. After an intense conversation about the meeting, they decided to send a messenger to Jerusalem to convey news of the meeting to Salama. Abu prepared a written summary of the discussion he'd overheard, including Abdullah's remarks about preferring the Jews to Amin. When he was finished preparing it, he gave it to the messenger. "Guard this with your life," he ordered.

The following day, Salama received the message and delivered it to Amin, who read it quickly. "So, Namir attended this meeting?"

"Yes," Salama replied.

"I knew he was a traitor," Amin groaned.

"Should we deal with him now?"

"No," Amin answered. "We will deal with both of them when the time comes."

Salama frowned. "Both?"

"Abdullah is a traitor, too."

✦ ✦ ✦ ✦ ✦

In December, Herbert Samuel issued an order establishing the Supreme Muslim Council, a five-member group that would govern and administer daily details of the Mandatory Authority as they pertained to Arabs. The Council was given exclusive control over Muslim waqf and Sharia courts, to administer them within the framework of the British Mandate for Palestine. Members of the Council were to be selected by the former Palestinian electors who served in the Ottoman Parliament.

In January 1922, the fifty-three former electors to the Ottoman Parliament met to choose the five members for the Supreme Muslim Council. Amin al-Husseini was elected president. The other members were Muhammad Effendi Murad, Abd al-Latif Bey Salah, Sa'id al-Shawa, and Abd al-Latif al-Dajani. As one of its first acts, the Supreme Muslim Council, with Amin in control, announced plans to renovate Al-Aqsa Mosque and the Dome of the Rock, both of which had fallen into disrepair during the war. In conjunction with that plan, they launched an international campaign to raise money to fund the project.

Both Al-Aqsa Mosque and the Dome of the Rock sat atop Temple Mount in Jerusalem, a site important to both Jews and Muslims. Amin saw the renovations as a way of asserting Arab authority over the area. "In order to have real authority, to exert actual control over our destiny, we must take what we want."

"Are you now favoring direct military action?"

"Not direct military action. Not now," Amin replied. "But that does not prevent us from seizing power by others means."

Privately, Latif expressed frustration over his position. "You seem to favor action, then it turns out to be non-action."

"My position is the same as it always has been," Amin replied curtly.

"But when others seem on the verge of confronting the Jews, or the British, you appear to agree with them, only to divert the entire affair to nothing."

"Have I called for such a confrontation as you suggest others want?"

"No," Latif replied.

"As I have said many times," Amin continued, "we must use the strength of the British to strengthen our position."

"But what are we doing to accomplish that? The Jews train armies. We do nothing and it seems your rhetoric is only that— words and nothing else."

"The Jews prepare their armies. The British prepare their policies and position papers. We prepare our hearts."

Latif frowned. "What does that mean?"

"The British are our enemy only to the extent that they are pawns of the Jews. The Jews are our real enemy. The British will leave. We do not have to confront them to make that happen. We only have to wait, which is precisely the action we are taking. We are waiting. Once the British are gone, then we can eliminate the Jews."

✦ ✦ ✦ ✦ ✦

In response to the Supreme Muslim Council's action regarding the buildings on Temple Mount, Jews associated with the Jewish Agency moved to establish greater access to the plaza around the Western Wall, the only portion of the temple compound left standing. Their hope was to make the area more conducive to worship and to create an ambiance of prayer and solemnity. Several proposed going so far as to removing surrounding structures that limited access.

However, the Western Wall was controlled by Muslims and had been donated in trust for Islamic religious purposes. As a waqf, the area around the wall was subject to the Council's administration. Jews, however, saw the site as holy for their own purposes, and their claims to the area became a point of contention between the two sides. Numerous speeches were made regarding the subject, which resulted in incidents of pushing and shoving between Arabs and Jews.

Fearing a repeat of the Nabi Musa riots, Samuel called Amin and Weizmann to a meeting. Both men were determined to have their way. "Haram al-Sharif is Muslim property," Amin argued. "It was set aside for religious purposes hundreds of years ago. The entire world accepts this as settled history. Now the Jews want to rewrite history to take it for their own purposes."

"We do not want to rewrite history," Weizmann argued. "We only want access to the area around the Western Wall. Our religious practices forbid any Jew from gaining access to the mount itself for fear of violating the holy of holies."

The argument continued for several hours, followed by Samuel's attempt at arm-twisting, then cajoling them toward a workable solution. Finally, he succeeded in convincing both men to accept the status quo. "Jews will not alter the site or its surrounding area. Arabs will not block access to the Wall for worship and prayer by non-Muslims."

FOURTEEN

ON THE ARABIAN PENINSULA, tension between the Hashemi and Saudi clans, which had been simmering since the end of the Great War, broke into open warfare when forces under Ibn Saud launched an attack against the Sharif's position south of Mecca. The attack posed a direct assault on Hashemi authority in the Hejaz.

Within days, the Sharif and his army were driven from the city and forced to flee across the desert, with the Saudis close behind. A conflict that began as a local skirmish became a fight for control of the entire Arabian Peninsula and, as Churchill had predicted, the Sharif proved unable to counter the challenge.

In London, debate among cabinet members turned from British policy toward Palestine to focus on policy toward the Arabian Peninsula. Gone was the debate over whether to lend the Crown's support to an Arab kingdom. Now they faced the situation many had feared: a Middle East potentially dominated by Arabs who were ill-equipped to manage its great resources and disinclined to cooperate with British use of them.

"We must choose sides," one minister argued.

"No," another sided. "We must choose a winner."

"We have very little ability to influence the outcome, short of sending large numbers of troops, which I am certain no one wishes to do."

"Which is why our choice is all the more important."

"Then we must give our support to the Saudis. Clearly they are the better of the lot."

Foremost on everyone's mind was the strategic role petroleum had come to play in the UK economy. Oil was no longer a luxury, but a necessity for the UK's economic viability. The empire, however, had few locations from which to draw on proven petroleum reserves. The Middle East's abundant resources served only to cloud London's decision-making process.

Making matters even worse, the Sharif was a troublesome and unpredictable partner. Sitting atop large oil deposits, British officials had attempted to work with him but the Sharif seemed not to appreciate the limits of British policy options nor the limits of his own abilities. As the conflict wore on, Ibn Saud came to be more and more the British choice for the future.

Still, the government in London had a long history with the Sharif and in respect of that, cabinet members agreed to try once more to administer its policy through him. Success in that regard, however, required the Sharif to establish himself more firmly within the British fold and for that, his signature was required on the Treaty of Versailles. By then, terms of the treaty were permanently in place as the framework of British policy in the Middle East. Sharif's accession to those terms became a condition of further British support.

"We are through beating around the bush," Churchill asserted. "If we are to continue with our support of the Sharif, he must agree to the terms of the treaty and signify that agreement by affixing his signature to it."

Within the week, Denis Steed, a UK government representative, was dispatched by the foreign secretary to meet with the Sharif. He traveled by ship as far as Jazan, then by camel into the Hejaz interior until he located the Sharif at an encampment near the Dawasir Valley. There he presented a copy of the Treaty of Versailles and asked for the Sharif's signature. The Sharif refused. "I have told your predecessors that I will not sign that document. I meant it then, and I mean it now."

"Continued British support depends upon your agreement to the terms of the treaty," Steed reminded.

The Sharif still refused and repeated his earlier objections. "The document codifies the Jewish presence in Palestine. Even the creation of a Jewish state. Palestine lies at the heart of the region that was promised to me by your government as an Arab kingdom."

"You cannot hope to survive without British aid."

"If I surrender my kingdom to the Jews now, what reason is there to persevere?"

Despite the Sharif's refusal, Steed did not give up, but after a week of discussions he realized the Sharif would never change his mind. Reluctantly, Steed returned to London where he met with the foreign secretary and reported the Sharif's steadfast refusal to sign the treaty. "Then we have no choice," the foreign minister decided. "We must cut off all support to the Hashemite Kingdom."

Without British money or arms, the Sharif's army was quickly overrun by the Saudis. As a result, his kingdom collapsed and the Sharif was forced to flee to Damascus for safety. He resided there only temporarily before settling permanently in Amman, Jordan, where his son Abdullah was king.

When news that the Hashemite Kingdom had fallen reached Amin al-Husseini, many of his closest advisors urged him to respond. "This would not have happened unless the British abandoned him," Hadad argued. "They chose to let him fall."

"Was this because the Sharif refused to sign the treaty?" Aref asked.

Amin, who knew the truth, nodded. "The treaty includes a provision for a Jewish homeland in Palestine. The British demanded his signature to it and threatened to withdraw their support unless he did."

"And he refused."

"Yes," Amin replied. "Of course."

"And they let him fall to the Saudis."

Salama shook his head in disgust. "This is what the British do to friends who refuse to comply with their demands. They crush them. It is all a one-way relationship for them."

"We must act. You must call for a general strike," Hadad implored. "A strike against both the Jews and the British."

Others voiced their enthusiastic support for the idea, but Amin cut them off with a wave of his hand. "Confronting the British is precisely what the Jews want. They know that if we do that, British authorities will be forced to stop us with force. We cannot confront the British head-to-head. We must wait them out. I promise you, they will eventually leave."

"But will we survive until they are gone."

"Yes," Amin replied. "We will not only survive but prevail and thrive."

✦ ✦ ✦ ✦ ✦

In the fall of 1925, Latif traveled to Istanbul to visit a relative. While there, he went to the home of a friend for coffee. As he waited for the coffee to brew, he had a moment alone and noticed a book on the table near his chair. The title, *Mein Kampf,* seemed strange until he saw that it was written by a German author named Adolf Hitler. When his friend returned with their coffee, he saw that Latif was holding the book.

"This is a very good book," the friend insisted. "You should read it."

"I don't read much."

"I think you'll read this one," the friend replied confidently. "Take it with you and give it a try."

Latif took the book with him and read a few pages late one night. As his friend suggested, he was fascinated by the things Hitler had to say—how the Jews were the cause of the world's troubles, the way in which the Jews manipulated events to their advantage, and Jewish plans to rule the world. Latif still was reading it when he left Istanbul to return to Jerusalem but when he finished it, he gave the book to Amin and insisted that he read it, too.

Amin glanced through several of the chapters but laid the book aside, thinking it did not really interest him that much. A few weeks later, however, his wife, Karimeh, gave birth to a son whom they named Muhammad Salah el-Din. Amin and Karimeh had two daughters, but Muhammad Salah was their first son, and Amin was proud to have someone to carry on his name. He was present when the child was born, but Karimeh was attended by women who saw to her daily needs. Amin expected to continue with his work as usual while she recuperated.

As days went by, however, it became obvious that Karimeh was having a difficult time recovering from childbirth. Women came to help her during the day, but as weeks went by, constant care for her became a challenge. Amin stepped in to help and sat with her at night.

At first during those long nights, he was reminded of being in the room when his father was dying. The memory of those moments proved emotionally difficult, so he pushed them aside and tried to think of something else. Thinking of nothing, however, was impossible, and as he glanced around the room for a distraction, he noticed *Mein Kampf,* the book that Latif had given him. It was lying on a table in the corner across from the bed. Amin made his way to it and picked it up. As he returned to his chair beside the bed, he began to read. Before long, he was engrossed in all that Hitler had to say.

"This man's views are inspired by Allah," he whispered. "This is precisely the kind of thing I have wanted to articulate."

The following day, Amin wrote a letter to Hitler congratulating him on the publication of his book and praising him for its contents. He also asked where and how he might acquire additional copies of the book to distribute to the group of men—Nafez, Salah, Latif, Aref, Qadir, and Hadad—whom he referred to as his advisors.

In the days that followed, Amin spoke of things he'd learned from Hitler's book and read passages from it to Nafez and the others. "I will have copies for each of you soon," he assured. "And we will learn the things this man teaches until we know them by heart."

✦ ✦ ✦ ✦ ✦

As Amin became comfortable in his role as president of the Supreme Muslim Council, he used his position to exert influence throughout all of Palestine. By placing friends and family members in leadership positions of key Muslim organizations, he was able to consolidate power over those organizations and make them instruments of his will to dominate the region.

One of those organizations was the Young Men's Muslim Association (YMMA). With local organizations in all of the major population centers, controlling it was key to controlling Palestine. In 1928, Amin learned from Nafez that the presidency of YMMA in Haifa was up for election. He asked about potential candidates and learned that the current president, Rashid al-Haj Ibrahim, wanted to continue in office but was considering other options, too. "He is a leading local member of the Independence Party," Nafez advised.

"A secularist?"

"Apparently."

Amin had a troubled look. He knew Ibrahim by reputation, but the two had never met. "We need men in leadership who are committed to Islam and all of its implications."

"Many of the best are becoming increasingly disillusioned by the situation in Palestine," Nafez replied. "They are turning more and more toward violence. Particularly the secularists."

"As I have said many times," Amin responded, "violence will not work. Not yet. Is anyone challenging Ibrahim for the YMMA position?"

"There have been rumors that Qassam is interested."

"Do you think he could win?"

"Only if Ibrahim does not run for the position."

Amin was intrigued. "Ask Ibrahim to come for a visit. And send Salama to see me."

Later that day, Salama appeared at Amin's residence. They sat together in the courtyard, and Amin outlined the situation with YMMA. "An election is coming up in Haifa for their president. I want you to make certain Qassam wins that election."

"I did not know he was running for office."

Amin smiled. "You will tell him that when you see him."

Salama looked surprised. "When am I to see him?"

"Tomorrow."

"Does he know I am coming?"

"No."

Salama seemed amused. "So, I am to arrive unannounced and tell Qassam that he is running for election as president of YMMA?"

"Yes, YMMA president in Haifa."

"And I am to make certain that he wins?"

"Yes."

"Very well." Salama stood. "I will leave to go there at once."

✦ ✦ ✦ ✦ ✦

The following day, Rashid al-Haj Ibrahim arrived in Jerusalem to meet with Amin. They talked about the future of Palestine and the need for an independent Muslim authority to exert the strength of Islam throughout the region. The meeting was cordial, but finally Ibrahim said, "We agree on many things, but I do not think we agree on what it means that the region should remain under Muslim control."

"We both are Muslim," Amin frowned. "On what is there for us to disagree?"

"You seek adherence to Sharia law," Ibrahim explained.

"Is there any other?"

"I favor an accommodating view."

"A secularist government."

"Yes. With each person free to practice Islam or not."

"That is a deep division."

"I suspect so."

"But," Amin added, "I sense we are in agreement regarding one very important item."

"And what is that?"

"Our opposition to Jewish immigration."

"Yes." Ibrahim nodded. "And in our opposition to British domination of the region."

Amin shifted positions in his chair and placed his hands in his lap. "I think we must consider that you have gone as far as your position with the YMMA can take you." He spoke with a smile but his eyes bore in on Ibrahim with a steeled glare.

Ibrahim seemed not to catch the unstated message. "Really?" he asked in surprise. "I was thinking I might—"

"Really," Amin said, cutting him off. "You need a stronger position from which to articulate your ideas. Perhaps a place in the Independence Party."

"I would be glad for a stronger position." Ibrahim gave a bewildered shrug. "But that would not mean I could not serve the YMMA, too."

"I think you will be very busy when you are chairman of the Haifa party organization."

Ibrahim shook his head. "That would be a long way away. Perhaps too long for me."

"Trust me," Amin assured. "It is closer than you think."

"You are offering this to me?"

"You would do well to accept."

Ibrahim had a skeptical expression. "You have it in your power to make such a thing happen?"

Amin ignored the question. "The party will be stronger for your service and the YMMA will be invigorated by new leadership."

"But who will lead them? Who can do the job?"

Amin wondered how Ibrahim could have served so long and not developed at least one person who could take his place, but he avoided the comment and instead explained, "I believe Qassam will be a perfect fit for the task."

Ibrahim's eyes opened wide and he nodded slowly, as if finally he understood what Amin had been saying. "Yes. I believe he would do a great job."

Not long after that meeting, Ibrahim announced that he would not stand for reelection as president of the Haifa YMMA. That same day, Qassam announced his candidacy for the position. The election was held a few weeks later and, with Salama working behind the scenes, Qassam was chosen president. Two days later, Ibrahim was named to the executive committee of the Haifa branch of the Independence Party.

Although Qassam concentrated most YMMA activities on the lower classes—traditionally the most fertile ground for recruitment—Qassam's position in the YMMA afforded access to members of the middle class. Likewise, his education and training made him attractive to the city's most educated Muslims. The intellectuals were also drawn to the cosmopolitan approach of the Independence Party and its message of Arab nationalism without the ardent religious emphasis of conservative Islam. Because of these interlocking relationships, Qassam discovered a growing number of opportunities to work closely with Ibrahim and the party apparatus.

At first, the wide ideological gap between the secularists and Qassam's YMMA seemed insurmountable, but he soon discovered that the two shared a common view in two respects. One was their mutual view of the struggle against Zionist expansion in Palestine. The other was their opposition to British rule.

As time went by, however, Qassam developed an activist view that separated him from both the Independence Party, which sought to resolve Zionism through accommodation, and from Amin and the Muslim Council, which sought to resolve the matter with the British by avoiding confrontation.

Qassam's activities through YMMA, however, were financed by wealthy Haifa businessmen who shared his views of the need for a revival of true Islamic faith. They ignored his political ideology, valuing his theology for its own sake. Because of their association, Qassam soon became independent of Amin's largess and more independent of his control.

✦ ✦ ✦ ✦ ✦

In an attempt to administer its rights and duties under the Mandate for Syria, French authorities created the Syrian Constituent Assembly whose delegates were to address day-to-day issues regarding the Mandate and Syrian life. In August 1928, the Assembly was convened in Damascus for the first time.

As one of Syria's most prominent politicians, Hashim al-Atassi was elected to the Assembly. In the course of the body's proceedings, he introduced legislation calling for the reunification of Syria with Palestine. News of the measure energized delegates, who were quick to make speeches in support of the proposal. Not a single person spoke in opposition.

Alerted to the pending bill, and to its widespread support, French operatives conducted a quick head count of delegates. Results from their count indicated the measure was set to win approval by unanimous consent. Rather than allow that to happen, French authorities intervened and abruptly adjourned the Assembly. Protestors took to the Damascus streets immediately.

When Amin learned of the French action, he sent a message to Atassi and invited him to Jerusalem to discuss the matter. Atassi arrived with a delegation hoping to obtain swift and enthusiastic support for his proposed unification. Amin, however, was cautious. "Your proposal is admirable, but I wish you had spoken with me before you introduced it."

"Why?"

"A vote by the Assembly to approve the measure would lead to a confrontation with the British. That would be bad for the residents of Palestine."

"You don't want to confront the British?"

"We are not ready for it. And neither are the people of Syria."

"Why do you say such a thing?"

"Have you forgotten what happened when Faisal attempted to establish a kingdom?"

"Faisal was weak."

"Yes," Amin agreed, "but he was equipped with British arms and his men had been trained by British soldiers. Even then they could not withstand direct confrontation with French troops. Now you have none of that and only militant citizens."

"How dare you talk of our people in that manner!"

"I mean no offense," Amin assured. "The Syrian people and the people of Palestine are one people. And in attempting an armed response, they share the same problem. We are not prepared for a European-style war."

"But neither the British nor the French have done as they promised. Time and time again they have shown that they do not have our interests at heart."

"This is true."

"They should be supporting our desire for independence. Yet instead, they support the Jews, who, as you have said many times, wish to kill us all."

Unstated between the two men was the underlying issue of which one of them would lead a unified Levant. They talked around the issue and as the conversation mellowed, others in attendance made their own suggestions. Some favored a Hashemite Kingdom, but others thought the Hashemites had had their opportunity and failed. "Faisal proved too weak when the moment for bravery arrived," someone spoke up.

"And his father, the Sharif, is no longer a viable option." On that, they all agreed. And no one wanted to join forces with Abdullah in Transjordan. "He is a traitor to us all," Atassi added. Then he looked over at Amin. "Some even question whether you are committed to the cause."

"They question *me*?" Amin roared. "Why would anyone question my commitment?"

"They wonder if you are committed to accommodating the British instead of protecting your own people."

Amin grew angry and launched into a diatribe against Atassi, recounting his own experiences, the suffering he had endured, and reminding them all that he was the Grand Mufti. After a twenty-minute rant, he paused long enough for others to intervene.

"This discussion highlights an important point," someone explained. "We cannot merely propose unification without also preparing a plan for how to govern that unified country."

"That's why we are here," Atassi snarled.

"But as neither of you would be willing to serve the other, and no one wants the Hashemites, perhaps we should look for a third alternative."

"You have someone in mind?" Amin fumed.

"Ibn Saud."

The suggestion fell on the room like a soothing balm. Immediately everyone saw the wisdom of the proposal. The Saudis were supported by the British, which meant they could not discredit his abilities without endangering their policy in Arabia. The Saudis, likewise, were heavily influenced by the Wahabi, who were at the heart of a Salafi movement, to which Amin was deeply committed. And Ibn Saud was ruthless. The French, acting alone, could not stand against him in the Middle East.

"Should we consult the Saudis first?"

"No," Amin replied. "This is not a formal enactment of the Assembly but a call from our joint working group. We should issue a statement and invite them to send delegates to discuss the details." He knew that nothing would come of the measure, but he had seen there was little to be gained in confronting Atassi. A public announcement of their interest in exploring the matter would fall on deaf ears with Mandatory authorities in Syria and Palestine, but it would sideline Atassi also, at least for the moment.

The following week, Atassi's delegate committee and the Muslim Council's executive committee issued a joint proclamation calling for the unification of Syria and Palestine under the rule of a monarch. Ibn Saud was proposed as that ruler. The joint statement included an invitation for a Saudi delegation to join Atassi and Amin in discussing how to bring their proposal to pass. As Amin expected, nothing came of it.

FIFTEEN

BY THE SUMMER OF 1928, the first stage of the Muslim Council's renovation of Temple Mount was complete. In August, a celebration was held in Jerusalem to commemorate that work. Arabs in the city were energized by the accomplishment and by the festive atmosphere, which put Jews on the defensive. Once more, they felt compelled to guard their access to the Western Wall.

In September, Jewish leaders issued calls for the purchase and destruction of houses in the Moroccan Quarter near the Wall to improve access. That, in turn, fed Arab suspicions that the Jews intended to drive all Arabs from Jerusalem and, indeed, from all of Palestine. Repeating a familiar refrain, Arab activists shouted, "They mean to kill us and seize our land."

Later that month, during the celebration of Yom Kippur, a Jewish bedel, preparing the Western Wall plaza for regular worship, placed screens in the area to divide the space between male and female worshippers. Muslims saw it and were immediately incensed.

When Amin heard about the screens, he protested the action to Sir John Chancellor, the newly appointed High Commissioner of the British Mandate of Palestine. Later that day, Chancellor called him in for a meeting.

"The plaza is not theirs to control," Amin argued. "It is ours. We allow them to gather there for worship, but they cannot make changes to the physical characteristics of the area."

Chancellor downplayed the significance. "Is it that big of an issue?"

"Yes!" Amin roared. "It's not so much about the screens themselves but about Jewish assertion of authority over *our* property. They didn't ask; they simply erected the screens."

"But I mean—"

Amin interrupted. "How would you react if we suddenly camped at the entrance to this building?"

"I suppose you have a point," Chancellor conceded.

British authorities responded with an official request to the Jewish Agency for removal of the screens, but the request was refused. Thereafter, Mandatory authorities sent constables to remove the screens from the Plaza by force. When they attempted to seize them, pushing and shoving ensued with Jews attempting to hold on to the screens and a squad of constables attempting to remove them. As the struggle continued, Arabs appeared from nearby streets and began throwing rocks at both groups.

Eventually, the screens were removed from the plaza, but tensions were high. In the days that followed, there was continued argument back and forth between Jews and Muslims. Jews protesting Muslim renovation activities on Temple Mount. Muslims protesting Jewish attempts to secure greater access to the Western Wall. And British constables scuffling with both sides in an attempt to enforce peace.

Finally, Chancellor convened a meeting of Jewish and Arab leaders. Amin represented Arab interests and the Muslim Council. Chaim Weizmann spoke on behalf of the Jewish Agency. The discussion began amicably but soon devolved into an argument, with Amin adamant that Jews recognize Arab control of the Wall, and Weizmann asserting the historic Jewish claim to the area. Chancellor let them voice their frustration until the rhetoric ran its course, then he said, "I expect you gentlemen to keep your people under control." He looked over at Weizmann. "No more changes at the Wall." Then to Amin, "No more confrontations with Jewish worshippers."

Weizmann spoke up. "We are not—"

Chancellor cut him off. "No more changes," he snapped.

In the days that followed, an uneasy calm settled over central Palestine. No one was certain how long it would last. Amin, however, was growing increasingly frustrated with Jewish attitudes and his own strategy of patience. "Being patient," he confided to Nafez, "is trying my patience."

Nafez smiled. "You are thinking of taking a different approach?"

"I am thinking the Jews are the most stubborn people on earth."

Nafez laughed. "They probably think the same of us."

✦ ✦ ✦ ✦ ✦

As the end of the year approached, Qassam reached the end of his term as YMMA president in Haifa. Though wary of Qassam's activist tendencies, Amin liked him and thought he was a good ally. Keeping him involved and in a prominent position had the added advantage of allowing Amin to keep Qassam's activism in check, too. In order to do that, he arranged to have the Muslim Council appoint Qassam as the marriage registrar of the Sharia court in Haifa. As things sometimes happen, the appointment did not work out quite the way Amin hoped.

From his position as marriage registrar, Qassam toured the villages of northern Palestine. Most residents of the region were farmers. Farming in the northern region of Palestine always was a challenge, but as Qassam toured the region, he was appalled to find they had gone from an adequate, though arduous life to barely surviving.

"The Jewish farming cooperatives buy up the land," someone explained. "They produce crops in a large volume and sell at prices below market. We cannot compete."

As Qassam made his way across Galilee, he encountered farmer after farmer who told him the same story. A sense of outrage welled up in him over the way Arabs were being victimized by a system created by, and facilitated by, the British government. "They are no better than the Ottomans," he grumbled. "They give the Jews every advantage but do nothing to assist our people. And all they ask is for a chance to make a life for themselves."

After seeing how vulnerable they had become, and sensing that no one else would do anything for them, Qassam encouraged the farmers to establish agricultural cooperatives. "You need to adopt the tactics of the Jews," he instructed. At the same time, he petitioned the Mandatory government on behalf of Arab farmers, asking for the same assistance given to the Jews. But the sense of anger he felt fueled a quest for something more and he began to search for a way to radically and pervasively address the political solution in Palestine.

Before long, reports of Qassam's remarks reached Amin. He seemed untroubled. "Let him have his say." But when he learned of Qassam's attempts to gain assistance for Arab farmers from Mandatory authorities, Amin became concerned. Not long after that, Qassam delivered a series of fiery religious sermons encouraging villagers to organize resistance against further encroachment by Jews' farms on traditional Arab land. He followed it up with a speech encouraging Arabs to attack the British army as they patrolled the region. "And if the Jews won't act responsibly, you can attack them, too!"

Upon hearing of Qassam's most virulent diatribes, Amin sent Salama to convey his disapproval. Qassam listened politely but was unrelenting. Not long after Salama's visit, he obtained a *fatwah* from Shaykh Badr al-Din al-Hasani, the Mufti of Damascus, stating that the physical struggle against the British and the Jews was required of all faithful Muslims. After that, Qassam's messages became even more strident than before. Amin saw his appeal to a cleric from outside the region as an act of betrayal.

✦ ✦ ✦ ✦ ✦

Later that year, during a celebration of Tisha B'Av, memorializing the destruction of the Temple, Betar youth marched through Jerusalem shouting slogans and creating a disturbance. When they reached the Western Wall, they became more belligerent and began chanting, "The wall is ours! The wall is ours!"

The following day, Arabs held a celebration in Jerusalem to commemorate Mohammed's birthday. During that celebration, Muslims, in response to Jewish action the day before, marched through the plaza at the Western Wall and destroyed Jewish items stored there for use in weekly worship services.

Incited by the Jewish protest, and emboldened by the Arab counter protest, a group of Arabs attacked a young Jewish boy while he played in the Jewish Quarter. At first they merely beat him, but as the attack became more violent, they stabbed him to death. In retaliation, three young Arabs who had ventured into the Quarter the following day were killed.

Very quickly, rumors spread through Arab sections of Jerusalem that Jews were not satisfied by the revenge killing of the three young men and planned widespread attacks on Arabs throughout Palestine. Likewise, rumors were rife among Jews that Arabs planned more attacks against them.

Reports of trouble between Jews and Arabs reached Amin

within minutes of their occurrence. He was angry at the insensitivity of the Jews who marched near the wall and felt vindicated by the Arab response. News of the attack on the Jewish boy was unsettling, but the killing of three Arabs in response made him angry. Still, he did nothing and made no attempt to issue a statement demanding justice.

When news of the rumors about more Jewish attacks reached him, he was dismissive. "The Jews have no more ability to launch such an attack against us than we do against them."

Salama was unconvinced. "What if the reports are true?"

Nafez added, "All of the Jewish farming settlements have armed forces to protect them. They are well equipped and trained in the use of sophisticated arms. The British have done nothing to disarm them. What if they bring their weapons against us?"

"They will not," Amin countered.

Aref was frustrated. "You are willing to risk our future and the future of our families on your hunch?"

"It is not a hunch," Amin replied calmly. "There is no risk."

Chancellor heard news of the rumors, too, and sent a message to Amin asking for another meeting. Amin came to his office and, as he had before, sat across from the High Commissioner at his desk.

"I need your help in calming the Arab masses," Chancellor began. "I need you to put an end to the violence."

"I can speak to our people," Amin replied, "but they have every right to defend themselves."

"You know as well as I do that the Jews do not intend to attack Arab villages."

"And you know as well as I do that certain elements among the Jews are capable of anything."

Chancellor dismissed his concern. "These are just rumors."

"Yes," Amin agreed, "rumors instigated by the Jews to manipulate you into cracking down on us while letting the Jews go free."

"So far," Chancellor replied, "only Jews have been killed."

"That is not true. Last week three Arabs were killed. Do you think we killed them ourselves just to blame it on the Jews?"

"And do you think the Jews intend to do more?"

"I do not know. And neither do you." Amin was growing angry. "Your constables have done nothing to investigate the three Arab murders. Yet I hear reports of them ransacking our neighborhoods in search of those who attacked a single Jew."

Chancellor avoided the implication. "Will Arabs take revenge for those who have died?"

"Surely, you cannot expect us to do nothing. We must, at the very least, be prepared to defend ourselves."

"I know this much." Chancellor leaned over the desk and pointed with his finger. "If you don't calm your people, I will be forced to act."

After meeting with Chancellor, Amin met with Nafez and Aref. After briefing them on the discussion, he told them, "I am not sure what we should do next. I did not like the way he spoke to me."

"You cannot back down," Aref replied.

"We must go on the attack," Nafez added. "Qassam and the others are right."

"And you are right," Salama chimed in. "The British are nothing more than puppets. The Jews are the puppet masters. Whatever the Jews tell them to do, that is what they do."

"We must attack the Jews," Aref reiterated. "And we must attack the British. We cannot wait for them to leave. They will never leave."

Amin shook his head. "I have seen the armies of the British and the Germans. And even the Ottoman. I know how they operate and the way they are armed. If the British strike against us as they are capable of striking, they will destroy us."

Nafez glared at him. "What are you afraid of?"

"I am not afraid," Amin argued. "I am a realist."

"You do not think that Allah will take our side against these infidels?"

"I believe that Allah is as angry with them as we are," Amin responded. "But I have seen how the infidels fight and I have seen the tools of war they use to do it. We cannot drive them away with rocks and sticks."

✦ ✦ ✦ ✦ ✦

The following Thursday, Amin appeared at Al-Aqsa Mosque and instructed the cleric to deliver a pacifying sermon that Friday. With Amin present, the cleric did as he was instructed and preached a sermon calling for a non-violent response. The audience seemed receptive, but Arab radicals in attendance that day were disillusioned by the cleric's remarks. As Amin emerged from the mosque, they confronted him with angry shouts.

"Amin is an infidel! Amin is an infidel!"

"A lover of the British! A comforter of Jews!"

Amin shouted from the steps with the same message he had given most of his life—that violence against the British would only bring destruction to Arab villages. "We cannot oppose them with violence. They will crush us."

The crowd responded with chants of "Allah makes us great! Allah makes us great!"

As that died down, another chorus rose. "We can attack the Jews! We can attack the Jews!" Followed by shouts of "We can destroy the Jews!"

Amin tried to respond but no one heard anything else he said that day as the radicals shouted him down. Soon the crowd was whipped into a frenzied mob. From the mosque, they moved into the Jewish Quarter, beating Jews on the street, smashing windows, and setting fire to homes. With no one to stop them, they burned and pillaged their way through almost every house. News of the attack spread quickly and that evening, Arabs in Hebron attacked Jewish neighborhoods in that city. Similar attacks occurred in Safed and Haifa.

Jewish defense organizations responded with force and before morning, 136 Arabs were killed with more than two hundred injured. The Arabs, however, were not deterred, killing 135 Jews and injuring more than three hundred.

Fighting between Jews and Arabs continued for weeks until, finally, the British Mandatory Authority intervened with sufficient force to bring the conflict to a halt. As Amin had warned, many more Arabs were killed in the fighting. On the surface, calm returned to the villages of Palestine. Beneath the exterior, though, a split had emerged between Amin and others who wanted to take an accommodating stance with the Jews and those, like Qassam, who sought a radical confrontation against both the Jews and the British.

In northern Palestine, Qassam used the period of relative peace to recruit followers. Many were eager to join his call to arms. Rather than forming them into a single army, he organized them into a dozen different cells. Each group fully autonomous and unaware of the existence of the other groups. The majority of his men were peasant farmers and urban laborers. Most were based in Galilee, but he had disciples throughout the country, including Gaza and Jerusalem.

Qassam trained his men in the art of combat, teaching them tactics and drilling them on rudimentary skills of a soldier, but he framed the conflict as a religious struggle. For him, and for his men, the fight was moral, political, and military jihad. "Our goal," he told them repeatedly, "is to defend the sanctity of Allah by bringing to an end British rule in Palestine. And by destroying Zionist aspirations."

The moral component of Qassam's teaching was especially attractive to the young men of Haifa's labor slums. Living away from their families, they were exposed to activities considered immoral in Islam. He encouraged his men to grow beards as a sign of their commitment to jihad and to carry a copy of the Quran with them wherever they went. Many of his followers were illiterate, so he taught them to read and write, using the Quran as a textbook.

After several months of training, the cell groups reached a level of proficiency that made combat possible. As the time approached for their first engagements, Qassam attempted to gauge the depth of Amin's opposition to armed conflict against the British and the Jews. He was intent on pursing his plans no matter what, but he hoped to avoid an internal fight at the same time. He also was concerned that Amin was making a mistake, and he wanted to know why.

That spring, Qassam came to Jerusalem and confronted Amin about his reluctance to face the reality of the Arab situation. "We are being ruled by two masters," Qassam argued. "One is British, the other is Jewish. The Jews steal our land, and the British bind our hands from stopping them. But they bind our hands with your assistance. Your fear of the British is making *you* a pawn of the Jews."

"I admit I am reluctant to engage our enemies in combat," Amin replied. "But it is not from fear. And certainly not from fear of the Jews."

"Then, what is it? Why do you insist on holding us back?"

"My vantage point has given me a realistic assessment of the situation. The British are strong. We are not. Which convinces me that we cannot solve our problems by direct confrontation."

"But every day that we wait, the Jews grow stronger. They are training men. They are organizing armies. The British help them while they oppose us. Do you not think that Allah will help us?"

"My belief in Allah is as firm as anyone's. But I have seen what happens on the battlefield."

They talked. They debated. They argued. And finally, Qassam added, "Are you prohibiting me from organizing my men for defense?"

Amin knew full well that Qassam was doing more than preparing for a defense. His men had witnessed Qassam's training sessions and heard his fiery speeches, all of which they reported to him in great detail. But, like Qassam, he was not interested in fighting an internal fight that pitted Arab against Arab. "No, we must be prepared to defend ourselves against physical attacks."

As the meeting came to an end, the two men embraced and Amin sent Qassam away with a blessing, but he was not happy. Qassam had manipulated him into authorizing an escalation of the conflict. One that he was certain would engulf all of Palestine and for which he saw no easy conclusion.

In the months that followed, cells of young Arab fighters sponsored by Qassam attacked a train south of Haifa, blowing it up with improvised explosives. Six British soldiers were killed, along with four Jews. Two nights later, another cell attacked a farming settlement near Tiberias. Two Arabs were killed in the fight, but six buildings on the compound were destroyed by fire. Jewish vigilantes branded the attackers as the Black Hand, and the name stuck. When Qassam heard it, he adopted the name as their official moniker.

Throughout that year, Black Hand cells attacked farming settlements, irrigation systems, railways, and trucks carrying supplies and produce to and from Jewish markets. Emboldened by their success against those targets, they attacked Jewish homes on the outskirts of Haifa. The attacks continued through 1932, reaching a climax when bombs thrown into a café in Nahalal resulted in a dozen deaths.

SiXTEEN

IN JANUARY 1933, Adolf Hitler was named chancellor of Germany. News of his rise to power appeared on the front page of every Arab-language newspaper in Palestine. Amin was delighted. Since reading the copy of *Mein Kampf* that he had received from Latif, he had been studying the book every night, making notes and memorizing passages much as he did the Quran.

At least once every week, he discussed parts of the book with Salama, Latif, Nafez, and Aref. Only Latif was conversant in German, and when they began studying the book, it was not available in any other language. By the time Hitler came to power, however, it had been translated into Arabic and was the most popular book in the Middle East. Studying it became much easier and Amin pored over the book with his men, dissecting sentences and paragraphs as if it were a religious text, which it rapidly was becoming for them.

Within days of learning Hitler had become chancellor, Amin contacted the German consul general, Heinrich Wolff, and arranged an appointment at the consulate in Jerusalem. They sat together in Wolff's office.

"I wanted to meet with you in person," Amin began. "And tell you how delighted I am that Adolf Hitler has been named to the chancellorship."

Wolff nodded approvingly. "Many are glad for his rise to power. We see in him a new day for Germany and, indeed, all of Europe."

Amin continued. "I am particularly glad for what I believe will be the new regime's policy toward Jews."

Wolff appeared a bit uneasy and glanced away, fidgeting with items on the desktop. "The details of policy . . . have . . . not yet been determined."

"Yes. But I have read the book many times." He pointed to a copy of *Mein Kampf* on the shelf behind the desk. "I think we both know what is soon to occur."

Wolff's eyes brightened. "You have read the chancellor's book?"

"Many times," Amin replied. "And I have been studying it with a small group of men who are important to me."

Wolff nodded once more. "That is good. I will be sure to pass along a note about your enthusiasm."

"Please do. I would ask, too, that you suggest that officials in Germany no longer permit Jews to travel to Palestine."

The nervous look appeared again on Wolff's face and he fidgeted again with the items on his desk. "We have yet to send anyone anywhere."

"But you have issued travel documents that allow them to come here," Amin explained. "And your government has suggested Palestine as a destination to which Jews might go."

Wolff had a thin smile. "They must go somewhere."

"Yes, but the grave is preferable, don't you think?"

Now Wolff was *really* nervous. "I'm afraid I wouldn't be able to—"

Amin cut him off. "I am not so naive as to fail to grasp that

German policy against Jews in Europe is the driving force behind our problems with the Jews here in Palestine. I understand that. But sending them here need not be the solution to Germany's problem."

Wolff leaned away. "And what would you propose as the solution?"

"The same solution as your chancellor," Amin said in a matter-of-fact tone. "Eliminate them completely."

"Surely the world would never accept such a solution," Wolff replied. "Not something of that extreme nature."

"Then perhaps you could propose another location," Amin suggested. "Africa, for instance, where they could starve to death or be eaten by lions." He laughed at his own remark but stopped when he noticed Wolff didn't join in.

"Perhaps so," Wolff replied and stood, signaling an end to their meeting. "I am pleased that you dropped by to see me and I will pass along your suggestions to our offices in Berlin."

Amin stood and the two men shook hands. "And please convey my congratulations to Hitler, your chancellor."

"Yes." Wolff ushered him to the door. "I shall consider it a privilege to let him know."

From the consulate, Amin made his way to a café near Temple Mount, where he joined Aref for coffee. Amin briefed him on his visit with Wolff and the matters they had discussed. "Do you think you will be able to influence their policy?" Aref asked.

"I do not know. But I would like to make sure they understand my interests."

"How would you do that?"

Amin leaned closer and lowered his voice. "Do you think we could convince the newspapers in Palestine to serialize *Mein Kompf*? Print a chapter each week."

Aref seemed intrigued. "They would need permission to do that."

"Would they *require* permission?"

"Most."

"Then perhaps I can help with that."

"You think Wolff will convince Hitler's publisher to agree?"

"You find out if the newspapers are interested. I'll contact Wolff and find out what he can do."

After several weeks of negotiations and numerous meetings, Amin and Aref succeeded in gaining approval to serialize *Mein Kampf* in Arab-language newspapers. The final arrangement involved only a select group of four papers and they pooled the effort—taking turns publishing chapters alternately—but the entire book was made available to the public, and newspaper circulation improved dramatically.

For his effort, Amin received a handwritten note from Hitler thanking him for his support. He showed the letter to Aref and the others and kept it on his desk for all to see. "Now," he announced, "we are on our way to addressing the Jewish problem. Not just here, but throughout the entire world.

✦ ✦ ✦ ✦ ✦

In 1935, Hassan al-Banna, an imam from Ismailia, Egypt, contacted Amin and asked to meet with him. Amin was aware of Banna from his work with the Young Men's Muslim Association and from articles he wrote for the association's journal, *Majallat al-Fath*. They met at Amin's home in Jerusalem and sat outside in the shade, sipping tea and eating date bread.

"As you know," Banna began, "I have written and spoken many times about the secular influence our people have endured at Ismailia."

"From the influx of workers on the Suez Canal," Amin noted.

"Yes. And from the books and newspapers they brought with them."

"Similar problems have been experienced all across the region," Amin added.

Banna nodded. "The Great War opened our traditional lands to many outside influences. But we have formed an organization in Ismailia to address that issue. We call it the Muslim Brotherhood."

Amin smiled. "I like that name. We *are* a brotherhood."

"Yes, we are. The men of our group seek to rid our lands of corrupting Western influences."

"And how do you propose to do that?" Amin wondered.

"We intend to restore the true beliefs of Islam through cultural and social domination. That will make it impossible for Western influences to have an effect on our people because those influences would not be discouraged and the indulgence of them would not be permitted."

Amin raised an eyebrow at the suggestion. "And you would include political domination, too?"

Banna nodded. "We could not influence culture without influencing political control."

"Good," Amin replied. "I have always seen the two as connected."

"Interrelated," Banna added.

"Very much so."

"We intend to restore the imposition of Sharia law and traditional practices of the faith in all aspects of Muslim life," Banna continued. "Not only in Egypt, but throughout the Levant and Mesopotamia. And as far as we are able to go."

"That is an ambitious plan."

"Much like the plan to establish an Arab kingdom sponsored by the British." Banna's voice had a sarcastically wry tone.

Amin ignored the implication. "How can I help?"

"We have grown from the six men who originally formed the organization to more than a hundred thousand. We have constructed our own mosque in Ismailia and established groups in every major city in Egypt. Now we want to establish a presence in Jerusalem."

Amin nodded. "And that is why you came to see me."

"We would like to name you as leader of our work here."

Amin was glad to join with Banna. He had heard of the Muslim Brotherhood already and had followed its growth from a distance. Although he'd always considered it part of the Young Men's Muslim Association, he now saw that the Brotherhood had the potential to be much larger. If he joined with them now, he could rise with it and expand his influence. Perhaps becoming a world leader of Islam and not just a voice in Palestine.

Before Banna returned to Egypt, Amin met with Nafez, Salama, and the others and briefed them on Banna's proposal. They were even more excited than Amin to become the core of the Brotherhood's work in Palestine. Later that day, Banna formally accepted them as the Jerusalem chapter with Amin as its leader.

✦ ✦ ✦ ✦ ✦

Later in 1935, at the port of Jaffa, police discovered a cache of arms hidden among the cargo of a ship that arrived from Europe. An investigation revealed that the shipment originated in Belgium and was destined for Haganah, a Jewish paramilitary force. News of the discovery and its destination made the front page of Palestinian newspapers the following day.

Palestinian Arabs were indignant. Leaders of every stripe and level called for a general strike and demanded the Mandatory Authority disband the Jewish groups. Furor of a kind previously known only among radical Muslims in Palestine now swept through the public. Amin sensed that he would not be able to resist their outrage. Nafez did, too. "We may no longer be able to avoid the obvious," he suggested.

"Which is?"

"That more than waiting must be done to address the situation."

"I know," Amin sighed.

"Are you afraid?"

"No," Amin snapped. "How can you ask such a thing?"

"I'm trying to find the reason why you can't see that we need to act. To call a general strike. Are you worried our people can't handle direct action?"

"I am not worried about the Arab response to the Jews. We can handle the Jews, even with their paramilitary organizations."

"But the British?"

Amin nodded. "The British are the one unknowable risk. The nature of their response to our actions . . ." His voice trailed away and he folded his arms across his chest. "It all leaves me profoundly worried."

"But you do not deny that we must act." Nafez offered it as a statement, not a question.

"No," Amin replied. "I had hoped to avoid this day, but I think we are left with no choice."

"Then, shall I announce your support for a strike?"

"Not yet."

"Not yet?" Nafez blurted in frustration.

"Not yet," Amin repeated.

Like other Arab leaders, though, the arms shipment to Haganah served as the final impetus for Qassam. He had no hesitation about what to do next. In a matter of days following news of the arms discovery, he expanded the Black Hand from small cells to groups of hundreds. Each of them equipped with bombs and firearms, some of which they improvised, but most purloined from British stockpiles. Then, while others protested, and fretted, and called for strikes, Qassam and his men raided Jewish settlements and sabotaged British rail lines. News of their actions drew still more volunteers whom he dutifully incorporated into new training units.

Qassam's attacks struck a responsive chord among the rural poor and urban underclass. The violent nature of his actions, however, deeply angered members of the Muslim urban elite. They approached him, thinking they could restrain him with words and threats, but they were met by the defiance and anger of a prophet.

"You come to me because you think my actions threaten the patronage you receive from the British Mandatory Authority," Qassam shouted. "In your heart, you prefer England over Palestine. The British over your fellow Arabs. You know nothing of Allah and the path of the faithful. Money is your only god. Privilege your only lifestyle. Your devotion to the infidel's way has made you ten times more the corrupter of our people than the British."

"We only wish to preserve the lives of our families."

"Your families mean nothing to you," Qassam railed. "You hide behind your mother's apron while men of valor take up the sword and shield of Allah. The restraint you seek from me is for the sake of your children. If you valued them at all, you would join me in the fight. Instead, you offer me an invitation to join you in condoning British actions and the indignities foisted upon us by the Jews. You ask me to join you in asserting that money matters most. And that, I assure you, I will never do."

✦ ✦ ✦ ✦ ✦

A few weeks later, the body of a Palestine police constable was discovered near Ein Harod. Qassam and his followers were believed to be responsible. British authorities began searching for him. When Qassam learned of it, he decided to flee rather than risk the lives of his men. "Tell them I did it," he ordered, "and send them to find me."

None of his men wanted Qassam to go, but he persisted. When they couldn't persuade him otherwise, six insisted on joining him. Together, they departed Haifa and fled to the hills near Nablus. For ten days, they lived on the move, being fed by the residents of villages in the area.

Eventually, however, British police trapped Qassam and those who were with him in a cave near Ya'bad. After a standoff that lasted almost two weeks, the police assaulted the cave. Facing certain death, Qassam encouraged his men to die as martyrs, then he led by example and charged toward the mouth of the cave, his guns blazing. The police fired back and during the exchange, Qassam and three of his men were killed. Those who remained surrendered and were taken into custody.

News of Qassam's death, his defiance to the end, and the manner in which he died, saddened his followers but electrified Palestinian Arabs. His funeral, held a day later in Haifa, became a rally for Arabs throughout the region. A crowd of at least three thousand mourners, most of them from the peasant and working classes, crowded and shoved their way past police barricades to join in the procession. They followed behind Qassam's coffin and those of his slain comrades all the way from the mosque to the grave site. At the time, it was the largest political gathering ever to assemble in Mandatory Palestine.

SEVENTEEN

FOLLOWING QASSAM'S DEATH, radical Arab nationalists throughout Palestine and, indeed, throughout the entire Arab world, invoked his memory as the symbol of Arab resistance. They organized protests and demonstrations in the streets of Haifa, Jerusalem, and Gaza. As the demonstrations grew in size, a call went out for a general strike and leaders in all the major cities began organizing for them. Unlike before, when there was merely talk of strikes and no action, these actually occurred— and with effectiveness that surprised even the organizers. Places like Haifa, Nazareth, and villages around Jerusalem were paralyzed by them.

News of Qassam's death spread far and wide, with obituaries appearing in Arab newspapers everywhere. One of the most prominent was the Egyptian newspaper *Al-Ahram*, which eulogized Qassam as a martyr. "I heard you preaching from up in the pulpit," the article read. "Summoning us to the sword. Through your death you are more eloquent than ever you were in life." Upon hearing the news, Egyptians took to the streets of Cairo and Alexandria protesting his death. The Muslim Brotherhood led actions in both locations.

Two weeks after Qassam's death, Banna arrived in Jerusalem unannounced and summoned Amin to a meeting in a room off the main hall at Al-Aqsa Mosque. Amin was perturbed at being called to meet anyone—he was accustomed to issuing orders, not in obeying them—but he forced aside his feelings and conducted himself in a cordial manner. When he arrived at the mosque, he found Banna in the study, facing a window, his hands clasped together behind his back.

Banna glanced over his shoulder as Amin entered the room, but before Amin could speak, he asked, "You are aware of the clamor over Qassam's death?"

Amin frowned. "Certainly, I am aware of the response. How could I miss it?"

Banna continued, still facing the window, his hands still clasped behind his back. "And you are aware of the call for a general strike?"

"Yes." The furrow on Amin's brow deepened. "What is this about?"

"You are aware of these things and yet you are reluctant to join in them."

"I see no point—"

Banna turned to face him. "I understand you have expressed some reticence to engage the British?"

"The Jews are our enemy. Not the British."

"Yet it is the British who dominate the Levant. Not the Jews."

"The British have the power to crush us," Amin argued. "The Jews do not. We must endure for now. We must follow the path of patience. The British will grow tired of us and leave, then we can deal with the Jews as we please."

Banna shook his head. "Our people cannot wait."

"We must—"

Banna cut him off again. "While we delay, the Jews grow strong. And our actions are seen by them as a sign of weakness. Our inaction is seen as acceptance, by the Jews and by the British."

Amin cleared his throat. "You do not see my point?"

"The Brotherhood has called a strike in Egypt." The tone of Banna's voice indicated his growing impatience. "We have done this as an act of support for Palestinian Arabs and at considerable risk to ourselves. We are facing great opposition from King Fuad and his administration."

"We appreciate the support," Amin replied, "but I do not see—"

Banna cut him off yet again. "As a member of the Brotherhood, you and the Jerusalem chapter should be taking the lead in this matter. You should have been the first to call for a strike."

"As I said, we cannot confront—"

"You must participate in the strike," Banna snapped, stepping closer to Amin. "The Brotherhood has adopted a posture of opposition and defiance. You no longer have the option of waiting."

"We have attempted to—"

"You are attempting a political solution to a strategic problem." Banna's voice was louder than before. "You can only use politics successfully to influence fellow Arabs. They will respond to it. The Jews and the British will not. For them, you must use force."

"I do not—"

Banna raised his voice almost to a shout. "Are you not listening to me? This is the Brotherhood's position." He pointed toward the door. "Go now and issue the order for the general strike." They stood facing each other for a long, painful moment. Had anyone else spoken to him that way, Amin would have responded with defiance. But this was Hassan al-Banna. Someone he could not eliminate with the back of his hand. Instead, he wheeled around and started toward the door.

As Amin departed the meeting, his sense of anger rose, and he again considered leaving the Brotherhood altogether. They could make a go of it on their own if they dared, but he would withdraw his support. And if they came near Palestine, he would wipe them from the face of the earth.

Instead of taking a bus or car home, Amin walked all the way, and by the time he reached the neighborhood where he lived, his rational mind came to the fore. The Brotherhood had several hundred thousand members and was growing every day. Soon it would be the dominant political and cultural group among all Arab countries. He believed that when Banna first approached him, and he believed it even after their confrontational second meeting. If he did not participate, Amin would find himself excluded from every major event that occurred during the remainder of his life. And worse than that, he would be irrelevant to Arabs outside Jerusalem. Like it or not, he had little option but to fall in line with Banna's expectations and join the call for a general strike.

Later that evening, after dinner and a few minutes alone with Karimeh, Amin met with Nafez, Aref, Hadad, Salama, Latif, and his cousin Qadir. After hearing of these things Amin received, they, too, were angry with the way Banna treated Amin. But they also agreed with him about Banna's assessment of the general strike.

"It is true," Latif offered, "that the British are far stronger than we. And stronger than the Jews, too. And I think you are correct that the British eventually will grow tired of us and return to England and their British lifestyle. Other things being equal, waiting would be the best strategy, but other things are not equal."

"Time and circumstance often conspire to frustrate the best of plans, and that has happened to us," Hadad added. "We must accommodate circumstance or be destroyed by it."

"You do not think we should wait them out?" Amin asked.

"We cannot afford to wait any longer," Hadad said.

Amin glanced around at the others. "Do you all agree?" They all nodded in response. "Very well, then." He sighed. "We shall join the strike."

They talked awhile longer, then one by one the men left the room until only Amin and Qadir remained. Amin looked over at him. "I feel I owe you an explanation."

"You owe me nothing."

"You are my kinsman," Amin noted. "And so I will tell you. The Brotherhood is the future of the Arab cause. Their combination of Islamic faith and militancy will explode across the Middle East. We cannot oppose them without becoming either irrelevant or the target of their ire."

"What are you saying?"

"I'm saying this is why I have changed my position."

Qadir frowned. "You chose to support the strike in order to please Banna?"

"No. I did it in order to remain with the Brotherhood."

"But won't we be under Banna's thumb now?"

Amin smiled. "Only until we plan a strategy to take control of the Brotherhood."

Qadir smiled as only a cousin might. "You wish to fight against Banna?"

"Not at all." Amin shook his head. "We must be more creative than that."

Qadir's smile broadened to a grin. "With cunning and deceit."

"Yes," Amin responded. "You will help me with this?"

"Certainly." Qadir nodded enthusiastically. "As will the others who were here tonight."

"No." Amin shook his head. "Not them."

Qadir looked puzzled. "No?"

"This will be dangerous," Amin explained. "There are many among us who are competing for power and influence. Loyalties may come and go. A plan like this is for you and me. For family."

"Very well." Qadir grasped Amin by the shoulders. "For family."

"For family," Amin repeated.

✦ ✦ ✦ ✦ ✦

Amin was serious about taking control of the Muslim Brotherhood, but he was not serious about joining the call for a general strike. Only in *appearing* to join it. He made several appearances in towns and villages where strikes were ongoing, using the occasions to insinuate himself into the moment, speaking often, but saying very little.

That spring, however, members of the Nashashibi clan, who dominated the National Defense Party, called for a general strike against all Jewish interests. This time protesters turned out in even larger waves than before, all across Palestine. Jewish businesses were not merely boycotted but attacked, damaged, and in some cases destroyed. Riots erupted in numerous locations.

In Haifa, the strike was led by Farhan al-Sa'di, an activist who had been loyal to Qassam and, in fact, had been with Qassam at the cave until shortly before his death. Amin sensed the Nashashibi were not serious about obtaining Arab independence, or about solving the Jewish problem, but were simply making a play for power. In effect, elbowing him aside. Amin still was reluctant to get in a fight with the British, but he could ill afford to let the Nashashibi flank him on the issue. Nor could he issue a public call for a strike. Having finessed his way around doing that earlier, doing so now would make it obvious to everyone that control of the issue was passing to the Nashashibi.

Instead, Amin drew on his widely-known association with Qassam, and the memory of his heroic death, to negotiate an alliance with Farhan that gave Amin control of the Black Hand network and its financial interests. He still was uncomfortable with direct, public action that risked confrontation with the British, but he was inching in that direction.

After Amin and Farhan reached an agreement, Amin made a point of appearing with Farhan at strategic public gatherings, creating the notion that he supported the general strike, and even that he was leading it. All the while giving himself deniability with the British, should the need arise.

✦ ✦ ✦ ✦ ✦

In the midst of the general strike, his meetings with Banna, and the negotiations with Farhan, Amin received news that Benito Mussolini, Italy's prime minister-turned-dictatorial leader, had launched a brutal assault on the North African country of Libya. Rumors spread quickly about atrocities committed in that assault, on the one hand, and the good things Mussolini had done in wresting control of Italy from the monarchs.

Amin was curious to know how much of what he'd heard about Mussolini was actually true and asked Nafez to investigate. "Talk to people here in Jerusalem who might be familiar with him," Amin directed. "Travel to Libya if you can, to see for yourself. I want to know who he really is and what he is doing."

Over the next two weeks, Nafez interviewed contacts with the Italian consulate but, on their advice, avoided travel to Libya. Instead, they pointed him toward three prominent Italian families who lived near Jerusalem. "They can tell you want you need to know," it was suggested.

When Nafez finished his inquiry, he came to Amin. "Mussolini is a ruthless man. He became prime minister by force, more or less, then eliminated his political opposition."

"Eliminated?"

"Yes. He killed them or ran them out of the country."

"Interesting. So why are they in Libya?"

"After the Great War, the Italians wanted an empire. They chose Libya because it seemed like a likely place to begin."

"Just like that?"

"Just like that." Nafez looked troubled. "They landed an army at the coast and moved inland, systematically attacking villages and towns. Killing men, women, and children who got in their way."

"A decisive leader."

"This isn't leadership. Most of the Italian brutality was asserted against our own people."

Amin was puzzled. *"Our* people?"

"Against the Muslims who live in Libya. They killed great numbers of Muslims."

Amin could see Nafez was troubled by what he had learned. "These things have to happen."

"Against Muslims?"

"Mussolini is not an Arab. He was attempting to take over a country populated with Arabs. Naturally, Arabs would be killed in a situation like that."

"Many think he intentionally targeted Arabs."

Amin looked away. "You do realize that if events go the way of force here in Palestine, many Arabs will die, right here at our door."

"I thought you wanted to avoid brutality?"

Amin shook his head. "I wanted to avoid a confrontation with the British. But I never for a moment thought we should avoid bloodshed. Only that it should be the Jews who die, not us."

Nafez looked concerned. "And you think this Mussolini can help us?"

"Yes," Amin said confidently. "I think he may be just the person we need."

By then Amin had reached the conclusion that Pan-Arabism—the all-for-one-and-one-for-all approach they had tried before—would not solve their problems. Arabs striving to break free of European colonialism were too divided to fight for freedom as one. Each region would have to fight for it themselves. For assistance, they would have to look somewhere other than the Arabs who occupied the neighboring regions.

As Nafez recounted details of the Italian conquest in Libya, Amin's admiration for Mussolini and his brazen use of force became even stronger. He imagined what it might be like to have that kind of force available. To eliminate an entire people with a simple command. That was his real goal. To attain the kind of power that no one could resist, then use it against the Jews to destroy them once and for all, just as Mussolini used it against his opponents in Italy and against those who tried to resist him in Libya.

Amin glanced over at Nafez. "Is that all there was to it? Is that all you found?"

Nafez looked away. "Yes. That was all."

But Amin could tell he had more to say. "Tell me the rest of it," he insisted. "Tell me what you haven't already told me."

Nafez gave a heavy sigh. "The people I spoke with indicated Mussolini has expressed interest in expanding his influence to include Palestine."

Amin's eyes widened and a smile spread over his face. "That is great!" he exclaimed. "I want to make contact with him right away. Invite him for a visit."

Nafez shook his head. "He is not like the men we have dealt with thus far. Not like the British. Or even the Jews."

"He is a man," Amin insisted. "Do you think we can't handle him?"

Nafez shook his head again. "Not this one."

"Contact him anyway," Amin insisted. "Use the people you spoke with at the consulate. See if they can arrange a visit for him here in Jerusalem. I will issue a formal invitation."

Nafez squared his shoulders. "I will give you their names, but I want nothing to do with this. We have enough fighting here already. And enough European forces manipulating us to do their bidding. We do not need another."

"I am not inviting him to a war," Amin retorted. "I only want to talk."

"Mussolini is not the kind of man who talks. If he comes, he will bring his army and they will be ten times the trouble of the British."

Amin was angered by Nafez's attitude but because they were brothers-in-law, he felt there was little he could do to force the matter with him. Nafez did not make a scene, either. He simply turned toward the door and walked away, but he no longer participated in Amin's work.

✦ ✦ ✦ ✦ ✦

Despite Nafez's reaction, and in spite of continued reports from multiple sources about the nature of Italian action in Libya, Amin was convinced Mussolini was a leader he could solicit for support. With Nafez no longer available, he explained Mussolini's interest in Palestine to Hadad, carefully omitting the part about Italian brutality against Muslims in Libya. "We could offer the Italians an opportunity to participate in Palestine," Amin suggested. "Give them an opportunity to extend their reach to the Middle East."

Hadad seemed to grasp Amin's intentions immediately. "You mean dangle that possibility in order to obtain financial and military support from them?"

"Exactly."

"But how much control will they take from us in the end?" It was the same issue Nafez had pointed out earlier, and Amin seemed aggravated by it even as Hadad spoke. "Wouldn't we be swapping the dominance of one European country for another?"

Amin dismissed his concern with a wave of the hand. "We will worry about that when the time comes. In order to confront the British and Jews now, as the Brotherhood desires, we must have support from somewhere. The British will not support us in our fight against the British. And they will not support us in our fight against the Jews. So, to whom shall we turn?"

Hadad shrugged. "I see your point."

"Of course you see it," Amin chided. "It's obvious. We need help, and the Italians seem like the best possibility right now. So I want you to pursue this. See if they are interested."

With Hadad's help, Amin arranged a visit for the two of them with Quinto Mazzolini, the Italian consul general in Jerusalem. After a brief conversation, Mazzolini handed them off to his assistant, Dario Vendola. "He will help you with the details," Mazzolini explained. "I am sure, given the political climate in Rome these days, we can find a way to accommodate your suggestion."

While Vendola and Amin talked, Franco Ormando took Hadad aside. A mysterious figure, even to seasoned Italian diplomats, Ormando served as the Italian Foreign Office's fixer—the one who solved seemingly unsolvable problems. He was suspected of doing most of his work by unseemly means, but no one cared so long as the problems they faced went away, which they always did when Ormando was involved.

Amin's visit with Vendola didn't take much longer than his meeting with the consul general. Rather than leaving Hadad behind at the consulate, though, he chose to wait and took a seat in a room just off the building's main entrance. An hour later, Hadad appeared at the doorway and indicated with a nod that he was ready to leave. They walked from the building in silence and when they were well away, Amin prompted, "So? How did it go?"

"He says we will have their support."

"Financial support?"

"Yes. Probably in a matter of days. Perhaps a couple of weeks."

Amin was beside himself with excitement. "Do you think they will actually follow through?"

Hadad smiled. "He seems like the kind of man who makes things happen."

Amin rubbed his hands together in glee. "Very good." He slapped Hadad on the back. "I knew this would work out. I just knew it."

As the general strike continued, disparate Arab groups continued to engage in sporadic acts of violence. The need for coordination of their activities became apparent. If the attacks were going to be effective in asserting Arab priorities, someone needed to direct them in a systematic way.

After consulting with Hadad, Latif, and the others, Amin formed a coalition of Arab clans and organizations governed by a coordinating group called the Arab Higher Committee. Justified to the British as a way of curtailing violence, it was, in reality, a mechanism for effectively neutralizing leadership from the various Arab factions. The committee included representatives from each participating organization but also contained at-large members appointed by Amin. All of these members were loyal only to Amin. His cousin Qadir served as committee secretary.

To committee members, Amin made clear their substantive purpose was to focus action against strategic Jewish interests. "If we are to have a general strike," Amin advised, "and if there is to be violence, then let us make every effort to avoid killing Mandatory officials in the process. Let us concentrate on killing Jews."

Even though he'd stacked the committee membership in his favor, working with the committee proved more challenging than Amin expected. After a month of discussion and argument, the Higher Committee endorsed the general strike, which already was underway, and called for an end to Jewish immigration. Very quickly, however, logistics became an issue as the lack of arms and munitions at their disposal became apparent. So much so that the success of the committee seemed to hang in the balance. Either it supplied the needs of the activists and kept them under its control, or it failed altogether.

Just as the committee was about to crumble, Amin's overtures to the Italians paid off and financial aid arrived. Amin was elated and used the money to purchase German arms and munitions for the now openly rebelling Arab groups. The transaction was arranged by a contact at the German consulate.

EIGHTEEN

INVIGORATED BY SUPPORT from Italy, and by the willingness of Germany to sell him arms, Amin turned to his study of *Mein Kampf*, and all things German, with renewed vigor and diligence. The more he read, the more enthralled he became with the ideas and beliefs expressed by the Nazis, eventually adopting Hitler's writings as the guide not just for working with Salama and the others but for his role as Grand Mufti.

Very quickly, too, Amin became convinced that the Nazi approach was preferable to that of the Italians. Mussolini directed his wrath against Muslims, which, though unsettling, Amin ignored for the sake of gaining financial backing from the Italians. But Hitler and the Nazis, on the other hand, focused their attention on the Jews, whom Amin was convinced were the real problem. He was interested in continuing his association with Mussolini, but his mind was almost entirely focused on Nazi ideology. With Salama, Hadad, and the others, he made the point unmistakably clear: "Hitler's approach offers a quick path toward power. He uses a combination of patriotism, militancy, and hatred of the Jews to incite his people to action. That is our path to the domination of Palestine."

In the months that followed, Amin turned to Latif and Aref for help in organizing his speeches in a way that placed the British and the Jews in the role of scapegoat, just as Hitler did with Jews, Poles, and many others. "Our troubles come from the Jews," he said in addressing crowds of any size. "Jews and their enablers, the British Mandatory Authority, are corrupting our minds, stealing our faith, and taking our land. It is the Jews you can thank for the misery you experience, the poverty in which you are forced to dwell, the jobs you are forced to endure without. And it is the British you can thank for helping them." For emphasis, he even went so far as to mimic Hitler's enthusiastic delivery, including hand gestures and head movements, which he borrowed from scenes he'd observed in newsreels.

As expected, Arab violence against Jews escalated rapidly. The Black Hand, still active throughout Palestine even without Qassam, was especially energized by Amin's message. In direct response to his speeches, they launched attacks on oil pipelines, irrigation systems, electrical generators, and trains that serviced areas heavily populated by Jews. Other Arab groups stepped up attacks on Jewish businesses and initiated nighttime raids on Jewish homes.

Faced with an onslaught of Arab violence, British and Jewish defense agencies responded harshly. British constables and Jewish paramilitary organizations engaged Arab militants in pitched battles. Armed British troops patrolled villages and countryside, accosting anyone they thought looked suspicious and conducting raids on the offices of Arab organizations.

As casualties mounted on both sides, Arthur Grenfell Wauchope, the most recent appointee to the office of High Commissioner for Palestine, convened a meeting of Arab and Jewish leaders to seek an end to the conflict. Jews argued that Arabs were responsible. Arabs claimed the entire affair was instigated and facilitated by British favoritism. "You always take the Jewish side," Amin argued. "And every time we complain, you ask us to be tolerant while Haganah, Irgun, and a dozen other Jewish gangs plunder and murder our people."

After a week of intense and often hostile negotiations, Wauchope succeeded in obtaining an agreement from the participants to halt the violence while a supposedly neutral royal commission investigated Arab claims. "At least give us a chance to show our goodwill," he argued. Amin doubted anything would come from the effort but agreed to a cease-fire, explaining the move to his followers as an opportunity to regroup.

In London, the British cabinet created the Palestine Royal Commission and designated Lord William Robert Wellesley Peel as its chairman. Members were added from various aspects of government and charged with investigating circumstances in Mandatory Palestine. In particular, Arab claims of favoritism by the Mandatory government.

The following month, the Peel Commission arrived in Jerusalem and began conducting its investigation. Interviews were scheduled, records reviewed, and witnesses called to appear at formal hearings held in every major city in Palestine. Amin appeared in person and gave detailed testimony regarding instances of favoritism, all of which was couched in strident and accusatory language. Members of the Nashashibi clan, including Jerusalem's mayor, attempted to mollify commission members with a more moderate view of circumstances. Amin was incensed by their obvious pandering and by yet another attempt to gain power and influence by flanking him on the issues.

After weeks of review, the Peel Commission finished its work in Palestine and returned to London to prepare a written report. A month later, the report was submitted to the British cabinet. The cabinet duly adopted the commission's report and released it to the public. That's when the people of Palestine learned the report included a proposal to partition Palestine—to divide it into Arab and Jewish areas. Under its terms, both groups would obtain separate political states but neither group would acquire complete control of the region.

A few days after it was released, Amin received a copy of the Peel Commission's report and rejected the proposed division out of hand. Primarily because it gave the Jews a political state. "They are interlopers," he charged. "They came uninvited and stole our land. They deserve nothing."

Some Jewish spokesmen also rejected the proposal. "It institutionalizes Arab control over parts of Palestine," they argued, "all of which constitute a Jewish homeland." David Grün, one of Amin's former pupils when he tutored language students in Istanbul years before, thought the plan was workable. Living in Tel-Aviv under the name David Ben-Gurion, he was active in the Zionist Congress and a member of the Jewish Agency for Palestine's Executive Committee. Over the ensuing weeks, he convinced the Zionist Congress to accept the proposal, with exceptions designed to strengthen the contiguous nature of areas under Jewish control. As a result, Zionist Congress officials instructed Chaim Weizmann, president of the Jewish Agency, to adopt the proposal with the exceptions noted. He did as the Congress instructed and aligned the Jewish Agency with the British Mandatory Authority, offering support and cooperation for its proposal. Amin and other Arab organizations were aligned in opposition.

✦ ✦ ✦ ✦ ✦

Although the Peel Commission's plan of partition was viewed in London as the optimal solution to the Arab-Jewish situation, implementation of the plan required more than simply marking boundaries on a map. Governments had to be created.

Constitutions and organizing documents drafted and approved. Elections scheduled and held. All of that required time and meetings—lots of meetings—in London and in Palestine.

While the British cabinet deliberated over details, a new German consul general, Walter Döhle, was appointed to the German consulate in Jerusalem. Amin, by then thoroughly enamored of Hitler and all things Nazi, thought Hitler would be eager to support his cause against the Jews. "Germany," he told anyone who would listen, "is a country that understood the Jewish threat. They will support us even better than the Italians."

A few weeks after Döhle arrived at his post, Amin arranged a meeting with him at the consulate. As they talked, he dangled the prospect of German-Arab cooperation, just as he had with the Italians.

Döhle had a knowing smile. "And I assume you will want something in return."

"As I said," Amin responded, "we are looking for a cooperative partnership. So, yes, the relationship would flow in both directions."

"And what would you expect from us?"

"We need German support of our efforts to throw off British domination and remove the Jews from Palestine." Amin spoke in matter-of-fact terms and was unapologetic for his request.

"I see," Döhle nodded. "And how would this benefit Germany?"

"Germany would enjoy free reign over all of Palestine. Through us, of course," Amin added.

"I see."

"We must end all hope of a Jewish state in Palestine and, indeed, put an end to the Jewish presence in Palestine. If they succeed here, they will move on to dominate the entire world. The Führer's vision of world domination cannot be complete without control of Palestine."

"What makes you think the Führer wishes to dominate the world?"

"I have read his book." Amin had a satisfied smile. "Many times."

After their meeting, Döhle dutifully prepared a memo summarizing the contents of Amin's presentation and forwarded it to the German Foreign Ministry in Berlin. There it was reviewed and discussed at a routine interagency conference. Joachim von Ribbentrop, the Foreign Minister, chaired the meeting.

Officials from Abwehr, the German intelligence service, were initially opposed to involvement in Palestine. "The region would entangle us in many illusive factors without providing a sufficient payoff for our troubles. Jews. Arabs. British. They all hate each other. We would be stepping into an impossible situation."

Comments went around the room. Most of them negative.

"And," someone added, "the Jews have support from America. We do not need to confront the Americans right now."

"Arabs have support from other Arab countries and peoples in the region. Let them help themselves. We do not need to involve ourselves in the affairs of either of these groups any further than we already are."

"Yes. We have too many unresolved issues here in Europe to go looking for things to do in other places."

"Not yet, you mean."

"Yes. Of course. When the time is right, we shall resolve all problems."

After most in the room had expressed their opinion, Ribbentrop spoke up. "I would remind you, gentlemen," he said in a calm and even voice, "the Führer has expressed a desire to obtain concessions from European nations regarding our interests in Czechoslovakia." Heads nodded in response. Ribbentrop continued. "The British have been reluctant to grant us what we want in these matters. Perhaps we could use a feint toward Palestine, where the British have heavily invested themselves, as a way of prying them loose with regard to the Czech issue."

"How so?" someone wondered.

"We make overtures of support to the Arabs," Ribbentrop explained. "Give them support, in fact, though minimal. The British will notice it and bring it to our attention as an objection. We resist, initially, but ultimately offer to forego our interests in Palestine in exchange for concessions on our presence in Czechoslovakia."

Around the room, heads nodded once more. "Excellent idea," someone said. "Brilliant," another added. Ribbentrop smiled indulgently. "I shall present the matter to the Führer."

A few days later, Ribbentrop received instructions in the form of a memo signed by Hitler: "You are to proceed with the Palestinian plan. Provide support to Amin al-Husseini in Jerusalem as part of a larger gambit to place pressure on Great Britain for concessions regarding Czechoslovakia."

✦ ✦ ✦ ✦ ✦

Early the following month, a messenger delivered a note to Amin at his residence. The note was from Döhle inviting him to a meeting at the German Consulate. Amin glanced at the messenger who still was waiting by the door. "It doesn't say when he wants to meet."

"You are to come now," the messenger urged. "The consul general wishes to speak with you. I am to accompany you to his office."

Amin was taken aback by the abruptness of the invitation but chose not to protest. Instead, he followed the messenger up the street and collected Salama along the way.

At that meeting, Döhle informed Amin that his request for support from the German government had been granted. He offered Amin a memo from the Foreign Office that indicated the amount. Amin glanced at the document and was deeply disappointed by the amount but chose to push his emotions aside and smiled politely. "Please convey my deepest appreciation to Adolf Hitler and Joachim von Ribbentrop. This is a wonderful gesture."

As he left the meeting, Salama, who had sat quietly to one side, noticed that Amin was upset. "Did something happen in there?"

"Only this," Amin said as he handed Salama the memo.

Salama glanced at the paper, then looked over at Amin. "Ten thousand Reichsmarks? That is all they gave us?"

"Yes."

"We need more."

"I know."

"Where do you think we can get it?"

Amin shrugged. "Perhaps the Americans will help us."

Salama frowned. "The Americans? They love the Jews."

"They feign support for them," Amin replied. "But in their hearts, they really hate them as much as we do."

"And you think they will help us?"

"If we kill Jews over here," Amin smiled, "the Americans won't have to trouble themselves with doing it over there." Salama laughed in response.

As strange as the idea sounded, Amin was serious in seeking American assistance. A few days after his meeting with Döhle, he arranged a meeting with George Wadsworth, the US consul general. They sat across from each other in overstuffed leather chairs in the corner of Wadsworth's office at the consulate. "I am surprised you wanted to talk to me," Wadsworth commented as they began.

"You should not be," Amin replied.

"Oh?" Wadsworth seemed curious. "And why is that?"

"Americans and Arabs have much in common. Especially Arabs who live in Palestine."

Wadsworth frowned. "I'm not sure I understand what you mean."

"Americans and Arabs share an anti-imperialist proclivity."

"Oh." Wadsworth seemed to relax. "I suppose we—"

Amin cut him off. "We also share a common suspicion of the Jews."

"You think we are suspicious of them?"

Amin had an arrogant smile. "It is rather obvious from articles in your newspapers that Americans see Zionism as an imperialist attempt to dominate Palestine, if not the world. You would do well to avoid being swayed by Jewish rhetoric."

"You think they mean to harm the United States?"

"I think they intend to *control* the United States," Amin corrected, "just as they control Great Britain."

Wadsworth had a pensive expression. "And you can prevent that from happening?"

Amin nodded. "Given sufficient levels of support, we can eliminate the Jewish problem here in Palestine. That way you will not have to eliminate it on the streets of New York."

"You want us to support you?"

Amin nodded again. "The Arab Higher Committee."

Wadsworth shifted positions in the chair. "I'm afraid that would put us in the position of opposing the British. They are our strongest ally."

"But surely you can help us," Amin implored. "At least to prevent the Jews from stealing our land."

"Perhaps." Wadsworth shrugged. "What do you propose?"

"Persuade officials in the United States to refrain from overtly supporting the Jews. Prohibit the transfer of money to those who live in Palestine. Curb or prohibit the sale of arms to their paramilitary organizations."

Wadsworth nodded. "That might be a possibility."

Amin left the meeting uncertain whether Wadsworth would come through with the support he needed but, having listened to Wadsworth, he felt desperate. "The Jews have infiltrated the minds of everyone," he said to himself. The Arabs of Palestine faced a growing Jewish population that was supported by the British and, from Wadsworth's attitude, by the Americans, too, leaving Arabs no choice but to fight, even if it meant confronting the British. He had tried to avoid it. He had tried to finesse around it. Now he felt there was no option. They had to fight.

After his meeting at the US Consulate, Amin continued his quest for help, courting the French and anyone else who would give him an audience. All of them listened—he was the Grand Mufti of Jerusalem; they didn't want him as an overt enemy—then politely rebuffed his request.

In the weeks that followed, British officials continued to deliberate over implementation of the Peel partition plan, and pressure began to build among Arabs for a return to armed resistance. In the past, Amin would have resisted those calls and argued vehemently against resorting to violence, but that was when he still held out hope that they might solve the Jewish problem another way. Now after thoroughly reading *Mein Kampf,* and after talking with representatives from Western governments, he was convinced that Arabs would have to fight for the country they wanted to establish, fight to drive away the Jews, and fight to make the British miserable enough to leave.

In September 1937, lightly armed Arabs, including members of the Black Hand, resumed attacks on Jewish settlements. Others launched coordinated raids against railways, water distribution facilities, and other infrastructure that serviced Jewish communities. Misery and fear gripped Jewish villages throughout Palestine.

Later that month, as violence continued to escalate, Lewis Andrews, an official with the British Mandatory government, was assassinated. Jews were quick to blame Arabs for his death, and in response Irgun, one of the more radical Jewish paramilitary groups, initiated random attacks against Arab interests, calling it part of an "active defense."

Arabs blamed the Jews for Andrews's death and for the escalating violence, saying "active defense" was merely a euphemism for "military offensive." They appealed to Mandatory authorities for assistance in defending their homes.

British constables gave Arab protests of innocence and pleas for help scant attention and appeared to side with the Jews. Very quickly their investigation into Andrews's death focused exclusively on Arab suspects. Amin was incensed that the British ignored Jewish complicity in the matter, but his protests were to no avail.

Two days after Andrews's murder, Wauchope, the British High Commissioner, issued an order outlawing the Arab Higher Committee. The day after his order took effect, Mandatory constables began rounding up committee members and placing them under arrest. When news of the arrests reached Amin and he learned that constables were coming for him, he bid his wife and children a hasty good-bye and fled Jerusalem. This time he avoided taking refuge in Syria, as he had before, and made his way to Beirut, Lebanon. Aref and Qadir, fearing their names were on the arrest list, too, accompanied him.

NINETEEN

WHEN HE ARRIVED IN BEIRUT, Amin contacted the Lebanese prime minister's office and asked for assistance. "As you can see," Amin complained, "once again I have been forced to flee the British."

"We heard of your trouble," the prime minister replied. "How may we assist the Grand Mufti of Jerusalem?"

"The Grand Mufti needs a place to stay."

After a brief discussion about his needs, the prime minister provided a residence large enough for Amin, Aref, and Qadir, along with a staff to attend to their needs.

Once Amin and his entourage were settled, Amin reconstituted the Higher Committee and summoned its members to a meeting. Some, however, were unwilling to risk the ire of the British and refused to attend, a fact that angered Amin immensely. "See," he railed, "the British have made cowards of them!" Rather than concede the matter, though, Amin dismissed the members who were absent and appointed Hadad, Aref, and Latif to take their places. Qadir continued in his post as committee secretary.

Though relegated to exile, enthusiasm among committee members was extraordinarily high. Lack of funding for the committee's work, however, remained as great an existential threat as it had since the day the committee first was formed back in Jerusalem. With money, they could continue to promote an armed struggle against the Jews and, now, also against the British. Without it, they would be cast into the abyss of political irrelevancy. No one would listen to them or follow their lead unless they could back up their rhetoric with the materiel of war.

In order to address the funding issue, Amin looked again to Germany. Using Aref's connections, he sent a message to Fritz Grobba, who recently had become the German envoy to the court of Ibn Saud, and arranged a preliminary meeting in Arabia to discuss the matter. Unable to travel himself, he sent Qadir to open the discussion of aid for the committee's work. Ever the faithful servant and cousin, Qadir took a boat from Lebanon down the coast to Alexandria, then trekked across the desert in search of the Saudi camp and Grobba.

While he waited for Qadir's return, Amin dispatched Salama to Jerusalem to collect his wife, Karimeh, and their children. British Mandatory authorities had their residences under surveillance and when they learned Salama had arrived they were reluctant to grant him access to the house. Salama refused to back down and, after pressing the issue with the High Commissioner, succeeded in gathering Karimeh and the children. A week later, they were reunited with Amin at the residence in Beirut.

Three weeks after Karimeh arrived, Qadir returned from Arabia with news from Grobba. "He is scheduled to attend a meeting in Greece next month," Qadir reported. "He will stop in Beirut to see you on his way."

Amin was pleased. "Is he willing to forward our request to Berlin?"

"He is willing to listen. That is all he would commit to."

"Did he say whether Hitler is interested in establishing a presence in Palestine?"

Qadir nodded. "He *is* interested in the Middle East. Because of the oil."

"But?"

"They are put off by what they see as the tangled nature of relationships in Palestine. And by the British."

"Surely they are not afraid of the British."

Qadir shook his head. "I got the sense that they were following a strategy in Europe and hoped to accomplish it without British opposition."

Amin smiled. "That Hitler." He shook his head admiringly. "He is so smart and so cunning."

✦ ✦ ✦ ✦ ✦

For the next four weeks, Amin worried and fretted over funding for the committee, contacting everyone he could think of but only garnering small amounts in response. Karimeh tried to console him but he was deeply troubled. "I have seen these things from Allah. Money from Germany. The elimination of the Jews. The vanquishing of the British. I know it must be true. I have seen it in my mind."

"Whatever Allah has spoken," Karimeh replied, "it will come to pass."

Finally, the day of Grobba's arrival came. Amin and a delegation from the city met his ship at the port and escorted him to the hotel where he was staying. Later that afternoon, Amin met with him there.

"As you can see," Amin began, just as he had with the prime minister, "I once again have been forced to flee the British. This time, I chose Beirut over Damascus because I knew it would be easier to conduct meetings here. And because we have friends in the Lebanese government."

Grobba seemed not to understand precisely what Amin meant, but he knew the point of the meeting. "Your associate Salama says you are in need of funding for the Higher Committee's work."

"Yes," Amin replied.

Grobba looked puzzled. "Tell me again, what is it the committee does?"

Amin was perplexed by the question but smiled and related, "We are the official representative for Palestinian Arabs. We administer Palestine under the auspices of the illegal British occupation."

"And why should Germany support you?"

"We kill Jews," Amin answered flatly. "And we need your help to do it."

Grobba smiled nervously. "I'm afraid you have misunderstood—"

Amin cut him off. "If Germany insists on ridding itself of Jews by sending them here to Palestine, then Germany must supply the weapons and ammunition for those who live here so that we may kill them."

Grobba's expression turned serious. "I understand the presence of Jews in Palestine has created a problem for you. But my superiors in Berlin are focused on German expansion in Europe. They are reluctant to assign resources to further involvement in the affairs of Palestine."

Amin repeated his argument sternly. "Germany created our problem. Germany must pay to solve it."

They talked awhile longer but Grobba assured him that Hitler, though interested in Arabs and Muslims in general, was reluctant to undertake any substantive operations in the Middle East. Desperate to gain some form of concession, Amin managed to convince him that training for his men would be helpful. Later that month, Qadir departed for Berlin where he was set to receive instruction in the proper use of explosives and advanced weapons. Amin was glad for that much but deeply frustrated by the paltry response he'd elicited from Grobba. "I need to get to someone else," he insisted. "I need to reach Grobba's bosses."

"Perhaps Mussolini is the way to do that," Aref suggested.

Amin had a questioning frown. "How so?"

"Hitler likes to be the one in charge. The first. The one taking the lead."

"Yes."

"If you move closer to Mussolini, and Hitler knows it, maybe he will step in and scoop you up."

"You mean like a romance?"

"Yeah." Aref grinned. "Like a romance. I think you have to court him."

Amin was intrigued and began to wonder how he might accomplish the gambit.

✦ ✦ ✦ ✦ ✦

At the beginning of 1939, war in Europe seemed unavoidable. Officials in the United Kingdom were interested in avoiding another global conflict, but the apparent inevitability of war with Germany forced some in responsible positions to make preparations, even if only in a tangential way. Among seasoned diplomatic professionals, establishing peace in the Middle East and preventing Arabs from aligning with Nazi Germany became a priority. The trick to doing that lay in placating Arab nationalist forces while at the same time shoring up support from Jews.

As British officials turned their attention to that task, analysts at the Foreign Ministry noticed a change in German policy. Until then, the German government had encouraged Jews to emigrate, particularly to Palestine, which they presented in a favorable light. In 1939, though, German policy shifted. Officials became less interested in expelling Jews and more interested in simply eliminating them, after, of course, working them to death as a means of acquiring the human labor necessary to build the German Reich. As a result, fewer and fewer Jews were permitted to leave.

British officials were not altogether sad to see Jewish immigration to Palestine decline. A growing Jewish population in the region posed a potential threat, both to Arab cooperation, which the British now sought, and to British authority. Fewer immigrants also meant less tension with Arabs, which played into the plan to bring peace and stability to the region. Nevertheless, discovery of the reduced immigration levels was an unsettling revelation. Everyone who saw the statistics understood the horror being visited upon Jews who were trapped in Nazi Germany.

In May 1939, the British government took the first step under its new priority of winning support from Palestinian Arabs by issuing a White Paper announcing and clarifying its Palestinian policy. The paper, a blatant attempt to placate Arab concerns, largely repudiated the notion of an independent Jewish homeland as previously expressed in the Balfour Declaration. Instead, it proposed a Jewish homeland within the confines of an independent Palestine. Limits were imposed on Jewish immigration to Palestine, as well as on the ability of Jews to acquire additional land over the succeeding five years. After that, Jewish immigration would only continue with Arab approval. A typically British document, the paper in essence created an independent Palestinian-Arab state that included a Jewish autonomous region, but without partitioning Palestine into two separate political entities.

Most Arabs were encouraged by the White Paper, especially members of the Nashashibi clan. Amin, however, thought otherwise. "Once again, they are trying to undermine me."

Aref, who was sitting nearby, seemed not to understand. "Who? Who is trying to undermine you?"

"The Nashashibi. They're only saying they support the British because they think they can push me out of the way. They're worse than the British."

"You think it's just another game?"

"Yes." Amin glared at him. "It's just another plot to get me out of the way."

Aref shook his head. "I'm not so sure."

"It's just like every other time." Amin threw up his hands in a gesture of frustration. "Or a ploy of the Jews to trick us into trusting the word of London diplomats."

"How would that work? The paper undercuts the idea of British support for a Jewish homeland, which was one of the Jews' major accomplishments."

"A way of convincing us to rely on empty words," Amin explained. "Get us to refrain from asserting ourselves against them."

"Or," Aref countered, "it might be a genuine attempt to restore order. Things *are* unraveling in Europe. The British can't afford to fight everywhere."

Amin thought for a moment. "We should find out what the Jews really think of this."

"It's all over the newspapers."

"Not the official word from Chaim Weizmann or the others."

"We'd have to send someone to Jerusalem."

"Yes," Amin agreed. "I think I will."

With Qadir still in Germany, Amin dispatched Salama to Jerusalem to gauge the depth and nature of Jewish reaction to the White Paper. "We need to know what they *really* feel about it. Not just what they say in the newspapers."

Three weeks later, Salama reported that the Jews were outraged. "They feel they have been deceived by the British."

"Imagine that," Amin said dryly.

Salama continued. "They say they cooperated with England

in the Great War and believed promises in return about a future Jewish political state, which they were to receive in exchange for that cooperation. Now they feel they have been lied to."

Amin pressed the point. "But are they genuinely offended?"

"I think so," Salama agreed. "Many in the World Zionist Organization were persuaded to follow this path of cooperation by Chaim Weizmann. They have ousted him from leadership of the Jewish Agency."

Amin's eyes opened wide in a startled expression. "Oh?" he exclaimed. "Who did they get to replace him?"

"David Ben-Gurion."

Amin laughed. "They were played by the British, just as we were. And now Ben-Gurion is in charge."

Aref looked over at him. "You know Ben-Gurion?"

Amin nodded. "He was one of my pupils in Istanbul. I taught him Arabic so he could study law."

Salama shrugged. "He seems like a capable fellow. He fought with the Ottomans during the Great War, didn't he?"

"Yes," Amin replied. "Then switched sides and went with the British after they issued the Balfour Declaration."

"So," Aref commented, "he's an opportunist."

"I suppose," Amin mused. "Something of a pragmatist, actually."

"Makes him rare among the Jews," Aref noted. "Most of them are idealists. Like Jabotinsky."

"Jabotinsky would kill us all," Salama commented flatly.

Aref chuckled. "Ben-Gurion would figure out how to make money from us first."

Salama took a seat. "So," he asked, "what do we do about the White Paper?"

Aref spoke up. "Maybe we should support it."

Salama seemed startled. "Why would we do that?"

"It grants us a political state over all of Palestine. The Jews only get a zone within it, but they'd be subject to our sovereignty. It's everything we wanted."

"Not quite," Salama said. "The Jews would still be here."

"Well," Aref countered, "it's as much of what we wanted as the British are likely to give us. And much better than the Peel Commission's plan."

Amin shook his head. "I don't think it makes any room for me."

Aref frowned. "What do you mean?"

"I mean the Jews will never accept an Arab state with me in charge, no matter how it's configured. And I'll never accept one if I'm not."

With Latif's help, Amin drafted a formal statement rejecting the White Paper. Aref made sure it was disseminated to every newspaper in the Middle East. A copy also was sent to the British foreign secretary in London and to the High Commissioner in Jerusalem.

While the others were working on the response to the White Paper, Amin took Hadad aside. "I want you to go to Jerusalem for me."

"Very well," Hadad replied. "What would you like for me to do there?"

"I want you to spread the word that I view all who support the White Paper as traitors."

"Anyone I should speak to specifically?"

"Just make sure the word gets out. And I want you to meet in person with Farhan al-Sa'di in Haifa."

"Why am I meeting him?"

Amin lowered his voice. "I want you to give him a message from me."

"Okay." Hadad nodded. "What's the message?"

"Tell him, 'Kill them all.'"

Hadad looked puzzled. "He will know what that means?"

"I assure you"—Amin smiled—"Farhan will know *precisely* what it means."

✦ ✦ ✦ ✦ ✦

In 1939, Germany invaded Poland. Under the terms of various treaties, and faced with irrepressible German hostility, England and France stepped forward to defend Poland. Both countries declared war on Germany. With war at hand, British policy in the Middle East turned from nuanced attempts to coddle, promote, and coerce cooperation to threats, thinly veiled as requests, for allegiance from less-belligerent regional governments.

In Palestine, the British abruptly switched from the accommodating stance posed in the White Paper to the brutal use of force. Having given up on reconciliation by others means, the British army applied its military might against the Arabs of Palestine and quickly succeeded in putting down the revolt.

Amin, like many others, saw the change as a deeper turn of British perspective away from a policy toward the Middle Eastern plan that placed Arabs in the lead, toward a policy that was decidedly biased in favor of the Jews. Order was restored in Palestine, but in the process, all hope of peaceful coexistence between Jews, Arabs, and the British was lost. The heavy-handed British approach, however, had one benefit for Amin.

Having received the message that was delivered by Hadad, Farhan al-Sa'di and the Black Hand went to work, eliminating Amin's Arab rivals. The Nashashibi family was especially hard hit. However, with casualties mounting from British troops and Jewish paramilitary units busily putting down the Arab revolt, no one noticed the many Arabs being slain by Farhan and his men. When asked about it later, Amin's only comment was, "They were traitors. Why should anyone mourn their deaths?"

TWENTY

WITH ENGLAND PREPARING for what might become a long and violent war, Amin sensed that his safety in Lebanon could no longer be guaranteed. "The British are going to war," he told his entourage. "The French always follow their lead and they have great sway in Beirut. We need to find somewhere else to live."

After inquiring among the Arab governments he thought might offer him a place, Amin received a message from a friend in Iraq. "King Faisal II would be pleased to have you as a guest of the kingdom."

By then, Faisal I, whom Amin had advised during earlier attempts at establishing his rule, was dead from a supposed heart attack. He had been succeeded by Ghazi, but Ghazi had died in a sporting accident. His son, Faisal II, a minor, now served as king through a regent, Abdullah Hejaz.

Amin was unsure precisely who extended the offer of asylum to him, but he was in no position to debate the matter. Without much deliberation, Amin accepted the offer and, in October 1939, left Beirut with his wife, family, and compatriots. Following a hot and dusty journey through the desert, they reached Baghdad.

As ruler of a truly Arab kingdom—and in light of the favorable response he had received to his earlier inquiry—Amin assumed Faisal II, through Abdullah Hejaz, would welcome his arrival with a show of solidarity and support. He arrived in Baghdad to find quite a different situation. Having received a request of support from the British Foreign Ministry—a thinly veiled demand, in fact, that forced Arab governments throughout the Middle East to choose sides and take a stand against Germany or face the wrath of the United Kingdom—the administration of Faisal II had chosen to side with the British. As a result, Nuri al-Said, the Iraqi prime minister, had terminated diplomatic relations with Germany, expelled all German diplomats from the country, and interred German nationals. Once again, there seemed for Amin no escaping the long reach of the British government.

With Arab countries once again falling beneath the shadow of the British Empire, and with Arab leadership caving to the Empire's demands, Amin was seen by the public as a champion of Arab nationalism. The true political heir to the Hashemite throne. A symbol of what it meant to be genuinely Arabic and a devotee of Islam.

Although appreciative of Faisal II and his uncle, most Iraqis were deeply suspicious of Said and of what they viewed as pandering to the West for his own aggrandizement. The tension they felt became apparent to Amin within days of his arrival. Many talked openly of Said's replacement, and speculation was rampant over whether the kingdom could survive. Some thought a military intervention by their own soldiers was the only hope of maintaining the country's identity as a distinctly Arab nation.

For his part, Amin had found the elder Faisal to be a capable leader when they worked together in the past. He liked the younger Faisal, too, even though he was quite young, and was reluctant to voice opposition to him. At the same time, he understood the frustration Iraqis felt over the way their officials responded to European policy, always willing to compromise Arab identity and Islamic principles to appease Western nations. And he enjoyed the accolades they gave him.

As Amin threaded his way between public sentiment and political reality, he soon became aware of a group of army officers who shared the public's sentiment about the current government. Unlike most in the street, however, these men were in a position to actually do something about the situation.

Known as the Golden Square, Salah al-Din al-Sabbagh, Kamil Shabib, Fahmi Said, and Mahmud Salman were colonels in the kingdom's army. Not merely soldiers, they were men of outstanding military ability with personal reputations that were above reproach. They were also deeply opposed to Faisal II's decision to side with the British in opposition to Germany. That became apparent to Amin when he and Aref met with them at the home of a friend late one night.

Sabbagh spoke first. "It's not so much that they chose a policy we oppose. It's just that Nuri al-Said is nothing but a puppet of the British."

"Which makes him a tool of the Zionist Jews," Shabib added.

"You wish to replace him?" Amin asked.

"We have no choice," Salman replied.

"If we can remove him," Sabbagh explained, "we hope to use the war and the German need for allies to make an alliance with Germany and break free of the British."

Amin nodded thoughtfully. "Do you intend to assassinate Faisal?"

"We do not need to assassinate him," Shabib explained. "Only to make him irrelevant."

"Which he already is," Salman added.

Sabbagh looked over at Amin. "You think we are wrong?"

Amin thought for a moment. "I am sympathetic to the cause of Iraqi independence, but I think Iraq should abide by its treaty with the British."

Sabbagh frowned. "You want us to side with them once again?"

"And fight against the Germans?" Salman asked.

"The British can never defeat the Germans," Shabib noted.

"I think you should make peace with England," Amin smiled. "But I did not say you should join them in the fight."

Sabbagh frowned. "Then, what do you mean?"

"You should use peace with England as a way to avoid being drawn into the war in Europe. I think avoiding this war is more important for you than openly opposing the British."

"Become neutral," Sabbagh noted.

Amin nodded. "Maintain neutrality. Conserve your energy for *after* the war."

Later that evening, on their way home, Aref commented, "It seemed as if you were afraid for them to confront the British. I thought we left that behind and understood that conflict is inevitable."

"Conflict is inevitable, but Iraq and Faisal are in no position to face the British. And neither are those four officers we just met."

"They are weak?"

"Yes, Germany would be their ally in regard to the Jews, but they are some distance away and we do not have a strong relationship with them. I think it best if Iraq sits this war out. Besides, this is a European affair. It is of no concern to us."

Indeed, Amin was not afraid of conflict, and he was as zealous in opposition to the British as any Arab. More so than most, in fact. But he was a practical man, too, and realized that he, his family, and the inner circle who accompanied him—Salama, Hadad, Latif, Aref, and the others—were in a vulnerable position. If they adamantly opposed the British, the British would pressure

Faisal to have them arrested. If they publicly supported Germany, they would be subject to arrest, just like German nationals who resided in the country. But if they joined an attempted coup, they could be killed.

Amin did not explain all of that to Aref that night as they discussed their conversation with the Golden Square. Indeed, he felt he could not. For just as he knew he must draw a fine line between those issues with outsiders, he also must do so with even his closest advisors. There could be no loose or casual conversation about replacing Faisal, or Said, or on any other topic of domestic Iraqi policy. Not if they could avoid it.

✦ ✦ ✦ ✦ ✦

In the spring of 1940, Mussolini and Hitler reached a cooperative agreement that aligned Italy and Germany as joint allies. Italy declared war on England and France and prepared to move its army toward the French border. With his eastern flank thus covered, Hitler turned Germany's military might against France, attacking from the north. By June, France was overrun from both sides and forced to sign an armistice agreement with Germany, effectively surrendering the government to Hitler's control. He quickly appointed officials of his choosing to rule the country and began plundering the nation's resources to stoke the German war machine.

In the face of rampant German aggression, the British government with Neville Chamberlain as prime minister began to unravel. Chamberlain, hoping to avoid a repeat of the Great War, had pursued a policy of appeasement with Hitler and thus was blamed for the German rout that was sweeping across the European continent. When France formally capitulated, Chamberlain was forced to resign. Winston Churchill was appointed to replace him as prime minister.

With little hope of intervening in Europe, the United Kingdom cast about for a suitable place to engage the Germans in a way that might afford them the possibility of military victory. Before long, someone remembered that units from the Italian army occupied Libya, having remained there following the end of the Great War. British troops were stationed right next door in Egypt, they too having remained there since the Great War. With England and Italy now formally at war, Italian troops in such close proximity offered an easily accessible target in a location that made them ripe for defeat. Determined to find success against Germany and its Axis allies, British troops stationed in Egypt crossed the border and attacked the Italian positions.

Within days, the Italians were pinned down from the east by the British. The Italians fought valiantly but with little hope of holding out, Mussolini appealed to Hitler for help. Hitler wanted to remain focused on Europe, but he also did not want to lose Italy's support. Italy lay to Germany's east, which provided protection to Germany's flank and prevented the Allies from establishing multiple fronts. After deliberation with his generals, Hitler relented and sent Erwin Rommel with a small group of tanks, quickly dubbed the Afrika Korps, to bail out the Italians. Before long, Rommel was engaged in a major military operation across North Africa.

By the summer of 1940 the fall of Poland, France, and surrounding countries—along with the change of government in England and the engagement of German tanks in North Africa—created the sense that Germany was destined to rule over all of Europe and, perhaps, the entire world. Only the British Isles held out stubbornly against the onslaught, but they were enduring successive bombing raids from the German air force, and many thought it only a matter of time before the United Kingdom would fall also.

The world, it seemed, was crumbling and there appeared to be no obvious means of stopping the Germans by direct opposition. British officials were desperate to find success—anywhere and of any kind. In the hope of finding it, they returned to conditions in the Middle East and began to frantically rethink their strategy in the region. It had offered a path for success during the Great War. Perhaps it would again, but for that to happen, England needed to reassert itself with the Arabs.

Doing that meant picking up the pieces from the disastrous offensive that ended the Arab revolt and somehow assembling a working relationship that not only staved off German overtures toward the region but also gave England an effective platform from which to mount a counteroffensive. Making that happen required the right person, and for the task the British cabinet selected Colonel S. F. Newcombe.

Born in Wales, Stewart Francis Newcome attended the Royal Military Academy, then was commissioned as an officer in the Royal Engineers in 1898. He was dispatched to Africa and served during the Second Boer War. During the Great War, he served as chief of the British Military Mission in the Hejaz. In that capacity, he worked closely with the Shariff of Mecca, his sons, and T. E. Lawrence. By war's end, he had developed a reputation as one who understood Arabian culture and who had a good working relationship with key Arab leaders in the region.

Newcombe was summoned to a meeting at the office of Anthony Eden, secretary of state for foreign affairs in Churchill's government. At that meeting, Newcombe was given his orders. "You have been seconded to our office," Eden informed him. "Your assignment is to travel to the Middle East and obtain Arab cooperation with us in this present war." It was an order, not a request, but one Newcombe sensed arose from desperation rather than a realistic view of the situation.

"I'm not sure that's possible," Newcombe replied.

Eden was indignant. "And why not?"

"They have a bad memory of their interaction with us during the previous war."

"Yes, well." Eden cleared his throat. "You can paper all of that over when you get there."

"It won't be that easy."

Eden had a perturbed look. "What do you mean?"

"We offended Arabs throughout the entire region with the way we put down Husseini and the most recent Arab revolt."

"Nevertheless." Eden gave a dismissive wave with a flick of his wrist. "We need their cooperation and we want you to obtain it."

Newcombe was worried. Ministers had a tendency to want something until they got it and once they realized what they had they changed their minds, leaving the staff officer who did their bidding with the blame. He'd seen others caught in this position, and things never turned out well for them. "You are telling me, 'Whatever it takes'?" he asked.

"Yes," Eden replied. "Of course. Whatever it takes."

"And you will back me up on this?"

Eden glared at him. "Now, see here. Are you questioning my integrity?"

"I'm just asking because this was a problem in the past. Promises were made to the Arabs. They believed and accepted those promises. And we didn't follow through. We still haven't followed through," he added quickly.

"Even so." Eden looked away. "We can't be bound by the past now."

Newcombe pressed the point a little further, just to be sure. "So, even if I have to promise the Arabs a state, I should—"

"Promise them whatever you must!" Eden snapped. "Just get their cooperation with us."

"The only way this will work is to promise them a state. Now. Immediately."

"Then promise it!" Eden shouted.

Newcombe was uncertain Eden, or anyone else in the British government, ever meant for the Arabs to have an independent state, much less to have it immediately, but he was an officer and he'd been assigned a task. He departed London immediately and traveled to Jerusalem. Two days after arriving, he met with Nuri al-Said, prime minister of Iraq, and representatives from various Arab factions including Jamal al-Husseini, Amin's cousin, who attended as Amin's representative. Members of the Nashashibi family were present as well. As Newcombe expected, the Arabs were suspicious of his motives and leery of dealing again with the British, but he kept them talking, though the desired agreement seemed like a long shot.

By July 1940, having persisted against all odds, Newcombe had pieced together an agreement with Said, on behalf of the Iraqi government, and with Jamal al-Husseini on behalf of the major Arab factions from Palestine. Pursuant to that agreement, the Arab parties formally accepted the terms of the White Paper and the principles outlined in the Balfour Declaration, including the creation of a Jewish state. Arabs were to immediately receive a Palestinian-Arab state that controlled all of Palestine. The Jews would have to wait for a state until later. In exchange, Iraqi and Arab representatives from Palestine agreed to side with the British against Germany.

Newcombe had obtained everything from the Arabs that Eden wanted. Still, he was suspicious that London would follow through. *I fear this is going to make things worse than ever,* Newcombe thought to himself as he boarded a ship for the return trip to England.

As Newcombe sailed for home, news of the final arrangement reached Amin in Baghdad. To the surprise of many, he was hopeful. Although the agreement did not name him as head of the proposed Arab state—a condition that had torpedoed the

Peel Commission's plan—he was certain he could work that out in the details. He was also confident the question of a Jewish state would be a non-issue by the end of the European war. "If there are no Jews remaining in Palestine, there will be no need for a Jewish state."

With success in hand, Newcombe presented the agreement to the prime minister's cabinet. Almost immediately, terms of the agreement were leaked to Chaim Weizmann, David Ben-Gurion, and other Jewish leaders. Predictably, all were outraged, not only at the conditions being imposed upon them but also at having been excluded entirely from the negotiations.

"This was a secret agreement," they protested. "Reached through secret negotiations to which we were not a party. British and Arab representatives colluded to determine the political fate of hundreds of thousands of Jews. It is precisely the kind of anti-Semitic persecution Jews have endured at the hands of Europeans for hundreds of years. Now we are being treated this way by the British Crown. There can be no Arab state without a corresponding Jewish state. And no agreement on anything that affects us without our participation!"

The World Zionist Congress organized lobbying efforts to bring political pressure against key British ministers. Press releases and position papers made their point clear: "The government of the United Kingdom now favors Arabs over Jews. This reveals the vile underbelly of British prejudice and the underlying nature of aristocratic anti-Semitism."

Bowing to pressure, British officials refused to support the agreement they had sent Newcombe to negotiate, even though they had told him to obtain an agreement at all costs. On August 29, 1940, the British government officially rescinded its agreement with Iraq and the Arabs of Palestine. No one bothered to officially inform Newcombe of the decision.

Anticipating a negative reaction from Amin, and even an overt turn by him toward an alliance with Nazi Germany, the British War Office developed a plan to assassinate Amin. The plan, in the form of a proposal, was forwarded to the prime minister's office for approval. Churchill gave his assent, and the plan was set for implementation when news of it reached the Foreign Ministry. Eden demanded a meeting with Churchill.

"Killing Amin al-Husseini is the wrong move," Eden argued. "At the wrong time. In the wrong place."

Churchill appeared unmoved. "Why not? It seemed like a good idea to me. Eliminates the source of most of the resistance we have to our Middle East policy."

"Assassinating parliament would do that, too," Eden retorted. "Shall we execute members of the opposition?"

"Don't be ridiculous," Churchill growled.

"And that is precisely what this plan is," Eden retorted. "Ridiculous."

Churchill frowned. "Why do you say that?"

"In the first place, if we killed Amin al-Husseini, it would be obvious to everyone that *we* were the ones who did it."

"I doubt they would ever know," Churchill scoffed.

"Anyone who tells you they can kill him without the blame falling on us simply doesn't understand the Middle East."

"Our people are good at this sort of thing," Churchill assured.

"They aren't *that* good," Eden argued. "And even if they were, Husseini would be dead and every person in Iraq still would blame us."

"Then, what difference does that make?"

"It would be terribly disruptive. And tougher with the agreement we just strong-armed them into accepting and immediately rescinded, it would be the end of any Arab cooperation in the Middle East. Even an *attempt* on Husseini's life would have a severe impact on the situation in the Middle East. We have the support of Faisal and his government, but Amin al-Husseini's resistance to us is widely admired by the people on the street. Support for us is tenuous, and Said's hold on his office is in doubt. If Husseini were executed, or even if there is an *attempt* to execute him, the blame would fall on us and it would push things over the edge. Said would be out. People would take to the streets in protest. Faisal himself might become the object of a coup."

"And Iraq would be lost. . .." Churchill finished Eden's argument for him but the tone of his voice indicated he understood the seriousness of the situation.

"Iraq and the support of all of the Arab people throughout the Middle East would be irrevocably lost." Eden leaned over the desk and looked Churchill in the eye. "Don't do it, Winston. Don't even try."

Churchill put the plan on hold and a week or two later shelved the idea, but the damage already had been done. Offering the Arabs yet one more promise, then rescinding it when they agreed robbed England of influence in the Middle East from that point on. Politicians from Arab nations and leaders of Muslim organizations still sought British financial support and accepted British arms and other assistance, but Arabs on the street no longer believed a word the British said and certainly nothing they put in writing. The British, they believed, were incapable of keeping their word.

The experience with Newcombe, followed by the response in London, ended any interest Amin might still have harbored in favor of working with the British. "I'll never trust them again. The only thing they know is force. That is the only thing they respect and the only thing to which they will respond. From now on, we must deal with them from a position of power, and for that, we must turn to violence. We have no other choice."

TWENTYONE

BY 1941, GERMANY under Hitler's command had met with success upon success. In light of that, Amin restructured his office as Grand Mufti, modeling it after Hitler's example. More than ever before, he surrounded himself with men whose loyalty to him was unquestioned. Safwat al-Husseini traveled to Baghdad and assumed the post of security advisor. Musa al-Husseini, also Amin's cousin and the former mayor of Jerusalem, came to Baghdad as well and was placed in charge of propaganda. Kemal Hadad, who had been with him as long as any non-family member, served as staff secretary. Together with Aref, Salama, Latif, and Qadir, they formed a tight circle of advisors and operatives that functioned as a Palestinian government in exile.

With Hadad's help, Amin drafted a letter to Hitler. Positioning himself as the leader of Palestine, he asked for help in solving the Jewish problem in Palestine. He hoped to obtain access to Nazi technology and expanded training for himself and his people in Nazi techniques.

Before the letter was sent, Musa al-Husseini read it. "Heads of state issue declarations and deal in formal documents," he noted.

"I think you should forgo this letter and reformulate it as a formal declaration. Propose it as a joint declaration between the Grand Mufti, Germany, and Italy regarding the future of Palestine."

Amin nodded approvingly. "That's a good idea, but we have no relationship with Germany except through local diplomats."

"The Italians have a fine relationship with Hitler and the German government," Musa replied. "Begin with the Italians. They were the first to support us and seemed eager to work with us. Get them to agree to the declaration and use their assent as a way to gain German approval."

Amin was hesitant. "But what if the Italians will not approve a declaration like this?"

"At least we'll be able to use the process as a means of meeting important people. Develop new contacts with the Italians. Perhaps gain access to German officials. Open a dialogue. Nudge them toward our view." He looked over at Amin. "These things require patience."

Amin's eyes opened wide. "So, if they agree, we win. And as long as we are able to talk to them, we win something, too."

Musa nodded. "We certainly won't lose."

Amin was energized by the idea and put Hadad to work rewriting key points from the letter, fashioning them into a formal declaration. Musa helped with the language and with placing the document in proper form.

In February, the declaration was completed. Amin formally issued it to the public and distributed it through Aref's many contacts with newspapers in the Middle East. The document stated, among other things, that, "Germany and Italy recognize the right of the Arab countries to solve the question of the Jewish elements, which exist in Palestine and in the other Arab countries, as required by the national and ethnic interests of the Arabs, and as the Jewish question is being solved in Germany and Italy." Amin then called on Germany and Italy to adopt the declaration as official policy.

As the declaration made its way through government channels, news reached Iraq that Rommel, having beaten back British advances in Libya, had launched an offensive against French positions in Tunisia. Reports indicated German tanks rolled across Tunisia with very little resistance. Amin was ecstatic. "Hitler is a genius! German victory seems inevitable. This is a perfect time to be aligning our interests with them." And indeed, it seemed he had chosen the right moment to step forward as an ally of Hitler's cause.

✦ ✦ ✦ ✦ ✦

By spring, Amin still had not received a response from Germany or Italy to his proposed declaration. Both governments, however, were reportedly considering the matter and giving the document a thorough review.

In the meantime, Amin had begun to rethink his earlier opposition to a coup in Iraq. Removing Said from office would give him an opportunity to shape a new government—he was certain he had enough sway with Faisal's uncle for that. And, if the conspirators went so far as to depose the young Faisal from the throne, Amin might even become king, a position from which he could easily align the country with Germany and Italy. That was more than he could expect but just as the time seemed right for him as Grand Mufti to align publicly with Germany, it also seemed a good time for the Golden Square to make its move. Amin convened a series of meetings to push them in that direction. It didn't take much to prod them along.

On April 1, the Golden Square and their supporters launched a takeover of the government. Qadir, using explosives training obtained in Germany, worked with Amin's blessing in support of the effort. After a brief but intense struggle, the Golden Square succeeded in unseating Nuri al-Said, who departed Baghdad and fled to Tehran. With Said gone, the Golden Square installed Rashid Ali al-Kaylani as prime minister.

Amin quickly positioned himself as a principle advisor to Kaylani and urged him to seek an alliance with Germany and Italy. Kaylani agreed, and as one of his first official acts sent an urgent appeal for help to officials of both governments.

✦ ✦ ✦ ✦ ✦

When the message from Kaylani reached Berlin, the message was vetted by Joachim von Ribbentrop's staff at the German Foreign Ministry, then delivered to Hitler. He had heard of Amin and was aware of his position as Grand Mufti of Jerusalem. He considered the matter, musing aloud that an intervention in the Middle East might prove helpful. "Perhaps we could divert attention there instead of here. Or force the British and French to syphon assets from elsewhere to address our threat there."

Hitler's advisors, however, were unimpressed and tried to turn his attention elsewhere. "The Saudis might be a more capable ally," one suggested. "They have proved their ability in the field," another said. "And," a third offered, "they have oil in their territory."

Hitler turned away with his hands folded behind his back and stared out the window as he spoke. "The Saudis have only localized influence. The Grand Mufti is a transnational figure. He has influence throughout the Arab world. And perhaps beyond."

Heinrich Himmler, head of the German SS—a paramilitary organization of the Nazi Party—agreed. "We are interested in recruiting Arab support for a push into the Balkans. Perhaps a push into the Middle East against the British could follow after that. The Grand Mufti would be very important to such an effort."

Hitler glanced at Himmler and smiled. "You always understand me best."

Himmler bowed ever so slightly. "Your thoughts are inspired, my Führer."

Without further discussion, Hitler instructed Himmler to work with the Foreign Ministry to facilitate a relationship with Amin. "See that we give the Grand Mufti and this new man in Iraq . . ."

"Kaylani," Himmler suggested.

"Yes." Hitler nodded. "See that we give them as much support as possible."

Hermann Göring was present at that meeting, also. He had listened without comment but not because he was disinterested. Quite to the contrary, the discussion sent his thoughts in a different direction.

An early member of the Nazi Party, Göring had been present for the infamous Beer Hall Putsch when the Nazis first broke into public view as a political force. After Hitler became chancellor, Göring was named minister without portfolio. One of his first tasks involved the creation of the Gestapo, which he handed off to Himmler. Later, he became commander in chief of the Luftwaffe, Germany's vaunted air force. Beyond that, he gathered power and influence seemingly without effort and, by the time of the gathering to discuss the Grand Mufti, was the second most powerful official in the Nazi German government.

Since the inception of the Reich, Göring had seen that the Jewish problem was the key obstacle to the Nazi Party's plans for establishing a Greater German Empire. He had given serious thought to its implications for the Reich's future. That problem, he quickly realized, would only get worse as Germany extended its reach over neighboring countries and into the Balkans. Already, surrounding nations not yet under the Reich's control were reluctant to accept additional Jewish refugees. Even the United States, for all its public expressions of righteous indignation, refused to increase its immigration limits to accommodate more Jews.

As the conversation with Hitler seemed to move toward a close, Göring finally spoke up. "If we align with Arabs in the Middle East, we will be forced to solve the Jewish problem in Europe for ourselves. Palestine as an option for them will no longer be possible. Arabs already oppose the presence of Jews in the region as it is. If we say the Arabs are our friends, sending Jews to Palestine will no longer be available to us as a solution."

"I understand that," Hitler replied. "But I want to stay focused on the war for now. We can solve the Jew problem later." He gave Göring a knowing look, as if the two of them had already discussed the matter at length, and he didn't want to disclose that conversation to others in the room. Göring acknowledged the unspoken point with a nod.

After the meeting, Göring called Reinhard Heydrich to his office. Reinhard grew up in a musical family and enjoyed a life of both social status and financial security. He enlisted in the German navy but was wooed to the nascent Nazi Party by a girl-friend who already was a member. Later, he joined the SS and rose steadily through the ranks to become chief of the Reich Main Security Office, a post he held the day he was called to meet with Göring.

When Heydrich entered Göring's office, Göring instructed him to close the door. Once they were alone, Göring looked at him with an emotionless glare. "What I am about to tell you must never be repeated. Do you understand?"

"Certainly," Heydrich replied.

"We are faced with a serious and growing Jewish problem. They are enemies of the state. We have been allowing them to leave as they are able, but now no other countries want them. This is a problem that will only grow worse as our area of influence in Europe expands."

Heydrich nodded, more as an acknowledgment than agreement.

"Someone must begin working on a plan to address that problem." Göring looked Heydrich in the eye. "That duty is now yours."

"Very well. I will attempt to find a solution."

"No," Göring snapped. "There must be no attempt. There is only one solution available for us." He paused and lowered his voice. "I want you to begin planning for the systematic extermination of the Jews."

Heydrich's eyes opened wide. "Extermination?"

Göring explained in a businesslike tone, "The time will come when we must turn our concentration camps into extermination factories. We must be ready when that day arrives. Making us ready for it is now to be your primary responsibility."

"We will have no other choice?"

"All options have been exhausted. We can't feed them forever."

Heydrich pressed the matter. "But kill them?"

"They are enemies of the state," Göring repeated. "You will do this for the Führer and for me?"

Heydrich seemed nervous but answered firmly, "Of course. Anything for the Führer."

✦ ✦ ✦ ✦ ✦

In May, barely one month into the new Iraqi government, British troops launched an operation to remove the rebellious Golden Square faction from power and return Nuri al-Said to office. The conflict became known as the Anglo-Iraqi War. As part of that engagement, the British army included units comprised of Jewish soldiers brought up from Palestine. The presence of Jewish military units in Islamic Iraq became immediately obvious to everyone. Amin saw it as confirmation of his previous charge that

Jews controlled the British government and were out to conquer Arabs everywhere.

One of the Jewish units was from Irgun, a Jewish paramilitary unit organized ostensibly to protect farming collectives in Palestine. In conjunction with Irgun involvement, General Percival Wavell, commander of the British operation, concocted yet another plan to kill Amin. David Raziel, an Irgun member being held in Acre Prison, was known to have training and ability in clandestine operations. Wavell approached him about conducting an operation to either kidnap or kill Amin. Raziel agreed to undertake the operation if he was allowed to capture Amin and bring him back to Palestine to stand trial. Wavell agreed, and a few days later Raziel was released from prison, then transported to Iraq with half a dozen men of his choosing to begin the hunt for Amin.

While Wavell and Raziel worked to implement their plot, German operatives in London learned of the plan through employees of the UK government. A message was transmitted to Berlin providing details. German diplomats in Jerusalem were notified and asked to determine whether the plot was real.

A few days later, German diplomats confirmed the plot was real and active and that Raziel already was in Baghdad, along with a group of men who were to assist him. One of whom was Ya'akov Meridor, a fellow Irgun member. "These men have worked together on similar projects many times," the embassy reported. "They are considered proficient and effective. Reports indicate they intend to kidnap Amin al-Husseini and kill members of the Golden Square." At Berlin's insistence, a messenger was dispatched from Jerusalem to warn Amin of the threat.

In Berlin, members of the Wehrmacht High Command—the group of officers who controlled the unified German military—met to discuss measures to be taken to support the rebellion in Iraq.

To the dismay of many, an argument ensued over whether it was an appropriate use of resources.

Hitler was the supreme commander of all Germany and head of the Wehrmacht. However, the day of the discussion about Iraq, Alfred Jodl, chief of the Wehrmacht operations staff, chaired the meeting. Jodl was incensed about what he viewed as a waste of time discussing whether they should offer the requested help.

"The Führer has ordered us to intervene," Jodl shouted. "That should settle the matter for you over whether it is *appropriate* for us to do so. But for those of you who insist on wanting more—the British have recruited Jewish operatives and Jewish defense organizations to conduct their operation against the Grand Mufti and the new government. These British Jews are intent upon exerting control over Iraq. Current Iraqi officials have asked for our help in resisting them. They have pledged their support to us, and we have accepted that pledge. If we do not act to help them, we will have a difficult time exerting any influence whatsoever in the region."

Having been upbraided by Jodl, the Wehrmacht reached a quick and unanimous decision to provide the Golden Square group, and the government of Iraq that it formed, all assistance possible and to intensify the war against Great Britain in the Middle East. Diplomatic relations between the Third Reich and Iraq resumed immediately.

Meanwhile, a contingent of the German Luftwaffe arrived in Baghdad and began patrolling the skies above the city. Not long after that, German operatives on the ground learned that David Raziel was on his way by automobile to Fallujah, a city located about seventy kilometers west of Baghdad, where Amin was thought to be staying. Raziel was thought to be accompanied by at least one British agent who was there to provide directions to Amin's supposed location.

Upon learning of Raziel's activity, German operatives contacted the Luftwaffe commander in Baghdad and requested assistance in locating the automobile. A German airplane was dispatched to conduct reconnaissance of the area. Twenty minutes later, the pilot located the car and strafed it with machine-gun fire. The car veered off the road, overturned, and exploded. All occupants inside were killed.

The following day, Amin was informed of the incident with Raziel. He was not surprised that Raziel and the British had plotted to kill him—he knew Raziel by reputation and knew that he took great delight in that sort of covert operation. However, he *was* surprised that the plot had gone so far toward completion. And above all, he was proud that his safety, and that of his family, had been won by members of the German army acting on orders from the German high command in Berlin.

✦ ✦ ✦ ✦ ✦

Although events were going well for Amin, the same could not be said for Rashid Ali al-Kaylani and his new government. British troops had overcome the Golden Square's strongest positions and had cordoned off a portion of the city, leaving Kaylani trapped but for one way out.

When Amin learned of situation, he went to find Aref. "Kaylani is in trouble. We must go to him at once and help him."

Aref was hurriedly stuffing his belongings into a travel bag and didn't bother to look up. "For what? Everyone is preparing to leave for Persia."

Amin was perplexed. "Everyone?"

"All of us." Aref paused to glance in Amin's direction. "Karimeh and the children. Salama and Hadad. Even Kaylani is going."

Amin felt confused. "When was this planned?"

"While you were busy with the Germans. The situation is lost. The British are too strong for us. We have no choice but to get out while we still can."

The muscles along Amin's jawline flexed and he banged his fist in anger against the tabletop. "How could he do this?" he demanded.

"How could who do what?"

"I have gone to great personal lengths to obtain the assistance of the German government." Amin seethed. "The Führer himself ordered the government to help us. Members of the Luftwaffe are here with planes and officers and important officials." Amin's voice rose as the anger inside boiled over. "The Abwehr has agents in the city trying to help. And now he wants to run and hide?!"

Aref stopped what he was doing and turned to face Amin. "Shall I take you to him?"

Amin ordered, "Take me there immediately."

With British troops holding key intersections, travel across Baghdad was almost impossible, requiring lengthy delays and circuitous routes to avoid patrols. The trip across town took almost two hours to complete. Amin and Aref arrived at Kaylani's residence to find dozens of men hastily loading cars and trucks with boxes and bags of belongings.

Amin came from the car and pushed his way inside the house, then hurried down the hall. He found Kaylani in the dining room and stormed toward him. "What are you doing?" he demanded.

"We are leaving for Tehran," Kaylani answered. "You must go, too." He looked scared and sounded nervous.

"You can't go yet. There is still more I can do here."

Kaylani shook his head. "I cannot stay."

"Why not?"

"The situation has become too dangerous. I must go." Just then, two small children entered the room, followed by a woman Amin assumed was Kaylani's wife. Suddenly he understood.

Kaylani was anxious for their safety. "Very well. Go in peace." Without saying more, Amin turned away and started toward the car.

On the way back across town toward his own residence, Amin thought of his wife and children and their safety. Kaylani was correct. The situation was much too dangerous for wives and children. As they neared the house, he looked over at Aref. "I want you to take Karimeh and the children to Tehran. Any of the others who want to go can go with you, too."

Aref pointed out the window. "I think they are ready now."

Amin looked past Aref and saw a row of cars parked near the house. Through the side windows he saw that all of them were packed and ready. "Good. You must leave at once."

✦ ✦ ✦ ✦ ✦

With Kaylani no longer in the country, morale among Iraqi forces collapsed and hostilities with the British quickly came to an end. By noon the next day, the British army occupied all of Iraq. Amin, acting under the colors of authority as the Grand Mufti, declared a Farhud—a violent pogrom—against Jews living in Baghdad. His declaration incited members of the Futuwwa, a Nazi-styled youth organization, along with Kaylani's staunchest supporters, to go on a bloody rampage.

Violence was particularly heavy in Baghdad. Amin coordinated the effort, hoping to not only destroy property but also to kill as many Jews as possible. By the time British troops restored order two days later, Amin's marauding gangs had killed more than 180 Jews, injured a thousand others, and inflicted heavy damage to Jewish-owned property.

Once the streets were cleared of insurgents, British military units began rounding up suspects. Amin, once again sensing the time had come to leave, fled to Tehran with the remaining members of his entourage. When they arrived, they were granted legation asylum by the Italian embassy. Amin's wife, Karimeh, and their children joined him.

Having endured a Nazi-inspired rebellion in Iraq, British officials were loath to permit it room to happen elsewhere. Once matters were put to rest in Iraq, they stepped up efforts to curtail German interests and activities in the Middle East, generally. As part of that effort, UK representatives pressured Iran to sever all ties with Germany. Iranian leadership resisted as long as possible, but by October 1941 they could do so no longer and aligned, however reluctantly, with the British.

With the Iranian government's decision to follow England's lead, Amin knew it was only a matter of time before British officials demanded his arrest. Rather than waiting for that day to arrive, he turned to the Italians for assistance in leaving the country. Italian officials, still enamored of gaining a foothold somewhere in the region, were all too happy to help. Traveling under Italian diplomatic protection, they conveyed Amin with his wife, family, and most of his entourage through Istanbul to Rome.

TWENTYTWO

AMIN, HIS WIFE, KARIMEH, and those traveling with them arrived safely in Rome on October 10, 1941. After a day to rest and collect themselves, Amin rode across town to the Ministry of Foreign Affairs where he met with Galeazzo Ciano, the foreign minister, and officials from his office. They were familiar with the declaration Amin issued earlier, but Amin outlined it for them in person anyway. "Our offer in the declaration is this—on the condition that the Axis powers recognize in principle the unity, independence, and sovereignty of an Arab state in the Middle East, including the areas currently known as Iraq, Syria, Palestine, and Transjordan—I, as Grand Mufti of Jerusalem and as head of that Arab state, will support the Axis in its war against England, France, and any others who may align with them."

"And what assistance might we expect from you?" Ciano asked.

"I have contacts and operatives who can assist in confronting the British at key locations," Amin replied. "Such as the Suez Canal and the port at Aqaba."

After reviewing Amin's offer and discussing it with him further, Ciano approved the proposal. In addition, he recommended that Amin receive an annual grant of one million lira to assist with his living expenses. However, final approval lay with Mussolini. "I will present the declaration to him on your behalf," Ciano informed. "And I will arrange a meeting for you with him at his earliest convenience."

When Amin returned to the residence where they were staying, he explained the meeting to Aref, Hadad, and Salama. He was excited by what he'd heard, and the expression on his face conveyed that mood. After he'd finished, Hadad added, "You realize, this doesn't mean you have been approved."

"The Foreign Ministry says I am," Amin replied.

"You have *their* approval," Hadad cautioned. "But it is not complete or final."

Aref, who was seated nearby, joined the conversation. "And, I might add, it is an approval that costs them nothing."

Amin frowned. "What does that mean?"

"It means," Aref explained, "Ciano can tell you anything he thinks will satisfy you because he knows Mussolini has the final say. So he can give you whatever you ask for, and you leave his office feeling happy, but the actual answer lies with someone else."

"The only approval that counts," Hadad continued, "is Mussolini's approval."

Amin felt deflated. "They are scheduling a meeting for me with him." He slumped into a chair near the window and stared at the world outside. "We shall see what happens then."

Two weeks later, Amin met with Mussolini. It was an amicable meeting in which Mussolini reaffirmed his hostility toward the Jews and Zionism. However, he did not give immediate approval to the proposed declaration or Ciano's stipend recommendation. Amin was encouraged, but he remembered the earlier discussion with Aref, Hadad, and Salama and was at a loss for what to do next.

A few days later, Ciano contacted Amin and suggested he make a few changes to the written declaration. "Il Duce gave me some notes to go over with you." Amin was all too happy to consider anything that would move the matter toward an amicable agreement and went to work immediately to make the suggested revisions.

After a day or two with Hadad, the final version read in part, "Germany and Italy recognize the right of Arab countries to solve the Jewish question, which exists in Palestine and in the other Arab countries, as required by the national and ethnic interests of the Arabs, and in accord with the manner in which the Jewish question is being solved in Germany and Italy."

When Amin and Hadad finished, Salama delivered the document to Ciano's office. The following week, the amended version of the declaration received formal approval from Mussolini and was forwarded to the German Embassy in Rome for a response.

✦ ✦ ✦ ✦ ✦

Upon receipt of the declaration from Italian officials, Ernst Bruns, the German ambassador in Rome, realized that Amin was not merely present in Rome but was there as a guest of the Italian government. "This is a dangerous situation," Bruns warned as he handed the document to an assistant. "See that our staff analyzes it thoroughly and have someone prepare a report detailing the Grand Mufti's activities since he arrived here."

"I'm not sure how much they know about that," the assistant replied.

"Then tell them to find out!" Bruns shouted.

Officials at the embassy reviewed the declaration and

dispatched agents to surreptitiously collect information about Amin's presence in the city. When the analysts finished examining the document, they drafted a memo with their conclusions. A report was prepared to go with it that contained details regarding Amin's activities in Rome and his budding relationship with Mussolini. Bruns forward the declaration and both reports to the Foreign Ministry in Berlin by special courier.

When officials at the German Foreign Ministry in Berlin received a copy of the Grand Mufti's declaration and learned from Bruns's report of Amin's presence in Rome, they were concerned. Not so much about the written declaration—though it was troubling—but about the developing relationship between the Grand Mufti and Mussolini.

Through careful diplomacy and staged interaction, Hitler had established a working relationship with Mussolini. Both men, however, had mercurial temperaments and were subject to bouts of seemingly uncontrollable rage. Keeping Hitler's relationship with Mussolini functional required a delicate arrangement. Any change in Mussolini's perception of his position might easily upset the balance between the two leaders.

After a thorough review by staff, Joachim von Ribbentrop, the foreign minister, was briefed on the document and the mufti's interaction with Mussolini. While that briefing was taking place, Hermann Göring burst into the room. "I just now learned that the Grand Mufti is in Rome and he has been meeting with Mussolini. Are you aware of this?"

Ribbentrop took a copy of Amin's declaration from the corner of his desk and handed it to Göring. "Mussolini signed off on this joint communique with the mufti."

"This is not good," Göring growled. "The Führer had his own plans for the Grand Mufti."

Ribbentrop nodded. "I am fully aware of the Führer's opinions concerning Amin al-Husseini."

Göring gestured with the document. "When did this happen?"

"A few days ago."

"A few days ago?" Göring frowned. "And you have done nothing about it?"

"We were just discussing the matter when you arrived," Ribbentrop answered.

Göring glared at him. "And what do you propose we do?"

"The Führer has expressed an interest in building a Muslim corps for use in the East," Ribbentrop said. "We are thinking the Grand Mufti might be of great assistance in recruiting Muslims for that effort."

"Indeed." Göring smiled. "He could be essential to its success."

Ribbentrop grinned. "I was thinking we should invite him here to discuss the matter."

"Excellent," Göring said. "See that it happens." Then he turned away and left the room as abruptly as he'd entered it.

When Göring was gone, Ribbentrop called an assistant to his office. "Instruct the ambassador in Rome to invite the Grand Mufti to Berlin, and see that he arrives here safely."

"Certainly," the assistant replied. "I will do this right now."

"See that you do," Ribbentrop commanded in a snide tone.

Late that afternoon, Bruns received Ribbentrop's instructions by way of an encoded transmission received in the radio room in the basement of the embassy in Rome. The message, though couched in diplomatic language, was nothing less than an order. "Take charge of the mufti. See that he arrives in Berlin safely." Bruns understood completely. He was to offer Amin a cordial invitation, as if to a social gathering, then whisk him away from the Italians and convey him to Berlin without delay. Bruns sent a car at once to collect the mufti.

✦ ✦ ✦ ✦ ✦

Before the week ended, Amin and his entourage arrived in Berlin and were taken immediately to the Foreign Office. There he had a brief meeting with Volker Rüling, an assistant from the policy department. After coffee and pastries, Rüling accompanied Amin and the others to a suite at the Hotel Adlon. He also arranged for a car, driver, and a German assistant to help with logistics. Amin's wife was especially glad for the help.

The following day, Rüling brought Amin back to the Foreign Ministry, where they were joined by Ernst von Weizsäcker and other mid-level diplomatic officials. They discussed the text of his declaration and proposed their own adjustments to the language. In their final draft, which differed only marginally from Amin's original proposal, the Axis powers declared their readiness to approve the elimination of the *Jewish national home* in Palestine, rather than the *Jewish question*. Amin did not care for the softened language—he wanted to eliminate the Jews entirely—but he was more interested in obtaining German consent to the declaration than quibbling over words. Besides, once he was in control of Palestine, he could resolve the Jewish situation in any manner he chose.

Later that day, Amin met with Ribbentrop to discuss the declaration. They began their conversation as an analysis of the declaration but as they continued to talk, they moved on to a wider range of topics. Finally, Amin suggested they should work toward a more extensive German-Palestinian involvement. "I have many contacts and followers in the region. All of them are ready to rise up, on my word, and revolt against British control." Ribbentrop was intrigued and agreed to arrange a meeting with Hitler later that week.

Six days later, Amin was received by Hitler in his formal office, treating him with the pomp and dignity of a visiting head of state. Amin dutifully shook hands with the Führer, but he could hardly contain himself. Even as they were taking a seat opposite each other, Amin launched into a soliloquy, doing his best to impress Hitler with assurances of his devotion to the Nazi cause. Hitler seemed to take it in stride but looked relieved when Amin finally reached an end. "The Arabs are Germany's natural friends," Amin added by way of summary. "And that is because we share the same enemies—the English, the Jews, and the Communists."

"Yes," Hitler agreed, glad, it seemed, for an opportunity at last to speak. "They are the enemies of all people everywhere."

"That is why we need your help," Amin continued. "You understand the situation we face. I have proposed a joint declaration from Palestinian Arabs and Axis powers that conveys that understanding to the world and presents the three of us as a united opposition against the Jews, including opposition to a Jewish homeland in Palestine. Mussolini has signed the document. We need your signature, too."

"They have shown me this document," Hitler replied. His voice had a caustic edge—his patience apparently strained—but he quickly repressed it. "And while I agree with you in principle, this is not the time for Germany to issue such a declaration."

Amin was puzzled. "And why is that?"

"We are fighting the Russians on one front and the British on another," Hitler explained. "We cannot undertake war on a third front just now." Amin started to speak but Hitler cut him off. "You should always remember that Germany has resolved, at every step along the way, to ask every European nation to solve its Jewish problem, and at the proper time we shall direct a similar appeal to non-European nations as well."

Amin understood Hitler's use of the word *appeal* did not really mean he was making a suggestion. Rather, he was ordering governments under Nazi control to hand over the Jews in their territories. That policy was helpful, but Amin wanted more than goodwill from Hitler. He wanted something specific. Something tangible. Something he could use to show that he had gained the favor of the German leader. And so he pressed on. "Ribbentrop and I discussed the possibility of Palestinian Arabs rising up in revolt against the British. They would do that if I gave the word. Their actions against the British in the Middle East would disrupt British plans to control the region. Will Germany join us in that effort by supplying the arms and military assistance necessary for such an action?"

"That is an interesting possibility and one we already have discussed at length among ourselves," Hitler replied.

"If Germany supplied the weapons, Palestinian Arabs would supply the men."

"That is tempting. However, as I have said, at the moment we are fully engaged against the Soviets. Once Germany has defeated the Russians and broken through the Caucasus into the Middle East, we will have no further imperial goals of our own and would support Arab liberation with all our might."

Hitler had indicated his lack of immediate interest in several ways, but still Amin could not let go. "If a full engagement against the British presence in the Middle East is too much," he countered, "we would be glad to coordinate a series of covert operations against them. Or perhaps establish a spy network, at least in Palestine. As I have said, I have great influence there and many operatives placed throughout the region. I would put them all at your disposal."

This time Hitler seemed genuinely interested. "That might be something we could actually do. But we will consider it only within the context of our overall strategy." He leaned closer and softened his tone. "Listen, I know you are having a problem with the Jews. And I know you hate them at least as much as I do. And I assure you, after we have settled our business in Europe, Germany's sole objective will be the destruction of the Jewish element now residing within the Arab sphere of influence. Jews are not simply to be driven out of Europe." Hitler's expression hardened. "They are to be hunted down and destroyed wherever they are found. They are a blight on society. Because of the Jews, we were forced to suffer the Great War." His voice grew louder. "Because of the Jews, we faced humiliation at the hands of the British and the French and the Americans. Jews created the Marxists and funded their revolution and they are undermining descent societies around the world." Hitler leaned away, took a breath, and forced himself to relax. "But first," he inserted calmly, "we must stop the Russians."

"I think I might be able to help with that effort," Amin offered.

"Oh?" Hitler raised an eyebrow. "And how is that?"

"I could help you form an Arab league as a special unit of the German army," Amin suggested. "Right now, thousands of Arabs are being held in prison in France. They were arrested by French police before Germany liberated the country." Hitler smiled at that remark. Amin kept going. "Now, those imprisoned Arabs are under German control. If you release them, I am certain I could convince them to join the German army."

"We have thought of that, too," Hitler replied. "But, again, this is something that is not possible right now. Releasing those men from prison would only strengthen the *De Gaulle-ists* and create internal resistance to our government in France. We are trying to avoid further domestic disturbances just now in order to allow officials there to gain control of the people." He seemed to note the look of frustration on Amin's face and smiled. "There is something you can help with, though."

Amin sat up straight, his back stiff as if at attention. "What is it, my Führer? Only say the word."

"We are attempting to recruit Muslims from the Caucasus region for use against elements in the East. Your assistance in that regard would go a long way toward convincing them to join us willingly."

"I would be glad to do it," Amin beamed. "And to help with training, too."

"Good." Hitler stood. "Heinrich Himmler, head of the SS, will meet with you and explain what we have in mind." He stood, signaling the meeting had come to an end, then shook hands with Amin. They posed for a few pictures together, then Hitler said good-bye and left the room.

TWENTYTHREE

THE DAY AFTER AMIN'S meeting with Hitler, Himmler summoned him to the Foreign Ministry. They met in Himmler's office and sat across from each other at the desk. "We have decided to grant you the sum of fifty thousand marks per month as remuneration for your assistance with the war effort," Himmler began. "You may keep the suite at the hotel, but the Führer thought you also should have a permanent residence. He has assigned you to Castle Bellevue. It is large enough to accommodate you and your assistants and it comes with a staff."

Amin was elated. "That is most generous of you."

"I am sure you will more than earn your keep."

"What will I be doing?"

"We are experiencing lower than expected enlistment rates among ethnic groups. Particularly among Arabs . . . and Muslims," Himmler explained. "We want your help in creating radio and print pieces that might appeal to them."

Amin nodded. "When do I get started?"

"One of our staff members, Fritz Grobba, will act as liaison with you. He will arrange the details of your daily schedule."

"Good. When can I meet him?"

"He will come to your hotel room this afternoon to go over everything. He can assist you with the move to Castle Bellevue, also."

Fritz Grobba was born in Brandenburg, Germany, where his father worked as a nurseryman. After completing his secondary education, Grobba studied at the University of Berlin and in 1913, received a Doctor of Law degree. During the Great War, Grobba served as an officer in the Prussian army. Afterward, he joined the legal department with the German Foreign Ministry and was assigned to the Middle East section. He was appointed German consul to Kabul and later ambassador to Iraq and Saudi Arabia. When the government in Iraq collapsed, Grobba was recalled to Berlin where he served as Germany's leading expert on Arab affairs and, until Amin's arrival, as Hitler's sole liaison with the Arab world.

After meeting with Himmler, Amin returned to the hotel to await Grobba's arrival. Shortly after lunch, Grobba arrived at the hotel suite. Salama greeted him at the door and then sat with Amin as he and Grobba became acquainted. Aref, Hadad, and Latif joined them when the conversation turned to details regarding the things Amin was expected to do for the Reich.

The following day, Amin went to work recruiting Muslims. He began with those who lived in Berlin. The effort went slowly at first, almost a door-to-door, house-to-house effort, with very little to show from it. Many Muslims, having seen how the Nazis treated the Jews, were reluctant to believe anyone who spoke for the government, including Amin, and avoided even meeting with him, much less listening to what he had to say. Undeterred, Amin frequented coffee shops and bookstores that were popular among residents of Middle Eastern descent, talking, visiting, and engaging anyone who would sit and talk. Gradually, German Muslims became acquainted with him and slowly warmed to his proposal that they join a special unit of the German army designed just for them.

As the Muslim response grew, Amin did not merely hand them over to Himmler and the military apparatus. Instead, he did as he had in Jerusalem when recruiting for Faisal I's army—he organized those who responded into a group accountable only to himself. He labeled the group the Muslim Brotherhood of Berlin. In order to maintain his role with the German government, Amin placed Qadir in charge, then began searching for a purpose to keep them involved. "They aren't ready to enlist in the army just yet," he noted. "What can they do in the meantime?"

Qadir shrugged. "What if they established a mosque?"

"That is an excellent idea."

"But will the government let us do that?"

"I think so. But maybe we should call it something else, just to be safe."

"Like what?"

"It will come to us," Amin answered. "Ask the men for their ideas about a name."

When Qadir presented the idea of forming a mosque to the group, they responded enthusiastically and began work planning the project almost immediately. As plans proceeded, one of the first questions raised was that of a name for the building. Qadir invited suggestions and many names were proposed, most of them typical. Then someone suggested they call it the Islamic Institute. Another changed it slightly to Islamic Central Institute, and a cheer went up from everyone in the room.

Qadir presented the name to Amin for final approval. "Excellent choice," Amin concurred. When his approval was conveyed to the group, they responded by naming Amin honorary chairman.

Amin reveled in his leadership role, even if honorary, and regularly met with the men at the Institute, teaching a class on Islam and contemporary thought. As he had in Jerusalem, he used *Mein Kampf* and the Quran together, showing his students how the ideas contained in one were reflected in the other. "In fact, the Nazi hatred of Jews is reflected in many Islamic texts and traditions, not just the Quran," he explained. "The prophet Muhammad knew the Jews are the enemy and that true believers who followed him were the righteous. Today, Jews are little more than infidels. Worse even than that, for they have corrupted what Allah gave them. All over the world, Jews are the instigators of trouble and misery. In every nation where they are allowed to prosper and multiply, they feed on the population like rats. Like swine at the trough. Here in Germany, Hitler and the Nazis have stepped up to deal with the European Jews because the rest of us have not. We Muslims, we Arabs, we true believers in Allah have the truth. Allah is with us. We can wipe them out if we approach the problem with a view to the patient implementation of the plan that the Nazis are showing us."

✦ ✦ ✦ ✦ ✦

As Amin's recruitment effort gained interest among Muslims in Berlin, they began enlisting in growing numbers. However, Hitler did not merely want bodies to fill the ranks of his many divisions. He wanted to use Muslims—and particularly Arabs—for the specific purpose of winning the war in the East. Himmler knew this and realized that in order to achieve Hitler's goal, they would need a way to train and deploy Muslim recruits while maintaining their ethnic and religious identity. He brought up the idea with Hitler during a meeting in Hitler's office.

"Regarding the Muslims," he began tentatively. "We are recruiting them in larger numbers, but we are in danger of losing them to the ranks of the regular army. If we are going to use them specifically in the East, as we discussed, we need to create a special unit to coordinate their training and deployment."

"That is an excellent idea," Hitler replied. "A Muslim legion."

Himmler nodded in agreement. "I'm not sure whom to contact to make that happen, but shall I tell them it has your approval?"

"I will contact the Wehrmacht myself," Hitler responded.

At Hitler's insistence, Alfred Jodl, chief of operations staff for the Wehrmacht, established a special unit known as the 13th Waffen Mountain Division of the SS, comprised of Muslims from Croatia. Initially little more than an administrative designation, with Amin's help the unit soon became widely known and attracted large numbers of men who were eager to join.

Although Amin and Himmler made progress attracting Muslims to the army, the effort was not without its share of troubles. Much of the difficulty lay in the interethnic conflict that riddled the region. Prior to the war, Soviet influence over the Balkan and Caucasus regions had kept that violence to a minimum. With the war and subsequent German expansion, Russian influence had been diminished. Erased in some areas. In the confusion that followed, old ethnic prejudices, always simmering just beneath the surface, were let loose. The ensuing violence against Muslim communities had produced huge losses of life. Bosnian Muslims alone lost more than 85,000 from ethnic cleansing.

Desperate for help, and aware that Amin was working with Germany, Hasan Jerković, a leader of the Bosnian Muslims, came with a delegation to meet Amin and petition him for assistance. After hearing their pleas, Amin enlisted Grobba's help. A few days later, a meeting was arranged between Amin, members of the Foreign Ministry, and Himmler's staff.

After hearing a report from Amin regarding the trouble with Bosnian Muslims, German officials were eager to get involved. "Perhaps this situation gives us even greater access to recruit larger numbers for the army," one officer spoke up.

"But how?" someone else asked.

"We could propose an alliance between this Muslim faction

and suggest it is a way for Bosnia to obtain autonomy. A chance to break free of domination by Russia, once and for all. If they fight for us, after war they get their country back."

"And they would naturally be the ones to run it."

Something inside Amin cringed at the suggestion. He had heard that pitch before from the British. It sounded good, but the payoff never came. "If we make that offer," he cautioned, "we must be willing to follow through on it."

"You mean keep our end of the bargain?"

"Yes. Otherwise, you will only create more trouble for yourself."

A senior official gestured in Amin's direction. "Make the pitch. An alliance between Bosnian Muslims and Germany. When we are successful in the East, we will keep our bargain."

✦ ✦ ✦ ✦ ✦

The following week, Amin traveled to Bosnia and met with Hasan Jerković and a dozen other Muslim leaders from the area. He offered them the solution proposed at the meeting—an alliance with Germany to defeat the Soviets, and after the war, Bosnians would have a country free of foreign interference.

Jerković was interested but cautious. "They mean we will have our country subject to their overall authority."

Amin nodded. "That is probably correct."

"Probably?" Jerković sounded incredulous. "You were at the meeting. What did they say?"

Amin didn't care for the tone in his voice and gave a terse reply. "They said exactly what I told you."

"But you think they did not tell you everything." Jerković had a knowing look.

Amin hesitated at first but finally acknowledged, "They did not specify what they meant by the phrase *get their country back,* though I doubt they would merely hand it over, having fought hard and lost German lives to wrest it from the Soviets."

Jerković gave a nod. "Exactly. That's what I mean. They want us to fight and trust them to treat us right."

Someone else spoke up. "We could argue about language and terms all day. But we are in a difficult position. Gangs from neighboring countries are killing our people every night. We should take the German offer and deal with the consequences later."

"Yes," Jerković agreed. "I think we should, too, but I'm just making the point. This isn't a perfect solution. So we would like assurances from the officials in Berlin regarding several issues."

For the next thirty minutes, Amin listened while everyone gave him a list of their concerns. Hadad, who was with him, wrote them all down.

When Amin returned to Berlin, he met with Himmler to discuss the list. They sat, as usual, at the desk in Himmler's office. "There are a few issues regarding the Bosnian Muslims that we need to address," Amin began.

"And what is that?" Himmler asked with a hint of impatience in his voice.

"They want to make certain that the Muslim military operations for which they volunteer are operations restricted to the defense of the Muslim countries. Bosnia in particular."

"They will be enlisted in the German army," Himmler replied curtly. "As soldiers, they will be subject to the needs of Germany and the German army, as specified by our military commanders, same as everyone else. No more, no less."

"They have heard of others who were recruited into the Soviet army, only to be sent to the harshest fighting in defense of the western end of the country, far from where they lived. They do not want to have that experience."

"We will make every effort to accommodate them." Himmler sighed. "Anything else?"

"They want the partisans who previously were fighting against Germany under pressure from the Soviets to be granted amnesty if they lay down their arms and volunteer for service in the German army."

"Very well." Himmler nodded. "That will not be a problem."

"They want the civilian population not to be subject to vexatious harassment by German troops."

"We already have issued the strictest orders to our troops on these matters. We should now—"

Amin cut him off. "Apparently that *has* been a problem."

Himmler looked angry. "From German troops?"

"Yes."

"I'll look into it." Himmler stood.

Amin remained seated. "They also want assurances that harsh measures imposed in the East—like deportation, confiscation of goods, and executions—will be governed in accordance with the rule of law, same as with all other German civilians, and not by military officials making summary decisions in the field."

Himmler moved as far as the end of the desk. "They are asking too much. Do they—"

Again Amin interrupted. "I can get you the recruits you want, but to get them from Bosnian Muslims, they need assurance on these points."

Frustrated at the delay, Himmler returned to his place behind the desk and plopped into his chair. After a lengthy discussion, he agreed to the points Amin raised. But as he rode away from Himmler's office, he wondered, as he had at other times, if Himmler had not appeared to agree merely as a convenient way to conclude the meeting. Nothing would prevent him, or anyone else in the German army, from doing as they pleased once operations began, but he had pressed the matter as far as could. Further even than most would have dared go. He would have to trust the Bosnians to the future and see what happened.

✦ ✦ ✦ ✦ ✦

In the weeks that followed, Amin conducted numerous visits to the Caucasus and Balkan areas. He met with Jerković and leaders from all the Muslim groups in the region, conveying Himmler's response to their list of concerns. "I still think an alliance with Germany is in your best interests," Amin remarked when he'd finished. They were eager to commit and asked Amin to help them spread the word.

In speech after speech throughout the region, Amin declared, "Those lands suffering under the Bolshevist yoke and threatened by the British impatiently await the moment when the Axis will emerge victorious. We must dedicate ourselves to unceasing struggle against the Soviet Union and against the British Empire—that dungeon that oppresses all peoples with the yoke of colonialism—and complete their destruction. We must dedicate ourselves to an unceasing struggle against the infidels and their empires. Colonialism is incompatible with the teachings of the prophet Muhammad. Communism is incompatible with Islam. Capitalism is incompatible with the pursuit of Allah."

In conjunction with the effort to enlist help from Muslims and Arabs, Amin also began regular presentations on Radio Berlin. At first his remarks were impromptu, and he sounded unsure of himself. Latif suggested he plan each presentation before going on the air and make his remarks from a written text. "Write it down first," he suggested. "And say only what you've written." Amin decided to give it a try. Latif helped draft and edit his remarks. After the show, Nazi officials complimented him on the crispness of his presentation. Encouraged by their response, Amin continued to improve, as did the response.

A few months later, Amin used his radio time to call for an Arab uprising—the kind he had proposed to Hitler in their first meeting. "You Arabs of Palestine," he said. "Rise up against the British. Rise up against the Jews. Take back the land of our fathers. Germany is attacking the British Empire on every front and prevailing. We must do our part, too. The end is near for the Imperialist British. This is our opportunity. This is our sacred duty. Kill the Jews wherever you find them. Allah is with you."

In a follow-up broadcast, Amin announced, "It is the duty of Muslims in general and Arabs in particular to drive all Jews from Arab countries. Germany is also struggling against the Jews and has very clearly recognized them for what they are. They, under Nazi leadership, have resolved to find a definitive solution for the Jewish danger that will eliminate the scourge that Jews represent in the world."

Privately, Amin told Muslim leaders in the East and men at the Central Islamic Center to "learn all you can, train as well as you can, and be ready to join the fight to take back control of our lives from the Jews."

With Latif, Salama, Hadad, and Aref, he added, "We are taking back the land of Muhammad from the clutches of European powers. Reforming the greater Muslim Empire of old. But we must be diligent. This is a long-term project. Be patient. Use this opportunity with the Nazis to acquire all the strength and equipment you can."

Amin's speeches and charismatic personality proved instrumental in improving Arab and Muslim enlistment in the German army. The response was so strong, in fact, that Himmler was able to create three Muslim divisions—the 13th Handschar, the 21st Skanderbeg, and the 23rd Kama—mostly from Bosnian and Albanian Muslims.

✦ ✦ ✦ ✦ ✦

As Germany's work in recruiting Muslims continued to develop, Hitler authorized the creation of a Ministry for the

Occupied Eastern Territories to administer Poland and lands in the East taken from the Soviet Union. He intended for Germans to occupy the region as part of the Greater Germany he envisioned. One comprised of people of pure Aryan descent who would return to the Motherland in droves once the war was won. Alfred Rosenberg was placed in charge of the ministry.

Rosenberg held a PhD in architecture but thought of himself as an intellectual with a wide range of abilities. As a member of the Nazi Party, he became the chief racial theorist. He wrote extensively on race and religion, providing the racial hierarchy that justified Hitler's atrocities toward ethnic groups viewed as inferior and thus a threat. In addition, he reordered religion around his ideas of a *religion of the blood*—the supposed innate tendency of Nordics to assert their superiority.

Being theoretically oriented, Rosenberg had no intention of conducting or overseeing the ministry's day-to-day operations. Such menial tasks were left to administrators and others hired to attend to such mundane details. One of those was Gerhard von Mende, a Turkic scholar and professor at the University of Berlin.

Key to Mende's supposed usefulness was his friendship with a group of Turks who were part of a Turkic Muslim independence group. His relationship with them gave him access to Russian-born Muslims, which Himmler, Rosenberg, and others hoped to use against the Soviets in furtherance of Hitler's desire to employ some of the lesser-defective ethnic minorities in the war effort. Among the most capable of Mende's acquaintances was Veli Kayum Khan, a Muslim who had been captured from the Soviet army and turned to the Nazi cause.

Mende was already aware of Amin's presence in Germany and of his work with Muslims, particularly those in Bosnia. Not long after assuming his position at the new ministry, Mende contacted Grobba and asked to meet with the Grand Mufti. An appointment was arranged for the next afternoon at Castle Bellevue. Grobba attended the meeting.

After a few minutes to get acquainted, Mende turned the conversation to the reason for his visit. "I have been hired for the specific purpose of recruiting and working with dissident ethnic groups in the East who might support Germany and its cause. I have been following your work in recruiting Muslims from the same region. I like the idea of building a Muslim army to fight alongside our own and think the idea can be applied to many ethnic groups in other regions."

Amin sensed an opportunity. "Build on local dissent against our enemies?"

"Exactly. One obvious venture would be to build a Turkic-Muslim army to fight the Soviets."

"Or," Amin added, "Palestinian Arabs to fight the British in the Middle East."

Mende nodded approvingly. "An excellent choice."

"On the other hand," Amin continued, "a considerable number of Muslims already live here in Germany. In fact, right here in Berlin. We are working with them to establish a mosque as a place for them to worship."

"That is a good idea. I wonder if there might be a way the ministry could help?"

"Perhaps. What did you have in mind?"

"The Ministry for Occupied Eastern Territories is in charge of distributing property formerly owned by Jews, particularly those located in the East. The ministry has considerable resources at its disposal." Mende had a snide grin. "Those Jews are rich, you know."

"I like that idea," Amin replied. "Jewish money, stolen from Muslims, recovered and appropriated for the good of Muslims. How could we go about obtaining those resources for the mosque?"

Grobba spoke up. "We should discuss the matter with Rosenberg. He is the minister. We need to make certain he is amenable with the idea and include him in its development."

Mende looked over at Grobba. "You work for Himmler, right?"

"Yes."

"Do you think we should contact him, too?"

For a moment Grobba thought Mende was needling him—sending a message to point out that he, too, was under someone else's authority. Then he noticed the look in Mende's eyes and realized he was asking only because he was afraid of offending Himmler. "That will not be necessary. I think we should proceed with Rosenberg on our own. He is in charge of the ministry. He can decide these matters on his own."

"Very well," Mende nodded. "I will arrange the meeting."

✦ ✦ ✦ ✦ ✦

A few days later, Mende and Amin met with Rosenberg in Rosenberg's office. They sat in overstuffed leather chairs across from the desk and sipped coffee while they talked. Grobba attended as well, which put Rosenberg in a defensive mood. "I wasn't unaware Himmler had an interest in the work of our ministry."

Until that day, Grobba did not realize the fear that Himmler instilled so deeply in the government. He knew Himmler could be ruthless, but he never imagined that the awareness of it went so deep. "I am Himmler's liaison with the Grand Mufti," Grobba explained in a kind voice, hoping to ease Rosenberg's tension. "I am here because the mufti is here. Not because Himmler sent me."

That seemed to ease Rosenberg's mind enough for the moment and he turned to Amin. "I understand you have inquired about using some of the financial resources we have recovered."

"We are working to establish a mosque for the benefit of Berlin's Muslim community," Amin explained. "We hope to use it as a means of recruiting Muslims for the German army. Perhaps you have heard of our efforts to do that in the East."

Rosenberg nodded. "We are all aware of the tremendous success you've had in that regard."

Mende looked over at Rosenberg. "The mufti's work with Muslims here in Berlin and in the East fits perfectly with the work you and I have been coordinating toward Muslims as well." The comment seemed awkward, but no one pointed that out.

Rosenberg focused on Amin. "What specifically did you have in mind?"

"At the moment," Amin replied, "we are raising money for construction of a building to house the mosque. We were wondering if the ministry might help fund the construction project. This would not only help us attract and recruit Muslims who already live in Germany, but our closer involvement with them would provide the ministry a place from which to recruit operatives of a more particular kind. As well as a base of operations totally within our control and easily accessible."

The discussion continued, but Rosenberg was sold on the idea. He assigned the task of coordinating the effort to Mende. Amin was glad to have his help. He liked Mende and looked forward to working with him for years to come. "He is a good man," Amin commented as he and Grobba departed from the ministry. "I think he understands the Arab mind."

"Perhaps," Grobba said. "And in any event, I am sure you will have plenty of opportunity to get to know him well."

"Do you think the Führer will be pleased with our arrangement?"

Grobba patted Amin on the shoulder. "I think the Führer is delighted to have you here and delighted by the work you are doing."

TWENTYFOUR

AS HERMANN GÖRING suggested earlier, with Amin now firmly aligned with Nazi Germany and deeply involved in German affairs, emigration and expulsion of Jews to Palestine was no longer an option for the Reich. By the close of 1941, this fact became unavoidably obvious to everyone, including Hitler. Late in December of that year, Hitler and Göring met to once again discuss the matter and the possibility of an ultimate solution to the question of removing the Jews from Germany.

"As you are aware," Hitler began, "your earlier suggestion that Germany would be forced to solve the Jewish problem itself has now become a reality. Other countries have refused to accept even the paltry number of Jewish refugees that they were before."

"Yes, my Führer. I'm afraid we have reached that moment."

"Afraid?" Hitler chuckled. "I am not afraid. This is a wonderful opportunity for us. Now Germany can put the Jews behind it and move on to achieve true greatness!"

Göring smiled. "What would you have me do, my Führer?"

Hitler stood facing the window, as he always did when

discussing matters that took them beyond the pale of traditional policy. Hands folded behind his back. Eyes focused somewhere in the distance, beyond the panes of glass. "I want you to formulate a plan for the extermination of the Jews," he directed calmly.

"Yes, sir." Göring's voice had a hint of jubilance.

"The other countries of Europe," Hitler continued, "and the Americans with their pompous, self-righteous attitude have left us no alternative. The Jews must be dealt with, once and for all."

Göring stood quickly, snapped to attention, and saluted. "I will attend to it at once."

From his meeting with Hitler, Göring hurried to find Reinhard Heydrich, whom he had previously directed to begin work on just such a solution as the one Hitler now authorized. He found Heydrich seated at the desk in his office. Göring flung open the door and entered the room unannounced. "The time has come to deal with the Jews."

Heydrich jumped to his feet. "The Führer has ordered it?"

"I just now came from his office. Formalize your plans and organize a meeting to get everyone on board."

"Certainly," Heydrich replied, but almost before the words left his lips, Göring was at the door and gone.

✦ ✦ ✦ ✦ ✦

The meeting Göring requested was arranged by Heydrich for January 20, 1942, at Wannsee, a site on the outskirts of Berlin. Göring presided.

"This meeting," Göring began, "has been convened for one purpose and one purpose only: to announce our new policy toward the Jews and to devise among ourselves a plan for its execution. We are not here to debate the substantive policy. That already has been decided by the Führer. We are here solely and only to decide how that policy should be implemented. Does everyone understand?" Göring waited, his eyes moving slowly around the room, while everyone nodded in agreement.

For the remainder of the day, Heydrich presented the Reich's new policy—the extermination of all Jews living in Germany and the occupied lands—and his initial ideas about how to implement it. Those in attendance reviewed the proposed plan and, as expected, gave it unanimous approval. Adolf Eichmann, an assistant to Heydrich, was placed in charge of determining the precise details—camp locations, transportation processes, execution methods, disposal of the bodies.

After the conference ended, Heydrich took Eichmann aside. "I want you to brief Amin al-Husseini on what we have decided here today."

Eichmann had a troubled frown. "Are you certain of that?"

"Yes. Someone must tell him and that someone is you."

✦ ✦ ✦ ✦ ✦

Late that evening, Amin received Eichmann in the study at Castle Bellevue. When he heard the details of what the Germans planned to do, he was elated. "You have no idea how happy this makes me!" he exclaimed.

"This is a big plan," Eichmann noted. "We will not be able to put it all in place instantly."

"I understand. But you have started."

Eichmann nodded. "We have started."

After he finished with Eichmann, Amin met with Salama and reviewed the matter, providing as much detail as he had received. Salama seemed interested but not overjoyed. "Do you think they will actually do it?"

Amin was caught off guard by the remark. "What do you mean?"

"This is a very big plan. Millions of Jews still live in Europe.

Merely disposing of the dead bodies will be a problem."

"These are Germans." Amin gave a dismissive gesture. "They can handle the logistics without any problem. I wonder if they might develop a similar plan for Jews in Palestine."

Salama shook his head. "That would be more problematic, don't you think?"

"How so?"

"The Jews in Palestine have access to the media—newspapers, radio. If the Germans tried something like that, they would alert the world. And their friends in America," Salama added. "Germany would have to first control the region. Which means they would have to defeat the British."

Amin had a playful look. "Unless we did it for them."

"You mean kidnap Jews and kill them?"

"Something like that."

"We'd have the same problem. The Jews would find out about it and they would never stop talking about it. Shouting about it. Screaming about it." He laughed. "They would let the world know what we were doing."

"But the world hasn't had anything to say about what Hitler and the Germans are doing."

"The world doesn't know the full extent of what he's doing," Salama noted. "If they did, they would do more than just complain."

"Well . . ." Amin's voice trailed away as he thought. "See what you can learn about how they implement this plan. And find out how they do it without the world knowing the extent of what they're doing. We will need to know these things when we take control of Palestine."

"How would I go about doing that?" Salama asked. "Who should I talk to?"

"See if Grobba can put you in touch with someone who can answer your questions."

✦ ✦ ✦ ✦ ✦

A month after his meeting with Salama, Amin was contacted by Walter Rauff. A former naval officer, Rauff was a lifelong friend of Heydrich. As Heydrich rose to the top of the SS, he brought Rauff with him, first as an assistant at the Reich Security Main Office and then as lead officer in charge of implementing the Final Solution to the Jewish Question. Amin and Rauff arranged to meet at Castle Bellevue.

"As you are aware," Rauff began, "we have extended our reach into North Africa. Rommel is there with his tanks even as we speak."

Amin smiled. "I understand he is having a splendid time shredding the British army."

"Reports would indicate that is so," Rauff noted. "Which is why I wanted to see you. We are considering extending the Jewish solution to the Jews of Tunisia, just as we did here in Germany. I was wondering if you might have someone who is knowledgeable of the area, who speaks the language, and who would be willing to assist us."

"Certainly." Amin stood. "Just one moment and I will get him for you." He left the room and a few minutes later returned with Salama at his side. After introducing them to each other, Amin brought Salama into the discussion. "Salama has been working on a plan for extending the solution to the Jews of Palestine," he explained. "Perhaps his plan would work in Tunisia."

"Perhaps it would," Rauff said. He looked over at Salama. "Do you have anything specific worked out?"

Salama nodded in response. "I have plans." He crossed the room to a cabinet and took down a notebook. "The estimates are rough, and the maps might not be up-to-date, but the ideas appear to be solid."

Rauff was excited. "This could be of great help. Let's see what you have prepared so far."

Amin looked over at Salama and grinned. "Think of it as a test," he suggested. "To see if your plan will work."

"And the interesting thing about plans," Rauff added, "is that you can always change them."

Salama placed his notebook and maps on a table at the far side of the room and the three of them huddled around it. The plan he had put together included a network of collection points each within easy traveling distance of slave-labor camps. The camps were complete with barracks, gas chambers, and crematoria. Salama pointed out potential sites for each of them. "The camps would be nothing more than wasting facilities."

Rauff looked puzzled. "Wasting facilities?"

"Places for them to die," Salama explained. "We have very little in the way of work that could be accomplished in camps. These camps would be located in remote areas."

Rauff still had a questioning look. "And the wasting part?"

"More work, less food."

"Ah." Rauff nodded. "I see."

"Physical exertion is not difficult to concoct," Salama continued. "Dig a hole. Fill it up. Anything to make the prisoners exert energy. Then we would feed them less than they expend. You can imagine the result."

"Death camps," Rauff said by way of summation. He seemed to be thinking of more than he said, but no one pressed the point.

"Yes," Salama responded. "And if we could think of something useful or productive for them to do with their effort, then all the better for us."

Rauff pointed to a section of detailed drawings. "What are these?"

"Small sealed buildings with connections on each side." Salama pointed to a place on the page. "This is a pipe that extends from the building. We would connect it to the exhaust pipe from a truck. It would take a little time, but fumes from the engine are deadly and we would use that to exterminate the people inside the building."

"Exhaust *is* effective."

"Especially for the ones who are old or sick."

Rauff nodded thoughtfully. "I have been working on a design for a mobile gas chamber."

Salama was puzzled. "A mobile chamber?"

"A truck with a van body on back."

Amin was intrigued. "How does that work?"

"Run a tube from the exhaust into the truck. Fill the truck with Jews and close the doors tightly. Then drive around for an hour or two." Rauff laughed as he described how it worked. "They'll all be dead before you've gone ten kilometers. Then dump them out and get some more."

Salama laughed. "Have you tried it?"

"Yes," Rauff answered in a businesslike tone. "Killed them all in a very short time."

Rauff and Salama got along especially well and after a while Rauff suggested, "Why don't you come with me to Tunisia? We can learn something from each other, and you would be a great help in implementing the plan." Salama agreed on the spot to join him.

✦ ✦ ✦ ✦ ✦

With recruitment of Muslims in the East going well, establishment of the mosque in Berlin proceeding on pace, and Salama in Tunisia exporting the Final Solution to the Jews of North Africa, Amin decided the time had come again to broach the subject of an Arab uprising. This time he mentioned it to Grobba. "No one was interested in it before," he observed after suggesting the details. "But an uprising in Palestine might be beneficial to German interests."

Grobba was not encouraging. "Most of the focus still is on North Africa right now."

"We can enlist the aid of the Muslim Brotherhood." Amin offered it as an added enticement, thinking everyone was as familiar with the Brotherhood as he.

Grobba responded with a puzzled expression. "I am not familiar with that organization."

Amin found that hard to believe. "It's one of the largest Muslim groups in the world. It has hundreds of thousands of members, all of them devout Muslims. All of them committed to an Islamic perspective and to Arab independence. Surely you have heard of it."

Grobba's eyes opened wide at the mention of such a large number. "I have not heard of them. But with numbers like that, I will discuss it with my superiors. Perhaps they would be interested in hearing more."

✦ ✦ ✦ ✦ ✦

A few days later, Grobba arrived at Castle Bellevue with Karl Rahm from the Foreign Ministry and Hanns Bruckner from the Wehrmacht. "We understand from Grobba that you could help us with an uprising among the Arabs."

"Yes," Amin replied. "I would be happy to assist in that regard."

"We are not interested just yet in Palestine," Bruckner said. "But we are very interested in Egypt. You mentioned something called the Muslim Brotherhood."

"Yes."

"We investigated them, and you are right. They have many members. Do you know how to contact the leadership?"

Amin smiled. "I am the guide of the Brotherhood in Palestine."

"The guide?"

"Like the director or president."

"Oh." Rahm had a look of sudden realization. "Then I am certain you would know how to reach whomever we wanted to contact."

They spent the remainder of the day discussing the proposed plan for a German operation in Egypt. Bruckner and Rahm seemed to think Rommel would have little difficulty mopping up the other major North African states that lay along the Mediterranean. They were certain he would soon turn his full attention on Egypt. Perhaps before the year's end.

When their discussion concluded, Amin met with Latif and took him for a walk on the grounds of the estate. "I want you to go to Cairo."

"Very well," Latif replied. "What would be the purpose?"

"I want you to meet with the Brotherhood in Cairo and brief them fully on developments that are happening here. The Institute and the Brotherhood chapter we have formed in Berlin, recruitment of Muslims in the East to serve with the German army. Give them the details of that."

"That shouldn't be too difficult to explain. I suspect they would all be very supportive of those efforts. Should I tell them about Salama and his work in Tunisia?"

Amin thought for a moment, then shook his head. "Keep that to yourself for now."

"As you wish."

"But there is one other thing I want you to discuss with them."

"What is that?"

As they walked toward the far side of the grounds, Amin told Latif about German plans for a major operation in Egypt and the desire for an Arab uprising to bolster their operation.

"You want me to tell them about this?"

"Absolutely. Brief Hassan al-Banna and I think there is a new man involved. Anwar Sadat. Discuss the plan with them in private. Hint at a Jewish genocide once the Germans are in control of the country, but don't get into details."

Latif looked surprised. "Is there going to be a Jewish genocide?"

Amin smiled. "Once we are in control, anything is possible. But first we must obtain control, and for that, the Germans need the Brotherhood's help."

"I assume there will be some kind of support for this?"

"Yes, the Wehrmacht will supply weapons and ammunition. Perhaps additional training. I'm not certain what more they will do, but tell Banna and the others to be ready."

"Certainly. When should I leave for Cairo?"

"As soon as possible; tomorrow would not be too early."

By then they were at the wall at the edge of the property. They turned around to start back toward the residence when Amin leaned closer and lowered his voice. "Tell Banna that he should stockpile any weapons and ammunition he receives for this and wait until German forces break out against the Allies. If something happens and they fail to gain the advantage they think is in their grasp, we will use the weapons later for our own purposes."

Latif grinned. "I will certainly tell them that."

✦ ✦ ✦ ✦ ✦

With Salama in Tunisia and Latif in Egypt, Amin thought more and more about the Final Solution. Soon his thoughts went beyond North Africa and Palestine to the question of how he could apply the solution to Jews everywhere. One day, in the summer of 1942, as he and Grobba traveled across town to yet another Muslim recruitment meeting, he seized the opportunity to express an interest in learning for himself how the Germans handled their Jewish problem.

Grobba was not encouraging. "They don't really let people see what they're doing, other than fellow soldiers. And then only those who need to know."

"I think it would add detail to my ideas about applying the Final Solution to Jews in Palestine."

"Maybe so." Grobba shrugged. "I'll ask Himmler about it."

The following week, Grobba notified Amin that Himmler had directed him to give Amin a tour of a concentration camp. "We can go on Monday," Grobba suggested. "We've been authorized to visit Sachsenhausen-Oranienburg." Amin was delighted.

Sachsenhausen-Oranienburg was a German concentration camp originally constructed on the grounds of an abandoned brewery in Oranienburg, a town located forty kilometers north of Berlin. It was created to house political dissidents who opposed the Nazi Party. Later, the prison was moved from the center of town to a site five kilometers farther north where a newly constructed facility eventually housed not only political prisoners but also captured Russian soldiers.

Inmates at the prison were made to work for various industries, including aircraft manufacturers, brick factories, and in conjunction with an enormous counterfeiting operation designed to undermine Allied currency. Others were used to test military footwear by means of rigorous forced physical activity. Experimental drug trials were conducted there, too. Punishment, either for sport or for supposed infractions, was cruel and unusual and many prisoners were executed. By war's end, more than thirty thousand inmates died at the prison, their bodies reduced to ashes in the prison crematorium.

It was a horrible facility, exhibiting some of the worst Nazi cruelties. Directors of the prison and many of its guards would eventually stand trial as war criminals. However, it was not a Nazi death camp for Jews, and whatever Amin saw during his visit, he did not witness the atrocities visited upon Jews. Those were reserved for other prisons in other places, to which no outsiders were permitted. Not even the Grand Mufti.

On the way back to Berlin from Sachsenhausen, Amin asked Grobba about training his associates in the German methods of dealing with Jews. Grobba must have known there were no Jews at the prison, but he did not point that out to Amin. Instead, he said simply, "I will ask. I suspect Himmler would be willing to show them some of the operational details."

As with the earlier request, Himmler agreed to provide training for three men from Amin's entourage. He and Qadir selected them and three weeks later they were sent to Sachsenhausen, where they participated in a training course for guards and police.

Meanwhile, at Grobba's request, Amin prepared a pamphlet for use with the 13th SS Handschar division. The pamphlet detailed the historic clash between Islam and Judaism and extolled Islamic virtues, incorporating ideas gleaned from Nazi racial theory. It ended with a quote from the hadith of Sunni Islam. "The Day of Judgment will come, when the Muslims will crush the Jews completely. And when every tree behind which a Jew hides will say: 'There is a Jew behind me, kill him!'"

Whether by Amin's urging or by the opportunity to settle age-old grudges, Handschar units were responsible for killing some ninety percent of the Jews in Bosnia. Among the most ruthless units under German control, their reputation for brutality extended to other ethnic groups as well. They were particularly ruthless in ridding northeastern Bosnia of Serbs.

✦ ✦ ✦ ✦ ✦

The year 1942 was a golden year for Amin. He had obtained the support of Adolf Hitler and, although he had been unable to interest the Führer in a Palestinian campaign, he *had* captured Hitler's interest in working with Muslims as a key component of German war strategy. At the same time, he had gained the friendship and support of officials at the highest levels of the German government. Men like Göring, Himmler, Heydrich, and Eichmann who could make things happen for him, and did. But that was about to change. Not dramatically at first. Amin would ride the Nazi train until the bitter end. But later when he and others looked back, they saw that 1942 was their zenith in Nazi Germany. The height of the glory days.

The turn in Amin's life came in November. That month, Allied forces finally succeeded in defeating Rommel on the sandy hills of North Africa. His defeat, though by no means catastrophic for Germany's overall war effort, put an end to plans for widespread Jewish genocide in Tunisia. It also ended thoughts of an Arab uprising in Egypt.

As the German army in North Africa collapsed, Banna, Sadat, and the Muslim Brotherhood in Cairo did as Amin suggested. They held on to the several truckloads of arms and ammunition that they had received from German sources, caching them for use at a later date.

Latif, still in Egypt, melded into the population and slowly worked his way back through Palestine. At Haifa, he boarded a boat to Greece, then started toward Berlin. Salama and Rauff fled Tunisia by boat, escaping capture by the narrowest of margins, and sailed to Spain. From there the journey northward to Germany was event-free.

TWENTYFIVE

IN DECEMBER 1942, construction of a building to house the Islamic Central Institute was finally completed. A celebration was planned for the opening, and notices were sent to leading figures and publications throughout the Muslim world. International travel was restricted in many areas because of the war, but Amin wanted everyone to know about the mosque even if they could not attend.

On the day of the event, a large crowd gathered in the main hall of the building. Most were Muslims from Berlin and the surrounding area, but a number of government officials were there as well, among them Gerhard von Mende and three of his assistants. Rosenberg made an appearance, too, though he did not stay for the entire time.

Hasan al-Banna, founder of the Muslim Brotherhood, was present, having arrived from Egypt two days earlier. No one was certain how he was able to make the trip, but he was there and participated in the dedication ceremony. Amin gave the only speech of the day, an address that extolled the virtues of mosque members and Nazi officials, then finished with harshly critical remarks for those he considered aggressors against Muslims—Jews, Bolsheviks, and Anglo-Saxons. The event was highly publicized, well received, and captured the interest of a broad audience throughout Germany.

After the public ceremony concluded, a private time of worship and prayer was held in one of the rooms off the main hall. Open only to members of the Institute and Muslim clerics, it included an official rite of induction into the Brotherhood for those whom Amin and Qadir had been teaching.

Afterwards Amin and Banna returned to Castle Bellevue, where they relaxed in the solarium and sipped coffee. "You have done well here in Berlin," Banna noted.

"Allah has blessed us," Amin replied.

"This is the first Brotherhood chapter we have formed outside our traditional Arab domain," Banna noted.

"We should spread the Brotherhood throughout the world. And we will be in a much better position to do that after the Germans win the war."

Banna shook his head. "I am not convinced they will win, and even if they prevail in Europe, I'm not certain they will be able to accomplish the kind of world domination they desired at the beginning."

"The German people are far superior to any of the races represented by the Allies."

"Perhaps in intellect. But not in economic power. In any regard, they are only a means to an end for us."

"I agree." Amin nodded. "We are the true Reich. The Muslims. The Brotherhood. Islam. We are the true nation of Allah and the true race of his making. Now we must work to unite all of Islam and force the infidels either to convert or be killed."

"We are making good progress with the Brotherhood. But not everyone in Islam is attracted to our organization."

Amin shrugged. "Perhaps we do not want everyone. Under Sharia law, yes. But perhaps not in the Brotherhood."

"Good point. But we need broad acceptance and appreciation among our people even if they do not support our lifestyle enough to adopt it. Everyone working toward the singular aim of establishing Allah's rule over the world."

"Even though they might have a different view of what that might be?"

"There's room for a difference of opinion."

"But how do we do that?" Amin asked. "How do we bring everyone with us even though they have a different view of Islam?"

"I think our effort might benefit from yet another organization."

Amin frowned. "Another organization?"

"One that is broad enough to include all aspects of the Islamic world. Sunni. Shia. An organization with a broader range of perspectives than the Brotherhood offers. Sacred as well as secular. Religious as well as political."

Amin's eyes opened wide in a look of realization. "A league of Islamic peoples."

"A league of Arabs," Banna suggested. "We should leave off reference to Islam. And we want people, not nations."

"Then perhaps we should call it simply the Arab League."

Banna smiled. "I like that."

"Forming it would require another Arab Congress. We'll need representatives from all areas to approve the organization." He gestured to Banna. "You should issue the call for the meeting when you return to Cairo."

Banna shook his head. "You have the name and title. You should issue a notice for it in your capacity as Grand Mufti of Jerusalem. Announce it; don't ask. People know you everywhere now. They look to you for guidance. They're more apt to follow your lead. They don't know me."

Amin was flattered by the comment but did his best to hide it. "I can announce a meeting and urge people to send delegates. But I will need your help to arrange the actual event. Right now travel beyond Germany's border is difficult for me. Communicating beyond Europe is cumbersome, too."

"All right," Banna replied. "I will be glad to help."

In the months that followed, Amin worked on the details of calling a congress of Arab leaders to approve the formation of an Arab League. He contacted Mende and brought him into the planning effort, hoping his position with the Ministry for the Occupied Eastern Territories would give them access to more German resources. Mende was glad to help. "This is a good idea and a great way for the Reich to reach a wider Arab audience."

"Then, you will help?"

"Yes. Of course."

As Amin had hoped, through Mende he was able to use German consul officials stationed around the globe to assist in sending notices to leaders in Arab countries of the Middle East and North Africa. Amin's own family members living in Jerusalem helped spread the word, too.

✦ ✦ ✦ ✦ ✦

While Amin continued to work on convening an Arab Congress and forming the Arab League, Qadir continued to recruit members for the Berlin chapter of the Muslim Brotherhood, which now had solidified its control over the Islamic Central Institute. The ranks of the Brotherhood chapter grew stronger almost every day and soon the Institute operated at full capacity.

By then Qadir was thoroughly indoctrinated in the Nazi viewpoint regarding Jews and in the methods they used to impose their perspective on Jews and on German society. He had been instructed earlier by Amin, before they left Jerusalem, in the correlation between the Quran and *Mein Kampf*. Now, as head of the Institute, he blended that earlier training with the things he'd learned from direct engagement with the Nazis to create a version of Islam that went beyond mere anti-Semitism to include a virulent hatred for Jews and the desire to see them extinguished as a race. A particularly vile blend of ideas culled and assimilated from the worst of the various Nazi racial theories wrapped in passages from *Mein Kampf* and covered with quotes from the Quran that seemed to echo the same sentiment.

At Amin's insistence, Qadir began instructing men at the mosque in his views. Before long, two of his students—Imad Kazim and Khalil Tibi—distinguished themselves as serious-minded devotees to Qadir's views. He viewed them as potential leaders. Superior in intellect, determination, and discipline, they were obviously well ahead of the others. Qadir and Amin focused on developing them further in hopes that they might be able to assist in expanding the Institute's reach, or even assume responsibility for the Institute's daily functions.

✦ ✦ ✦ ✦ ✦

Later that year, Latif arrived in Berlin from his ordeal in Egypt and the trek through Palestine to Greece. He appeared at Castle Bellevue unannounced and exhausted. After time to eat, rest, and recuperate, he and Amin sat in the solarium and talked about his experience working directly with the Germans, the condition of the Muslim Brotherhood in Egypt, and Banna's leadership ability.

Latif was taken aback by the question about Banna. "Do you think Banna is not suited for the job?"

"I think he was been very well suited to this point," Amin replied. "But in order to expand to the next level, the Brotherhood will require leadership from someone with more vision than Banna."

"He had vision enough to contact you and bring the Brother-hood to Jerusalem."

Amin nodded. "He came here to dedicate the Institute. And we are working together to convene an Arab Congress. But he lacks that *something* in leadership that the Brotherhood will require as it develops into its next form."

"You may be right," Latif conceded. "But they seem to be strong in Egypt. A threat to the monarchy, actually."

"Good." Amin paused to sip from his cup of coffee. "The mon-archy in Egypt needs to be threatened. It is a disgrace to Islam."

"Banna doesn't care much for the king, either."

Amin changed subjects. "You came back through Palestine?"

"Yes."

"Did you notice anything out of the ordinary?"

Latif thought for a moment. "Not much. There was something odd in Haifa, though."

"What was that?"

"A celebration for Jews who had arrived from the East."

A scowl wrinkled Amin's forehead. "From the East?"

"Yes."

"Where in the East?" Amin demanded.

"Most were from Bulgaria, I think. But a few were from Hun-gary and Romania, too."

"How many?"

"The people I talked to said they were about four thousand."

"Four thousand!" Amin shouted. "Four thousand?" Muscles along his jawline were tense and his eyes had an angry glare. "How did they arrive?"

"By ship."

"And the British did not turn them away?"

"No, I don't think they made any attempt to."

"Did these Jews have papers?"

"I didn't see any of them, so I can't say for a fact. But no one seemed afraid of detection. They had a celebration to welcome them that was a public event. No one seemed worried about it."

Amin seethed. "This cannot happen."

Latif shrugged. "What can we do about it? They won't send them back. Not with the war and all."

"We can make sure no more are allowed to leave," Amin declared.

That evening, Amin met with Grobba and told him what Latif had reported about Jews arriving in Palestine from the East. Grobba did not seem upset—certainly not as upset as Amin—but agreed to check into the matter.

Three days later, Grobba informed Amin that, indeed, Jewish refugees had come from the East and traveled to Palestine. "Where were they from?" Amin asked.

"Primarily from Bulgaria. But some were from Hungary and Romania."

"How many?"

"Not quite four thousand."

"Then it is just as Latif reported."

"Yes. I think so."

Amin frowned. "I thought Bulgaria was a signatory to the Tripartite Pact."

"They are. Now."

"But not in the beginning."

"No." Grobba shook his head. "When the war started, they attempted to maintain a posture of neutrality, but as things in Europe grew more challenging, Hitler demanded that they join us and permit the army to freely cross through their territory. They joined the Axis bloc, but they have been a reluctant partner."

Amin arched an eyebrow. "Perhaps it is time for the Jewish solution to be visited upon them."

Grobba seemed uncomfortable and looked away. "You would have to speak to Himmler about that yourself."

"I would be glad to take it up with him. Can you arrange an appointment for me?"

"Certainly."

✦ ✦ ✦ ✦ ✦

The following week, Amin met with Himmler and told him of Latif's report from Palestine and of Grobba's confirmation that Jewish refugees from the East had arrived in Haifa. "And I fear that is not all," Amin added. "If four thousand made it, with papers, there must be many thousands more getting through."

"This is troublesome indeed," Himmler replied. "Jews leaving is bad enough, but leaving with government-issued documents is unthinkable."

"Is there something that can be done about it?"

"We can order them to stop allowing Jews to leave. But that will create a second issue we must solve."

"What is that?"

"Jews will have to go somewhere. They can't stay where they are."

"Better to send the Jews to concentration camps in Poland than to Palestine."

Himmler stared at Amin a moment before saying, "Do you know what happens to Jews in the camps?"

"I assume they eventually die there."

Himmler nodded. "And so far, three million have died."

Amin's mouth fell open in a look of surprise. "Three million?"

"Yes. As of the most recent head count."

"Only another eight or ten million to go before they are all gone from Europe." Amin smiled. "Then we can begin eliminating them from the Middle East."

✦ ✦ ✦ ✦ ✦

After talking with Amin, Himmler met with Hitler and discussed the situation in the Balkans and reports of Jews leaving from there for Palestine. "Reports indicate they are arriving in Palestine with papers, and the British are not objecting."

Hitler stood near the window, looking out on the lawn. When Himmler finished describing the situation, he turned back with a frown. "These Jews have papers?" Himmler nodded in the affirmative.

"Government papers?"

"Apparently so."

"How is this possible?"

"It's Bulgaria," Himmler grumbled. "The Bulgarians are weak."

Hitler turned away and stared out the window again. "Does the Grand Mufti know about this situation?"

"He is the one who brought it to my attention."

"What does he think?"

"He thinks it must be stopped."

"The Grand Mufti is correct." Hitler turned away from the window and took a seat at his desk. "The Jews must be prevented from leaving anywhere within the Reich."

"How should we do this?"

"I will speak with Ribbentrop."

"Do you want me to handle it?"

"No!" Hitler snapped. "I told Ribbentrop earlier that this must be ended, and he did nothing about it. I will speak with him myself."

Himmler pressed the matter further. "If we prevent Jews in the East from leaving, something will need to be done about them. They can't remain where they are. We need the space for others."

"I will order all countries in the Balkans to deliver their Jews to us." Hitler glanced over at him with a smile. "We will take them off their hands."

"Good. We can solve the problem ourselves and not lose any time on the relocation schedule."

The following day, Hitler ordered Ribbentrop to direct Hungary, Romania, and Bulgaria to prohibit further Jewish emigration. "Also," he continued, "instruct them that they are to immediately begin collecting every Jew who resides or is found within their borders and assemble them for transport."

"We shall transmit the order today," Ribbentrop replied. "Shall I inform Himmler?"

"He already knows. Get the Jews to him. He knows what to do with them."

TWENTYSIX

AFTER A STRING OF STUNNING military successes from 1939 through 1940, Hitler turned his attention to the Soviet Union, and in the spring of 1941 Germany launched an attack against them, striking from the south and east. By doing so, Hitler hoped to gain additional territory in which he could resettle Germans returning home from other parts of the world, acquire raw material necessary to sustain Germany's military, and eliminate the Soviet Union as a strategic threat.

The attack caught the Soviet Union off guard but was not a total surprise. Germany's lightning-fast advance, however, was. By winter, the German army had advanced far beyond the Russian border, surrounding both Leningrad and Moscow. There, however, the initiative stalled.

Unable or unwilling to withdraw, Hitler ordered repeated attempts to capture the remaining portion of the Soviet Union that lay to the west. Those attempts failed miserably and only served to deplete much of Germany's ability to make war. By 1943, Hitler was forced to abandon the Russia invasion. Germany's withdrawal from that campaign marked the turning point of the war in favor of the Allies.

While Germany's prospects for winning the war took a turn for the worse, Amin continued to advocate for covert operations in Palestine. He renewed his earlier offer to help establish a spy network. Offered to supply agents willing to attack infrastructure. Suggested he might create special squads to roam the countryside, killing Jews on sight. Anything to catch the interest of German leadership, but to no avail.

"No one is interested in operations of that kind," Grobba explained. "Not now. They have all they can manage right now trying to stave off the Russians, the British, and the Americans."

As Allied forces continued to press their advantage against Germany, Hitler convened meeting after meeting in an attempt to devise a strategy that would turn the war back in his favor. Somewhere in the discussion, Göring remembered Amin's suggestion from one of their earliest meetings that he would be willing to promote an Arab uprising in Palestine. It didn't make much sense at the time but now, with the German army pressed from every direction, the idea seemed worth exploring.

In a planning session with Hitler, Göring reminded him of Amin's earlier suggestion that they attempt covert operations in Palestine. "What of it?" Hitler snapped. "The mufti is always promoting some idea he thinks will kill Jews."

"Some of his ideas are a little crazy," Göring agreed. "But if we can get the Arabs in Palestine to revolt in sufficient numbers, we might be able to create the impression that we are mounting an offensive in the region. That would force the Allies to reposition some of their forces away from Europe and toward the Middle East, to counter our supposed offensive."

Hitler appeared interested. "And you think that would work?"

"As a way to create trouble. Trouble that might require the Allies to divert some of their strength elsewhere. I do not propose it as an ultimate solution. Just a way for us to gain some time to prepare and execute our true plan to defend the Reich."

The more they talked the more interested Hitler became until finally he decided to give the operation a try. "Operation Atlas," he decided. "We shall call it Operation Atlas." Himmler was assigned the task of designing it. Göring gave him instructions. "When you are ready, tell Grobba to brief the mufti and enlist his cooperation."

Normally, an operation the size of Atlas would have involved several agencies. Abwehr, Germany's intelligence agency, would have been one of the principal players. However, Abwehr was run by Admiral Wilhelm Canaris, a naval officer who had come to political prominence early in the Nazi era and was named chief of the intelligence service.

At first, Himmler was enthusiastic about having Canaris in such a strategic position, but before long he grew suspicious that Canaris was less than supportive of the Hitler regime. Because of those suspicions, Himmler kept Operation Atlas solely within his control.

Absolute secrecy, however, was impossible and before long Erich Vermehren, an Abwehr agent, learned through a friend at SS that several pending operations were being closely guarded by Himmler to the exclusion of other agencies, including the Abwehr. Among those top-secret plans was Operation Atlas. Vermehren, of course, informed Canaris immediately.

✦ ✦ ✦ ✦ ✦

In December, Himmler was ready to proceed with the operation. Grobba came to see Amin. "You have been advocating for covert operations in Palestine since you arrived here."

"Yes, I have," Amin replied. "Has something happened?"

A grin spread over Grobba's face. "You will be pleased to know Himmler is ready to authorize such an action."

Amin's eyes opened wide. "Himmler? The operation will be under SS control, not the Abwehr?"

"Yes. We are of the opinion Canaris cannot be trusted," Grobba explained. "Himmler wants this under his control."

"Does this operation have a name?"

"Operation Atlas. The name was chosen by Hitler himself."

"That is a great honor."

"Yes, it is."

"Who will actually conduct this mission?"

"They will use a special commando unit established within the Waffen-SS. A five-man team, the last I heard. It will enter Palestine by parachute and establish an intelligence-gathering base that can radio information from the region back to Germany. At the same time, the unit will create a network of observers and informants to help gather that information and engender support for Germany among Arabs. If they are successful, they hope to recruit and arm Arabs to take action against the Jews with the intention of causing conflict between Jews and Arabs. If all works well, it will disrupt the British Mandatory Authority and create at least the illusion that Germany is planning a major operation in the Middle East."

"A rather ambitious plan," Amin noted.

"Yes. Quite ambitious. And while they're doing all of that, members of the original unit will strike Jewish targets, sabotage infrastructure, and do all it can possibly do to incite, confuse, and kill Jews."

"I wish I were going with them."

"I'm afraid that will not be possible."

"I understand," Amin chuckled. "But who will be on the team?"

"The mission unit will be composed of three members from the SS who lived in Palestine."

Amin was surprised. "They have SS members who actually lived in Palestine?"

Grobba nodded. "They are from the Templer religious sect. Are you familiar with that group?"

"Germans who were members of the Lutheran Church?"

"Yes," Grobba replied.

"They had several places. They came to Palestine because they were expelled from the church due to their views of the apocalypse. They thought they were supposed to come to Israel and establish themselves as prophets. Like in the Jewish writings." Amin shook his head. "Sometimes the Christians are crazier than the Jews."

Grobba ignored the comment and continued his briefing on the covert operation. "These three men grew up in Palestine. They have been trained in this sort of operation and will carry the brunt of the covert work. But they need at least two Palestinian Arabs to go with them. People who know the terrain, have contacts that they can draw upon for support, and who know the location of usable assets. They should be people who are living outside Palestine, though. Less risk of tipping someone off about plans if they aren't there already. Do you have someone in your group who could go?"

"I have two men available," Amin replied. "They would be great for the task."

"Do I know them?"

"Hasan Salama and Abdul Latif."

Grobba nodded. "Excellent choices."

When he finished discussing the operation with Grobba, Amin informed Salama and Latif of their selection for the unit. Both were excited to participate and began training with the SS that same week.

The Atlas mission unit was led by Kurt Wieland, a Palestinian-born German from the Templer community at Sarona on the outskirts of Tel Aviv. As a young man, he was head of the Palestinian Hitler Youth. In 1940, he left Palestine and moved to Germany where he then joined the Brandenburg regiment, an SS unit comprised of German foreign nationals loyal to the Nazi party. Wieland was assigned to the military intelligence corps due to his knowledge of languages. He rapidly advanced in position and eventually obtained the rank of major, serving in the commando unit of the Waffen-SS under Otto Skorzeny. As a Brandenburg member, Wieland took part in a covert German mission to Iraq in 1941, in support of the coup. He was in charge of the technical side of the Atlas operation.

In addition to Wieland, two more German soldiers, also raised in Palestinian Templer communities, were assigned to the unit. They both knew the region well and belonged to the Brandenburg regiment—Werner Frank, the unit's radio operator, and Friedrich Deininger. Frank was born in Haifa. Deininger was born in Waldheim, a German colony located northwest of Nazareth.

After the Atlas Unit trained for a few weeks, Amin met with them to brief them on possible mission objectives, political aspects of Palestinian life, and key people they should contact upon arrival. He specifically mentioned two of his cousins, Nafith and Ali Bey al-Husseini. "They live in Jerusalem. They loath the British and will be of enormous assistance to you."

✦ ✦ ✦ ✦ ✦

While work proceeded on Operation Atlas, the pace of activity in Berlin grew frantic. Ministers and officials with whom Amin had enjoyed easy access and an amicable relationship became more distant and less ebullient at his appearing. Amin noted the shift in attitude and raised the issue with Grobba. "It's not you," he was told. "It's the war. Everyone is worried about what will happen next."

In the midst of that, Gerhard von Mende visited Amin at Castle Bellevue to discuss the ongoing effort to organize Muslims in the East. "We need to continue forming them into military units. Their assistance is vital to the fight against the Russians."

Amin was suspicious. Since arriving in Germany, he had spent most of his time recruiting Muslims for that very same fight and had heard reports about poorly trained, ill-equipped units being hurled into the thick of the fight. Many thought they were being used solely as a buffer to shield German regular troops from what was becoming a Soviet onslaught. Rather than ignoring the issue, as he might have earlier, he addressed it.

"Does the army have sufficient time and resources to train new units now?" Amin asked. "Or will these men be merely thrown at the Russian front as a human shield, to slow the Soviet advance?"

The look on Mende's face indicated he did not care for the question. "It's a rather hectic pace."

"Rather like what the Russians did with them when the Germans advanced into the East a few years ago."

Mende kept going. "We've had some discussions about whether it is time to organize the Muslims you've been working with at the Institute."

"Who has been discussing this topic?"

"Officials at the ministry."

"Rosenberg?"

Mende nodded. "Among others."

Amin was troubled by the news that he had been the subject of a conversation at the ministry. A conversation that did not sound at all flattering. "Most of the men who attend prayers regularly are students. Many of them are not German citizens.

In the past, that has been an issue for enlistment. Will they be allowed to enlist now?"

Mende sighed. "Look, the war is not going well. Many are feeling desperate. Some think that if we use all available resources, perhaps we can still prevail, but others are not convinced. Those who think we still have a chance of winning, or at least fighting to a stalemate, see the Islamic Central Institute and realize it is now fully operational and quite successful, full of able-bodied men. They think it is time to begin recruiting the mosque's members to the Reich's work."

Amin was even more worried than before. Mende's visit now sounded like an attempt to let him know that others in the government knew what he was doing—creating a Muslim power base rather than assisting the Reich—and were telling him to align more perfectly with Nazi priorities. Amin, however, kept his deepest concerns to himself and agreed to assist Mende by organizing Arab students in Berlin into a military unit.

Privately, Amin had grown leery of the recruitment project and worried that the Germans would lose the war. "If the Germans are defeated," he told Qadir as he explained Mende's visit, "the Brotherhood might lose control of the mosque and most of its members."

"We have no choice but to provide them the men they ask for," Qadir replied. "If we don't, the Germans will take control of it."

"This is a tenuous moment."

"Perhaps we can do as you have suggested many times," Qadir suggested. "Use the Germans to make our people strong and then no one will be able to stop us. We can return with them to Palestine and drive the Jews into the sea."

"Perhaps." Amin was not convinced that could happen now. "In any regard, we must be prepared in case things go a different way."

"And how do we do that?"

"We must establish local leadership that can survive even if we are absent. I know we have discussed this in the past, but I think we should put it in place now."

Qadir looked troubled. "Do you think we will be forced to leave Germany?"

"The war is going worse for the Germans than I thought."

Qadir nodded. "The Allies are pushing them back on every front."

"And whether we leave or stay," Amin continued, "the Allies will know that we have worked with the Nazis. The records will show it and our enemies will make sure the Allies know it." Amin took Qadir by the shoulders and did his best to give a reassuring smile. "We have trained Kazim and Tibi to take over for us. Do you still have confidence in them?"

"Yes," Qadir replied.

"And I do, too. So perhaps we should work to protect the most promising members of the Brotherhood from service, assign only the least-acceptable students to the unit Mende wants to establish, and see if that will buy us some time."

Qadir smiled. "That is an excellent idea."

With that in mind, Amin and Qadir selected from among the mosque's members those students who had shown the least promise, the least interest, the least discipline and offered them in a group to Mende. They were accepted without question, trained sparingly, and within weeks sent to the Balkans as the *Arabisches Freiheitkorps*—the Arab Free Corps. Once deployed, the corps served as an auxiliary unit of the German army and was assigned the task of hunting down Allied parachutists.

✦ ✦ ✦ ✦ ✦

Operation Atlas began on October 6, 1944. The five-member commando unit parachuted into Palestine from a captured B-17

Flying Fortress flown by Luftwaffe pilots. They landed in Jericho near an area known as Wadi Qelt. Unit members became separated during the drop, three landing in one area and two in another.

The unit's equipment, packed in two wooden shipping crates, had been dropped by parachute also. It landed in a separate area of the wadi. The first crate held a cache of submachine guns, cartons of dynamite, a radio, and a duplicating machine. The other held clothing, a German-Arabic dictionary, five thousand pounds in British sterling notes of various denominations, and other items including gold coins, explosives, and a quantity of poison for use in a planned attempt to poison the Tel Aviv water supply.

Salama, having never landed by parachute at all, much less under operational conditions, injured his ankle when he hit the ground. He was separated from the others but, unlike the others, knew exactly where he was located. Rather than attempting to find the group, he started toward Jerusalem at a hobbled pace. Latif and the Germans made their way to a cave in a wadi cliff and began salvaging equipment from the crate that held the guns, dynamite, and radio. Latif devoted much of his time to putting the radio into operational order.

The day after the unit landed, shepherds tending their sheep discovered the second crate and pried it open. Inside, they found the currency and gold coins. They stuffed their bags full and started toward Jericho, intending to return for the rest later. In Jericho, one of the men bought a dozen sheep from his neighbor and paid for it with some of the gold coins. The neighbor was suspicious and mentioned the coins to a friend who was an officer with the Jericho police.

When the Jericho police chief learned that gold coins were being circulated in the city, he initiated an investigation. Two policemen called on the man who had received the coins and examined them. After a few questions, they determined the identity of the shepherd who used the coins to pay for the sheep.

The shepherds were searched, and the remaining gold coins were seized. Under harsh interrogation, the shepherds reluctantly told the policemen the location of the site where they discovered the coins and agreed to lead the police to it.

A full report of the discovery was submitted to the Jericho police chief, who immediately informed British military commanders. That same day, a manhunt was launched involving British military units and members of the Jericho police force. In the course of the hunt, searchers learned from British Intelligence that an Abwehr agent, Erich Vermehren, defected several months earlier. Among the things he disclosed was information about German plans for a supposed covert operation in Palestine. At the time, no one was able to verify the details. Now it seemed the defector might have been correct after all.

British and Mandatory police units involved in the manhunt discovered more of the Atlas Unit's dispersed cargo. An analysis of the equipment indicated to British officers that a covert operation really was underway, though no one was certain just what that operation might entail. Based on that information, the search teams were bolstered and the hunt intensified.

✦ ✦ ✦ ✦ ✦

Meanwhile, after catching a ride on a delivery truck, Salama arrived in Jerusalem and arranged to meet with Amin's cousins, Nafith and Ali Bey al-Husseini. They took him to Nafith's home and bandaged his ankle, then fed him. While he ate, Salama told them about Operation Atlas. "Amin said we should ask you for help, which is why I am here."

Nafith shook his head. "We are not interested in any such operation."

"Absolutely not," Ali Bey reiterated.

Salama was puzzled. "Why not?"

"We are angry with the British," Nafith explained, "but not angry enough to provide support to the Germans."

Salama was astounded. "Amin thought you would be eager to help."

"Amin has been gone from Jerusalem for quite some time," Ali Bey explained. "He misunderstands the nature of the current political relationship between Arabs and the British."

Nafith added, "It is a terrible mistake to participate in such an adventure with the Germans."

Salama was bewildered, and Ali Bey seemed to notice it from the look on Salama's face. "But don't worry. You should remain with us. We have heard that the British are looking for men who parachuted into the country."

Nafith looked over at him. "Men who landed in the wadi near Jericho."

Ali Bey grinned. "I assume that is how you damaged your ankle."

"Yes." Salama leaned over to rub his ankle. "And it hurts."

"We will get you going again," Nafith promised. "We'll have you in good shape before anyone knows you are here."

Ali Bey leaned closer and lowered his voice for emphasis. "But we are not interested in helping the Germans."

"Not at all," Nafith added.

✦ ✦ ✦ ✦ ✦

A few days later, members of the Transjordan Frontier Force participating in the manhunt noticed a man standing at the entrance to a cave in Wadi Qelt. The man wore traditional Arab garb but cradled a firearm in the crook of his arm. They confronted the man and discovered he was a German. On further inquiry they learned he was Kurt Wieland. Just inside the cave they found Werner Frank, Friedrich Deininger, and Abdul Latif.

Outnumbered, they surrendered without resistance.

Shortly after the men were captured, Grobba brought the news to Amin. "Hitler, Himmler, and Göring are angry over the entire affair. They feel they were goaded into it by you."

Amin's eyes opened wide. "By me?" he blurted.

"That's what they think."

"I suggested it when I first arrived," Amin reminded. "And no one thought it was a good idea. I continued to mention it but every time I tried to talk about it, you or someone else told me it was not the right time and that no one was interested in the region. You said everyone was focused on something else."

"I know."

"I mentioned my ideas," Amin railed. "But I by no means goaded anyone into doing anything. They acted on their own. In fact, this particular operation was Göring's idea."

Grobba agreed. "And I think they know that, but they are embarrassed by the operation's failure. And on top of that, the war is going badly for us everywhere now."

Amin was still upset. "Am I facing any risk over this?"

"No," Grobba replied calmly. "They are angry, but they are mostly angry with themselves." He stood to leave, then paused and took a note from his pocket. "This came for you." He handed the note to Amin. "It was in a diplomatic pouch from Turkey."

When Grobba was gone, Amin glanced at the note to see it was from a relative. The language of the message was guarded and cryptic, but from it Amin learned that Salama was alive and living in a village near Jerusalem. No one had any news about Latif.

TWENTYSEVEN

AS THE ALLIED ARMIES continued their advance across Europe, conditions in Germany grew increasingly dire. For the first time since the Nazis came to power, public confidence in Hitler waned. Sensing that political situation left him vulnerable—that Arabs might become the scapegoat the Jews were before the war—Amin focused his attention on strengthening the work at the Islamic Central Institute in preparation for the day when he would no longer be present to lead it.

Daily, Amin met with Kazim and Tibi, shaping their education, understanding, discipline, and thought. Cultivating in them the same intense hatred of the Jews that he had, the sense of entitlement he held for the establishment of an Arab homeland in Palestine, and the determination to make that homeland a political reality.

"With so many opposed to us," Tibi noted, "it seems we shall always face armed conflict."

"Yes," Amin agreed. "The kingdom envisioned by the Quran will come to pass only by means of struggle and conflict. That will be the work of the Brotherhood. A network of Muslim men, all of them devoted to Allah. All of them devoted to the singular purpose of eliminating the Jewish race from the earth."

Tibi frowned. "Eliminating them?"

"Yes, we must kill all of the Jews. Every last one of them. That much the Nazis got right. The Jews cannot be allowed to survive. Not here in Europe and certainly not in Palestine."

With events moving quickly, and not in a good way, Amin lost track of the effort to convene an Arab Congress. Hassan al-Banna, however, did not, and in the midst of German disarray, a message arrived from him reminding Amin of their intention to form the Arab League and their desire to convene an Arab Congress.

"I have made tentative arrangements for us to gather at Alexandria," the message from Banna read. "I know the situation has become desperate where you are, but that only highlights the need for the league we discussed earlier. We must be prepared to operate in a world where Germany is powerless to protect us. For that, we need to convene the congress."

Although hard-pressed to do more than work with those who remained at the Institute and attend to his personal daily routine, Amin issued the call for the Arab Congress. Against great odds, he even succeeded in obtaining help from the German Foreign Ministry in disseminating that announcement to every country with a significant Arab population.

When that was done, Amin sent a reply message to Banna and asked him to bring Salama from Jerusalem. "Have him come to Alexandria for the congress," Amin instructed. "I need him in attendance at the meeting as my official representative."

✦ ✦ ✦ ✦ ✦

Two months later, delegates from Egypt, Iraq, Syria, Jordan, and Lebanon gathered in Alexandria for the meeting. Salama attended as Amin's official envoy. The group referred to themselves as the preliminary committee of the General Arab Conference. Delegates were interested in the proposed Arab League but spent most of their time discussing the rapidly changing state of world affairs and what that might mean for Arab nations and Islam.

"Germany and the Axis powers are in complete disarray," someone noted.

Another spoke up. "They are facing total defeat and yet Hitler is unwilling to surrender."

"His refusal to accept reality will lead to the complete destruction of Europe."

"And misery for many people."

"And perhaps an opportunity for us," someone added.

Between discussion of the war, attendees reached an agreement to cooperate together to fill any void in the Middle East left by the demise of Germany. They also committed to establishing an Islamic kingdom throughout the Middle East. A resolution stating again Muslim and Arab opposition to a Jewish state in Palestine and opposition to further Jewish immigration to Palestine won unanimous approval.

In its final session, the gathering approved the formation of the Arab League. However, delegates felt the league should have an official diplomatic entity. Someone suggested they should all return to their home countries, gain the approval and authority of their governing bodies, then return for a second meeting. A resolution to that effect passed without opposition and a second meeting was set for Cairo to ratify the league's formation.

✦ ✦ ✦ ✦ ✦

In January 1945, Soviet troops entered Germany. Amin could see that nothing would stop their advance and that it was only a matter of time—perhaps a short time—before the Allies entered Berlin. Despite all of that, Hitler insisted that no one surrender. Officers who attempted to convince him otherwise were arrested. Many of them were executed.

With conditions so unsettled, Amin limited his activities even further, forgoing trips to the Institute to remain at his residence. He hoped doing so would help him avoid the internal controversy that now plagued the German government. His only contact beyond the castle grounds was through Grobba, from whom he learned that Mende and Rosenberg had disappeared.

"Grobba says they do not think foul play was involved," Amin commented as he relayed the news to Qadir.

"Maybe we should leave, too," Qadir suggested. "While we have the time."

Amin did not want to abandon the Islamic Central Institute but realized Qadir was right. They had no choice but to leave Germany. Doing so, however, required planning, and as a first step in arranging an orderly departure, Amin asked Aref to accompany Karimeh and the children to Egypt. "They will be safe there. Salama is still there and he will be able to help."

"Will you join us later?"

"I suspect so," Amin replied. "But I do not know for certain how things will end here."

After a teary good-bye with his wife and family, Amin told Qadir to notify Kazim and Tibi that they were now in charge of the Institute. Qadir looked surprised. "Don't you want to meet with them one last time? Give them some words of advice?"

Amin gave an emphatic shake of his head. "No, I do not want to provide Hitler or anyone else a reason to suspect me of anything. We should begin sorting through our papers and belongings and determine what we must keep."

"That could take a while," Qadir said.

"We will have to work quickly. We need to leave soon."

✦ ✦ ✦ ✦ ✦

In March 1945, heads of state from Egypt, Iraq, Transjordan, Lebanon, Syria, and Saudi Arabia met in Cairo as an extension of the Arab Congress. At that meeting, they officially signed articles forming the League of Arab Nations—the Arab League—as envisioned by the congress held at Alexandria a few months earlier. Salama attended the gathering, as did Banna. Though they had no official role, both men worked to keep delegate discussions focused on conditions in Palestine and on the need for urgency in addressing how the Middle East would be handled once the war finally ended.

Members of the League were primarily concerned about Jewish immigration to Palestine and the international momentum building for the creation of a Jewish state in Palestine. In one of its first policy statements, the Arab League announced its adamant opposition to both. Amin followed events in Cairo through periodic telegrams from Salama.

The following month, Allied aircraft began a concerted bombing campaign against Berlin. As bombs exploded around them, Amin and Qadir loaded boxes and bags into a car parked in front of the residence.

"We must hurry," Amin urged.

"I think we waited too long," Qadir replied.

"We must at least attempt to escape."

"Where are we going?"

"To Switzerland."

"Why not Egypt?"

"Too risky."

"No riskier than traveling by car across Germany with the Allied army lurking behind every tree."

"Too risky for Karimeh and the children," Amin explained.

"You think the Egyptians will not welcome you?"

"I think the Jews and the British will use them to force me out in the open." Qadir seemed not to agree with Amin's assessment but said nothing.

When they had packed as much as the car would hold, Amin, Qadir, and Hadad left Castle Bellevue and drove south, dodging German and Allied military units as they made their way toward the Swiss border.

At Konstanz, a city in southern Germany near the Swiss border, they found the area was held by French troops. Amin and Qadir hid in an abandoned farmhouse on the outskirts of town while Hadad made his way to the border outpost in an attempt to make contact with the Swiss government to ask for asylum.

Two days later, someone spotted Amin. Not long after that, he and Qadir were taken into custody. When the French learned his identity, Amin told them he had an asylum petition pending in Switzerland. French officials detained him anyway but agreed to check with Swiss officials regarding the status of his petition. A few days later, they learned that Amin's attempt for asylum in Switzerland had been refused and made arrangements to transfer him to Paris. They had no reason to detain Hadad or Qadir, but neither of them wanted to leave Amin's side. So the French agreed to send them to Paris, also.

✦ ✦ ✦ ✦ ✦

Meanwhile, on May 8, 1945, Germany officially surrendered to the Allies. By then, Amin, Hadad, and Qadir were in Paris, where they lived under house arrest in a private residence provided by a Muslim Brotherhood member.

After a review of Amin and his status, French authorities notified US and British officials that Amin was in custody. Representatives from all three countries met to discuss what to do with him. The French government was represented in those talks by

Henri Ponsot, a former ambassador of France in Syria, "I would note," Ponsot began, "that Amin al-Husseini is not charged with any war crime. In fact, he is not charged with anything at all. Our agents only detained him because he is a known figure. We have nothing on which to continue to hold him."

Edwin Anderson represented the United States. "You may not have specific charges against him, but he is suspected of plenty and he collaborated with the Nazis for the entire duration of the war. We're holding German citizens who did far less than Husseini. We can't just let him go free."

Lewis Carlyle, for the British, suggested Amin might be a unique asset. "He could be the only person capable of uniting Palestinian Arabs. If he did that, Arabs would cool off the Zionists. Act as a counterweight to their zealous approach." Everyone in the room knew what Carlyle really meant. The British were keenly interested in an amicable resolution of matters in the Middle East in order to facilitate access to the region's oil. They also had several thousand troops in Palestine to enforce the Mandate, which presented its own demands.

French authorities presented themselves as taking the morally superior high ground, which is why Ponsot made a point of telling the others about the lack of charges against Amin and the groundless nature of continued detention. Nevertheless, the French government, like the British, had its own ulterior motivation for dealing graciously with him. Chief among them was the notion that they could capitalize on good treatment of Amin as a means of improving their situation with the Arab world. A way to redeem themselves from the disastrous Sykes-Picot debacle and the sense of betrayal among Arabs.

Negotiations over what to do with Amin dragged on for several weeks. Ponsot took the lead and was the group's primary representative in dealing directly with Amin. Because of that, and because the French government had physical custody of him, Ponsot had a decisive influence on how the matter played out.

After lengthy internal discussions, the French government granted Amin special detention conditions and important privileges. As part of that, the government assumed responsibility for the care and well-being of Amin and his entourage. Through intermediaries, they let the Arab world know that they had accorded him this status.

News of France's boasting eventually got back to Amin, who realized French officials were being gracious to him not out of respect or because they saw him as a meritorious individual, but in an attempt to use him for their own purposes. Qadir and the others were angry, but Amin calmed them quickly. "We should think of this as a gift. A gift from Allah that we should use to our advantage."

The British opposed any special treatment for Amin and filed a request for extradition, arguing that he was a British citizen—albeit from Mandatory Palestine—who collaborated with the Nazis. Despite the fact that Amin appeared on official Allied lists of war criminals, French officials decided to consider him a political prisoner and refused to comply with the British request.

Yugoslavia also requested extradition of Amin in order to prosecute him for his role in the massacre of Serbs in the Balkans. Zionist representatives, fearing that Amin might escape prosecution altogether, supported the Yugoslav request. Zionists also claimed that Amin was responsible for massacres in Greece and pointed out his action against the Allies in Iraq in 1941. In an attempt to strengthen their claims, they requested the support of the United States in the matter.

In response to the Yugoslav extradition request, Amin argued that the massacre of Serbs was performed by General Mihailović and not by him. He also stated that more than two hundred thousand Muslims and forty thousand Christians were assassinated by the Serbs and that he had established a division of soldiers in Bosnia only after Bosnian Muslims had asked for his help. Ponsot accepted Amin's explanation and convinced French officials to refuse the Yugoslav request, too.

With the French government harboring Amin, Jewish leaders in Palestine decided to do what they had wanted to do before and eliminate him. Operatives in Paris located Amin's residence and prepared to assassinate him. Before they could kill him, French officials learned of the plan and moved to thwart the attempt by notifying Jewish contacts that they had discovered the plot. Upon learning that others knew what they were about to do, the operation to assassinate Amin was canceled on orders from David Ben-Gurion. He didn't really care about the international community's response to the action but had become concerned about the nature of an Arab response, which would bode ill for Jews living in Palestine. He also was concerned that killing Amin would only make him a martyr.

By September 1945, despite their interest in exploiting Amin's situation to their advantage, French officials decided to transfer him to an Arab country. At the instruction of his superiors, Ponsot discussed the matter with Amin in an effort to determine which country he preferred. Ponsot suggested Egypt, Saudi Arabia, or Yemen as possible locations. Amin was agreeable with either Egypt or Iraq, and even Transjordan, but not the others on the list. Diplomatic contacts were established with authorities in the respective countries and with the Arab League.

In the course of their discussions, Amin, always on the lookout for advantages in every situation, suggested to Ponsot that France might consider sponsoring provocations in Palestine designed to goad the British into a response against Palestinian Arabs. "As a way of forcing Arab countries to pay closer attention to British policy than to that of France," he explained, "I could coordinate such an action for you."

When Ponsot relayed Amin's offer, French officials were intrigued by the suggestion but not really interested in following through with it. "The plan," one official proffered, "is too nuanced to succeed." In the meantime, however, they granted Amin permission to buy a car and eased restrictions on his movements, allowing him to meet with whomever he wanted, though he was under constant police surveillance.

Amin was very satisfied with his situation in France but sensed, as he had at times in the past, that circumstances were turning against him and that the moment had come for him to move on. He had no hard evidence of it. Just the tone in the voice of a British diplomat, the look in the eyes of the Americans. Something had shifted. Things would not be pleasant for him in Paris forever. Perhaps not for long at all.

In addition, Amin also had the sense that he needed to reassert his authority and control over Palestinian affairs. Many years had passed since he fled Jerusalem for Lebanon and then made his way to Berlin. He had attempted to keep his hand in the political machinations of Palestinian Arabs, but distance and time had an effect. If he stayed away much longer, those who had filled the leadership gap created by his absence would begin to think of their position and power as permanent. He needed to remind everyone in a dramatic manner that *he* was the Grand Mufti, and they were not.

No longer hindered by restrictions that limited the people with whom he could meet, he contacted Banna and inquired about using the Arab League to intervene with the British to reconstitute the Arab Higher Committee. Banna was supportive of that idea and visited Amin in Paris, where they discussed the matter further. After hammering out an arrangement to cover the necessary details, Banna agreed to help.

✦ ✦ ✦ ✦ ✦

In November 1945, the Arab League intervened with the British Mandatory Authority and asked to reestablish the Arab Higher Committee. The British agreed to do so and to recognize it as the supreme executive body representing all Arabs in Mandatory Palestine. With Banna's help, Amin supporters were appointed to a majority of the positions on the twelve-member body. Among those was Jamal al-Husseini, his cousin who spent the war in Jerusalem. Although absent, Amin was named chairman of the committee. Members from opposing political factions were relegated to a frustrated minority. Jamal served as co-chairman and functioned as Amin's proxy.

As might be expected, the committee was quickly engulfed in disagreements about bias in favor of Amin and his proposals. The stated dispute was over allocation of waqf money and the appointment of officials for the Sharia courts, but underlying that was the raw and sometimes brutal struggle among Arabs for control of Palestine.

Unable to contain the trouble, Jamal, acting on his authority as co-chairman, disbanded the Arab Higher Committee. After the committee was disbanded, he quickly reconstituted it as an organization exclusively staffed by Amin's family members and political allies. Rather than fight for control again, the opposition responded by forming its own organization known as the Arab Higher Front. It was staffed exclusively with those who opposed Amin.

To settle the dispute and stabilize the situation, Arab League foreign ministers intervened, replacing both the Arab Higher Committee and the Arab Higher Front with the Arab Higher Executive as the official Mandatory representative of Palestinian-Arab interests. Once again, even though he was absent, Amin was chosen chairman. Jamal was selected as vice chairman and continued to exercise Amin's authority over the group.

✦ ✦ ✦ ✦ ✦

In May 1946, the question of Amin's ultimate destination and fate remained in limbo. Amin, convinced by then that he needed to act immediately to change his situation, contacted Salem Elbaz, an influential Moroccan businessman who resided in Paris, and asked him to help arrange travel for Amin and Hadad to Cairo. Elbaz was eager to assist them.

Through relatives and friends, Elbaz, under the guise of organizing a hotel development in Damascus, contacted a Syrian politician who worked in Paris. Through him, Elbaz procured Syrian travel documents for Amin and Hadad. Next, he obtained tickets for them on a TWA flight bound for Cairo. Then, with the help of Muslim Brotherhood members who resided in Paris, and with the cooperation of sympathetic officials, the French police, who already had lifted restrictions on Amin, were persuaded to suspend their surveillance of him.

On the appointed departure date, with police no longer present to stop them and no longer in a position to alert anyone, Hadad and Amin left the residence and drove to the airport. There they boarded the TWA flight to Cairo and were gone.

When Amin arrived in Cairo, he was reunited with Karimeh and their children. Aref was there, too. After greeting them and catching Karimeh up on the latest news, Amin asked about Latif. "I have heard nothing of him since he left Germany on Operation Atlas."

"Latif was captured by the British and imprisoned," Aref explained.

Amin looked worried. "But he survived?"

"Yes." Aref nodded. "He is alive."

"Where is he?" Amin frowned. "Do the British still have him?"

Aref smiled. "One of his relatives in Jerusalem helped him

escape. Last anyone heard, he was living in Pakistan, but no one is certain exactly where."

"Find him," Amin ordered. "And help him get back here to Cairo. We will need him."

A few days later, the Egyptian government officially granted Amin asylum. It also provided a residence large enough for Amin, Karimeh, the children, and the others to live together, as they had in Berlin. Hadad served as Amin's secretary. Salama and Qadir joined them.

Amin's cousin Jamal shuttled back and forth between Cairo and Jerusalem, acting as ambassador for the Grand Mufti in exile. Through his position as co-chairman of the Arab Higher Executive, he kept Amin abreast of events in Jerusalem and the latest news from Mandatory officials. Amin still was chairman but was unable to leave Egypt for fear of arrest. Or worse.

Said Ramadan, Hassan al-Banna's son-in-law, was assigned as Amin's liaison with the Muslim Brotherhood. Ramadan was a student at Cairo University with friends who gave him access to several key administrators in King Farouk's government. Among those was Ismail Sabry, son of the king's official domestic policy advisor, and Hosni Tantaway, son of the king's closest international advisor. Ramadan attended to Amin and his entourage's personal needs. He also introduced them to Brotherhood members, briefed them on the current state of Egyptian politics, and served as a practical guide to help them negotiate the streets of Cairo. Amin liked him from the start.

TWENTYEIGHT

IN MAY 1947, the British government notified the United Nations that it wanted to withdraw from the Palestinian mandate it had held since the end of the Great War. That month, the British foreign secretary filed a formal request with the United Nations, asking that the General Assembly take up the matter and prepare recommendations regarding the future of Palestine.

The General Assembly responded by forming the United Nations Special Committee on Palestine—UNSCOP, as it became known—which was charged with the duty of reviewing the situation and formulating recommendations. Comprised of delegates from Australia, Canada, Czechoslovakia, Guatemala, India, Iran, Netherlands, Sweden, and Yugoslavia, the committee was intended to be politically neutral. Emile Sandstrom, the Swedish delegate, served as chairman. The committee wasted little time getting to work and in June traveled to Palestine to begin a fact-finding tour.

As chairman of the Arab Higher Executive, and in his capacity as Grand Mufti, Amin refused to cooperate with UNSCOP.

"Palestine has belonged to Arabs for thousands of years," he argued. "Jews who want to divide it and take it away from us are interlopers, late-comers, and criminals. Their actions violate international law. The United Nations is obligated by its charter to defend our sovereignty and maintain the integrity of our borders. No committee, nor even the General Assembly, of any international body is empowered to change our borders or steal our land."

To reinforce his position, Amin ordered all Arabs of Palestine to avoid contact with UNSCOP and directed members of the Arab Higher Executive to make certain everyone abided by his directive. Privately, he sent Jamal to deliver a message to dissident factions, including members of the Nashashibi clan. "If you attempt to cooperate with UNSCOP, you shall pay for it with your lives."

Events in Palestine now seemed to move forward at an ever-quickening pace. Even from Cairo, Amin sensed it and he also sensed the need for additional help to keep up. Said Ramadan, Hassan al-Banna's son-in-law, had served well as his liaison to Egyptian life and politics. Now Amin took him deeper into his confidence, teaching him the peculiar blend of Islam that he had come to embrace and that he had taught the others—a Nazi-inspired hatred of Jews cloaked in passages from the Quran. When he wasn't studying, Ramadan helped Hadad craft those beliefs into a message that Amin used to appeal to the masses.

"The Jews are our enemy," Amin maintained. "In these latter days, they are not only using their friends the British, whom they have blinded and deceived by Jewish spells and magic, but also the United Nations—an assembly of great promise but now corrupted by Jewish desire—to impose their will on us. To steal from us land that has been the home of Arab peoples for thousands of years. We must not allow this to happen. We must stand up. We must take our place in the great sweep of history. We must rise up and wipe the Jews from the face of the earth by any means necessary."

The message was an intoxicating brew of hatred, lies, and ancient writings, infused with lofty rhetoric that stirred the crowds to an almost uncontrollable frenzy. Wherever Amin spoke, people rushed to hear him, filling the streets, chanting and shouting and calling his name. Many fell prostrate at his feet as he passed by and proclaimed him the true leader of the Arab people, the true successor to Muhammad.

Throughout the Middle East, Arabs hung on Amin's every word. But in the halls of government in the Arab League's member states, ministers looked upon those crowds and loathed him. They were jealous of his favor with the public, jealous of his ability to sway the masses, and jealous of the way politicians from other regions seemed to defer to his opinion. "They act as if he is the Grand Deity, rather than merely the Grand Mufti," someone groused. "Any time a politician in Europe or Asia or America refers to the Middle East, they cite his opinion as if it is the final word on the matter."

"We should do something to stop him," another commented.

"That won't be necessary," a third replied.

"Why not?"

"The United Nations will do that for us."

"How so?"

"They are determined to give the Jews the homeland that they want. And now, more than ever, they are resolved to do it as payment for the debt they feel they owe from the Nazi holocaust."

"And what does that mean for the Grand Mufti?"

"The UN will divide Palestine. They will create a Jewish state. And they will create an Arab state. But they will never allow Amin al-Husseini to be anything more than Grand Mufti. Certainly not a head of government."

"Or even head of state," someone added.

"And when there is an Arab state in Palestine and the Grand

Mufti is not the head of it, he shall drift away into obscurity."
Everyone laughed in response.

✦ ✦ ✦ ✦ ✦

In September 1947, UNSCOP concluded its work in Palestine
and withdrew to The Hauge to prepare a report of its findings.
The following month, the committee issued its report, which gave
unanimous support to termination of the British mandate. The
UN General Assembly accepted the report and appointed an ad
hoc committee to address the question of what might happen if
Amin and other Arabs opposed the move vigorously and refused
to participate in the committee's deliberations.

As the committee deliberated Palestine's future, a minority of
the committee's members raised the question of whether the UN
had the authority to impose a government on Palestine that was
contrary to the wishes of the residents of Palestine. They asked
that the question be referred to the World Court for a ruling.
By a majority vote, that request was denied and the committee
went on to approve a plan for Palestine that included political
partition of the region, but with a unified economy. This plan was
substantially the same plan proposed by the Peel Commission
years earlier and one supported by the Jewish Agency. As it had
on previous occasions, the Jewish Agency accepted the committee's plan with only minor exceptions for adjustments to border
locations.

In November, the UN General Assembly adopted the
UNSCOP/Ad Hoc Committee plan as the future for Palestine.
After the plan was announced, Alan Cunningham, British High
Commissioner of Palestine, sent emissaries to Cairo to inquire
about Amin's position regarding the proposed action. Though
transferring any power of state to Amin was unthinkable, Cunningham was not sure the plan would work without Amin's

support. "We certainly won't have a smooth transition without it," he opined.

Amin listened to the delegation's presentation, then reviewed the matter with his associates. Later that week, he announced his opposition: "As we have stated on numerous occasions in the past, Palestine has been the home of the Arab people for thousands of years. Its borders are well established and our claim on it is without serious challenge. The United Nations has no authority whatsoever to seize our country, redefine its borders, and appropriate large portions of its territory to anyone. Much less to the Jewish interlopers who have invaded our lands."

British officials indicated they were prepared to go forward with the plan of partition without Amin's approval. A deadline of May 13, 1948, was set for British withdrawal. No one was certain what would happen next. They didn't have to wait long to find out.

✦ ✦ ✦ ✦ ✦

Faced with the real possibility that the UN would create a Jewish state in Palestine and impose it on Arabs living there, Amin directed Arabs to respond with acts of violence against Jews wherever and however targets were found. "The British have had enough. They are leaving. Just as I told you they would. They have had enough misery and are running back to England and their British lifestyle. We must do the same thing to the Jews—make life in Palestine so miserable for them that they prefer to leave rather than stay." Jamal, from his position as co-chairman of the Arab Higher Executive, made sure the message received wide distribution.

At first the response to Amin's call for violence was sporadic, but in the weeks that followed, it steadily grew in intensity. The first major attack came against a Jewish bus traveling on the coastal plain near Kfar Sirkin. An eight-man Arab squad from Jaffa ambushed the bus, killing five passengers and wounding many others. Half an hour later they ambushed a second bus, traveling southbound from Hadera, killing two more passengers. Not long after that, Arab snipers attacked Jewish buses as they rode along the streets of Jerusalem. Soon, attacks of that nature became a common occurrence.

As head of the Jewish Agency, David Ben-Gurion was hard-pressed by everyone to respond to the attacks. However, rather than simply calling on one of the paramilitary organizations to unleash retribution, Ben-Gurion chose to use the moment as a means of exerting his authority as putative head of a budding Jewish state. Instead of calling for attacks, he announced that henceforth all Jewish paramilitary organizations would now be under the authority of the Jewish Agency. Like many others, Ben-Gurion sensed that Jews were on the verge of establishing a political state, and he wanted their governing apparatus to look like a governing apparatus. That meant having a standing army capable of defending the state.

Since the establishment of the first Jewish settlements, Jewish paramilitary organizations had operated with almost complete autonomy. Naturally, Ben-Gurion's plan to make them accountable to the Jewish Agency met with resistance, but Ben-Gurion would not back down. "If we want to *be* a country, we have to *look* like a country," he often said. "And for that we need a standing army."

Of the paramilitary groups, Haganah was arguably the least aggressive of the defense groups and the one most nearly aligned with Ben-Gurion's views. Because of that, and because Haganah was the largest of the groups, Ben-Gurion hoped to fashion it into a military unit that could form the basis for the state's military. Haganah leaders did their best to comply with his expectation.

Irgun and Lehi were a different matter. Formed from a

Revisionist Zionist perspective—generally in accordance with the uncompromising views of Ze'ev Jabotinsky—they were less disciplined, more ruthless in tactics, and committed to obtaining Jewish control of Palestine in its entirety. They saw Ben-Gurion's practical approach as a compromise of Jewish identity and were adamantly opposed to a two-state scenario. Consequently, Lehi and Irgun leaders ignored Ben-Gurion's calls for reason and discipline and responded to Arab attacks in like manner. "They shoot us, we shoot them. They bomb us, we bomb them back." Their first responses to Arab violence included the placement of bombs in crowded Arab markets and at bus stops located in Arab districts.

✦ ✦ ✦ ✦ ✦

Like Ben-Gurion with the Jews, Amin understood that in order to be accepted as a political entity, Arabs in Palestine needed to conduct their corporate affairs as if they were a political state. Part of that included maintaining a disciplined, well-trained army. Using Jamal, who shuttled back and forth between Cairo and Jerusalem, Amin presented his desire to form an army to the Arab Higher Executive. "The UN will declare a Jewish state," he asserted. "We must be prepared to annihilate the Jews." After a brief debate, the executive agreed to raise an army, which they named the Army of the Holy War.

While Arab and Jewish paramilitary units continued to trade attacks in Palestine, Jamal, Salama, and Qadir began recruiting soldiers for an army. Amin, confined to Egypt and unable to travel freely, concentrated on raising money to supply and equip the army. Most of that effort was aimed at soliciting fellow Arabs, many of whom were hesitant to fund an army that ultimately benefited him. An army that perhaps might be used to their detriment one day in the not-so-distant future. Sensing their reluctance and suspicion, Amin encouraged members of the Arab League to form their own plan for the defense of Arab claims to the region. He preferred to do that for himself, without outside interference, but the cause of Palestine was a cause for the greater Arab community, too, and he thought they had a duty to participate in the region's defense.

In December 1947, Qadir and Salama traveled to Jerusalem for the first of many recruiting drives. Working from mosque to mosque, they traveled across the city and then the region in a systematized effort, informing each group about what they faced. "The British are leaving. The United Nations will declare a Jewish homeland, at least in parts of Palestine. For many thousands of years, this land has belonged to Arabs. Now, with one signature on a single piece of paper, they want to take it away from us. We must not let that happen. We must be prepared to fight to the death to save our families and their futures."

Audiences gave an overwhelming response to the appeal. Quicker than anyone thought possible, the army's ranks filled as Arabs rushed to prepare for the coming fight with the Jews. And still they kept coming. With so many able-bodied young men available, Qadir and Salama divided the recruits into two sections.

Qadir took one group and established a headquarters at Bir Zeit. From there he began attacking Jewish interests in and around the city. "We will train as we fight," he declared. "The day of war is at hand."

Salama took the second group, most of whom had military training of one form or another. With them, he assumed responsibility for operations in the Lydda and Ramla sectors, an area that included a portion of the main road between Tel-Aviv and Jerusalem. Both he and Qadir had impressive victories against Haganah units.

✦ ✦ ✦ ✦ ✦

As the Army of the Holy War enjoyed success, Arab League members grew worried. Although opposed to the creation of a Jewish state, members of the League were deeply divided by rivalry, suspicion, and jealousy. While Amin and his army triumphed in early clashes with the Jews, King Farouk gathered with the commander of the Egyptian army, General Ahmed al-Mawawi, to discuss the situation and mull over potential responses.

"I am deeply concerned by the growing power and influence of Amin al-Husseini," Farouk advised. "Not only is the Grand Mufti the most popular figure in Egypt, he is quickly becoming the most powerful."

"Yes, your majesty," General Mawawi replied. "Left unchecked, his success in Palestine will give him a tremendous base of support here in Cairo. Perhaps even enough to attempt a coup against the crown."

"What do you suggest as the proper way for us to go about battling the Jews and containing the mufti at the same time?"

"I think the Arab League should consider forming its own army," Mawawi answered. "That would provide the best solution to both situations. Give the League the ability to fight the Jews in its own name, while stifling the mufti's growing strength."

"Yes," Farouk agreed, "that is an excellent suggestion and one I have been contemplating for some time."

"It has the added advantage," Mawawi continued, "of putting the League in the position of controlling Palestine after victory is achieved."

Farouk smiled. "Yes, the League's army in control rather than the mufti's."

"You should suggest that when the ministers of the League meet again."

Farouk shook his head. "I think I shall not wait that long to address the situation but will contact him this afternoon."

After Farouk's meeting with General Mawawi was concluded, Ismail Sabry, son of the king's domestic policy advisor, contacted Said Ramadan. They met late that evening on a side street not far from Amin's residence. Sabry gave Ramadan a full account of the discussion he overheard. "The king is very worried about the Grand Mufti. He thinks the mufti's success in Palestine is making him too popular here in Egypt. His power is growing too strong. It is a view shared by all of the Arab League ministers."

Ramadan frowned. "Because of his popularity?"

"His popularity here, but that popularity is based on the victories of his army in Palestine."

Ramadan scowled. "Doesn't he realize the army is necessary for the defense of Arabs who live in Palestine?"

"They understand that, but it is seen also as a threat to neighboring Arab states."

"All of whom want to carve up pieces of Palestine for themselves."

Sabry nodded. "I am afraid so."

"What does Farouk plan to do?"

"He wants the Arab League to create its own army. That way, after victory, the Arab League will control Palestine."

"Do the others in the League want to follow Farouk's idea?"

"Farouk held several conversations by telephone with them this afternoon. Many of them have expressed an interest in such an army. They think it might be necessary to counter the perceived threat from the mufti. They do not like him and think he has ambitions beyond Palestine."

"How would they raise soldiers? Will the surrounding states contribute their own troops?"

"No. Farouk made that part very clear. He wants to recruit men for the army from Palestine. In the same areas as the Grand Mufti has been seeking recruits for his army. He says if they do that, they can keep the mufti's army from growing any larger."

Ramadan went directly from his meeting with Sabry to Amin's residence. It was late when he arrived, but Amin was waiting for him. "It is just as we suspected," Ramadan reported.

"They are building their own army?"

"Many of them want to. Farouk is behind it. General Mawawi supports the plan."

Amin rubbed his chin in thought. "How do they plan to do it?"

"They want to recruit soldiers from Palestine."

"From Palestine? They are not sending men from their own armies?"

Ramadan shook his head. "They want to get them from the same places we are recruiting. That's part of their plan to curtail us. Dry up our supply of recruits *and* outmaneuver us on the battlefield."

Amin was angry and once again felt betrayed by his fellow Arabs, but there was little he could do to stop the League, especially from his position in Cairo. All he could do was redouble his efforts to keep Salama and Qadir supplied with the weapons and ammunition they needed and hope their success continued.

✦ ✦ ✦ ✦ ✦

Not long after King Farouk polled Arab League ministers about forming an army, the League voted to do just that and created the Arab Salvation Army. Recruiters descended on Palestine and snapped up many, though by no means all, of the remaining volunteers not already enlisted with Amin's Army of the Holy War.

Much to Amin's dismay, Arabs living in Palestine quickly became confused about which army was which. As a result, many who might have joined the fight became frustrated and stayed at home. That, too, played into the Arab League's plan to contain Amin's ambitions while at least appearing to confront Jewish efforts to create a political state. They wanted to drive the Jews away, but they feared placing Amin in a position of military strength. He already held political power. That came from his considerable ability to sway an audience with his rhetoric. But an Amin al-Husseini with soldiers and weapons was more than they could bear. Or risk. For the League, expressions of Palestinian nationalism must be confined to only the options offered by the League.

TWENTYNINE

IN DECEMBER 1947, operatives from Irgun and Lehi threw pipe bombs at a crowd of Arab workers who were lining up to work at a refinery in Haifa. Six people were killed and forty-two injured. An angry Arab mob responded by roaming the streets randomly attacking Jews. Their actions left thirty-nine Jews dead. Fighting continued in Haifa until British soldiers intervened and reestablished order. That order was short-lived.

The following week, men from Palmach and the Carmeli Brigade, commando-style Jewish paramilitary units, attacked the Arab villages of Balad al-Sheikh and Hawassa. Dozens were killed and countless homes destroyed.

As fighting continued, most incidents occurred on the outskirts of the main towns. Snipers from both sides fired into houses, at pedestrians, and at vehicles traveling along the streets and highways. Bombs were planted and mines laid along suburban and rural roads. Despite attacks by Arab units and counterstrikes by Irgun and Lehi, most Jews maintained a primarily defensive posture, attacking only when attacked.

A few incidents, however, were indiscriminate. Arabs shot and killed a Jewish woman while she hung laundry on a line to dry, then shot at the ambulance that came to collect her body. And then at mourners attending her funeral. Roads between the Jewish settlements were blocked and, for some, food supplies became problematic. Those were uncoordinated attacks. Probing military operations in some instances, but nothing like a fully synchronized, well-laid strategic operation.

Beginning in January 1948, all of that changed as operations on both sides became increasingly militarized. Particularly in Jerusalem and Haifa, violent attacks increased. Riots, reprisals, and counter-reprisals followed each other in rapid succession. Isolated shootings faded, replaced by all-out battles between well-armed, well-trained units formed to fight in military style. Attacks against traffic, previously only a few indiscriminate rounds, became lethal ambushes with devastating consequences.

✦ ✦ ✦ ✦ ✦

By February, Amin convinced members of the Arab League that they had no choice but to defend Arab claims to Palestine with their national armies. "Your Arab Salvation Army will not be strong enough. Nor will my Army of the Holy War. You must commit regular troops to the cause. Fully-staffed armies equipped with modern weapons and modern machinery. And you must use it with the full intention of defeating the Jews and driving them into the sea!"

At last, Arab League ministers and generals realized the truth of Amin's plea and scheduled a meeting of military commanders to organize their coordinated military effort. Amin attended, accompanied by Hadad and Ramadan, who served as his advisors. Originally intended as a planning session, the meeting quickly devolved into petty arguments and endless negotiations over the organization of Palestinian field commands and the allocation of troops from the separate countries. Commanders of the Arab Salvation Army and of Amin's Army of the Holy War insisted on having command and control authority equal to that of their counterparts from other countries.

After intense debate, the Army of the Holy War, under the command of Salama and Qadir, was allocated the Lydda and Jerusalem districts, respectively. These were areas in which they already were active, and they lobbied hard to get them, rather than waiting to be handed an assignment to a remote location that would have sidelined their interests.

Ramadan was glad to have the assignment, given the other options, but the experience left him deeply suspicious of the Arab League in general and its military commanders in specific. "They have given us what we wanted, but the districts make the split in our army permanent and a matter of policy," he fretted. "That is why they finally agreed. They realized they could keep us permanently divided."

"We already are," Salama noted. "So the difference is the same for us. But why would they want to make sure we are separated?"

"Together, you and Qadir are a formidable force. Leaders from the Arab League think if you combined your forces you would take all of Palestine on your own. This way, you cannot combine your forces without League approval. It is a way of minimizing your involvement in the war and thus a way of minimizing your power and effectiveness."

Amin spoke up. "As you can see, leaders of the Arab League feel they are supplying the bulk of the troops and war materiel. They want to be in charge. Now *and* after the war. They want to control the entire region."

Qadir shook his head. "That will never happen."

✦ ✦ ✦ ✦ ✦

Four days after the Damascus meeting, the Arab League announced another meeting in Cairo. Amin met with Ramadan and Hadad to prepare for it. "We need five things from the Arab League," Amin outlined. "Greater Palestinian autonomy in areas evacuated by the British, appointment of a Palestinian-Arab representative to the League's general staff, formation of a Palestinian Provisional Government, a loan for the proposed Palestinian administration, and an appropriation of large sums to compensate Palestinian Arabs entitled to war damages."

"That's a lot to ask," Hadad worried.

"Yes, but we must be ready to declare our independence as soon as the British evacuate. And we must be ready to act like the legitimate state we claim to be. Ben-Gurion has been preparing the Jews to do this. We must do it, too. Not because they will do it, but because this is how governments act."

"I think you are correct," Ramadan commented. "But I agree with Hadad. It is a lot to ask from a partner as reluctant as the League has proven to be. I do not think ministers from the League will accept your terms. This is far beyond what they are willing to do."

Amin frowned. "You think they still see us as mere instruments of their design, for their purposes?"

Ramadan nodded. "We are window dressing. What they want is control of the entire Palestinian region. They only allow us to participate because they need you, the Grand Mufti, to manipulate the British and keep their withdrawal on schedule."

When the Arab League meeting was convened in Cairo a few days later, Amin made his demand. As Ramadan suggested, Arab leaders were not impressed. After the morning round of meetings, Amin took Hadad and Ramadan aside. "I do not like the way the meetings have gone."

"They are worried about an Arab state in Palestine under your control," Hadad agreed.

"And your time in Germany is becoming a problem," Ramadan added.

Amin was puzzled. "My time in Germany?"

"Yes," Hadad interjected. "They think you are more a disciple of Hitler than of Muhammad and that if you are the head of a strong and viable political state in Palestine, you will subsume all of your neighbors into a kingdom no one can resist, just as Hitler did."

"There is also a rumor," Ramadan added, "that you refuse to issue arms from the Higher Executive's cache to anyone except the Army of the Holy War."

Amin had a sheepish expression. "I have no choice. The League has not provided us with sufficient arms and munitions to meet our rising ranks. If I cannot supply my own army, why would I use what I have to supply someone else's?"

When the afternoon sessions began, Arab League members saw an opening with Amin's armament policy and used his refusal to arm other groups as a basis for rejecting all of his demands. Amin and those who were with him stormed from the meeting hall in protest.

✦ ✦ ✦ ✦ ✦

Though angry and bitterly disappointed by the Arab League's decision to deny his requests, Amin continued to plan and work to move his Army of the Holy War into an advantageous position. He reached out to others beyond the Arab League in an effort to locate funding. Forced to continue without League support, he used his position as Grand Mufti to cajole, convince, and badger the support he needed from non-governmental sources. And he made certain Qadir and Salama positioned the Army of the Holy War to assert control over Jerusalem and the surrounding region as soon as the British departed.

Late in February 1948, Salama and the troops under his command organized coordinated attacks against Jewish communities in central Palestine. Using car bombs aimed at the headquarters of the pro-Zionist *Palestine Post* newspaper, the Ben Yehuda Street market, and the Jewish Agency's offices, they killed eighty-five Jews and injured hundreds more. In response, Lehi placed mines on the Cairo-Haifa rail line near Rehovot. The resulting explosion killed twenty-eight and injured thirty-five, most of them Arabs.

With Haganah and other Jewish military groups distracted by Salama's action, Qadir and his unit occupied the citadel at Qastal Hill on the road from Tel-Aviv to Jerusalem. From there, high above the landscape, they rained down gunfire on all who attempted to pass, successfully prohibiting access to the Jewish sections of Jerusalem. A hundred thousand Jewish residents were trapped in the city and deprived of food.

To counter the Arab blockade, Jewish authorities attempted to supply the city using convoys of armored vehicles. They made multiple attempts to force their way past the hill, but each time suffered heavy losses of men and vehicles. Very quickly those attempts became futile.

Amin was encouraged by the results and thought it indicated that he was destined to be in power as the head of a Palestinian government. "Allah is with us," he averred. "Soon we will return to Jerusalem and take our rightful place among the heads of state."

By March, Qadir's blockade of Jerusalem placed Jewish residents in a dire situation. Low on food, without medical care, and unable to leave, they were desperate for relief. Equally desperate to reach them, Haganah resumed its attempts to run the blockade.

Using armored vehicles and driving at a high rate of speed, soldiers from Haganah attempted to roar past the hill and push through to the city with loads of supplies. Each time, however, just as before, Arab gunners inflicted a heavy toll. At most, only a few vehicles made it past. Most lay in ruins alongside the road, the supplies they carried strewn across the ground.

Early in April, Haganah gave up its attempts to get past Qastal Hill and launched a carefully planned assault to wrest control of it from Qadir and his men. After heavy fighting, they succeeded in taking the hill. One week later, though, Qadir and his men counterattacked and succeeded in retaking the top, forcing Haganah to retreat to the settlement of Motza below.

Tragically, during the fight, Qadir, the Army of the Holy War's most able field commander—Amin's cousin—was killed. His death left one half of Amin's army leaderless and demoralized. Two days later, troops from a Jewish commando unit arrived and recaptured the Qastal Hill. This time there was no Arab counterassault.

By then, members of the Arab League had withdrawn all support from the Army of the Holy War. Having exhausted its supplies in the attempt to defend Qastal Hill, and with nothing available for restocking the unit—and with Qadir dead—the men who had been under his command felt beaten down and defeated. The senior officers attempted to reorganize the unit on the plain between Jerusalem and Tel Aviv, but their hearts were no longer in the fight. A few days after the defeat at Qastal, the force that once had been Qadir's, the pride of the Army of the Holy War, collapsed and its members disappeared.

Upon learning the fate of Qadir and his unit, Salama's half of the army abandoned the fight, too. No one mutinied openly. No one challenged him for control. They simply camped one night, and when Salama awakened the next morning, they were gone. Vanished into the countryside, leaving him alone to face the rising sun.

With nothing more to do, Salama slipped away and made his way to Gaza. From there he returned to Cairo and reported to Amin.

Amin was distraught at news of the death of Qadir. They had been together a long time. War was approaching, however, and he knew he must move quickly to save his position. "Find Yasser Arafat," he directed Ramadan. "And bring him to me." Arafat was Amin's cousin. These were challenging times. When loyalty counted most, he often turned to family members, as he had with Qadir. Now he would with Arafat, too.

"Where is he?"

"He's a student at the university. Tell him I need him."

Ramadan had little difficulty locating Arafat and brought him to Amin the next day. Amin met with him alone. "As you are aware, our kinsman Qadir is dead."

"I heard the tragic news," Arafat replied. "Will you travel to Jerusalem to mourn his loss?"

"There is no time for that. And it is much too risky for me right now. If the British found me there, they would arrest me on the spot. And then where would we be?"

Arafat nodded thoughtfully. "I see your point."

"The Jews will declare their independence soon." Amin returned to the point of the conversation. "We must be ready."

"War is inevitable. Your father knew that when the Jews first started arriving."

Amin ignored the reference to his father. "War already is here," he corrected. "Qadir died defending our hold on the hill outside Jerusalem."

Arafat nodded once more. "You are so very right. How can I help?"

"I need you to assume leadership of the Army of the Holy War."

Arafat's eyes opened wide, but he made no attempt to decline. "As you wish. But I understand the army is in disarray."

"We will rejuvenate it," Amin assured. "We have no choice. This must be done."

"From where shall we find soldiers?"

"Salama will help you locate those who were with him. The

best should not be difficult to find. I will help you locate others to fill the ranks."

"From where?"

Amin smiled. "The Muslim Brotherhood. We can recruit them from right here in Egypt and train here as well." Arafat liked that idea.

With Ramadan and Hadad helping, Amin recruited members of the Brotherhood to fill the ranks of Arafat's army. On his own initiative, he approached the Saudis for financial support. "We must be ready," he told them. "War is at hand. The Jews intend to steal our land and wipe us out. We are the Fedayeen. The ones who sacrifice themselves for the sake of Islam. We must not allow those who oppose Allah to prevail."

Ibn Saud was not interested in helping, but many of his warlords were eager to assist. "The Jews are a blight on the world," they said. "Whatever we can supply, we do so as a gift." From them Amin received arms, armaments, and money. Most of the arms came from British stockpiles accumulated during the First and Second World Wars.

✦ ✦ ✦ ✦ ✦

On May 13, 1948, the British Mandate for Palestine expired, and the last remaining British army units boarded ships and withdrew. Just past midnight—early on the morning of May 14, 1948—prominent Jewish residents gathered at a theater in Tel Aviv where David Ben-Gurion and executives from the Jewish Agency proclaimed the creation of a Jewish state in Palestine.

Reading from the text of the official declaration establishing the state, Ben-Gurion intoned, "We declare that, with effect from the moment of the termination of the Mandate being tonight, the eve of Sabbath, the 6th Iyar, 5708, the 15th of May, 1948, until the establishment of the elected regular authorities of the state in accordance with the constitution which shall be adopted by the elected Constituent Assembly not later than the October 1, 1948, the People's Council shall act as a Provisional Council of State, and its executive organ, the People's Administration, shall be the Provisional Government of the Jewish State, to be called Israel."

As members of the Jewish Agency gathered at a table to sign the official documents, a tumultuous celebration broke out among the 250 invited guests. After a long and determined struggle, the state that Jews of Palestine and, indeed, Jews from all over the world had longed for was finally a reality.

THiRTY

ON MAY 15, 1948, the day after Ben-Gurion and executives from the Jewish Agency announced the formation of the state of Israel, the armies of Iraq, Syria, Jordan, and Egypt invaded Palestine. Units of the Egyptian army entered from the south, coming up the coast through Gaza. They advanced quickly and with devastating results.

Jordanian forces invaded from the east, crossing the Jordan River and approaching Jerusalem at a rapid pace. In a matter of days, they seized control of the region that lay beyond the Jordan in eastern Palestine. Stoked with the rush of almost instant success, King Abdullah's advisors urged him to press on. "Drive the Jews into the sea," one said.

"Divide the region across the middle and trap the Jews," another encouraged.

But despite their insistence, Abdullah was reluctant to press the fight and ordered his army to solidify control of the region known as the West Bank. "But linger to the east of Jerusalem," he cautioned. His primary concern was to deter other Arab states from thinking he was weak and thus attacking him. Secretly, he really did prefer the Jews to any of the Arab options at the time. Having made his statement, he was content to occupy the eastern side of Central Palestine, which was heavily populated by Arabs.

Having recently concluded the largest, most costly war in human history, major nations of the West were appalled at the outbreak of yet another conflict. Representatives from the US, UK, and a dozen other nations called for a meeting of the UN Security Council. Israel was not a UN member but had representatives present when the Security Council convened to address the situation. Abba Eban, a veteran Jewish diplomat, was deeply involved in the proceedings. The Arab cause was equally well represented, both from member states and from special envoys representing a number of Arab factions. Debate and negotiations were heated.

As Arab nations sent their armies into battle with Israel, Yasser Arafat and the newly rejuvenated Army of the Holy War joined the fight, too. Entering Palestine from the Sinai Desert where they had been training, they surged across the border, quickly seizing crucial towns and roads in the Negev. Rather than occupying the region, they attacked infrastructure—water supplies, electrical distribution lines, telephone and telegraph facilities—striking first one, then the other, then quickly moving on to the next target. They hit hard, moved fast, and lived off the land, supplying themselves with weapons, vehicles, and food captured along the way.

While Arab troops advanced from every direction against the newly declared state of Israel, Amin continued to lobby Arab League members to declare all of Palestine an Arab state. "We must issue our own declaration of independence," he stressed. "Create an Arab state and give our people something definite to fight for."

Arab leaders listened politely but declined to go that far. "First, we must win the war. Then we can talk about a political entity to govern the region."

Privately, Amin ranted to Salama. "I knew they were suspicious of me, but I did not know until today how deep that suspicion ran."

"Perhaps they will come around," Salama suggested. "A strong showing on the ground by Arafat will change things for us."

"I don't know." Amin sighed. "I am not sure we can ever create a Palestinian state with them as our sponsors. They have shown that they are not our allies."

Salama nodded. "I think we also have very different ideas about what Palestine should be."

"They treat me the way the British treated the Sharif—promise of support but always with their own interests in mind. Talking one way in public, while in private planning to act in an entirely different way."

✦ ✦ ✦ ✦ ✦

After enduring two weeks of humiliating defeat, Israeli forces obtained aircraft from Czechoslovakia and from agents operating surreptitiously in the United States. Within days of their arrival, the airplanes were made ready for combat and deployed against the Egyptian army in Gaza. With help from close air support, Israeli troops finally succeeded in halting the advance of Egyptian troops along the coast. With the Egyptians stymied, Israeli commanders turned their new air power toward the Negev and unleashed it against Arafat and the Army of the Holy War, containing them south of Beersheba.

With fighting at a stalemate, the UN Security Council took action, approving a measure declaring a truce. Folke Bernadotte, a veteran international diplomat from Sweden, was sent to Palestine to negotiate a permanent cessation in the fighting. Abba Eban accompanied him as his assistant. Bernadotte met with Israelis and Arabs but made no progress, and on July 8, 1948, fighting resumed.

After ten days more of fighting, a second truce was declared. The UN sent Bernadotte and Eban back again to negotiate. Bernadotte met with Jewish leaders and traveled to Cairo to meet with Amin. During those meetings, he proposed a different partition of Palestine from the one originally approved by the UN. All sides rejected the idea.

As armies prepared to resume fighting, Amin and his men leaked details of King Abdullah's previous discussions with Israeli representatives, including summaries of his conversations with Golda Meir in which King Abdullah indicated his preference for Jews over a government led by Amin. Using that information, Salama, Hadad, and others spread rumors among Arab leaders that Abdullah planned to reopen the bilateral negotiations he conducted with Israel before the war began.

In mock indignation, Amin confronted members of the Arab League about the matter. "He intends to sell all of us out to the Jews. Not only the Arabs living in Palestine but also those in Lebanon and Syria."

Members were at a loss to counter the accusation. "So, what do you propose?" someone asked.

"The only way forward for the Arab League now," Amin responded, "is to declare an independent Arab state and then fight for it with all our might."

✦ ✦ ✦ ✦ ✦

As the controversy about King Abdullah raged among members of the Arab League, Saleem Namir obtained a copy of the transcripts from Abdullah's meetings with Jewish Agency leaders. After reading it, he showed the documents to Abdullah. "This is the work of Amin al-Husseini."

Abdullah dismissed Namir's concern with a wave of his hand. "You might be right about the mufti, but it is nothing. We do not need to worry about him. He does not even have the support of the Arab League."

"He didn't before this," Namir responded. "But now that they have seen in print the things you said to Golda Meir, Arab League members are incensed."

"Why should they be worried about what I said to her?"

"Because it validates their opinion of you and your intentions toward them."

Abdullah arched an eyebrow. "And what do they think my intentions are?"

"They think that you wish to rule all of Palestine. And that you would rule over them if you were able."

Abdullah nodded. "I *do* wish to rule all of Palestine."

"But you can't say that," Namir argued. "Or let them believe it unchallenged."

Abdullah shrugged. "Why not?"

"Because if they see you as a threat, they will come against you. All of them as one."

Abdullah seemed to consider the point. "Then, what do you suggest I do?" he asked after a moment.

"Move against the Jews. Step up the attacks. In a single thrust, your army could slice Palestine in half. The Jews will be trapped."

Abdullah frowned. "But won't the others see that as exactly what they are afraid of? Jordan controlling all of Palestine?"

"No," Namir countered. "Arab League members think you favor the Jews over them and will not destroy the Jews. And they fear that once you have boxed in the Jews, you will turn on them and defeat them. The only way to disabuse them of that notion is to attack the Jews with ruthless power."

Abdullah considered the suggestion and, reluctantly, agreed. The following day, he ordered his army to engage the Israelis and continue its march westward. Very quickly, the army seized the eastern half of Jerusalem.

✦ ✦ ✦ ✦ ✦

Before the controversy with Abdullah faded, and before the full extent of Abdullah's military action was evident, Amin used the situation to pressure Arab League members for greater military action.

"See what he is doing?" Amin argued. "He is advancing westward. He intends to take all of Palestine for himself. You must act before he seizes everything. You must declare an Arab state over all of Palestine. And you must do it quickly."

Reluctantly, Arab League members acquiesced to Amin's demands. With unanimous support, they approved the establishment of the All-Palestine Government to take control of Palestine.

As a first step toward establishing that government, the Arab League convened a Palestinian National Council in Gaza. Amin, though absent from the proceedings, was appointed chairman. Jamal al-Husseini, Amin's cousin, once again stood in his place as proxy. At that gathering, the council enacted a series of resolutions forming the new government. Amin was unanimously elected its president. The government existed largely only on paper—it had no army, no legislature, and the only territory it controlled were areas secured by the Egyptian army.

Making matters even more tenuous, in assigning Amin the role of president, the Palestinian National Council made him only the head of state, not the head of government. The role of head of government—the office that ran the government on a day-to-day basis—was vested in the office of prime minister. To fill the post of prime minister, at least on a temporary basis, the council turned to Hussein Pasha, a former prime minister of Egypt. Thus, the All-Palestine Government relied on the Egyptian army for security, and a former Egyptian politician controlled its daily function.

When the initial meeting ended, Jamal, Arafat, Ramadan, and the others traveled to Cairo to explain the results to Amin. He listened attentively, then commented, "At least they have taken a step in the right direction. One that should have been taken from the start, but at least we are moving toward an Arab government for Palestine and one that is under our direction."

After an exchange of glances among the others, Arafat argued, "That is not exactly how the League sees it."

Amin frowned. "What do you mean?"

"League members view creation of the All-Palestine Government primarily as a way to prevent Abdullah from incorporating the entire region into a Jordanian federation."

Amin nodded. "I understand that."

"But that's not all," Arafat added.

Amin was irritated. "What more could there be?"

"They don't want Abdullah to control the region, but they don't want *you* to have power over it, either."

Amin was exasperated. "They just named me head of the All-Palestine Government."

Arafat concurred. "Yes. But they made you head of state, not head of government. And they installed that government in an area solely under the control of the Egyptian army."

Ramadan spoke up. "The real power is with Pasha. The prime minister."

Amin looked away. "An Egyptian."

"Yes."

"Egypt is in control of everything," Amin sighed.

"Very much so," Arafat said.

"And," Salama added, "it's a little worse than that."

Amin scowled at him. "Worse?"

"We have learned that Saleem Namir is Abdullah's advisor. He has great influence over Abdullah and is coordinating his efforts with the League."

Arafat added, "Namir knows what the League members want and rather than fighting them over it or exposing their true intentions, he is coordinating with them to limit your effectiveness as a means of increasing Abdullah's control."

Ramadan added, "The All-Palestine Government is merely a means for all of them to keep you in check and get what they want."

Amin stared out the window. The thought that Namir, his childhood nemesis, still was working against him filled him with rage to the core of his being. So childish. So evil. So utterly. . .inexpressible. And yet he chose to leave it there, unexpressed, and instead asked coldly, "They are that afraid of me?"

"Yes," Arafat replied. "They are very afraid of you."

✦ ✦ ✦ ✦ ✦

Although still living in Cairo when elected as president of the All-Palestine Government, and fully aware of the government's limitations, Amin began at once to plan his administration. Working with Hadad, Salama, and Ramadan, he settled on the appointment of administration officials and arranged the details necessary for a move to Gaza, where the government planned to establish its temporary capital, pending a final move to Jerusalem. He also developed a plan to help with the war effort.

One day, as they paused for lunch, Amin related, "I know this war has gone badly for us. But I think we can turn it around in a moment."

Ramadan looked curious. "How will we do that?"

"First, we must put an end to this latest effort by the UN to impose the Jews on us."

"There is not much we can do about the UN," Hadad said.

"Of course there is," Amin responded.

"What can we do?"

"We can assassinate the UN negotiator," Amin suggested.

Hadad had a startled expression. "Bernadotte?"

"Yes."

"Impossible."

Amin shook his head. "Not impossible. Just a bit of a challenge." He was serious about assassinating Bernadotte and asked a servant to bring Aref to the study. When he arrived, Amin excused himself from the others and met with Aref alone.

"How may I help you today?" Aref asked.

Amin avoided eye contact. "I have come to the conclusion that someone must eliminate Bernadotte."

"The UN negotiator?"

"Yes."

"How might that happen?"

Amin glanced toward the door. "Perhaps a car bomb," he suggested. "Or a lone gunman rushes his car. Something like that."

They talked awhile longer, but the meeting didn't last long, and Amin never issued a direct order, but Aref left the residence with the sense that he had been directed to assassinate Bernadotte. He began that day planning how to do it.

✦ ✦ ✦ ✦ ✦

Aref worked fast and within days left Cairo for Jerusalem. Before he reached the city, however, gunmen from Lehi, one of the radical Jewish paramilitary units, did his job for him. As Bernadotte traveled through Jerusalem in an open car, a jeep blocked the street, then someone from the jeep rushed the car and discharged a barrage of gunfire into the back seat where Bernadotte sat next to a French army officer. Bernadotte was killed instantly. The French officer next to him was critically wounded. Both men were transported to Mount Scopus Hospital, where they were both pronounced dead on arrival.

The United Nations and most nations of the world condemned the action. Israeli authorities launched a manhunt to locate and capture those who were responsible for the attack. Amin was distraught, but not over grief at the loss of human life. He had planned to use the assassination as a means of gaining leverage with Arab League members. To show them he was a man of decision and authority. "Now," he lamented, "that advantage is lost."

✦ ✦ ✦ ✦ ✦

On October 1, 1948, the All-Palestine Government issued a declaration of independence and asserted its authority over the whole of Palestine, with Jerusalem as its eventual capital once the war was won. At the same time, Amin named Ahmed Hilmi Abd al-Baqi as prime minister. Hilmi then announced his cabinet members, comprised of people previously selected by Amin, most of whom were Amin's relatives and followers, though he also included representatives of other factions of the Palestinian ruling class. Jamal al-Husseini was designated foreign minister. Raja al-Husseini was appointed defense minister. Michael Abcarius would serve as finance minister and Anwar Nusseibeh secretary of the cabinet. Once the declaration was issued and the positions announced, Amin and the ministers who lived outside of Palestine headed for Gaza to take up their new posts.

At Amin's insistence, one of the new government's first acts was to designate the Army of the Holy War the new country's official national army. An army for the stated purpose of liberating

Palestine from Jewish control. Amin wanted to name Yasser Arafat as the army's official commander but was forced by the Egyptians, who still controlled the only areas over which the government could rule, to name someone else. After deliberation, Amin settled on Umar al-Husseini, a distant cousin.

Egyptian officials took the matter under consideration and debated how to handle the situation. "The mufti thinks he is in control of an actual government. In reality, he is the titular head of an Egyptian zone."

"We provide security. The only area he controls is the area we have established."

Mohamed Naguib, commander of Egyptian forces in Palestine, was in attendance. "Nevertheless," he advised, "we should attempt to work with the Army of the Holy War. They control a great many men, and the Grand Mufti is popular among them all."

Reluctantly, the others conceded the point. Over the next several days, they worked out the details of coordinating actions involving the various national armies with those of the All-Palestine Government.

Afterward, Naguib was sent to brief Amin on military arrangements for the new government. In the discussion with Naguib, Amin learned that Naguib was a member of the Muslim Brotherhood and very dissatisfied with the direction events had taken.

"We should have occupied Palestine as soon as the British left," Naguib groused. "And declared the establishment of an independent Arab state over the entire region."

"I tried to convince members of the Arab League to do that very thing," Amin replied. "But they would not."

Naguib nodded. "I know. King Farouk is weak and Egyptian society is corrupt. The others are much the same."

"The Muslim Brotherhood must change that."

"We are doing our best to restore the integrity of our people,"

Naguib assured. "But it is difficult when they see the conduct of their leaders."

"Then the leaders must be replaced," Amin replied. "Leadership must be given to men of upright hearts and devoted purposes."

"Yes," Naguib agreed, "but I do not think the time is right for such a huge undertaking."

Amin gave an indulgent smile. "The time is never right for those who seek to avoid it."

Naguib seemed to agree but said, "Let us conclude this war, then we will make changes."

✦ ✦ ✦ ✦ ✦

King Abdullah responded to the formation of the All-Palestine Government and the establishment of an army for it by convening a Palestinian Congress. Saleem Namir served as secretary. At Abdullah's direction, delegates to that congress asserted authority over all of Palestine. Their action posed a direct challenge to the decisions made by Amin and ministers in Gaza. At Namir's urging, Abdullah ordered Lieutenant-General John Bagot Glubb—known as Glubb Pasha, one of Jordan's most courageous leaders—to disarm the Army of the Holy War.

That order was carried out by the Jordanian army with ruthless efficiency. Arab League members, forced to either stand aside or openly confront Abdullah's army, chose to yield to the king's desire and watch as he systematically disarmed many of the best units of the All-Palestine Government's army.

Once again, Amin found he had been betrayed by those who were supposedly sworn to help him. Dejected and dismayed, he renewed his earlier commitment to kill Abdullah. This time adding Saleem Namir to the threat.

✦ ✦ ✦ ✦ ✦

When the All-Palestine Government issued its declaration of independence, Arab League members quickly recognized the new government. Great Britain and the United States, however, refused. In a joint communique, representatives from both governments stated, "Amin al-Husseini's role in World War II can be neither forgotten nor pardoned and precludes him from further involvement in Palestine's political future."

Following the lead of the US and UK, other non-Arab nations refused to recognize the new government. Isolated and totally dependent upon Egypt for survival, the All-Palestine Government quickly became irrelevant among the nations of the world. Things were not much better for the government on a regional basis, either.

The government had no money of its own and operated only under the supervision of Egypt. As a result, units of the Army of the Holy War that remained after Abdullah's disarmament were generally ineffective in battle. Poorly equipped and poorly trained, the ranks gradually dwindled away.

By late October, the All-Palestine Government was a nonentity, once again existing only in theory. With the Israeli army advancing into Gaza, Amin and the ministers were forced to flee. They relocated the government to Cairo, becoming a government-in-exile, but by then the impotence of the effort was obvious. Gradually, the All-Palestine Government lost all importance.

THIRTYONE

MEANWHILE, IN EGYPT, Hassan al-Banna and the Muslim Brotherhood were deeply dissatisfied with King Farouk. Having come to power at the age of sixteen, he was too young and too immature to rule effectively without proper guidance, which he did not receive, and spent most of his reign indulging in Western pleasures, rather than devoting himself to Islamic teaching and the proper Muslim lifestyle. Time and again, Banna spoke against him, telling men of the Brotherhood, "Our king has forsaken Allah. He does nothing to lead the country in righteousness and devotion to the teachings of our forebears."

Finally someone asked, "Then what should we do?"

"As men of Allah," Banna replied, "as men of the Quran, we must cut him off from influencing our people."

"Cut him off?"

"A man who has the Quran and does not follow it is no better than the infidel who does not believe at all."

"The king is an infidel?"

"He is to us."

"And you are saying he should be executed?"

Banna hesitated. "It is a terrible thing to kill the king, and that I should not like to do. But he must be placed in a position from which he can no longer influence our people. We must act to purge our country of his corrupt leadership. Otherwise, we will be validating the message of his actions. We will be saying to our people that the way he lives is the proper way for us all to live. And *that* we cannot do."

Meanwhile across town, Amin, his dreams and visions for Palestine in ruins, struggled between periods of deep depression and seemingly uncontrollable anger. He was supposed to be the ruler of Palestine. To do great things. Be a man of note. His own father had said so from his deathbed. After years of struggle, and at no small risk to himself, he had succeeded in orchestrating events in his favor. Members of the Arab League promised to help. Promised to send men. Armies, even. Pledged themselves to do it. To support an Arab government—by Arabs, for Arabs—in a land that had been the Arab ancestral home for thousands of years. But when the moment came for his fellow Arabs to act, they had acted only out of their own self-interests. Greed and avarice ruled the day. And all to his humiliation. How could they do that? How could they forsake all that he had done? All that they had done. All that Allah had done.

After days of alternately sitting in a chair, staring out the window, and raging around like an animal, shouting at everyone and everything, Amin had a moment of peace and calm. In that moment, he became keenly aware of his circumstances. The precariousness of his position. "Members of the Arab League don't merely want me on the sideline," he mumbled to himself. "They want me dead." His eyes opened wide in panic. "They mean to kill me. But what can I do? How can I stop them?"

After a moment, a smile came to Amin. Not a kind smile. Or a happy smile. Not even a sane smile. And more than a sinister smile. "I must get to them first," he whispered. And for that there was only one person who could help. "Banna."

With a sudden sense of urgency, even desperation, Amin called for a car and hurried across town. He found Banna at home, seated in a chair in the corner of his study, and equally discomfited.

"Just the person I need to see!" Banna exclaimed as Amin entered the room.

"And you are the person *I* need to see."

"What has happened?"

"The Egyptian government has shown us no support for the All-Palestine Government."

"I think they—"

"They sent the army to fight the Jews," Amin acknowledged. "And yes, they've occupied Gaza. But not for the sake of a Palestinian government. Not for the sake of giving Palestinian Arabs control of their own destiny. And certainly not in furtherance of a plan they received from Allah."

Banna nodded his head slowly. "Only to spread and enlarge their own power. The Egyptian government is morally corrupt and devoid of any purpose except indulging in an orgy of Western pleasures."

"And *we* are utterly humiliated because of it," Amin responded.

"Yes, it is a disgrace."

"I am humiliated!" Amin shouted. "Farouk. Abdullah. All of them. They talk and talk and do nothing. And now I fear they mean to kill me." He looked over at Banna with a crazed expression. "I *know* they mean to kill me."

Banna sat up straight. "You have some news of this?"

"I feel it in my heart."

"Then we should not wait. We should do something about it now."

That afternoon, Amin and Banna devised a scheme of bombings meant to end Farouk once and for all. "And if we cannot kill him," Banna said, "at least we can destabilize the government and remove him from power."

"I want him dead," Amin snarled. "I want them *all* dead."

Banna frowned. "All?"

"All of the heads of the governments who call themselves the Arab League."

✦ ✦ ✦ ✦ ✦

In November 1948, operatives from the Muslim Brotherhood launched a series of bombings that rocked Egypt, killing an array of government ministers. Authorities suspected the Muslim Brotherhood was behind the blasts and, although they had no proof to substantiate their suspicions, began arresting members of the Brotherhood wherever they were found. With King Farouk's blessing, Mahmoud el-Nokrashy, the prime minister, issued an order banning the Muslim Brotherhood from Egypt.

Wave after wave of arrests swept across Egypt, each more intense than the others. Banna avoided the police but after a month of dodging them and hiding, he made his way to Amin's residence. "Can you help?" he asked in desperation.

Amin was all too glad to help and, after a day to make arrangements, transported Banna in the back of a produce truck to a safe house on the outskirts of the city. With Banna out of the way, Amin assumed control of the bombing plot. Using Salama, Hadad, and others, the bombings continued despite the arrests and despite efforts of the police to discover the identity of the assailants.

After repeated attempts to eliminate senior government officials, and finding only partial success, Amin turned to a more precise method. "We need a gunman," he told Ramadan.

"For what purpose?"

"Bombings are good, but we need to target specific people. For that, bombing is imprecise. You can find me an assassin?"

"Trained?"

"It does not matter," Amin said. "Find someone willing to do whatever it takes and send him to me."

A few days later, Abdel Meguid Ahmed Hassan, a student at King Fuad University, came to Amin. "You wished to speak with me?"

"Yes," Amin replied.

They sat in the study that day and talked, and in Ahmed, Amin found precisely the person he wanted. A member of the Brotherhood who was incensed at the government crackdown. "We cannot allow this to continue," Ahmed vowed. "Something must be done." And with that, the plan began.

✦ ✦ ✦ ✦ ✦

Three weeks later, as Nokrashy ambled along the corridor of the Interior Ministry building, Ahmed appeared. Dressed in an army uniform, he encountered no difficulty in gaining close proximity to the prime minister. As Nokrashy drew near, Ahmed drew a pistol from a holster at this side and fired five shots. Nokrashy collapsed to the floor and was dead.

✦ ✦ ✦ ✦ ✦

With Banna under his protection—and having successfully orchestrated the assassination of the prime minister—Amin realized he was in a position to seize control of the Muslim Brotherhood. He'd already done that in one sense, but most Brotherhood members expected Banna to one day return. Some already were planning for that very day. In order to take control, Amin would have to remove Banna permanently. Doing that would be tricky. Banna was loved and respected by everyone. Eliminating him would be risky. For an operation such as that, he would need a devious, underhanded, conniving person and he knew just the one—Yasser Arafat, his cousin.

With the Army of the Holy War once more in disarray, Arafat had retreated to Cairo when the All-Palestine Government departed Gaza. Amin sent for him and Arafat responded immediately. They met at Amin's residence, where he explained the situation. Arafat was glad to participate, and a plan quickly developed.

The following day, Amin called Salama to the study. When they were alone, he spoke, "I have received word that Banna's location has been disclosed."

Salama looked worried. "He is in danger?"

"Yes."

"What should we do?"

"Find Yasser. Tell him to send a detachment of men to move him to a new location."

"Do we have a new location?"

"Yes."

"Does Arafat know of it?"

"You will tell him."

"Me?" Salama was startled. "I know of no such place."

Amin smiled. "I will tell you the location." Then he whispered the location in Salama's ear.

The following day, a detachment of men under Yasser Arafat's command arrived at the safe house to move Banna. Salama was there to assist in packing his belongings. When everything was loaded and ready, Banna was placed in the back seat of a car with a man seated on either side. A driver and guard rode up front. Arafat led the way in a separate car. Salama followed in a third.

From the safe house, the three cars made their way toward

the opposite side of town. As they turned the corner on a busy street, a rocket was fired from a rooftop. The rocket struck the car in which Banna rode and exploded. Pieces of the automobile and parts from the bodies of its occupants were tossed into the air by the blast. Arafat leapt from his car and began shooting in the direction from which the rocket came, but by then the assailants had disappeared.

When news of Banna's death reached Amin, he tore his clothes and fell to the floor, weeping and wailing in grief. "How many more of us must die?" he lamented. "How many more of us must give our lives for the cause of Islam?"

The next day, Amin issued a public statement blaming Banna's death on King Farouk and the climate of injustice fomented by his government. "They have persecuted members of the Muslim Brotherhood solely because they are more devoted to Allah than to the king, just as the Quran commands us. Because they seek to live a holy life—a life in service to Allah and not in servitude to the monarchy—they are slaughtered on the streets of this great city. This is a sad day for Islam, a sad day for Arabs, and a sad day for the people of Egypt. They deserve a government that promotes the worship of Allah and encourages the life of devotion to the Muslim lifestyle. Instead, they have received a king more profligate that any Western infidel, and more corrupt than the Jews who threaten our brethren in Palestine."

Farouk was outraged by the statement and, but for the fact that he was the Grand Mufti of Jerusalem, would have ordered Amin's death immediately. That, however, would have caused more trouble for him than he already faced. Instead, death squads were let loose and went on a rampage through the city, arresting members of the Muslim Brotherhood that had been missed before. Several were executed on the spot. A great commotion followed and, in the turmoil, rumors about Amin's involvement in Banna's death were lost.

✦ ✦ ✦ ✦ ✦

With Banna no longer present, Amin stepped forward to fill the Muslim Brotherhood leadership void. He did not assume formal leadership, but as the Grand Mufti of Jerusalem, he was in the unique position of being a member of the organization and enjoying the freedom to move about openly in public. He used that position and access to assert dominion and control over the Brotherhood. Likewise, as the Grand Mufti, members of the Brotherhood turned to him for guidance and direction, never once suspecting that he was the one who orchestrated Banna's demise.

As Amin solidified his position of leadership with the Muslim Brotherhood, he still harbored resentment against members of the Arab League, and his thoughts turned to settling matters in a more dramatic fashion. Particularly regarding King Abdullah of Jordan and Saleem Namir, Abdullah's most trusted advisor.

Once again, he turned to Salama for assistance. They discussed the matter while seated in the garden behind the residence. "I have been thinking lately of this matter with King Abdullah," he began.

"And of his lackey, Saleem Namir, no doubt," Salama added.

"Very much so."

"This would be an excellent time to address that matter."

"Yes." Amin nodded. "Rather a drastic measure but one that must be done, I'm afraid."

"An operation of that type would require serious men."

"With discipline."

"And training."

Amin looked over at Salama and smiled. "Then we should get to it. Now while we have men of that type available."

Salama pushed himself up from his chair and stood. "Consider it done." He turned to leave, then paused and glanced back at Amin. "This will take a while to put together. You understand that, don't you?"

"I realize the logistics of the matter pose a challenge." Amin smiled once more. "But I have every confidence you, of all people, are equal to the task."

✦ ✦ ✦ ✦ ✦

After careful observation and inquiry, Salama singled out four Muslim Brotherhood members who appeared to be the most capable. One an expert in explosives, another an expert marksman, and a third a notable driver. The fourth, Mustafa Ashu, who grew up in Jerusalem but came to Egypt during the war with Israel, was regarded as a utility man, capable of handling almost any situation with adequate effect. He was the one with whom Salama chose to coordinate the group's activities. Salama made the decisions himself, avoiding any further involvement of Amin in the matter.

When he'd settled on the team members, Salama arranged a meeting with Ashu to inform him of the mission. "We are interested in settling some old scores," Salama explained. "You have been chosen to participate."

Ashu had a puzzled expression. "What kind of scores?"

"No one who makes peace with the Jews can be allowed to live."

Amin's revenge was deeper, going back to the insults Abdullah uttered during his earlier meetings with Golda Meir, who was the primary mediator between the Jews in Palestine and British authorities. And also to the antagonistic nature of his childhood relationship with Namir, but Salama did not mention any of that. "You and the team will conduct an operation to address Abdullah's betrayal of the Arab people in his overtures to the Jews."

"I hate the Jews," Ashu muttered.

"Which makes you the perfect person to lead this mission."

"I should be happy to take the revenge myself."

"Allah takes revenge," Salama said. "We are but the instruments of his wrath."

"Then we shall be a sharp sword in the executioner's hand."

With the team selected, and Ashu in place as its leader, Salama took them aside to begin research and training for the mission.

THIRTYTWO

BY WINTER OF 1948, Israel's battle for independence was winding down toward an obvious end. Fighting between organized armies gradually ceased and, in the spring of 1949, negotiations for a formal settlement began. As those talks proceeded, an overarching agreement between all individual parties proved elusive, resulting in separate agreements between Israel and each of its combatants.

On February 24, 1949, Israel signed an armistice agreement with Egypt, ending the conflict with its primary opponent. In March, an armistice was reached with Lebanon. The following month, Israel and Jordan signed an agreement as well, and in July a settlement was finally obtained with Syria.

At the war's end, Israel possessed all of the area assigned to it by the UN plan of partition, along with significant sections of Palestine that had been originally reserved for the proposed Arab state. When asked if Israel intended to relinquish those additional areas, Ben-Gurion replied, "If the war had resulted in Arab forces controlling part of the land originally allocated for us, do you think they would give it back?"

The defeat suffered by Arab forces and the resulting territorial changes cast doubt on the leadership capabilities of Amin and the Arab Higher Executive. Those doubts were not only felt by officials outside of Palestine but also by many Arabs within Palestine who wondered if they might not be better served by someone else. Amin seemed oblivious to the implications of the resounding Jewish victory and to the doubts of Palestinian Arabs.

News of the final settlement between Israel and its Arab neighbors reached Amin at his residence in Cairo. That news sent him into yet another fit of rage. "Once again, our fellow Arabs have betrayed us," he roared. "First, they pledged to defend Arab sovereignty, then they refused to fight the war as if to win it. Then they pledged to support and defend the All-Palestine Government, only to use it as a device to control us and even then, they withdrew their support when we needed it the most. And now, after stating they would never accept a Jewish state, they have negotiated and signed formal agreements with it."

"The Arab forces were beaten," Ramadan noted.

"Because they would not fight to win," Amin retorted. "They only fought to protect their own positions and interests. They only fought to enlarge their borders. They didn't fight to defeat the Jews. They only fought to obtain a little slice of Palestine for themselves."

"And now we have a Jewish state."

"Yes," Amin continued. "A Jewish state they all swore they would never allow."

"But they haven't actually recognized that state."

"In signing agreements with the Jews, they recognized their state's legitimacy." Amin shook his head in disgust. "A Jewish political state in Palestine, legitimized before all the world by its Arab neighbors. Again, something all of them swore they would not do."

Ramadan nodded. "The Arab League is rather like the British."

"Exactly," Amin replied. "They are traitors to us just as the British were and just as the French were. But unlike the French and British, members of the Arab League are fellow Arabs. Which makes their traitorous acts a betrayal of Allah. They have made themselves twice the evil of the infidels." Amin paused to consider the point. "No, they are ten times the evil of the infidels."

✦ ✦ ✦ ✦ ✦

If the Arab League and its constituent ministers proved inadequate in expressing the Islamic sentiment that Amin sought, the Muslim Brotherhood did not. Its Salafi message of a lifestyle devoted to Allah and the teachings of the Quran continued strong and unabated, despite the outcome of the war in Palestine. Because of its clear and concise call, the Brotherhood appealed to Arab men of every age who were eager to join.

Despite persecution from the Egyptian government, or perhaps because of it, Brotherhood membership steadily increased across the Arabian Peninsula, where it found its most radical expression and deepest support among the Wahabi. The Brotherhood also found acceptance in nations beyond Egypt where it enjoyed strong growth, though not at the pace apparent in Arab countries.

One of the men to whom the Brotherhood's message appealed strongly was Sayyid Qutb, an Egyptian civil servant. Inspired by the things he heard from Brotherhood members, he joined the Muslim Brotherhood at the height of the war with Israel. The group's call to devotion of oneself in service to Allah in a way that penetrated every aspect of life was particularly appealing to him. And, as a civil servant, the Brotherhood's intention to return Egypt to the true Islamic way, as a political entity, convinced

Qutb that the Brotherhood was the real and actual nation of Islam.

Right from the beginning, Qutb was a devoted Brotherhood member, volunteering for any task that needed attention. Through that involvement, he caught Ramadan's attention, and after learning of Qutb's superior intellect and ability, he mentioned Qutb to Amin. Always interested in new talent, Amin arranged for the two of them to talk.

At that meeting, Qutb showed Amin an article he recently published entitled "The America That I Have Seen." Amin glanced over it, then asked, "You have been to America?"

"Yes," Qutb replied. "I only recently returned."

"So, this article is based on your personal observations."

"Yes, the things I saw and experienced."

The article was critical of life in the United States—American materialism, its preoccupation with individual freedom over all else, a pervasive desire for the attainment of wealth, and rampant racism convinced—and vividly portrayed the underbelly of American society as rotten to the core. Amin was energized by what he read. "'They are the Great Satan,'" he quoted from the article.

"The one who has corrupted the world," Qutb added.

"Jews corrupted the United States. Then the United States corrupted its allies."

Qutb agreed. "Precisely what I saw."

Amin looked over at him. "Come to work for us."

"To work for you?"

"The Muslim Brotherhood," Amin explained. "Come to work for us full time." It sounded more like a command than a request.

Qutb was caught off guard. "Doing what?" he asked finally.

Amin pointed to the article. "Doing this."

A few days later, Qutb resigned from his position with the Egyptian civil service and reported for duty with the Muslim Brotherhood. Amin assigned him as a writer for the Brotherhood's weekly paper, *Al-Ikhwan al-Muslimin*. Before long, Qutb was the paper's editor. Not long after that, he was placed in charge of the Brotherhood's propaganda operations, too.

From there, Qutb's intellect and training helped him rise quickly through the Brotherhood's ranks. Not long after taking over the propaganda operation, he was added to the working committee—the standing committee that oversaw the Brotherhood's day-to-day operations. Based on his work in that capacity, he was elevated to the guidance council, which had assumed formal responsibility for the supreme leadership of the Brotherhood. From new member to the highest levels of leadership, his was a meteoric rise.

✦ ✦ ✦ ✦ ✦

By July 1951, Salama and the assassination team sent to deal revenge to Abdullah were in place, situated and unnoticed in Amman, the capital of Jordan. Informants had been obtained, and all was going well for their plan to kill the king with a catastrophic explosion, probably in the Eid al-Adha, a huge festival that celebrated the willingness of Abraham to sacrifice his son in obedience to God's command. That festival was scheduled for September.

With everything running on schedule, Salama was set to enjoy a relaxing moment, perhaps even a vacation to the mountains. Then, in July, Riad Bey al-Solh, a former Lebanese prime minister, was attacked and killed by three gunmen as he made his way through the Amman airport. The gunmen were members of the Syrian Social Nationalist Party who acted in revenge for the execution of Antoun Saadeh, a Lebanese politician who had been executed by the Lebanese government for alleged subversive activity. Saadeh had been instrumental in founding a Lebanese opposition political party. His death was widely viewed as a political reprisal. Solh's death was an attempt to settle that score.

Solh was a close personal friend of King Abdullah, and although he was Lebanese, he was killed on Jordanian soil. Abdullah, no doubt, felt a sense of responsibility for his old friend's death and insisted that Solh be accorded every honor available, including burial in East Jerusalem, an area of the city that Jordan controlled. At Abdullah's insistence, Solh's body was transported to Jerusalem, where an elaborate funeral service was planned. Abdullah announced that he would attend the service.

Abdullah's attendance at the funeral placed him on Jerusalem soil, which Salama knew very well. It also placed him in a city where Salama had access to many resources not available to him in Amman. Namely, family and friends who would supply anything he lacked and cover for him if things went wrong. The possibility of assassinating Abdullah during that trip was tantalizing, but more information was needed.

Salama contacted his network of Jordanian informants to find out if funeral details were available. Within hours, he received a copy of the king's official schedule providing details of the funeral and the king's associated activities afterward.

The funeral was set for a weekday at Al-Aqsa Mosque on Temple Mount. Crowds were expected to be enormous. Amin thought that might offer a great opportunity to kill Abdullah but with little hope of escaping, as the streets would be filled with mourners. The following Friday, Abdullah was scheduled to return to the mosque for weekly prayers, then attend a private meeting with Israeli officials. No one in the Jordanian cabinet supported the Israeli meeting but there was little they could do to stop the king or persuade him otherwise.

Having considered the king's schedule, Salama decided the Friday prayer service might afford the better opportunity for them. They still could attend the funeral, prepared to act, but if they were unable to get close enough, they would try again on Friday. With little time to waste and no time to prepare, Salama swung into action. He obtained a pistol and an automobile, then picked up Mustafa Ashu and they started toward Jerusalem.

As planned, Salama and Ashu attended the funeral for Solh but, as Salama expected, the area was packed shoulder to shoulder with mourners and onlookers. He and Ashu watched from a distance, hoping not to call attention to themselves. Afterward, they spent the night with Salama's family. He told no one why they were there except that they had business to attend to regarding their work with the Muslim Brotherhood.

On Friday, King Abdullah attended the prayer service at Al-Aqsa Mosque on Temple Mount, just as indicated by the schedule Salama had received. During the service, a crowd gathered outside the building, but nothing like the size of the one earlier that week for the funeral. Security, however, was tight around the building. Salama and Ashu were not able to enter it, but they found a place to stand near a spot where Salama was certain Abdullah would pass as he departed.

When the service ended, people who'd been inside began leaving. Salama took the pistol from the waistband of his trousers and pressed the grip into Ashu's hand. "Take it," he whispered. "And do what must be done."

Ashu took the pistol from Salama, tucked it behind the belt of his trousers, and covered it with his shirt, then made his way through the crowd toward the mosque entrance. Moments later, Abdullah appeared in the doorway as he emerged from the building, flanked by bodyguards. Salma watched from a distance as Ashu stepped forward boldly, drew the pistol from beneath his shirt, and fired three shots at point-blank range into Abdullah's body. As the hot lead ripped through his flesh, the king shrank back, his eyes wide with fright. He seemed to stand there for a moment, as if he'd been turned into a statue, then a shudder ran through him and he collapsed.

At the same time, and seemingly in the same moment, Abdullah's bodyguards returned gunfire. Ashu's body wheeled first this way, then that as the men emptied their side arms in anger. The hail of gunfire seemed so complete, so intense, and so awful that it held his body erect merely by the momentum and force of the bullets. As if gravity somehow were startled and confused, too, and forgot to do its job. But when the shooting stopped and Ashu's body was suddenly motionless, he dropped to the ground in a crumpled heap.

At first the crowd was aghast and stared at the scene as it unfolded, as if they, too, were frozen in place. Then all at once they turned in unison and stampeded from the mount, screaming and shouting in a panic-stricken melee. In the confusion that followed, Salama blended into the crowd and hurried away as one of them.

The following week, Jordanian police rounded up ten men they claimed were responsible for the murder of King Abdullah. Six of them were Amin's cousins. One of them was Musa Kazim al-Husseini, the cousin who once served as mayor of Jerusalem. When Amin learned of the arrests, he was angry. "This is the work of Saleem Namir," he seethed. "He is sending me a message."

Salama, who by then had returned to Cairo, looked doubtful. "You think Namir believes you orchestrated the shooting?"

"He suspects, but he knows he cannot prove it."

"Then, why make the arrest of innocent people? Won't their innocence be obvious to everyone?"

"Namir doesn't care about guilt or innocence. The king has been killed. Someone has to pay. This arrest is merely an attempt to force me to confess. He thinks that by placing them in danger I will come forward to take the blame and save my family members." Amin had a sinister smile. "He wants me to pay for the death of the king, but it will not work. Those men they have arrested did not kill Abdullah and neither did I. I am not going to confess just to save them. And certainly not to satisfy Namir."

"And what if he executes them?"

"Even Namir would not be so foolish," Amin scoffed. "They will be sent to prison, and I don't mind telling you, they will not mind spending time in prison for the sake of the cause. In our family—even our extended family—we know the important things must come first."

With the death of King Abdullah, his son Talal was poised to take the throne. Talal, however, had a troubled relationship with his father and younger brother, Naif. Because of that, Abdullah had made several attempts to remove Talal from the line of succession. At the time of Abdullah's death, Talal was out of the country seeking medical treatment and, in his absence, Naif made a play for the crown. His attempted revolt was quickly put down, and Talal assumed the role of king. Tawfik Abu al-Huda was appointed Jordan's prime minister.

Not long after Huda was confirmed as prime minister, he gave notice that he intended to execute all who were involved in Abdullah's death. Amin dismissed the notice as merely another threat. "They are only trying to pressure me. They will kill no one."

Again, Salama appeared unconvinced. "Imagine if it were some other king in some other country. Or a president. Wouldn't their permanent government want someone to answer?"

"Perhaps."

"And wouldn't they want the supposed assailants to answer with their lives?"

"Maybe." Amin shrugged. "But this is not some other country. This is Jordan."

"If it is Namir's doing, he is in a position to have what he wants."

"What do you mean?"

"He has the backing of the Jordanian royal family. He has

six of your family members in prison. If you come forward and accept the blame, he will execute you. If you do nothing, he will execute six of your kinsmen, clearing the path for more of his family members to take influential positions in Jerusalem."

"And?"

"Either way, he wins."

Amin shook his head. "That only works if Huda executes them, which he will never do."

Later that month, those who were arrested were hanged, including Amin's cousins. Amin learned of it within hours of their deaths but never acknowledged that he'd been wrong in his assessment. Instead, he insisted, "This was the work of Saleem Namir. He is the one behind this."

"You are certain it was not King Talal, Abdullah's son?" Salama asked.

"Talal is mentally incompetent," Amin hissed.

"And not Tawfik al-Huda?"

Amin shook his head. "Huda would never stoop to something like this. Not the murder of innocent civilians. This was Namir." Amin smiled. "But do not worry. I will make him pay. He will pay for Kazim's death. And he will pay for all the others, too."

✦ ✦ ✦ ✦ ✦

Following Hassan al-Banna's death, Amin had stepped forward to fill the resulting leadership void in the Muslim Brotherhood. Gradually, however, as the organization recovered, the Brotherhood's guidance council asserted its prerogative and assumed formal responsibility for the organization's direction. It was an amicable arrangement; all were grateful for Amin's assistance.

After an appropriate time of consideration and reflection, the Brotherhood moved on from the era of Banna and readied itself for whatever might come next. In that transformation, the council turned its attention to the issue of naming a permanent leader. A position they designated as the General Guide—a single individual who would serve as the group's executive.

When the council announced its decision to consider filling the post, Amin raised the issue with Hadad. "Do you think they will consider me for General Guide?"

"It's doubtful," Hadad replied.

A puzzled frown wrinkled Amin's brow. "Why is that?"

"You are not Egyptian."

Amin's frown deepened. "You think they are limiting their consideration to only Egyptians?"

"Senior members view the Brotherhood as an Egyptian organization."

"But we are expanding far beyond Egypt now."

Hadad nodded. "This is true. But members of the council still are Egyptian, and they are in control."

"Then shouldn't I force them to confront that issue?" Amin argued. "Challenge them to see that their prejudices limit their effectiveness?"

Hadad shook his head. "It is a battle you cannot win."

Amin was exasperated. "Then, what are you saying? That I give up and let it go?"

"It would be better for you to expend your energy advising the council. Solidify your position as a key Brotherhood member. A statesman. One with relationships and influence on a broad international scale rather than expending your energy as a candidate for the General Guide position. One is a position you already have. The other is a position you cannot attain."

Hadad's advice struck a positive note with Amin. "Then, who should have the position? Whom should they appoint?"

"Maher Alam."

Amin shook his head in disagreement. "He is a nice fellow, but he is too weak for a position like this. The General Guide must be able to assert himself across a divergent group of people. Not just among amicable Egyptians."

"Then, who?"

Amin smiled. "Hassan al-Hudaybi."

"He is a good man," Hadad noted. "And he has a broader vision for the Brotherhood than merely encouraging Egyptians to follow the teachings of the Quran."

"Exactly." Amin grinned. "And that is why he is perfect for the job."

In the following weeks, Amin carefully insinuated himself into the council's deliberations as it considered the person to fill the post of General Guide. With tact and cunning, he steered council members away from other candidates and toward Hassan al-Hudaybi. When the final decision was made, they chose Hudaybi. Amin was quite satisfied—with Hudaybi and with himself.

THIRTYTHREE

BY THE FOLLOWING YEAR, corruption of the Egyptian monarchy had become an issue the Muslim Brotherhood could no longer avoid. Further inaction on the matter threatened the Brotherhood's underlying purpose and integrity. Addressing the guidance council, Hassan al-Hudaybi, the new General Guide, raised the question in poignant and direct terms. "How can we continue to call for a return to the teachings of the Quran, yet fail to address this issue? Direct action is required, either to bring the monarchy in line with the teachings of the Quran or to eliminate it."

At the same time, a group of young but experienced Egyptian army officers, led by Abdel Nasser, raised the same question. Could they tolerate the king's conduct—indulging in Western corruption—and remain true to the teachings of the Quran? They also raised the more troubling question of whether the army might be compelled, on moral grounds, to act in the interest of the people to effect change in the civilian government. Their consideration of the issues led to the formation of a cell known as the Free Officers Movement, which sought to break Egypt free of corruption and imperialist influence, both from the Egyptian monarchy and from England, which remained in control of the Suez Canal.

Although not formed as an official arm of the Brotherhood, being comprised primarily of Brotherhood members, the Free Officers Movement came to Amin's attention very early in its development. The revolutionary potential of such a group was immediately obvious to him and he insinuated himself into their meetings. Before long, he began conducting regular sessions with its members, teaching them his blend of ideas gleaned from the Quran and *Mein Kampf.*

"Corruption is a major problem throughout the world," Amin taught. "Not just here in Egypt, but everywhere. It has a common source and that source is the Jews. The Jews are the most corrupt of all people, and from them all corruption emanates. First to their neighbors in Europe and then gradually throughout all nations of the West. And from the West, through the presence of the British, to our very own Egyptian monarchy. And from the monarchy to Egyptian society."

After attending several of Amin's teaching sessions, Nasser came to him for assistance and to discuss options for the Free Officers Movement. Amin listened as Nasser outlined what the group had done to that point, then asked, "Is Mohamed Naguib involved with your efforts?" Amin made no effort to disclose the extent of his prior dealings with Naguib or the conversations they shared during the attempt to form the All-Palestine Government.

"No," Nasser replied. "He is not."

"I think Naguib would be a good person to have," Amin suggested.

"And why is that?"

Amin was determined to insinuate Naguib into the discussion

and into the Free Officers Movement. "From what I have seen, the men in the Free Officers Movement are all young. Naguib is older. And he has a widely accepted reputation."

Nasser seemed to bristle at that comment. "All our men are of the highest integrity."

"I do not doubt that," Amin responded. "But they lack the . . . heft of broad experience."

"And you think Naguib would bring that heft?"

"Despite the outcome of the war with Israel," Amin explained, "Naguib achieved a measure of success against the Jews. His exploits are widely known. The public views him as a hero. I think his involvement with your group would make it easier for the public to accept the changes I believe you want to make."

"And what changes do you think those are?"

Amin smiled. "I think we both know what your real intentions are. To remove the monarchy from power and to end the corrupting influence of the British."

Nasser showed no emotion. "There is only one way to eliminate the influence of the British."

"Yes." Amin nodded. "And we both know what that means."

"You think Naguib would be of assistance in that regard?"

"Yes, I do."

"If we approach him, we will expose our group to him. Our discussion even here today is treasonous. To raise these matters with him, only to find that he supports the monarchy, would mean certain death. Will he accept our invitation?"

"I think if you ask, you will find a favorable response."

✦ ✦ ✦ ✦ ✦

After talking with Nasser, Amin met with Naguib. "Abdel Nasser came to see me," he began. "Do you know him?"

"I know of him," Naguib replied.

"You are aware that he and others have formed an organization they call the Free Officers Movement?"

Naguib nodded. "I have heard of them."

"Have you considered joining that organization?"

"I thought about it."

"But?"

Naguib had a stern expression. "Nasser is not a man easily satisfied with second place."

"And you are not satisfied with anything other than first place."

Naguib smiled. "That has usually been my experience. Why do you ask about this?"

"I mentioned you to Nasser," Amin replied.

"In what context?"

"In the context of you joining their association."

Naguib raised an eyebrow. "The Free Officers Movement?"

"Yes."

"Why would you discuss that with Nasser?"

"They need you."

"You do realize, don't you, that they mean to overthrow the monarchy and take control of the government."

Amin looked away. "I understand they intend to take radical steps toward turning Egypt in a new direction."

"What they're talking about is treason."

Amin looked Naguib in the eye. "Only if they fail."

"And that is the problem they face. They must succeed if they hope to survive."

"And you are not convinced they can succeed."

"Not entirely."

"But you *are* convinced the monarchy must be replaced."

Naguib lowered his voice. "The king is a blight on the country that can only be cured by removal."

"The Free Officers Movement needs the wisdom of your

experience. You understood long ago that the true enemy of Islam is corruption of the lifestyle ordered by the Quran. And you understand that after the Jews, the West is the most corrupting influence we face. I do not think the others are as aware of this as you; they need your wisdom to guide them."

"What are you saying, Amin?"

"I'm saying I would like for you to participate in the work of the Free Officers Movement."

"I will consider it."

"One more thing," Amin added. "Nasser does not know of our previous dealings. I think it would be best not to tell him."

✦ ✦ ✦ ✦ ✦

As Naguib suspected, settling the question of leadership with Nasser proved to be a troublesome matter. Nasser, however, realized Amin was correct in his assessment that the Free Officers Movement needed the public weight Naguib's reputation afforded. They were, after all, in an all-or-nothing situation. The Free Officers Movement either succeeded, and they all lived to tell about it, or it failed, in which case they all would be hanged.

With Naguib and Nasser in the lead, the Free Officers Movement engineered the take-over of the Egyptian government. Opposition was light and the Egyptian monarchy was abolished forthwith. King Farouk and his family fled the palace for Naples.

Control of the country was placed in the hands of a Revolutionary Council, which was charged with making both policy and law. Officials in the permanent government—ministers, clerks, and other administrative personnel—were glad for the change and readily accepted the council's leadership. Sayyid Qutb, whose role in the Muslim Brotherhood had been encouraged and promoted by Amin, was appointed to membership in the Revolutionary Council.

In its first act, the council installed Naguib as Egypt's president. Despite titles and publicly announced roles, however, Nasser held great sway over key members of the council. Behind the scenes, he was actually the one wielding power and controlling the country's future.

Although initially enthusiastic, Amin became deeply suspicious of Nasser's intentions and motives in the days following the ouster of the king. To plumb the depths of those suspicions, Amin met regularly with Qutb to keep tabs on the situation. He also hoped to use Qutb's interaction with the council as a means of containing Nasser's actions.

At first, Qutb was on the inside, serving as a close advisor to Nasser. Access to power at that level was intoxicating for him and he had every confidence in the new government. "I think Naguib and Nasser will move the entire government toward a system based on Sharia law," he reported. "Just as the Brotherhood has sought for many years."

As months passed, however, and that did not happen—even after the installation of Naguib—Qutb began to doubt the new leaders were any different from the king. As his doubts and concerns deepened, he went to see Amin. "At first, Naguib seemed committed to fundamental Islamic teachings. I had the sense he was sponsored by you and so I had great hopes for the government under his leadership and direction. I also had great expectations."

"And now?"

"Now I do not understand what has happened."

"I think we both know what happened," Amin replied.

"What?"

"Nasser," Amin groaned.

"You think he is somehow prohibiting Naguib from making the necessary changes?"

"On the outside, Nasser seems like a true revolutionary and a devoted follower of Islam. But on the inside, he understands the revolution only from a political perspective, not religious."

Qutb lowered his head. "This is disheartening."

"I know." Amin sighed. "Everywhere we turn we find men of good intentions. Men who seem to want the best for all. For the Brotherhood. For Islam. For Allah. But upon closer examination we find they are only a fleshly bag filled with bones and human frailty."

Not long after talking to Amin, Qutb resigned from the Council. Within weeks, Naguib resigned from the presidency. With no one left to stop him, Nasser seized control of the Revolutionary Council and of Egypt.

✦ ✦ ✦ ✦ ✦

By the summer of 1954, not only Qutb but also many others were deeply disappointed in the policy and direction of Nasser's government. Qutb talked many times with Amin about the state of Egyptian affairs and the things they might do to change it.

Amin was equally concerned. "I should have suspected this."

"But how could you have known?" Qutb asked.

"I could have paid closer attention," Amin replied. "I am certain now that Nasser was one of the commanders who opposed my formation of the All-Palestine Government. One of the primary reasons the Egyptian government would not commit to it at the level necessary for it to succeed." Amin only suspected that was the issue—he had no proof—but Qutb was now in a position from which he could be manipulated for many purposes. Amin wanted to make certain he did not return to Nasser's orbit.

Qutb seemed puzzled. "But why would he do such a thing?"

"I have power that is not limited by borders or governments," Amin said. "Because of that, many see me as a threat."

"So, what should we do? I and others want to know."

Amin rested his hands in his lap. "Sometimes an occasion arises when circumstances require one to take action. Action that others would think of as extreme or unwarranted but which we know are absolutely necessary."

"There is no choice but to remove Nasser from office. I am convinced of that. And the only way to do that is by killing him." He looked over at Amin. "But can that even be accomplished?"

"As an initial matter," Amin replied, "an assassination of the kind you're contemplating can only be accomplished with careful planning and absolute secrecy. Do you have others you can trust? Perhaps only one or two?"

"Yes, I do."

"Can you trust them with your life?"

"Yes."

Amin pressed the matter closer. "Can you really trust them? Trust them to protect you when their own future hangs in the balance? When their own interests are at risk?"

"Yes."

"Then confine your discussions and planning to them and do not talk about it to anyone else. Not even to me."

✦ ✦ ✦ ✦ ✦

In the weeks that followed, Qutb gathered regularly with a small group of supporters, all of them from the Muslim Brotherhood. With a solemn oath, they committed themselves to a plot to assassinate Nasser.

After an initial survey of the problem, Qutb and his companions decided on a car bomb as their preferred method of execution. Nasser's schedule was studied, his usual routes were noted and mapped, and bombing material was acquired. A date of attack was chosen and all was in place, including the attachment of the bomb to Nasser's automobile. However, at the last minute Nasser deviated from his schedule and was delayed in leaving. Nasser's driver came from the building to move the car. When he started the engine, the car exploded. Nasser rushed to a nearby window and looked out to see what had happened, only to find the remains of his car in flames. That same day, he ordered an investigation into the attempt on his life.

Very quickly, investigators discovered Qutb and the group of men with whom he'd been meeting. Hours after learning of them, they tracked down two members of the group and learned the details of the group's plot to kill Nasser. Qutb was in hiding, but Nasser's investigators persisted and soon succeeded in arresting him along with others from the group.

Many who knew of Amin's close association with Qutb suspected Amin was involved in the assassination plot. Nasser suspected him, too, and wanted to arrest him, but having only a hunch and no proof, he could ill afford to move against the Grand Mufti of Jerusalem. Nevertheless, he knew Ramadan and Amin enjoyed a close personal relationship and, although it was impossible to prosecute Amin, Ramadan was vulnerable to any scheme Nasser might develop. With Amin out of reach, Nasser claimed Ramadan had been implicated in the investigation and ordered Ramadan to leave Egypt immediately.

When Amin learned that Ramadan had been ordered to leave, he sent for him, and the two met at the residence. "These are troubling times for us all," Amin began. "But regardless of what happens to us or what difficulties we may face, the Brotherhood must survive."

"Yes," Ramadan replied. "Always."

"And so," Amin continued, "you must step up and assume your rightful position. You must use this as an opportunity. An opportunity to expand the Brotherhood's power base beyond Egypt. We have broad support in many places. Syria, Saudi Arabia, Pakistan. Even in Europe we have a growing presence. Brotherhood members in all of those locations will support you. But there are many other countries where we have not yet entered. You must seize the initiative and reach those countries."

"You really think I can do that?"

"I know you can." Amin reached to a shelf behind him and took down a copy of *Mein Kampf*. "This is a copy given to me personally by Hitler." He handed it to Ramadan. "This book and the Quran are all you need to understand your role. They will be your guide. Your companion to show you the way you must go."

"But where should I go?" Ramadan had a look of desperation and a quiver in his voice. "I mean first. Now. I must leave immediately. Where will I live?"

"I have made arrangements." Amin smiled. "You will travel first to Syria. There you will find a residence prepared and waiting for you. Rest there. Stay as long as you need. But do not make it your permanent home."

"And then?"

"Then you begin your journey. Just as I have instructed you. Taking the Brotherhood to new places. You will be our ambassador to the world."

✦ ✦ ✦ ✦ ✦

Once Ramadan was on his way to Syria, Amin located Hassan al-Hudaybi, the Brotherhood's newly appointed General Guide, and suggested Hudaybi should go into hiding. "But where?" Hudaybi asked.

"Berlin."

Deep furrows appeared on Hudaybi's forehead. "Berlin? I know no one in Berlin."

"Others have gone before you to make a way."

"I am aware of our work there, but are they willing to receive me?"

"Our people at the Islamic Central Institute will help you," Amin replied. "But you must go there right away."

Hudaybi shrugged. "But how?"

"I have taken care of that for you." Amin called for Salama. A moment later he appeared at the doorway, and Amin explained, "Salama will see you on your way."

"Now?"

"Yes." Amin hesitated. "Is that a problem?"

"No." Hudaybi shook his head. "It is not a problem at all. In fact, it is a very great blessing and relief. But I would like to say good-bye to the council."

"There are not many who remain free and they are being hunted night and day. Gathering them would be dangerous."

"Then perhaps I may write a farewell note."

"That would be better."

Hudaybi spent an hour composing a letter to the Brotherhood's guidance council, instructing them to cease all public activities, to concentrate on personal study of the Quran, and to focus on strengthening Brotherhood membership. "One day, we will rise up even stronger than before in Egypt. But for now we must keep quiet and stay out of sight."

When Hudaybi was finished, he handed the note to Amin, said good-bye, and left the house with Salama. Sometime after midnight, he boarded a cargo ship bound for France where Brotherhood members were prepared to receive him.

✦　✦　✦　✦　✦

Meanwhile, because of his association with Qutb and the Brotherhood—and because of Nasser's suspicions about him—Amin's influence in Cairo was marginalized. Police and soldiers followed him around the clock and several times his house was searched. As scrutiny of him intensified, Amin became worried that yet another crackdown on the Brotherhood might be coming. Ramadan had been sent away and was safely out of Nasser's reach. Hudaybi was also. But as Amin's worry grew deeper, he became concerned for his cousin Yasser Arafat.

Arafat was young, often impetuous, but dashing and coura-geous enough to accept any challenge. With so many members now in jail, the Brotherhood could not afford to lose someone as capable and willing as he. And Amin had more hopes for him than merely the Brotherhood. Arafat was someone he considered a potential successor to his own position. If not as mufti, then as the future leader of the Palestinian people. Perhaps a future Palestinian-Arab government. But first, Arafat must survive the current crisis.

For that reason, Amin contacted friends abroad, then sum-moned Arafat to the residence. They met in his study. With little by way of greeting or introduction, Amin instructed, "You must leave the country immediately."

Arafat seemed taken aback but recovered quickly. "I will go wherever you send me."

"Good," Amin said. "I have arranged a place for you in Kuwait."

"May I ask, why the sense of urgency? Has something happened?"

"I have received nothing that implicates you directly," Amin blustered. "But they are increasing their scrutiny of me and if—"

Arafat snarled. "Then we must hit back."

"There is no time for that," Amin dismissed his concern with the wave of his hand. "We must concentrate on preserving the leadership we have left. Better opportunities will arise in the future, but first we must survive the present."

Arafat seemed to relax. "And you want me to leave?"

"Yes. You are the future. Not just of the Brotherhood, but more importantly of the work in Palestine. We cannot afford to lose you, Yasser. *I* cannot afford to lose you."

Arafat's chest seemed to swell with pride at the comment. "Very well. But I know no one in Kuwait."

"I have made calls on your behalf."

"Nasser's people listen to our phone calls."

Amin nodded. "I am aware of that. But the people to whom I have spoken are people I have known for a long time and we talk to each other in a way that even if someone overheard us, they would not know what we were discussing." He handed Arafat a slip of paper with two names on it. "These two." He pointed at the paper. "Salah Khalaf and Khalil al-Wazir. They will be waiting for you when you arrive. They are Brotherhood members. They will help you."

"And what should I do after that?"

"Prepare for the future and be ready when an opportunity arises. I will call on you. So be ready."

The two embraced, then Amin walked Arafat to the door and said one last good-bye. Arafat stepped out to the driveway, where Hadad was waiting with a car. As they drove away, Amin whispered a prayer to Allah.

✦ ✦ ✦ ✦ ✦

With Ramadan, Hudaybi, and now Arafat safely out of Egypt, Amin retreated even further from public involvement. He left home only for Friday prayers at a nearby mosque and spent the remainder of his time working behind the scenes to encourage the Brotherhood members who remained in Egypt. As he had done many times before, he formed a small group of devoted members and met with them weekly, teaching them his blend of ideas from the Quran and *Mein Kampf*.

"Corruption is the problem," he repeated. "The Jews are the most corrupt of all. They corrupted the West and now they are using the West to corrupt us. Eliminate the Jews and all of our problems will go away."

It was an idea he had taught many times before, but with it Amin hoped to preserve a remnant of the Brotherhood and lay a foundation for its eventual rise. "We must take the long view," he said to Salama, who remained always at his side. "And work for a future we may never see. In that way, we can empower and inspire those of the future to accept our dream and make it a reality." He flashed a curious smile. "In effect, through our ideas and our ideals, we can go with them into the future long after our bodies have expired."

THIRTYFOUR

THE FOLLOWING YEAR, Gerhard von Mende—the former Nazi official with whom Amin worked closely during his time in Germany—arrived in Cairo. The two had not talked since the war's end and were glad to see each other again.

"So, tell me," Amin commenced when they were settled in the study. "What happened after we all left Berlin?"

"I am sure you know about the death of the Führer."

Amin nodded slowly. "That was a very sad ending to a brilliant man."

"Many of the others—Himmler, Rosenberg, Göring—met with a similar fate at Nuremburg. I am sure you followed news of them."

"They were good men, too," Amin noted. "And you? What happened to you?"

"I did my best to stay out of the way of British and American forces."

"And the Soviets, too, I suspect."

"Yes. The Soviets most of all. I was worried for my own safety, but I also was concerned for members of the Muslim units we had created and wanted to do my best to see that they were not captured by the Soviets, either."

"I suspect the Russians would have murdered them all."

"Yes. Most definitely," Mende agreed. "In an effort to see that that did not happen, I eventually came to the conclusion that I should contact one of the Allied powers to see if I might work for them and find a way to bring the others with me."

"Oh? Wasn't that risky, contacting the Allies?"

"Somewhat, but by then I had heard that both the British and the Americans were offering specialists an opportunity to work with them. Rocket scientists, physicists, and the like."

"The Soviets, too, I understand."

"Yes, though the Soviets were outmaneuvered in that regard. The Americans obtained the best minds."

"So you thought they might be interested in you, too?"

"I thought there might be a chance of it. By then I had reached the conclusion that I could not go on hiding in Europe. And I was not interested in relocating to South America with the others. So I contacted the British and told them about the vast network of Muslim operatives we had assembled during the war to fight against the Soviets in the East. Trying to capitalize on their growing anti-Soviet feelings."

"And they bought that story?"

Mende grinned. "Completely."

"Interesting."

"I told them we promised to help the Muslims obtain freedom for their countries if they fought against the Soviets, which they did. And then I suggested the British and other Allies might benefit from my expertise and from access to that network, much of which remained intact and in place, in their efforts to stop the spread of Communism."

"They view Communism as a serious threat to the West," Amin said. "And rightly so."

"It is particularly threatening to the stability of Europe," Mende added.

"And the British agreed to take you on?"

"Yes. For a time, I worked with the British and through them I was able to protect most of the men with whom we worked during the war. Eventually, though, the British grew uncomfortable with me. Several in London raised objections to my Nazi past. And they cut me loose."

"But not to prison."

"No." Mende grinned. "They simply said they no longer needed my services and that was that."

"What did you do next?"

"By then I had developed contacts with the Americans. A few army officials and half a dozen operatives in their new Central Intelligence Agency. And I had also begun working with officials from the West German government. They were very interested in developing a relationship with European Muslims as a way to combat the spread of Communism."

"Doing the same thing as you did before with the British."

"Yes. And the same thing we both did when you were in Germany, though now for others. Not for the Reich."

Amin was glad to receive an update of the situation in Europe and on the events that transpired in Mende's life after the end of the war but mention of the CIA left him uneasy and suspicious. The CIA was an American intelligence institution, and the Americans, after all, were corrupt pawns of the Jews. They also had vast resources and the ability to make trouble where none existed before.

"What does the CIA want with me?" he asked in a dry, emotionless tone.

Mende shook his head. "The CIA did not send me here. Nor did the West Germans. I came on my own initiative."

"For what purpose?"

"I thought we might be able to work together again."

Amin was surprised. "Oh? In what regard?"

"You are a key leader in the Muslim community, and you have access to people throughout the Middle East. You have connections to people who might help me with what *I* am doing. I have connections to financial assets that might help you in the things *you* are doing."

"Keeping the Communists out of Europe?"

"Yes."

"An intriguing idea. I will need time to consider the suggestion."

"Certainly. Shall we meet again?"

"I will send for you in a few days. You can remain in Cairo that long?"

"For you," Mende smiled, "it would be a pleasure."

✦ ✦ ✦ ✦ ✦

That night, Amin met with Hadad and discussed Mende's offer. "It could be a way to fund Brotherhood activity in Europe," Hadad noted.

"I suppose." Amin shrugged. "But I am not certain it is that straightforward."

"The Americans have money. As do the West Germans. We could use them to obtain funding the way we used the Germans when we built the Institute in Berlin."

Amin sighed. "I don't know."

"You seem suspicious."

"Mende is involved with the CIA."

Hadad's countenance changed. "Oh."

"The Americans are very powerful. And they can be quite devious. Working with them would require someone who is alert to more than what they say."

"With them," Hadad noted, "the true meaning, the true intention, always lies four levels beneath the words that come from their mouths."

"They are corrupt."

"Corrupt and powerful." Hadad had a tight smile. "Rather like the British. And yet we used them successfully."

"But not without consequence," Amin responded. "They did not follow through on many of their promises. And I don't think the CIA will, either."

"Life is imperfect. People are imperfect. The British gave us arms and training. As did the Italians and Germans. And we are stronger now than we were then." He looked over at Amin with a satisfied expression. "Just think of all we have accomplished."

"We *have* come a long way."

"And there is much farther for us to go. Perhaps we just didn't understand at the beginning how far we had to go."

"Perhaps." Amin nodded. "So you are in favor of working with Mende?"

"I think the opportunities for us are few here in Egypt. Our ability to reach beyond Cairo is continually limited by Nasser and his personal ambitions. And neither the UK nor the US is our central problem."

"The Jews?"

"The Jews," Hadad agreed.

"And our Arab colleagues. They all want a piece of us so they can get a piece of Palestine."

"I agree."

"If we agree to work with Mende, the effort would be located primarily in Berlin. We would need additional leadership there to do this."

"Imad Kazim and Khalil Tibi have done a good job."

"Yes, but they are busy with the basic work of the Institute," Amin replied. "This thing with Mende would require more attention than they could give. I fear if we placed this in their hands, things would get overlooked and trouble would result."

"What about Aref?" Hadad suggested. "I haven't seen him lately. Could we use him for this?"

Amin shook his head. "Aref has left us."

Hadad frowned. "For what? Where did he go?"

"I am not certain where he is."

"Nasser got him?"

"No. He was gone before the trouble with Nasser began."

Hadad's eyes opened wide. "Was he working for Nasser?"

Amin shook his head vigorously. "It was nothing like that. Do not worry about Aref. He is no longer available to us. We will need someone else."

"What about Ramadan?"

Amin grinned. "An excellent choice. And I know exactly where *he* is."

A few days later, Mende returned to Amin's residence for dinner. Afterward, the two men went for a walk on the residence grounds. "I have agreed to explore the possibility of working with you," Amin offered.

"That is excellent news."

"I would like to send someone to Berlin to lead our participation, but I am not sure that is possible right now. So, for the meantime, I will send Salama to get things started."

"I shall look forward to working with him."

"He and the others already in Berlin will be able to explore this effort in detail with you, and based on their reports to me, I will open doors for you among our wider group of associates."

Mende turned to face Amin. "I think we shall enjoy a long and very fruitful association." The two men shook hands, then Amin led the way back to the house.

✦ ✦ ✦ ✦ ✦

After his visit with Mende, Amin sent his nephew, Bassem Darwaza, to locate Ramadan and arrange a meeting for them to discuss the proposed Mende collaboration. By then, Ramadan had moved to Pakistan and was emerging as a major leader of the Muslim Brotherhood in Asia, in effect functioning as the Brotherhood's unofficial foreign minister. A global ambassador. Just as Amin had hoped. Darwaza traveled from Cairo to Karachi, located Ramadan, and arranged for him to meet Amin in Algiers.

A week later, posing as an Egyptian businessman, Amin traveled to Algiers and met with Ramadan. They discussed the possibility of working in Germany, the growing Muslim population in Europe, and other opportunities working with Mende might present for the Brotherhood. Amin gave his usual explanation of what they might accomplish—use the money and resources of the West, this time from the United States and Germany, to strengthen their own organization.

Ramadan listened attentively. "The West has always taken advantage of us and never keeps its promises. We must be careful to ensure that doesn't happen again."

"In the past, the West gave us promise. I am not looking for promises this time. Only resources and opportunities. We will make our own success."

"And do it with their assistance?"

"On the one hand, we shall give them exactly what they say they want—access to Arabs who will help them oppose Communism. At the same time, we shall acquire for ourselves the resources and contacts we need to spread Islam and Sharia law throughout the world." Amin gestured for emphasis. "At the *same time*. Not exchange for their promises of future action."

"Well," Ramadan contemplated, "it is an intriguing proposition, but I will need time to get into position. Right now I am engaged in activities in Pakistan that cannot be immediately disentangled."

"But you will take charge of the matter with Mende?"

"Of course I will take charge of it."

"And you will relocate to Berlin as soon as possible?"

"Yes."

✦ ✦ ✦ ✦ ✦

When Amin returned to Cairo, he sent Salama to Germany to begin work with Mende. Before Salama departed, they met at a mosque near Amin's residence. "Our goal," he explained, "is to expand the reach of the Islamic Central Institute."

"Use Mende's money for our purposes."

"Yes, but you must do so in a manner that gives him what he wants, too."

"Right."

"You should meet with Mende as soon as you arrive. Get to know him. Work with him as much as possible. Perhaps get to know his contacts, too. They might be useful to us in the future."

"What about Imad Kazim and Khalil Tibi?"

"Make certain they continue their normal activities. You will need their assistance in learning the lay of the land but maintain the integrity of your own work and keep it separate from theirs, at least for now. Make it appear as though the Institute is involved, but in reality, make certain it is protected. I do not wish to risk tarnishing the Institute's image."

As he had with Arafat and the others he'd sent out, Amin gave Salama the names of a few people in Germany who might be able to help him. "Make sure they understand the nature of our work," he cautioned. "Our primary focus is the expansion of the Muslim Brotherhood, not opposition to Communism or the Soviet Union."

"We're using Germany and the US to get what *we* want."

"Precisely. I do not intend to be manipulated by the West ever again. And remember what I have said many times before: We have two guides in this work of ours—the Quran and *Mein Kampf.* Keep them both close to your heart."

THIRTYFIVE

WITH EVENTS FORCING Muslim Brotherhood activities away from Egypt, and with most of its key members now living in other areas of the world, Amin decided the time had come to relocate his own center of operations. Early in 1959, he discussed the matter with Hadad over lunch.

"Returning to Jerusalem is not possible. Going abroad to North or South America would only take us farther away from Palestine, which is the place we really want to change."

"You are thinking you need to leave Egypt? Live somewhere else?"

"Yes. But I'm not certain where."

"Perhaps we should consider a return to Beirut," Hadad suggested.

"I hadn't thought of that. Lebanon was good to us once before."

"Yes. It was," Hadad agreed. "And Fuad Chehab, your old friend, is now the president of Lebanon."

"He is, indeed." Amin liked the idea of returning there.

"Lebanon might be a good place. Could you make a few inquiries for us and see if they would accept us?"

"Certainly," Hadad replied. "I'll contact Chehab's office and see if they are willing to entertain the idea."

Hadad made calls not only to Chehab's office but also to several other officials in the Lebanese government. Through those conversations, he learned that Chehab was scheduled to travel to Cairo for official meetings with Nasser. "He would be delighted to discuss your requests during that visit," an aide offered.

✦ ✦ ✦ ✦ ✦

A few months later, Chehab arrived in Egypt. He and Nasser participated in official functions associated with a state visit and toured the country together. Before leaving to return to Beirut, he came to Amin's residence, where the two renewed their old friendship. After a long conversation about people and events of the past, Amin broached the subject of returning to Beirut. "For a short visit?" Chehab asked.

"No," Amin replied. "I would like to relocate there. On a permanent basis."

"We would be delighted to have you and Karimeh as residents. I will see that arrangements are made."

Later that year, Amin took Karimeh and their youngest children to Beirut. Hadad joined them. Chehab provided a home for them—a spacious residence on a large estate near the edge of the city. With friendly and accommodating ties to the Lebanese government, he was able to come and go as he pleased.

✦ ✦ ✦ ✦ ✦

When Ramadan arrived in Berlin, he took control of the Islamic Central Institute and began assessing its accomplishments and potential as a base for an expanded view of the Brotherhood's mission in Europe. Since its founding, the Institute had grown in both size and influence.

During the war, it provided much-needed instruction for Muslims living in Nazi Germany. After the war ended, workers from the Middle East flocked to Germany seeking jobs on the many construction projects that dotted the landscape, rebuilding the damage inflicted by Allied bombing and the retreating Nazi army's scorched-earth policy. Many of those workers found the Institute a vital source of religious and emotional support. Even more recently, it had become a place of refuge for Muslims fleeing the Arab-Israeli War in Palestine and Nasser's crackdown in Egypt.

Amin had hoped that with Ramadan's arrival at the Institute, Salama might be free to join him in Beirut. Ramadan, however, thought otherwise. "I would like to use Salama to establish a presence in Hamburg," Ramadan related in a phone call.

This was the first Amin had heard of such an effort, though he was not opposed to it. "Do we have enough people there to establish a mosque?"

"More than," Ramadan replied.

"Very well."

"I was thinking also of sending Kazim and Tibi to Munich," Ramadan continued. "We have a group there that is ready to establish a mosque. Kazim and Tibi could show them how to do it."

Amin disliked the idea of moving Kazim and Tibi to a different city. They had been faithful and never asked him for anything, always taking care of the Institute and the needs of its members on their own. Moving them now, after all of that, seemed disrespectful of their work and sacrifice. They also were no longer as young as they once were. Moving would be difficult for them. "Would they be required to relocate permanently?"

Ramadan was hesitant. "Well, I suppose not."

"They have been with us in Berlin a long time," Amin explained. "Moving now would be a big imposition for them."

Ramadan took a plaintive tone. "Well, if you would rather that I sent someone else—"

Amin cut him off. "No, I think they will do a good job. And I think establishing a group in Munich is an excellent idea. But I would prefer, for Kazim and Tibi's sake, that it be a temporary assignment. One they could perform without having to relocate. So they could maintain their Berlin residence."

"I will work it out with them." Ramadan sounded less than enthusiastic about the change, but not combative.

"Good. Perhaps I can come there one day and help as well." Amin meant it as a word of encouragement for Ramadan, but both men knew he would never see Germany again.

"That would be a great help to everyone."

Amin came away from the conversation with as many questions as he had before the call. Only, after their talk, the questions went in the opposite direction. Before the call, he had been confident of Ramadan's ability as a leader and of his commitment to the Brotherhood. After talking to him, however, he began to wonder if Ramadan wasn't attempting to do something with the work in Germany that was solely for the benefit of Ramadan.

Despite those concerns, after arriving in Berlin, Salama developed a close relationship with Mende, just as Amin hoped. That relationship afforded him an opportunity to fund expansion of the Institute's work and shore up its finances. Money flowed freely from Mende, and Salama made the most of it.

Mende's money, in turn, came from the US government and was handled through a CIA front organization known as the American Committee for the Freedom of Russia. The money was paid by the CIA ostensibly for the recruitment of Muslims who were supposed to assist in the fight against Communism in

Europe. Instead, Salama used the money to recruit new members for the Brotherhood, make necessary repairs to the Institute's property, and otherwise shore up finances.

When Ramadan arrived, the improved financial stability Salama had obtained enabled him to consider the expansion plans he now sought to implement. Sending Salama to Hamburg and occupying Kazim and Tibi with expansion into Munich meant Ramadan was left alone in Berlin. Alone with a continuous supply of money. Amin did not like the risk that situation posed.

✦ ✦ ✦ ✦ ✦

Meanwhile, within hours of arriving in Kuwait, Yasser Arafat met the two people Amin had suggested—Salah Khalaf and Khalil al-Wazir. Originally from Palestine, they were members of the Muslim Brotherhood and were glad to help, eventually finding a job for him as a schoolteacher.

Once settled in his position as a teacher, Arafat quickly expanded his circle of friends to include other Palestinian expatriates—men who had fled to Kuwait following collapse of the war against Israel. With Amin's support, Arafat began meeting with Wazir and the others, teaching them the blend of hatred of Jews for which Amin had become widely known. Hatred based on a lethal fusion of *Mein Kampf* and the Quran. Arafat's new friends devoured the ideas with an ever-increasing appetite. Before long, he directed that appetite toward the creation of an organization dedicated to the liberation of Palestine.

"Established Arab states," Arafat argued, "have proved themselves incapable of doing the things necessary to win independence for our people in Palestine. Each time they have tried, they have been unable to put aside their petty differences and consuming greed. In the end, they spend their time and energy trying to dominate us, rather than win against the Jews. We must not let that happen again."

Wazir spoke up, "Whatever we do, I suggest we refuse contributions from them. That way, they won't have a hold on us."

"And," Khalaf added, "we should refrain from making ideological alliances with them."

"Then we are agreed that we should form an organization?" Arafat asked.

"Yes," they replied in unison.

"But what is the name?" Wazir asked.

Various names were offered as suggestions, but none seemed acceptable until Wazir said, "Maybe we should call it what it is. The Palestinian National Liberation Movement."

Everyone liked that name, and there were drinks to celebrate the establishment of the group. Somewhere late in the night, someone—no one remembers who—began referring to it as FATAH, a reverse acronym for the group's name in Arabic.

Over the next twelve months Fatah, with its insidious doctrine of hatred for the Jews, attracted additional members to their group. Radical Muslims who viewed Islam through a political lens and none other. They conducted military maneuvers, staged mock raids, and worked to perfect their skills at creating improvised explosives using readily available material. Before long, a division became apparent between those who relished military operations and those who preferred other roles. By the end of the year, Fatah had formed a separate organization for its aggressive operations. That unit became known as Al-Assifa.

With the group becoming more specialized and with a broader organization in place to facilitate its diverse activities, Arafat and Wazir decided to move Fatah and its military wing from Kuwait to Syria. "We will construct a camp outside Damascus," Arafat explained. "Far enough away to give us anonymity.

Close enough to the city to make provisioning easy. And much nearer our target—Israel."

The move to Syria also put Arafat closer to Beirut and allowed him to meet regularly with Amin. With Amin's help and approval, Al-Assifa recruited additional members and began staging real and very deadly attacks against remote Jewish villages in the Galilee.

One of Arafat's key recruits was Abu Daoud, who came from a wealthy family near Haifa. Daoud gave Fatah access to a ready supply of money, along with businesses and suppliers who were eager to help, once they learned of Fatah's true purpose. "Finally," Daoud boasted, "an organization willing to actually exterminate the Jews."

More importantly to Fatah's long-term goals was the access Daoud gave to Middle Eastern arms dealers. Dealers with genuine connections to the best arms in the world. Automatic weapons from the United States, France, and Germany. Missiles, rockets, and plastique, too. With the money he obtained from Daoud, and access to quality arms, Arafat was able to keep Al-Assifa well supplied and free to conduct operations without the added constraint of minimizing the expenditure of scarce material.

✦ ✦ ✦ ✦ ✦

With events once again moving toward the ultimate goal of liberating Palestinian Arabs from the Jews, Amin turned to the strategic nature of the work and how to proceed in an organized and thoughtful manner. After considering the issue on his own, he summoned Ramadan and Arafat to Beirut for a conference.

"After being harassed by Nasser and the Egyptians," Amin began, "we are now in a better position and have perhaps moved beyond that trouble. Some of our people are in Germany. Some here in Lebanon. Others in Syria."

"Though some are still in Egypt," Arafat noted. "And some are in Jerusalem."

"And that is something I wanted to address," Amin continued. "We are no longer centrally located, as we were in Cairo. Now we are scattered about. To coordinate our effort, I think we must consider again the need for an umbrella organization."

"That was the purpose in forming the Arab League," Ramadan noted.

"This time I would like to form an organization that will bring us together, rather than divide as the League, oddly enough, has done. And one that will actually fight, rather than merely protect its own interests."

"For that to work, we must create an organization free from interference by the established Arab states."

"Precisely what I had in mind," Amin agreed. "An organization without ties to the Arab states, and one that will risk everything in order to confront the Jews with force."

"Kill as many of them as possible," Arafat growled. "Just as they kill us."

Amin smiled. "But it must be an organization that we control."

"Should we separate this organization from the Brotherhood?"

"Definitely," Arafat spoke up. "Keep it separate."

"I have considerable influence with the Brotherhood. I see merit in working within its framework."

Ramadan frowned. "You mean an organization formed by the Brotherhood and accountable to the Brotherhood?"

"Accountable to no one but ourselves. And not formed by the Brotherhood, officially, but closely associated with it in a manner that insinuates an overt connection."

Arafat grinned. "Form our own organization but do it in a way that makes people think we're connected with the Brotherhood. Mooch off the Brotherhood's credibility but keep it under our control."

Amin laughed. "You know me too well."

Ramadan looked troubled. "We may face opposition."

Amin was alert. "From where?"

"I have heard rumors that the Arab League is in discussions to form just such an organization as the one we propose."

"The Arab League is dominated by Egypt," Arafat responded. "Any organization they create will be dominated by Nasser."

"Any word on when they intend to do this?" Amin asked.

"They have a meeting in January," Ramadan noted. "Most who know about it expect they'll do something then."

"Where will they meet?"

"Cairo," Ramadan answered.

Amin looked over at him. "I can see by the expression on your face that you want to attend."

"I do, but I don't think I should."

"You'd be arrested upon arrival," Amin warned. "Send someone in your place."

✦ ✦ ✦ ✦ ✦

In January of the following year, just as Ramadan had suggested, the Arab League held a summit in Cairo to consider the Palestinian situation. After hearing reports from the ministers of member nations and from several Arab factions, the League turned its attention to the question of creating yet one more organization to represent the Palestinian people. Nasser proposed they call it the Palestinian National Council. "Comprised of delegates to represent both the Arab League and Palestinian Arabs. To function as an administrative body. Promulgating policy and legislating rules on behalf of the people of Palestine."

Khaled Alluba, Ramadan's cousin, attended the meeting and reported the results to him. Ramadan met with Amin and

Arafat shortly thereafter. "In many ways," Ramadan disclosed, "the meeting in Cairo produced nothing more than another version of the All-Palestine Government, only with a new name. The Palestinian National Council."

"Who are the members?"

"Each of the League members choose a delegate, and others are elected by the people of Palestine."

"So, once again, it is a government dominated by Arab states."

"And once again," Arafat complained, "Nasser and his colleagues are set to impose their will on the Palestinians."

Amin nodded. "It will be ineffective in every regard except for that."

"Perhaps," Ramadan replied. "But couldn't we handle them the same way we handled the British and now are handling the Americans?"

Amin frowned. "What do you mean?"

"Work with them. And while we do that, we use them for our own purposes. Let the Arab League think they are in control but all the time we would be getting exactly what we want from the arrangement."

"We tried that before," Amin reminded. "That was our approach with the All-Palestine Government."

"I don't think it would work very well with Nasser."

Ramadan seemed puzzled. "Nasser?"

"Whatever the Arab League is doing with this, you can be sure Nasser is in charge of it."

"Still," Ramadan said, "it might be worth a try."

"It would not be easy to do," Amin pointed out. "They are aware of us and have a history with us. I don't think they will allow us to simply walk in and take over. Was there anything else decided at the meeting?"

"Nothing was decided," Ramadan answered. "But they discussed taking a two-part approach to Palestine. The council as an administrative arm, and a second organization as the military wing."

Amin raised an eyebrow. "A military aspect, subject to the League?"

"Nasser suggested it should be a separate organization under the League, but no one else would agree. I think they want to place it under the council."

"Interesting," Amin mused.

"Most of those in attendance seemed to understand the reasons why the All-Palestine Government failed. Structurally, they realize it was not created to win." Ramadan gave Amin a wary look. "They also blame you."

"Me?"

"Yes."

"Why?"

"They think you tried to use it for your own purposes and not for the greater good of all Arabs living in Palestine."

Amin bristled. "I am the Grand Mufti of Jerusalem. They should conform their expectations to mine, rather than expecting me to conform to theirs."

✦ ✦ ✦ ✦ ✦

In May 1964, the newly formed Palestinian National Council met in East Jerusalem, an area controlled by Jordan. During that meeting, the council established the Palestine Liberation Organization—PLO for short—to carry out its military and security function. The PLO's stated goal was the liberation of Palestine through armed struggle. Ahmad Shukeiri was named as the PLO's chairman. To effect that purpose, the PLO created yet another organization known as the Palestine Liberation Army.

When Arafat learned of these developments, he traveled to Beirut and met with Amin. "I like the idea, but I do not think

Shukeiri is capable of waging the kind of warfare necessary to be successful."

Amin nodded. "I agree. Shukeiri is a diplomat, not a warlord. And Nasser will never supply enough money or arms to make it work without also taking full control of the operation."

"And full credit for its success," Arafat added.

Amin agreed. "Nasser's goal has always been to dominate as much of the region as possible. Egypt. The Sinai. Palestine. Syria and Jordan if given the chance. Even Lebanon."

"What do you think about Ramadan's suggestion that we find a way to work with them?"

"I think we should remain apart from them for now," Amin replied. "If they are what we think they are, this effort will fail just like the others."

✦ ✦ ✦ ✦ ✦

In January 1965, with Shukeiri's approval and direction, the PLO attacked the National Water Carrier of Israel—a major irrigation system that moved water from the Sea of Galilee, near Tiberias in the north, to farms in the Negev, south of Jerusalem. The attack was poorly planned and ineptly executed. It caused damage to the facility but failed to render it useless. A few days later, the PLO followed up with attacks on additional infrastructure sites—a power station, a bridge, and other facilities—but neglected to return to finish destruction of the water carrier.

In response, Israeli military units attacked the Arab village of As-Samu in the Jordanian-occupied area of the West Bank. Jordanian security troops attempted to repel the assault and defend the village but were overwhelmed and forced to retreat. A number of Jordanian troops were killed in the fight, along with many of the village's inhabitants. More than 125 homes were destroyed.

The following day, Jordanian officials filed a formal complaint, arguing that the attack amounted to an invasion of Jordan and an affront to its sovereignty. Arab citizens protested, too. Some against the attack, others against what they saw as inadequate protection from the Jordan army. To address the situation, Jordan sent additional troops into the area and called up reserves to the region.

Israel countered Jordanian military adjustments by repositioning troops to better interdict PLO activity and protect vulnerable settlements in the Negev against possible reprisals. As a result, large contingents of Jordanian and Israeli troops were encamped opposite each other, alert to the slightest provocation.

With conditions in the region already tense, Egyptian military officials received a report from their Soviet counterparts of Israeli troop movements in the Negev. "Apparently massing on the Sinai border," an attaché suggested. "These movements, and others farther to the north, seem to portend an Israeli invasion." The reports were erroneous and the analysis altogether unfounded, but Egyptian officials had no data of their own against which to compare it. Nasser, trapped in his obsession with power, blinded by the humiliation he'd experienced in the previous war, and duped by his devotion to all things Soviet, issued an immediate order closing the Straits of Tiran to Israeli shipping, effectively closing the Gulf of Aqaba. At the same time, he mobilized Egyptian troops and positioned them in large numbers along the Israeli border.

Israeli leaders perceived Egyptian troop movements as unprovoked and as preparation for an attack. Very much aware that its neighbors were its enemies and close at hand, the Israel Defense Forces developed a preemptive policy: When faced with a verifiable threat from its neighbors, Israel would strike first rather than wait to see what the other side might do. In accordance with that policy, on June 5, 1967, Israel launched preemptive air strikes against Egyptian air force bases. Caught by surprise, most of Egypt's aircraft were destroyed on the ground. Israeli forces followed those air strikes by attacking Egyptian troops along its southern border and by invading Gaza.

The Egyptian, Jordanian, and Syrian armies attempted to respond, but over the next six days, Israeli troops proved too strong to resist. They seized control of Gaza, occupied the Golan Heights at the Syrian border, and succeeded in driving the Jordanian army out of East Jerusalem. By the end of the week, Israel controlled all of Palestine—southward from the Lebanese-Syrian border, eastward to the Jordan River, along with Gaza and a large portion of the Sinai Peninsula.

The conflict, known as the Six-Day War, was one of Israel's greatest military triumphs and one of the most crushing defeats the Arab world had ever known. When the fighting ended, Israel controlled all of the territory apportioned to Arabs under the 1948 UN Partition Plan for Palestine, having more than doubled its size in less than one week's time. The armies of Egypt, Jordan, and Syria lay in ruins.

THIRTYSIX

HAVING RECEIVED YET ANOTHER defeat at the hands of the Israelis—this time in only six days—the Arab world was in disarray. The military prestige of its established Arab states was in tatters. Sentiment toward Arafat and Fatah, however, was on the rise. From the Galilee to the Negev and at all points in between, Palestinians at every social level agreed with Arafat's view—that Palestinians should break alliances with individual Arab governments and find a truly Palestinian solution to their dilemma. Some even went so far as to suggest that Palestinians were the only ones who could solve the issues that Arabs of the Levant faced.

Amin joined in the public disdain for Nasser and the Arab League, ranting and raving to anyone who would listen about how the Arab League had, once again, betrayed the cause of Palestinian nationalism. "And in doing so," he added, "they have forsaken the true teaching of Islam." In private he even went so far as to suggest that Arafat was wrong, too. Insisting that he, the Grand Mufti of Jerusalem, was the only one who could rally Palestinian support for the Palestinian cause—though he reserved that opinion for his innermost group of advisors.

After a week spent castigating the League, Nasser, the West, and the Jews, Amin calmed down enough to send for Arafat. They met a few days later at Amin's residence in Beirut.

"Once again," Amin began, "the Arab statesmen have failed the people of Palestine."

"Yes," Arafat agreed. "They get to go home to Syria or Jordan or Egypt while Palestinians are left to inhabit a ruined homeland with the Jews in complete control."

Amin shook his head. "Such an utter and complete failure."

"There's no other explanation for it except their own stupidity."

Amin nodded. "They were fighting a bunch of ragtag Jews. How difficult could that be for an Arab army as well equipped as Nasser's? If you had been that well supplied, that well equipped, that heavily staffed, it would have been a two-day war and we would have won."

Arafat liked that compliment at first, though the longer he considered it the less sure he was that it was a compliment at all. "Muslims," he replied, "should win against Jews every time."

"And it wasn't just Nasser and the usual ministers from the Arab League this time," Amin continued. "The PLO failed, too. It failed to defend Arabs from attack by the Jews. Failed to fight to win. Failed to throw themselves at the enemy with the abandon total war requires."

"Nasser relied too heavily on the Soviet Union," Arafat noted. "This whole thing started because of bad intelligence from them."

"And bad analysis by the Egyptians."

"And poor leadership in the PLO. Shukeiri is a diplomat, not a general. He might be at home in a negotiating room, but he's lost on the battlefield."

"And he's in Nasser's pocket all the way."

"Which makes the PLO merely an arm of the Egyptian government," Arafat added.

"Which is why *you* must take control of the situation," Amin said.

Arafat's eyes opened wide. "Me?"

"Yes, you. You are the only one who is willing to do what must be done to finally end this debacle."

Arafat was delighted with Amin's endorsement and ecstatic at having the opportunity to take charge, but he wanted to know precisely what Amin expected of him. "And what is it that I should do?" he asked.

"Kill them all," Amin growled.

"All of whom?"

"The Jews! Kill every Jew. Drive the ones who won't die into the sea. Cleanse the land of the Jewish pestilence and give it back to us."

Arafat looked Amin in the eye. "Do you mean that? Literally?"

"Yes," Amin replied. "I mean it. Kill them all."

✦ ✦ ✦ ✦ ✦

Arafat was excited to do just as Amin ordered—take the fight to the Jews. Kill them all. Drive those who remained into the sea. It was a mission he felt he'd been born to do and an undertaking about which he had dreamed for years—arrive in a Jewish village with trucks, throw back the tarps to reveal automatic weapons, and fire them until every man, woman, and child lay dead on the ground. "At last," he muttered, "I can get on with the purpose of my life."

✦ ✦ ✦ ✦ ✦

With renewed energy and enthusiasm, Arafat returned to Syria, gathered Khalaf, Wazir, and Daoud, and went to work making plans for action. "We can conceal our true intentions," he suggested, "by moving through Jordan and entering Israel from the east side of the Jordan River." Visions of what they would do had been in his mind for so long, he forgot the others did not have the same context and launched into a description without taking the time to inform them of his thoughts.

"And what are our true intentions?" Wazir asked.

"To fulfill our destiny. And the destiny of the PLO. To liberate Palestine from the Jewish plague that has descended on it." Then Arafat realized he had been thinking and dreaming of this operation for so long that he had lost track of the people he might have discussed it with or the ones who'd been with him when he articulated it before. With a sigh, he stopped himself and began at the beginning. "To take control of Palestine we must assemble, train, and equip a force that is lean, hard, and capable of moving fast. One that supplies itself and resupplies itself from what it finds along the way." He took a map from his satchel, unfolded it, spread it over the table, and pointed to a spot on the map. "This is how we will do it. But we must move quickly before Nasser or the others have time to regroup."

The discussion continued for the remainder of that day and into the night. Others offered suggestions but the final strategy followed the model suggested by Arafat. A light force, capable of moving fast but hitting hard, targeting strategic sites, then moving on to whatever was ahead.

"This will require key men and time to train," Wazir noted.

"We don't have that. We must begin with whatever we have on hand and fill in the gaps as we go." Khalaf and Daoud thought they were moving too quickly, but no one wanted to argue the point.

A few days later, Arafat and his men departed Syria and traveled through Jordan, gathering new recruits as they went. A week later, they crossed the Jordan River in disguises. On the West Bank, they established recruitment centers in Hebron, Jerusalem, and Nablus and attracted both fighters and financiers for the cause of Palestinian liberation.

After a month or two of final preparation, Arafat and the men of Fatah began nighttime raids on Jewish villages. Moving with unrelenting speed, they killed men, women, and children in every place they went. Seized weapons where they found them. Destroyed buildings, bridges, power stations, and communications lines with alarming efficiency. And when they found nothing else to plunder, pillage, or destroy, they attacked buses filled with Jewish passengers, killing them in broad daylight.

As Fatah attacks increased, Amin used its success as proof that Palestinian Arabs were the ones needed to liberate Palestine. "The men of Fatah are showing us the way forward. These are men of action. Men who get things done. Palestinians fighting for Palestine."

To financiers and the businessmen of Lebanon, he said, "Give us guns. Give us ammunition. We will solve the Israeli problem ourselves. We will rid the land of Jews ourselves. Just give us the means to do so."

And to visitors from throughout the region he argued, "Members of the Arab League have proven themselves impotent in matters of war and have shown they have no regard for us. They fought in Palestine only because they wanted to control us. We do not want their help and we certainly don't want their control. We want only to choose our own destiny. The PLO cannot give us that under Shukeiri. We need a PLO leader who is Palestinian by birth and Palestinian at heart."

Amin's message struck a chord with all who heard it and as a result, political pressure was brought to bear on Shukeiri and senior PLO leadership. They resisted at first but by December 1967, calls for their ouster mounted and they could stand it no more.

Shukeiri was forced to resign his post as PLO chairman. Senior leaders of the PLO went with him.

With Shukeiri gone, Yahya Hammuda took his place and, after consultations with Amin, invited Arafat to join the organization. Not long after Arafat joined the PLO, Khalaf and Wazir were installed in key positions. Daoud was placed in charge of PLO security. And within a month, Hammuda resigned. Arafat became chairman, giving Fatah control over the PLO.

After taking control of the PLO, Arafat contacted King Hussein of Jordan and sought a formal agreement allowing him to relocate PLO operations to a remote area in western Jordan, near the border. King Hussein, eager to accommodate Palestinian enthusiasm—and equally eager to avoid falling victim to Palestinian anger—agreed to let them into the country.

Within weeks, Arafat and the PLO occupied a large swath of territory on the west side of Jordan, effectively controlling access to Amman from all but a narrow corridor that led into Jerusalem. With Jordan's tacit approval, they began a war of attrition against Israel, crossing the border at will to continue the hit-and-run attacks they had begun as Fatah the year before.

As the PLO proved effective in fighting the Jews, it attracted money from powerful and wealthy Muslims who lived outside the region, most of whom, like King Hussein, were eager to keep radical Arabs at bay. Saudi princes channeled large sums to Arafat under the unspoken agreement that he would keep his interests away from Saudi Arabia. Businessmen in Egypt, Libya, and Morocco did the same.

With financing no longer an issue, the PLO steadily grew in power and influence, functioning as a state within a state. Although located on Jordanian territory, its members showed flagrant disregard for Jordanian law, especially in the western regions of the country. The PLO established its own system of Sharia courts, imposed its own rules, and exacted its own taxes in the form of tribute. Those who resisted met with the organization's full might and power. Few survived to resist again.

By 1970, Arafat and the PLO branched out from Palestine with members conducting airline hijackings and kidnappings throughout the world, all in the name of Palestinian liberation. Removed from its geographical context, the PLO became known as an international terrorist organization. Its members appeared on terrorist lists throughout the Western Hemisphere. Arafat seemed to revel in the notoriety. "This is how we show the world we mean what we say," he boasted. "This is how we take our message to a wider audience."

Wazir seemed to question the strategy. "But why do we need the rest of the world? Can't we solve our problems by ourselves?"

"Perhaps," Arafat replied. "But nations beyond the Middle East can help us do that more quickly."

Wazir frowned. "How is that possible?"

"European democracies are allies of Israel," Arafat explained. "Israel is their trading partner. The Jews rely on international commerce for hard currency. Those countries that do business with them can apply pressure where the Jews feel it the most." He grinned. "In the pocketbook and bank account. They have leverage with Israel that we do not."

"But will it really work?"

"Oh yes," Arafat smiled sardonically. "Liberal Americans are always looking for a cause to support. It's the way they salve their conscience for the guilt they feel over the profligate lifestyle they live."

Khalaf seemed unconvinced, too. "Hijacking an airplane does that?"

"When we take over an airplane and make our demands, they sympathize with us."

"How so?"

"Liberal news outlets broadcast reports of our demands and

back up those reports with scenes from Gaza and other areas, showing the desperate conditions in which our people are forced to live. When the liberals see that, they do not get angry at us for trashing the aircraft or threatening the lives of the passengers or even for killing the passengers."

"No?"

Arafat shook his head. "They get mad at the Jews. And when they get mad at the Jews, they send us money. They also write letters to politicians and that's where the pressure on Israel comes from."

"From the guilt wealthy Americans feel about the way they live?"

Arafat had a sinister grin. "Guilt is a terrible thing. It rots their minds and prevents them from seeing us as the enemy. Instead, they see us as a people in need of their help. The prophet Muhammad was right about how corruption works. It makes one fear the thing one enjoys the most and hate your closest enemy. It turns a friend into a foe and a foe into a friend. And that is what we are doing with the Americans. The British. The Europeans."

For the PLO, that time in the wilds of western Jordan was a time of great success. Success that brought power and influence like nothing Arafat had imagined. Amin had imagined it, because he imagined one day ruling Palestine as a king, but Arafat had only imagined war. Rampant and relentless killing, looting, and destroying was the end of his understanding and it blinded him to the arrogance that surrounded him. An arrogance that did not escape the attention of Saleem Namir.

After serving King Faisal in the quest for a Hashemite Kingdom, Namir had switched allegiance to Faisal's brother Abdullah. As Amin suspected, Namir was the one behind the attempts to draw him out when Abdullah was assassinated, and it was Namir who had orchestrated the execution of Amin's relatives when he refused to respond.

Following King Abdullah's death, his son Talal took the throne but was forced to resign following only a short reign. When Talal's son Hussein took his father's place, Namir deftly maneuvered his way into the new king's court, where he quickly became one of king's closest advisors.

Namir had been opposed to allowing the PLO into Jordan and predicted Arafat would one day threaten King Hussein's control of the country. "He sees you as young and naïve," Namir counseled. "Someone who is unable to resist his aggression." But King Hussein did not believe Namir and no one else could convince him otherwise.

In the summer of 1970, with PLO operatives aggressively hijacking airlines, bombing Israeli villages, and engaging in random acts of terror throughout the region and the world, the pressure Arafat imagined he could bring on the Jews came to rest instead on King Hussein. Arab governments, Israeli officials, and representatives from nations on every continent pointed to Jordan as the cause of the problem. "You give Arafat and his terrorists sanctuary," they said. "And you enable the PLO to kill our people, destroy our property, and terrorize our nations." They demanded that Hussein take action.

Namir thought the king had reached a critical juncture. "If you continue to allow Arafat and the PLO to use Jordan as a staging area, other Arab leaders will think you are planning to use the PLO to move against them. That you intend to use Arafat and the PLO as an instrument for expanding Jordan's control over the region. And perhaps beyond."

"That is ridiculous," Hussein scoffed. "We would never attempt such a thing."

"You might not. But if this keeps up much longer, they will not believe you when you say it. And even the Americans have come to wonder if you are after something bigger than merely supporting Arafat."

King Hussein continued to resist pressure to curtail the PLO, but then Namir learned of a plot among PLO members to assassinate Hussein. After confirming the plot was real, Namir brought the matter to the king's attention. "Abu Daoud and other members of the PLO have plotted with certain members of your government to kill you and install a government sympathetic to the PLO."

"Daoud?"

"Yes."

"You are certain of it?"

"Absolutely."

"And Arafat is behind it?"

"No. But the faction supporting Daoud would like to name Arafat as head of the government. They have not yet convinced their conspirators from your government to go along with that plan but it is the only thing that has prevented them thus far."

King Hussein looked worried. "You are certain they are working with members of my own government?"

"I am positive."

Hussein thought for a moment, then shook his head. "I do not believe it."

"Conduct your own investigation," Namir insisted. "Ask Wasfi Tal or Habis Majali to investigate and see if I am not telling the king the truth." Tal was the prime minister. Majali was the army chief of staff. Either of them could have discovered the truth with no difficulty. "But do not let this matter rest until you learn the truth. If I am right, you are in grave danger."

As Namir suggested, King Hussein ordered an investigation of the government to see if a coup d'etat was afoot. To his horror, he learned that the allegations Namir had made were true. Crucial elements of his own government, though at a sub-ministerial level, were meeting regularly with PLO members. Apparently, only the final details remained to be addressed before a take-over would be launched. One that was planned to include Hussein's execution.

Faced with a mortal threat, King Hussein ordered the army to expel the PLO. On September 17, 1970, Jordanian troops surrounded PLO positions in the western hills and attacked. Members of the PLO fought back, but after a week of heavy fighting, the Jordanian army prevailed. PLO members who were not killed fled Jordan for Lebanon. Arafat was among them.

✦ ✦ ✦ ✦ ✦

When Arafat reached Beirut, he found Amin in a fit of rage. "How could he do this?" Amin asked. "How could an Arab attack a fellow Arab?"

"I have heard reports that he was advised to do this by Saleem Namir."

At the mention of Namir, Amin became even angrier and appeared on the verge of collapse. His body shook and his face turned red. "I will have his head!" Amin shouted. "I will have his head on a platter and eat it for dinner!" He turned to Arafat. "You must go back."

"That is not—"

"You must go back and bring me both their heads. Hussein *and* Namir."

Arafat shook his head. "That is not possible."

Amin glared at him. "Why not?" he demanded.

"Because the Jordanian army now occupies all of the territory we once controlled."

Amin's eyes flashed with anger. "Is there no one from the PLO left in Jordan?"

"Daoud and two dozen men remained behind to gather up the last of the weapons and ammunition. They are all that is left in Jordan."

"Tell them to wait," Amin cautioned.

"For what?"

"Tell them to wait," Amin insisted. "And tell them to meet us in the desert."

"But where?"

"I will give you directions." Amin made his way to his desk and took a seat. "You can get a message to them?"

"Yes."

"Good." Amin took a notepad from a drawer and began to write. "I will give you the message."

Arafat sent the message, and a few days later he and Amin met Daoud in the desert near the Bedouin site where Amin once lived with Aref when they were in hiding. "I want you to assassinate Hussein," Amin directed. "And I want you to kill Saleem Namir."

Daoud grinned. "I will be all too glad to do it."

"You could die in the process," Arafat warned.

"I would gladly take that risk."

After discussing other matters, Daoud returned to the PLO encampment where he'd been hiding, high in the hills near Jerash. The men who remained with him were even more eager than he to take revenge on King Hussein and went to work planning the operation in meticulous detail. In the course of their work, they adopted the name Black September Organization. "In remembrance of the month in which the Jordanian army turned traitor and attacked us," or so they said.

Assassinating King Hussein proved more difficult than Daoud imagined, and as the weeks went by, many of his men became discouraged. However, Wasfi Tal, the prime minister, seemed an easier target and equally culpable in the attacks against the PLO. With Hussein proving an unlikely target, Daoud turned their attention to Tal and assigned men to track his movements.

In November of the following year, they learned that Tal was scheduled to travel to Cairo for high-level meetings. Many thought another invasion of Israel was being planned and someone suggested they should delay taking action. "We've heard this before,"

Daoud reflected. "Even if they attack, the Jews will destroy them once again. We must follow through as planned.

Later that month, Daoud and members of Black September traveled to Cairo, entering Egypt as consultants for a Saudi construction firm. They located Tal outside a government building and followed him to the Sheraton Cairo Hotel. Later that day, as Tal came from the elevator and crossed the lobby, two of Daoud's men opened fire on him at close range. Tal was dead before his body hit the floor.

News of Tal's death reached Amin at the residence in Beirut. He was delighted to hear it, and when he learned that the assailants were members of Black September acting on orders from Daoud, he was overjoyed and summoned Daoud to Beirut.

Daoud returned to Lebanon where he met with Amin and Arafat to discuss potential targets for additional attacks. "Most big targets inside Israel are heavily guarded," Arafat reminded. "As are the important ones in Arab countries. We need a target that affects Israel but is located outside Israeli territory. A meaningful one, but one to which we have access."

Daoud mentioned the Olympic Games were set for the following year in Munich. "Israel has a team. They are scheduled to compete."

Amin nodded. "I have many contacts in Germany who can provide important help. Inside information. Logistical support. Transportation."

"That location is better than any we have. Even better than sites right here in the Middle East."

With tentative approval from Amin and Arafat, Daoud began to plan an operation against the Israeli Olympic team for the following year. Amin assisted by contacting Salama in Hamburg and Ramadan in Berlin, then Kazim and Tibi in Munich to tell them that Daoud would be arriving there soon. "Give him all the assistance he requires."

✦ ✦ ✦ ✦ ✦

Over the next several months, Daoud traveled to Munich. Kazim and Tibi gave him a place to stay and helped familiarize him with the city. Posing as a security advisor for an Olympic team from Pakistan, Daoud obtained preliminary schedules for upcoming Olympic events and the location for the facilities where team members would be staying. The site still was under construction but Daoud learned the basic layout, noting potential access and exit points for infiltration and escape routes.

On a later visit, Kazim introduced Daoud to Mounir Samad, a Muslim Brotherhood member who worked with the Munich police. Through Samad, Daoud obtained details about Olympic security, including maps, schedules, and a manual of police procedures being developed for use during the games. With that information, Daoud adjusted the routes he'd previously noted and developed ideas and strategies for what might actually improve the plan. He also thought of how they might escape.

When he returned to Beirut, Daoud met with members of Black September. "I think we could infiltrate the dorms where the Olympic teams will be staying," he advised.

Someone questioned, "And what would we do inside?"

"We could do anything we like," Daoud replied. "I suggest we take them hostage, make a big show of it, then kill them all as we escape."

"Why wait around?" another member asked. "Why not just shoot them or blow them up while they lie in bed?"

"Be a lot easier to escape that way," another person interjected. "We could even shoot them from a distance."

Daoud shook his head emphatically. "No! This has to be dramatic. Something that catches everyone's attention. Television crews will be everywhere. We have to take advantage of that. Let the world see that something needs to be done about the Jews."

Daoud and two of his men returned to Munich. They spent a week surveying the site, taking pictures, and discussing options. By the time they concluded that visit, the others were convinced that Daoud's idea of something dramatic—kidnapping and taking hostages—would never work. "It's a recipe for disaster," one of them opined.

"We have to hit hard and move fast," another added. "Just like we did at the beginning when we used to cross from Jordan and hit Jewish villages. This is just another village. We need to inflict maximum damage, in the shortest possible time, and get out."

After reviewing the information they had collected, Daoud reluctantly agreed. By the time they left Munich for Lebanon, the improved plan was in place. "We will infiltrate the dorm, slaughter as many Israelis as possible, and get out quickly."

The next year, Daoud and members of the Black September Organization traveled to Munich for the Olympics. On September 17, 1972—a date chosen especially to commemorate their fellow PLO members who had been killed by the Jordanian army attack—slipped into the dorm where the Israeli Olympic team slept and, in a blaze of gunfire, massacred eleven members of the team. Daoud and the assassination crew escaped unharmed.

THIRTYSEVEN

BY THE WINTER OF 1973, Amin had fallen into poor health. As the following summer approached, he was obviously dying. Karimeh sent word to Salama informing him of Amin's condition. Salama came immediately from Hamburg to be by his side. He arrived in Beirut to find Amin in bed and on the verge of death. Hadad, who had served faithfully as his secretary, was with Amin. The two of them, Hadad and Salama, sat on either side of Amin's bed, the three of them talking for what they knew would be the final time.

In the midst of their conversation, Amin turned to Salama. "It is your duty to stop the Jews now. Hadad has been with me all these years, helping me, but you are the one with the strategic relationships to keep our work going. Hadad will assist you, as he has me, but you must take the lead."

Salama looked perplexed. "How do I do that?"

Amin smiled weakly. "It is an easy task. Kill all of the Jews, then the land will be ours."

Over the next week and a half, Amin repeated that instruction several times, then, near the end of June, his energy faded even more. Most days, he seemed to struggle just to draw a breath. On July 2, he rallied briefly, then lapsed into a coma and by July 4, Amin al-Husseini was dead. The official cause of death was listed as heart failure.

As with many devout Muslims, Amin had wanted to be buried on Haram ash-Sharif—Temple Mount—near Al-Aqsa Mosque in Jerusalem. When Jordan controlled East Jerusalem, such a burial would have been easily arranged. However, after the Six-Day War, Israel controlled the entire city, including access to Temple Mount. Approval for burials at that site required the approval of the Israeli government, especially in Amin's case because of the contentious relationship he'd had with the Jews.

Hadad contacted the Supreme Muslim Council and submitted a request for approval. The council forwarded that request to Yitzhak Rabin, the Israeli prime minister. Rabin declined to authorize the burial.

With the return of Amin's body for burial in Jerusalem no longer possible, Karimeh and Hadad arranged a funeral for him in Beirut. Three days after his death, Amin's body was laid to rest in the Martyrs' Cemetery, a place of honor for thousands who died in the cause of Palestinian nationalism.

After Amin was buried, Salama departed Beirut for the return trip to Hamburg. On the way, he thought about the things he and Amin had done together and about the statement Amin made to him—the charge he had given him—in their final conversation. *"It is your duty to stop the Jews now."* And the follow-up explanation: *"Kill all the Jews."*

They had tried many things to prevent the Jews from establishing a state. Alignment with the British, then the Germans. Alliances with surrounding Arab states. And revolution driven from within by Palestinian Arabs. Of these attempts, only the revolts that came from within gave them any satisfaction, though they produced only limited results on the ground. Yet despite their many and repeated attempts, they had never come near killing *all* of the Jews. "We must have missed something," Salama mumbled to himself. Or perhaps the times changed faster than they could keep up, and they just never quite got on top of an evolving situation. The thought of opportunities had, and opportunities missed, only amplified the sense of loneliness that he felt. Amin had been a leader, a guide, and a prophet. He also had been the dearest friend Salama had ever known. Now he was gone, and Salama felt very much alone.

After a day at home to recover from the trip, Salama made his way to the room he used as a study. He sat at his desk awhile, staring out the window, sipping from a cup of tea, his mind still on the events of the past and the void he felt when looking into the future. Who could possibly replace Amin al-Husseini, the Haj, the Grand Mufti of Jerusalem? How was he to carry on the work they'd started together?

From somewhere in the blackness of the morose abyss that lay before him, Salama remembered the words Amin said to him every time sent him out on his own. *"The Quran and Mein Kampf will be your guide."*

A copy of *Mein Kampf* rested on a shelf just beyond the end of the desk. He leaned forward and took it down, then flipped through the pages. The book had originally belonged to Aref—one of the copies Amin gave them when he first discovered it, way back when they all still lived in Jerusalem.

Like the others, Salama noticed Aref was gone from Cairo but he never knew why and never felt free to press the issue. One day he was there, the next he was not. But not long after Salama moved from Cairo to Germany, he met by chance an acquaintance from Tel Aviv, a newspaper editor who was also friends with Aref. From him, Salama learned that Aref was living in Germany, too. After an extensive search, Salama located him in the village of

Bliesdorf in Brandenburg on the east side of the country, not far from the Polish border.

During their only visit, Salama learned that while Aref still was living in Cairo, he had fallen in love with a German woman whose husband had come there to work on one of Nasser's hydro-electric dam projects. She found Cairo a miserable city and longed to return to Germany but had no way to do so. Then one day she learned that a relative—an uncle or cousin or something, Aref couldn't remember which—had died and left her a house in Blies-dorf. By then she and Aref were deeply involved. With the house in Bliesdorf as an option, she decided to abandon her husband and return to live in Germany. She took Aref with her.

"I don't suppose Amin ever talked about it with you," Aref had commented.

"No," Salama had replied. "He refused."

"He was very angry with me. For taking up with a non-Arab, and a non-Muslim, and a married woman. So angry, in fact, I thought he might kill me rather than let me go."

Salama had found the story highly unusual and wondered many times how much of it was true, but he liked Aref, so he kept the information to himself. A year or two after that visit, Aref died. His widow gave him Aref's copy of *Mein Kampf.* "He used to talk about you all the time," she related. "I suspect that book means something to you. It means nothing to me."

As Salama flipped through the pages of the book that day after returning from Amin's funeral, he came to a letter that was tucked between the pages near the center. He'd read it many times before but had forgotten it was there. The letter was from Latif and had been sent from Kohat, a city in western Pakistan not far from the Afghan border. Salama had been surprised to find it when he first obtained the book and was surprised again to see it just then.

Carefully and gently, Salama removed the envelope and placed the book on the desk, then he slipped the letter out, unfolded the page, and began to read. With every word from the page, he heard in his mind Latif's voice talking to him. The sound of it brought tears to his eyes and took him back again to a time when they all were together, risking their lives for whatever Amin told them they had to do. A smile came over him and he wiped the corners of his eyes with his fingers. "I wonder if Latif is still alive," he whispered.

After a moment, Salama folded the letter and returned it to the envelope, then picked up the book and began to read. Before he reached the end of the first page, he took a notepad from a desk drawer and began making notes. Amin was right. Even though thirty years had passed, the book still spoke to him.

Over the next several weeks, Salama delved into the study of *Mein Kampf*, spending hours at his desk reading and making notes in between his duties at the Hamburg mosque. He thought often of Amin and remembered how Amin took advantage of every opportunity afforded him. Salama wondered if there were opportunities that he might avail himself of to rid Palestine of Jews. To fulfill the mandate given to him by Amin.

At noon one day, he left the house and walked up the street to the mosque. As he did, he saw a group of young people on the sidewalk across the street. Students from the nearby Hamburg University, he supposed. Students came from all over the world to the university. Most of them arrived, gained an education, then returned home. Or moved on to somewhere else. He had worked with some of them, recruiting them for the Brotherhood, but he had not taught them about the lessons of *Mein Kampf*, partly because he was distracted by other things, and partly because the Germans had an aversion for that part of their history. He didn't want to risk causing trouble with the other things they had been doing—growing the Brotherhood's membership, supporting Ramadan and his activities. The last thing they needed was for rumors to start about people at the mosque teaching from Hitler's book. Now, however, he felt emboldened by Amin's final words to him and by the example from Amin's life, which was fresh on his mind.

A few days later, Salama announced a new class at the mosque. "A class designed to teach university students about the lessons Amin al-Husseini gleaned from Hitler's book *Mein Kampf.* We'll explore the ways those teachings reinforce similar ideas from the Quran." It was a risky thing to conduct such a class, even twenty years after the war, but he thought by couching it as an academic inquiry, he might avoid trouble from meddlesome personnel who closely followed policy guidelines.

The class was offered in the evenings, and attendance on the first night was sparse. Perhaps five people showed up. Salama was unsure what to do with them, so he decided to begin at the beginning and told them how his friend, the Grand Mufti of Jeruslem, discovered the book and taught a class just like the one he was teaching them. "Most of what I'm going to tell you came from the Grand Mufti. In many ways, he is here with us, teaching us ideas that he began to develop fifty years ago."

The class met weekly. At the following session, four extra people attended. Ten more came the week after that. And finally Salama had to limit attendance to no more than twenty or so. There was never an empty chair.

✦ ✦ ✦ ✦ ✦

In 1979, following a decade of coups and revolution, the Soviet Union invaded Afghanistan and placed the government of the country in the hands of a socialist regime. Policies implemented by that regime led to reforms of traditional Muslim practices, including the grant of greater political rights to women and universal education. It also meant domination of the country by a foreign power. Though not traditionally thought of as Western, influences from Soviet Russia changed the way people dressed, the kinds of entertainment they sought, and the degree of social mobility they came to expect. Islamic restrictions about social interaction were lifted.

Those changes were particularly evident in Kabul, but residents living in rural areas held on to traditional practices and beliefs. They were angered by what they viewed as the degrading transformation of their people and felt the country was being corrupted. When Ramadan learned of the coup and resulting Soviet intervention, he came to see Salama.

After discussing the latest news reports, Ramadan said, "I was more familiar with the region before I moved to Germany. Since then, I have concentrated on our work here and have not kept in touch with the people I know in Pakistan and the border area. But this situation in Afghanistan seems very much like the one you and Amin and the others faced in Palestine with the British. A foreign power occupying our native lands."

"Yes," Salama replied. "It would seem so."

"If that is the case," Ramadan continued, "this situation might present not only a tragedy but also an opportunity. The kind of ambiguity in which Allah often chooses to work."

Salama frowned. "For us?"

Ramadan shook his head. "For the Brotherhood."

"We would need a report from the area," Salama cautioned, "rather than relying on rumors and thirdhand information."

"I agree," Ramadan replied. "But I have things scheduled in the weeks ahead that prevent me from traveling there anytime soon."

That's when Salama realized the point of the meeting. "I can go," he offered.

The following week, Salama made travel arrangements and found someone to cover his duties at the mosque. The week after that, he departed Hamburg and traveled to Islamabad,

Pakistan, then hired a truck to take him over the mountains into Afghanistan.

For the first few days Salama simply sat and listened. By a campfire, in the tent of a warlord, at a shop in a village. Gradually he pieced together the stories he heard. Brutality from the government—a puppet state installed for the purpose of administering the country with a pro-Soviet policy. Brutality from occupying Soviet troops. Frustration that no one seemed capable of mounting an effective response. It was just as he and Ramadan had suspected; a repeat of the situation they faced with the British in Palestine fifty years earlier.

After another week of listening, Salama met with a group of young Afghanis in Jalalabad. "You have a sense of purpose," he began. "The purpose to rid your country of foreigners and traitors and return it to Islamic rule. What you lack is the underlying instruction in how to do that. I am here to give it."

For the next three weeks, Salama instructed them in the tenets of Islamic faith and the need for strict adherence to Sharia law. Taking the familiar and setting it in the context of the struggle between Islam and the West. As he did, he introduced them to the major themes of Amin's teaching regarding Hitler's concepts in *Mein Kampf* and those of Islam as reflected in the Quran. His young students absorbed every word that came from his lips. That first group became two and before long he was traveling around the outskirts of the city, meeting with a new group every day.

Inspired and empowered by what they learned, Salama's study groups took on a militant characteristic. Before long, they talked of jihad. "Like the men of old," they reminisced. "Like you and the Grand Mufti in Palestine." They adopted a military-training regimen, referred to themselves as the mujahideen—those on a jihad—and blended the idea of spiritual jihad with military fervor. "We will take back the country for Allah!" they shouted. "Take back the country for Allah!"

After weeks of training, the mujahideen grew restless and began scouring the countryside, searching for government targets they could raid to express their displeasure with the secular, socialist government. As they grew more aggressive, Salama instructed them on the approach used in Palestine by the first resistors and by the PLO. "Move fast. Hit hard. And do your best to capture better weapons, more explosives. Live off the land in every way."

With practice, mostly by trial and error, the mujahideen slowly broadened their attacks and increased the damage inflicted on Soviet and government outposts. Unrest increased also and, as the men grew more and more comfortable with their roles in fighting for the cause of Islam, they began to talk of toppling the current regime.

By then Salama had been in Afghanistan for almost six months. He was weary from the constant travel, always moving from one site to the next, and from the rigors of being constantly on guard against Soviet troops, spies, and snipers. He also was concerned about the mosque in Hamburg, and so he made one final visit to each of the seven groups he'd established, then hired a truck to take him over the mountain to Islamabad, Pakistan. From there, after a short delay, he returned to Germany.

In Hamburg, Salama rejoined the weekly study group he'd formed there, addressed several details at the mosque that had gone lacking in his absence, and rested. *This wasn't so difficult in years past,* he thought. But he no longer was a young man.

THIRTYEIGHT

AS TROUBLE CONTINUED in Afghanistan, the Soviet Union sent additional troops into the country. Tanks and armored personnel carriers patrolled the roads. Warplanes and helicopters patrolled the sky. Soldiers and government officials applied ever-increasing pressure in an attempt to quell the uprising, rounding up militants and executing them on site. Still, the violence grew more intense with each passing day.

Salama watched reports on television and read about them in the newspaper. He also received personal accounts through letters smuggled to him from the people he'd met and worked with. Friends. Acquaintances. Fellow Muslims. Forced to live in the horrors of a society subjected to the worst forms of brutality and repression. At first, Salama thought the worst of it might be an anomaly that would subside with time, but when reports of escalating atrocities persisted, he decided to go back and see for himself what was happening.

Once again, Salama made his way to Islamabad, Pakistan, then hired a truck to take him over the mountains into Afghanistan.

After a day to recover from the journey, he started around the region, meeting with the groups he had previously established. From them he heard personal accounts of how oppressive the Soviet occupation had become. "The Soviets were invited by the socialists to help them destroy our traditional way of life, or so they said. They are doing a good job of it, too."

"They are opposed to everything Islam teaches."

"The soldiers are worse than pigs," someone said. "But government agents are even worse. They rape the women. Kill the men. Take whatever they want."

"Men who once were devout Muslims, using their position to steal, plunder, and devour whatever they like."

As Salama had instructed before, the men had engaged in hit-and-run attacks, but most of the attacks had been against patrols of less than a dozen men and on unoccupied government buildings. "That is as much as we can do," they lamented. "We do not have the kinds of weapons we need."

Salama repeated again stories of how he and others had struggled in Palestine against a British occupation and how, more recently, the PLO fought against the Jews. "Move fast. Hit as hard as you can," he stressed, "but always with an eye toward capturing the next biggest weapon. Light arms and ammunition. Then heavier. A fifty-caliber machine gun. A grenade launcher. Shoulder-fired missiles if you can find them. Missiles would be best. That way you could attack from a safer distance and have time to get away before anyone could respond. You have to fight, but you also have to survive to fight again. That's how you gain the upper hand."

"It's very frustrating, though," someone responded. "We hit them, but they can hit back much harder."

"You must take the long view," Salama warned, "and work to improve your position one step at a time, one day at a time, one attack at a time. But always hit hard and kill as many of them as you can. Make the Soviet soldiers' lives so miserable they will want to leave and go back to where they came from."

Salama remained in Afghanistan three months, encouraging the people he knew to keep fighting. He also worked to discover whether the rumors of missiles from America were true, but he was unable to find anyone who had personally seen the weapons.

✦ ✦ ✦ ✦ ✦

At the end of his third month, Salama departed Afghanistan, resolved to find a way to supply the mujahideen with the arms and munitions they needed to win against the Soviets. As had become his custom, he hired a driver to take him over the mountains to Islamabad. This time, however, instead of going straight to the airport in Islamabad, as originally planned, he went to Kohat, the place where Latif was living when he wrote to Aref in the letter Salama found in his copy of *Mein Kampf.*

After discreet inquiries, Salama succeeded in locating Latif, his old friend from Palestine, and soon reached the residence. Latif was excited to see Salama, and the two talked late into the night. In that conversation, Salama learned the details of Operation Atlas—the failed Nazi plan to insert spies into Palestine.

"We had trouble from the beginning," Latif recalled. "We were dropped in the wrong place. Our equipment and supplies were scattered everywhere. It was a disaster right from the start." The rough start left them vulnerable to discovery, which led to their arrest and imprisonment. Latif laughed. "But my cousin worked at the prison. He helped me escape. And another cousin worked on the docks. He got me on a boat that brought me here to Pakistan."

"But you never tried to rejoin us?"

"By then, it was obvious the Germans were not going to win,

so I chose to stay here until the war ended. When the end came, I was married and had two children." His wife entered the room with tea. He smiled at her.

Salama nodded. "We wondered what happened to you."

"Amin never told you?"

Salama was surprised. "He knew?"

"I wrote him several times."

"He never said."

Latif had a kind expression. "I think he was disappointed."

"But you found peace."

"Yes, very much so."

Salama intended to stay with Latif only one more day but as they continued to talk, Latif told him of a young man with whom he had been working. "Abdullah Azzam. He grew up in Palestine. In the West Bank."

"A member of the Brotherhood?" Salama asked.

"Oh yes. And he was trained at the University of Damascus."

Salama nodded approvingly. "An educated man."

"He has taught many places. Most recently, he has been lecturing at the university in Jeddah."

"I thought you said he was a young man?"

Latif grinned. "To us, he is very young."

Salama felt a pang of loneliness. "Time is passing much too quickly."

Latif nodded. "Which is why we must do our best to pass on to the next generation the things we learned."

"Amin taught us much."

"He did. And we have learned much on our own, too."

"But what of this young man? Abdullah Azzam. He is your pupil?"

"Not quite. But I am trying to be a guide."

"How often do you see him?"

"Every few months. He will be here later this week. You

should delay your return. Stay with me until he comes, so you can meet him."

Salama was weary and he had been gone from the mosque in Hamburg far too long, but he enjoyed visiting with Latif and was intrigued by Latif's description of Azzam. He also enjoyed the setting at Latif's house, with the mountains in the distance and the cool shade in back, so he decided to stay awhile longer.

✦ ✦ ✦ ✦ ✦

Later that week, Azzam arrived at Latif's house. Salama liked him immediately and the feeling seemed to be mutual. At first, they talked of their experiences and the friends they had in common, but gradually the conversation turned to the trouble in Afghanistan.

"When foreigners occupy your homeland," Azzam said, "you have a duty to kill them to defend your way of life."

Salama glanced in Latif's direction. "We have heard that before."

"'Kill them all,'" Latif responded, quoting Amin.

"Our mentor," Salama explained. "Amin told us many times the remedy for the situation in Palestine was to kill the Jews. 'Kill them all,' he said."

"'And those who won't die,'" Latif added, "'drive them into the sea.'"

"I heard him speak once," Azzam recalled, "when I was younger. In Cairo."

"That was a good place for him then," Latif noted.

"Until Nasser took over," Salama added. "Until then, Amin's popularity was an asset. After Nasser took over, it became a threat."

They were silent a moment, then Azzam asked, "Do you think that's a realistic strategy? To kill them all. A war of attrition."

"I'm not sure we can kill all the Soviets in Afghanistan. They will only bring in replacements and they are a huge country."

"But you could make their life miserable enough that they will want to return home."

"I have been telling them that," Salama responded.

Azzam looked over at him. "Telling who?"

"The people with whom I've been working in Afghanistan."

"You have been to Afghanistan?"

"Yes. Teaching some of the men."

"I like that idea," Azzam commented. "Of making the Soviets so miserable they want to go home."

"It worked with the British in Palestine," Latif insisted.

"But for that strategy to work," Salama contended, "we would need widespread resistance. Not just the efforts of fighters in the mountains."

"I have considered issuing a fatwah," Azzam said. "To rally public support against the Soviets. Telling Afghanis that it is their duty to rise up and defend their country."

"It would take something like that to make the Russians want to leave," Latif agreed. "Widespread, unrelenting opposition from the public. Always attacking. Giving them no reprieve."

"Whatever the strategy," Salama persisted, "we must find a way to help our brothers in Afghanistan. They need guns and ammunition. And those things cost money."

"I know people in Saudi Arabia," Azzam added cautiously. "People with lots of money."

Latif raised an eyebrow. "Would any of them be interested in helping?"

"One of my students might be helpful. Osama bin Laden. He is the son of a wealthy man who owns a construction business. They build things all over the country. I could ask him."

"That would be good. Will you ask him?"

"Yes, I will."

✦ ✦ ✦ ✦ ✦

After a few months in Hamburg, Salama was rested and ready to return to Afghanistan. He was especially interested in returning to Latif's home in Kohat. This time, however, he asked Imad Kazim, from the mosque in Munich, to join him. Kazim had heard about the work Salama was doing and was eager to make the trip.

Salama and Kazim arrived at Kohat to find Azzam was there with his student bin Laden. Another man, bin Laden's friend Ayman al-Zawahiri, was also there. As they became acquainted, Salama learned that Zawahiri was born in Cairo and joined the Brotherhood when he was fourteen, the same year Qutb was executed as one of the conspirators in the attempted assassination of Nasser. "That was the event that inspired me," Zawahiri recalled. "We were very young then, but several of my classmates and I formed our own cell. Dedicated to the overthrow of the Egyptian government."

Zawahiri continued with his education, attended medical school, and became a surgeon. When civil war broke out in Afghanistan, Zawahiri began making trips to the region to treat wounded Fedayeen, which is how he came to know Azzam and how he came to be at Latif's house that day with bin Laden.

Bin Laden was interested in hearing stories from Latif and Salama's association with Amin al-Husseini. It didn't take much coaxing to get them started. Latif told of how they first met, and Salama told about their life in Cairo when they were in school. As their stories moved on to their days in Palestine, the discussion turned to Amin's approach to occupation by foreign powers. "He always said," Latif recounted, "'Get what you can from them, use them to make yourself strong, but never surrender your soul to them.'"

"What did he hope to gain from the British?" bin Laden asked.

"Weapons," Salama interjected.

"And training," Latif added. "Those were the two things we needed from the outside. Motivation was not a problem. Commitment was not a problem. But at that time the British fought the Ottomans, some of our people still were committed to warfare in the old ways. The British and, indeed, all of the West had moved to mechanized warfare."

"Industrial warfare," Zawahiri commented.

"Exactly." Latif nodded. "Back then, the region was not stocked with automatic weapons or sophisticated explosives, as it is now."

"He taught you well," bin Laden added.

"Yes," Latif replied. "He taught us constantly."

"One of the primary things he taught," Salama continued, "was the idea of pairing teachings from the Quran and the prophet Muhammad with ideas from *Mein Kampf* and the teachings of Adolf Hitler.

Bin Laden raised an eyebrow. "I have heard mention of this, but I have not heard any exposition of the things he actually said. Just that he matched the two."

"Latif was the one who first introduced him to *Mein Kampf.* Stole a copy from the house of a friend in Istanbul and brought it to him."

Bin Laden laughed out loud at the comment, but Latif waved him off good-naturedly. "I didn't steal it," he said with a grin. "My friend gave it to me. But I *was* the one who gave the book to Amin."

"He didn't read it at first," Salama remembered. "It took some time for him to pick it up."

"He was sitting with his wife one night as she recovered from the birth of their child," Latif said. "He saw the book on a table and began reading. After that, he never stopped reading and rereading it."

Salama chuckled. "And he never stopped talking to us about it, either."

Kazim listened attentively. He'd heard many of their stories before but that day, with the five of them sitting together, he was especially alert. Bin Laden, however, seemed thoroughly energized by the conversation. "I have heard bits and pieces of Amin and his band of followers. Some from older members of the Muslim Brotherhood. Some from relatives of the Sharif of Mecca. But hearing them now, from two who were there at the beginning, is very special to me. As if we are connecting the present to the past."

They talked into the night, with Kazim telling about the work Amin started in Germany, the Institute in Berlin and the mosques in Munich and Hamburg. Gradually, though, the discussion turned to the Afghan resistance and the need for arms and munitions. Bin Laden had spent the past several months attempting to supply arms to the Fedayeen, but the logistics of paying for supplies and transporting them to the region was daunting. "We need a quicker, more efficient means of paying for the items they need," he reminded.

"First," Salama put in, "we need money to pay for them."

"Money is not a problem," bin Laden replied. "I have access to money. I brought a large sum with me. All of it in US twenty-dollar bills."

"Good," Salama responded. "That will help."

"But it is not nearly enough," Zawahiri injected. "Which is the problem we were discussing earlier. A better form of payment that does not require lugging sacks of cash over the mountains."

"We have been blessed so far," bin Laden said. "No one has attempted to take it from us. But the mountains are full of people with agendas. Encounter the wrong ones and life could become . . . difficult."

Salama spoke up. "I can help with that."

"What would you propose?"

"We need an organization. An entity," Salama replied. "With a name, I can open a bank account in Germany. We can collect and disburse the money through it."

Latif grinned. "This is another of Amin's devices." He gestured with a finger for emphasis. "Whenever he wanted to do something, he always formed an entity for it. Sometimes a legally separate entity. Sometimes just a name. But either way, when he started something, he named it."

"Then we should have a name," Kazim decided. "What shall we call it?"

They discussed the matter for an hour and finally agreed to call their collaboration the Afghan Services Bureau. "An organization to raise money for the Afghan resistance effort," bin Laden said. Then they consecrated the venture with prayers to Allah.

THiRTYNiNE

WHEN SALAMA AND KAZIM returned to Hamburg, they contacted an attorney who was a member of the Muslim Brotherhood and, with his assistance, formed the Afghan Services Bureau as a legitimate legal entity dedicated to the purpose of furthering education opportunities in Afghanistan.

With legal documents in hand, Salama and Kazim encountered no difficulty in establishing a bank account at a financial institution with offices located just up the street from the mosque. As promised, bin Laden's friends and family members in Saudi Arabia contributed large sums of money to the bureau, all of which was funneled into the account, then to banks in Switzerland, the United Kingdom, and the United States before moving through the financial system to the accounts of arms dealers and suppliers around the world.

Before long, shoulder-fired rockets arrived in the mountains of Afghanistan, along with the latest in automatic weapons, ammunition, and explosives. Not long after that, life for the occupying Soviet troops became unbearable and they began retreating toward the Soviet Union.

✦ ✦ ✦ ✦ ✦

In the meantime, bin Laden, Zawahiri, and Azzam moved to Afghanistan, established a training site in the mountains, and melded disparate Afghan resistance groups into an international organization known as Al-Qaeda. These Salafist Jihadists stood in direct succession to the teachings of Rashid Rida, the Egyptian cleric who shaped the beliefs of Izz ad-Din al-Qassam and Amin al-Husseini and spawned a revolution in Palestine. An intellectual and doctrinal descendant of Hassan al-Banna and the Muslim Brotherhood, and the teachings of Amin al-Husseini that infused the Quran with Hitler's radical Nazi hatred for the Jews. All of that found a place in bin Laden's Al-Qaeda.

By then, Salama, Latif, Hadad, and all the others who had been with Amin from the beginning were dead. Only Kazim and Tibi remained from the time Amin spent in Germany. They knew him personally and worked with him intimately.

In the final years of his life, Kazim visited the mosque in Berlin, which he helped found, and the one in Munich, which he and Tibi founded together. Most of his time, however, was spent in Hamburg where he continued to lead students in the study of the Quran and *Mein Kampf*, showing them how the Quran applied to current society through the teachings of Muhammad and Hitler, always with the focus of the lessons on the evil and corrupt Jews and their Western facilitators. "This," he taught, "is the most important contribution I can make now. Ensuring that the teachings of Amin al-Husseini continue to influence the minds of those who follow." He used Salama's notes to make certain he left nothing out.

In Afghanistan, a group calling themselves the Taliban took root. Teaching strict adherence to Sharia law, they gradually gained control of the entire country. With Taliban approval and support, bin Laden's camp, high up in the mountains, operated openly without fear of government reprisals. As the training program developed, bin Laden remembered the teachings of Amin al-Husseini that Salama had presented that day at Latif's home in Pakistan. He obtained his own copy of *Mein Kampf* and did his best to remember the details Salama shared and to find his own connections between the two documents. Finally, though, he decided, "We should have them come and teach our people."

Zawahiri shook his head sadly. "Latif and Salama are both dead."

"So the teaching is lost?"

"I think Kazim, the man who came with Salama that day, continues to teach the same thing."

"Find him," bin Laden instructed. "And see if he will come and teach us those things again."

✦ ✦ ✦ ✦ ✦

A month later, Zawahiri appeared at the mosque in Hamburg. Kazim remembered him from the time they met at Latif's home in Kohat. As they sat together in Kazim's office and had coffee, Zawahiri asked about whether Kazim would come to Afghanistan to teach at their training camp in the mountains.

"What sort of training camp?" Kazim wondered.

"Training men for the jihad against Western corruption." Kazim was interested and they talked about details of the plan. The length of time he might stay in the country. The need for someone to cover his absence at the mosque. And the arrangements used by Zawahiri and others for traveling to and from the base.

Zawahiri stayed a few days with Kazim, and while he was there attended a session of the student class where Kazim taught about the Quran and principles gleaned from *Mein Kampf.* "Together, they provide a theological and philosophical framework that supports a political jihad," he noted, "not merely an expression of personal piety but of political righteousness." The notion that in Islam one could and should remove corruption from one's personal life and also from society at large, rooting it out even before it becomes strong enough to be apparent to others.

In his lessons, Kazim relentlessly attacked the Jews. "Even the civilians who have heretofore been thought of as innocent bystanders are to be treated as the enemy," he emphasized. "They facilitate a government who hates us. They elect the officials who kill our people and wage war against us. They must be made to stop. They promote a culture made weak by inbreeding with slime. They must be made to stop." Zawahiri was enthralled.

✦ ✦ ✦ ✦ ✦

A few months later, Kazim arranged for Tibi to cover his obligations in Hamburg and traveled to Afghanistan, following the route he and Salama used on their earlier journey. He remained at bin Laden's camp for almost two months and spent his days teaching about the things he had learned from Amin—ideas from the Quran mixed with Hitler's ideology from *Mein Kampf.*

While he was at the camp, Kazim spent many long nights talking with bin Laden and Zawahiri about the West and the United States in particular. "Politicians in America cannot get elected without Jewish support," he opined. "Conservative candidates must support Israel in order to gain the Christian vote. And liberal candidates must give support to Israel in order to gain the support of East Coast moneyed elite."

"Either way," Zawahiri averred, "it is an unholy alliance."

Kazim agreed. "I am not certain the Americans understand the depth to which they are being manipulated by the Jews. The Christians seem especially blind to it."

"But as you have said," bin Laden noted, "even the civilians are to be seen as complicit now."

"We no longer have the luxury of ignoring their role in facilitating Jewish corruption."

"But how do we stop them?" bin Laden asked. "What is the best way?" It seemed to be more than an academic question.

"I think we must consider a major attack against the Americans," Zawahiri said.

"But will that only bring a response against us? We cannot inflict enough damage on the United States to prevent it from striking back." They continued to discuss the topic in their nightly meetings, but no one had a definitive solution.

A few weeks later, Khalid Sheikh Mohammed arrived at the camp. Zawahiri introduced him to Kazim—the two had not previously met. That night, they sat together as usual in bin Laden's tent. After they talked of many things, the topic turned to the question of an attack on America. Khalid responded quickly. "Airplanes," he said.

Bin Laden frowned. "Airplanes?"

"Yes," Khalid reiterated. "Airplanes. Commercial aircraft. They can easily be weaponized. Get a person onboard. Take control of the flight. Fly the plane into a target. They are loaded with fuel, especially the ones on long flights. They're like flying gas bombs."

"We would need to find a weak access point. Security is tight in Europe. Many checks are now in place."

"That might be an issue," Khalid conceded. "But we do not need to use an armed person. He could use whatever he found. A plastic knife will easily lodge in a person's throat, given enough pressure. And not every location is as strict as Europe. I am sure we could find a place to get some of our people aboard. They fly all the time. Continue to discuss the matter."

Bin Laden's eyes sparkled with interest. "But we would need

the right kind of people. Intelligent enough to fly a commercial airplane. Accustomed to Western life so they would blend in without being detected beforehand."

"And fluent in English," Kazim added.

Zawahiri frowned. "Why English?"

"If we are attacking sites in the United States," Kazim said, "they would need to be in the country already. Before boarding the flight. That way, they could all board the same day and the attacks could be coordinated."

"That is a good point," Khalid acknowledged.

"I meet with students every week at the mosque in Hamburg," Kazim added. "I teach them the same thing I have been teaching here. Perhaps some of them would be acceptable."

"Are they committed enough to do this?" bin Laden asked. "They would be making the ultimate sacrifice."

"Some of them are," Kazim replied.

Bin Laden appeared hesitant as they discussed operational aspects of the attacks. Khalid, however, was enthusiastic. "We must plan this meticulously. And perhaps make several dry runs from airports in other countries to see what might be required, how airline employees react in certain situations, and the kinds of things that might be onboard the flight that could be used as weapons."

"And," Kazim said, "we must choose a site for such an attack that would produce dramatic consequences. They will surely strike back and we must make it worth the sacrifice."

Zawahiri wagged his finger. "I would not be so quick to think our attack would have no consequence."

"What do you mean?"

"New York is the financial capital of the world. With some of the tallest buildings in the world. If we hit the right places, we could bring the American financial system to a halt. And when it stops, the world stops."

Kazim frowned. "You said *places*. Are you thinking of multiple locations?"

"As you said." Zawahiri smiled. "If we are going to this much trouble, we should make it worth our while. And worth the sacrifice."

✦ ✦ ✦ ✦ ✦

Khalid Sheikh Mohammed had seemed beside himself with enthusiasm at the prospect of planning an attack on the United States. Over the next several weeks, he and Kazim met almost daily to discuss the plot, which Khalid now referred to simply as "the planes."

Kazim returned to Hamburg expecting to hear from Khalid immediately about moving forward with the details—choosing students to participate, vetting them carefully, presenting them to bin Laden for approval, placing them in the United States. But first one year, then the next passed without so much as a message or a note.

Then one warm spring day, Ramadan appeared at the mosque in Berlin. He was accompanied by Khalid Sheikh Mohammed. They ate lunch together and Kazim tried to get Khalid to tell him news from Afghanistan, but Khalid gave only evasive answers, relegating their conversation to small talk. But after Ramadan left to return to Berlin, Khalid suggested, "Show me the students in your class. The ones you are teaching about the Quran and *Mein Kampf*."

That evening, at the appointed time for the Quran, *Mein Kampf* class, Khalid sat to one side of the room and watched the students while Kazim taught the lesson. When the class ended, he waited until everyone was gone, then asked, "Who was the young man who sat on the front row? The one with the intense eyes and permanent scowl."

"That is Mohamed Atta," Kazim replied. "He arrived in Hamburg not too long ago and enrolled in a graduate architectural program at Hamburg University of Technology. He's a serious student. Very devout."

"A member of the Brotherhood?"

"Yes."

"Works hard?"

"Very hard. Fluent in German, Arabic. Gets good grades."

"And English?"

Kazim nodded. "He is fluent in English, too. But he eschews Western life and all of its influences. Appalled more than most by the extent to which Western life has corrupted Arabs and Muslims in particular. He has said several times that the only way to rid the world of the corruption is to rid the world of the Americans."

Khalid smiled. "He sounds like the kind of person for which we have been searching."

At first, Kazim was puzzled by the comment. Then he remembered their discussions about a plot against the United States. "You mean the planes?"

"Yes. The planes."

Kazim beamed with satisfaction. "He would be perfect for it. And his friends, too."

"Who are they?"

"The men seated with him tonight, near the front. Marwan al-Shehhi and Ziad Jarrah. They are friends of his from school. He recruited them for the class."

"And they are committed to our cause?"

"Very much so."

That Friday after prayer, Kazim introduced Khalid to Atta. They talked alone for a while and were joined by the others—Marwan al-Shehhi and Ziad Jarrah.

A few days later, Khalid left Hamburg to return to Afghanistan. Nothing much happened after he was gone, but a few months later, Kazim noticed that Atta and the others were not present at the class or at Friday prayers. He asked around and learned that they had gone on a trip together, but no one knew where or when they would return.

FORTY

EARLY ON THE MORNING of September 11, 2001, Mohamed Atta boarded a flight from Boston's Logan Airport that would carry him to New York City. He made his way down the aisle to his assigned seat, then squeezed into it and placed the seat belt across his lap. Moments later, the aircraft pushed back from the gate and rolled down the taxiway. Atta was nervous. Almost jittery. The veins in his neck throbbed and his skin felt clammy. He flexed his fingers a few times, balling them into a fist and tensing the muscles in his forearm. *Nothing to worry about,* he told himself. The others would take care of the rough stuff. He and Omari would fly the plane. That's all he needed to think about. Flying the plane.

To his left was Abdulaziz al-Omari, a Saudi Arabian. They had traveled together that morning on the flight to Boston, but the others—Wail al-Shehri, Waleed al-Shehri, and Satam al-Suqami—were seated a few rows behind him. Atta caught sight of them as he entered the plane but avoided making eye contact. Even now he resisted the urge to crane his head around for one last reassuring look in their direction.

At the end of the runway, the aircraft came to a stop. It sat there a moment, then Atta heard the engines whine as they revved to full throttle. There was a lurch as the pilot released the brakes, and the aircraft started forward. It lumbered down the runway, picked up speed, and finally leapt into the air. Atta felt his back pressed against the seat and he gripped the armrests tightly with both hands. He hated flying.

As the plane gained altitude, it banked slowly to the right. Out the window, Atta caught sight of the city lights as the plane turned away from Boston. They were turning westward, he surmised. Steering to a heading that would take them toward California. He glanced around at the passengers seated near him. A smile tightened the muscles in his cheeks. They had no idea what was about to happen. No notion of never reaching their destination. At least, not the destination they planned. For a moment he felt sorry for them, but he pushed that thought aside. They were Americans. They benefited from America's corruption. They enabled it. Now they must pay the price. That was what he had been taught at the camp in Afghanistan. That is what he believed.

Fifteen minutes into the flight, the seat belt sign on the bulkhead turned off, and the pilot announced that beverage service would begin soon. Atta unfastened his seat belt and stood, then glanced in Waleed's direction. Of the three men brought onboard for muscle, Waleed was his favorite and the one in whom he had the most confidence. A look, a gesture, a nod was all it took to communicate with Waleed and he never hesitated. He acted. Swiftly. Powerfully. Decisively.

Without lingering, Atta stepped from his seat into the aisle and started toward the cockpit door. He reached it just as two attendants appeared in first class with a beverage cart. One moved toward him, a look of concern on her face, as if she meant to block his way. Before she could act or speak, Waleed grabbed her arms and pinned them behind her back while Wail secured her wrists with a zip tie he produced from his pocket. Atta heard a commotion behind him, then a scream. Nothing would stop them now.

By then, Atta was at the cockpit door and he grasped the knob with his right hand, gave it a twist, and pushed, forcing his way into the cockpit. Atta and the three men with him rushed inside. Without pause, Wail reached over the pilot's shoulder and slit his throat with a box cutter. Satam did the same to the co-pilot. Blood gushed from the gaping wounds in their necks, spilled down their clothes, and dripped onto the flight deck. Waleed unbuckled the pilot's harness and dragged his body from the seat, then threw it down to block the door. Satam did the same with the co-pilot. While they did that, Atta climbed into the pilot's seat.

Once seated in the cockpit, Atta grasped the wheel with both hands and felt the weight of the plane pull against his arms as the autopilot disengaged and the flight controls came alive. A smile turned up the corners of his mouth as he banked the plane sharply to the left.

Seconds later, Atta glanced across the instrument panel and found it a bewildering sea of screens, gauges, and panels. He'd trained for months on a simulator at the school in Florida and was certain he understood what they all meant. One for the navigation system. Another for the engine controls. A dozen more he'd determined were unnecessary and had quickly forgotten. But now, in the moment when it all counted, he felt confused. Atta closed his eyes, took a deep breath, and forced his body to relax. He knew this. He had read the manuals. He could figure it out.

Atta opened his eyes and glanced once more across the indicators on the panel. The navigation display appeared to be in map mode and there was a button to press to change it. Somewhere. Somehow. The adrenaline coursing through his body caused his thoughts to bounce from one to the next to the next.

"Compass," he snarled. "Where's the compass?" The flight instructor had told him in an offhanded, almost joking manner that if all else failed he could use the magnetic compass. But where was it? His palms were sweaty, and he felt the fabric of his shirt stick to the skin of his back. Everyone had performed as planned. *They* were in control. Now the entire operation rested on *him* and—

Just then he caught sight of the compass. A round black ball with white letters and numbers. Mounted at the top of the windshield, near the center. Atta breathed a sigh of relief and hoped the others hadn't noticed how desperate he'd been.

Using the compass as his guide, he set the plane on a course to the south. Off to the left, far in the distance, the water of the Atlantic Ocean was barely visible. He turned the craft farther in that direction, pointing it on a path toward the coastline.

Minutes later, as the ocean drew nearer, Atta banked the plane to the right and followed the water, keeping it just off his left shoulder as they continued south toward New York, hoping not to fly past the city. It all looked much smaller from twenty thousand feet.

Fifteen minutes later, New York City came into view. "Look," Satam said, pointing over Atta's shoulder. "That is the city."

Atta smiled and pushed the wheel forward, causing the plane to gradually descend. "Not too much," Omari cautioned. "Not yet. We must get all the way there."

"I know," Atta growled. "I've done this many times in practice."

Over Yonkers, the Twin Towers of the World Trade Center came into view, standing stark and angular against the clear blue sky.

"There it is!" Omari exclaimed. "There it is!"

"Allahu Akbar!" Atta shouted and the others picked it up as a chant. "Allahu Akbar! Allahu Akbar! God is great! God is great!" And all the while, the Trade Center loomed larger and larger in the airplane's windshield. Atta stared ahead, praying for the strength to see the mission through to the end. All the while, the towers grew bigger and bigger before him.

As they flew over midtown, they passed other buildings on the left and right. They were so low that the buildings seemed so close he could reach out and touch them as they went by. Atta ignored the sights and focused his eyes on the first of the Twin Towers, the northernmost building of the World Trade Center. He knew it from the photos he'd seen online. The one with the radio tower on top. That's the one he wanted. That was his target. Others would be along in a few minutes to strike the building next to it.

By then, the North Tower was close. Still Atta did not deviate from the plan but kept the nose of the plane pointed toward the upper one-third of the building. The windows on the side loomed larger than ever. Atta wondered fleetingly if the people inside had any idea what was about to happen. Could those infidels know they were about to be sacrificed to Allah? Did they know—

Suddenly the nose of the plane struck the building and shattered its windows into thousands of pieces. With only the slightest loss of momentum, the plane ripped through the outer skin of the building and plowed forward, scattering people, desks, and office partitions aside. It pushed through a wall, then another, and then into a corridor near the elevators where it seemed to grind to a stop.

All of it, from collision to the opposite side of the building, took less time than it takes to catch a breath, and in his last moments, Atta wondered if that was all he'd done, merely gashing a hole through one wall. Then suddenly a roaring noise rose up around him. The seat on which Atta sat gave a shudder. Something white-hot and sharp pierced his right buttock and sliced through his hip. Pain shot through his body but no sooner had he felt it, orange and red flames swirled around him and it was instantly hotter than he'd ever known before. The skin on his arms seemed to bubble. Liquid inside his eyes burned the skin of his cheeks, but before he could cry out in agony, a steel beam came crashing through the top of the cockpit. The edge of it struck his forehead, ripping the top of his skull open from front to back, just above his ears.

✦ ✦ ✦ ✦ ✦

After years of service, first at the Islamic Central Institute in Berlin, then with the mosque in Munich, and later at the one in Hamburg, Kazim was growing old. He was also tired. Work at the mosque, teaching the classes Salama began, reminding students of the links between the Quran, Islam, and Nazi hatred for the Jews had become a wearisome task for him. Not the concepts or principles—he still very much believed in them—but the constant work required to prepare for class and the necessity of being there was no longer a joy for him. Repeated trips to Afghanistan had further drained him. During his most recent journey he had become ill, and only in the last month had he come to feel as good as he did before he left.

Now, with the energy slowly leaving his body, Kazim spent much of his time gazing out the window, thinking of the past. And sipping from a cup of coffee. He was doing just that late in the afternoon of September 11, when the door opened and one of the young men burst into the room. "Come!" he shouted. "Come quickly." His voice was loud and the expression on his face was one of excitement and glee.

"I'm resting," Kazim sighed, his eyes still focused out the window to a point in the distance.

"You must come," the young man repeated. "Quickly! Quickly!" He took hold of Kazim's arm and tugged at it to urge him along.

Reluctantly, Kazim set the cup on the ledge by the window and stood, then followed the young man out the door. They continued up the hall to a room where a laptop sat on a table. Images from the screen seemed to show a building on fire. Kazim wondered where it was located, but the screen was too far away for him to make out the details.

"Here," the young man pulled a chair up to the table. "Sit here." He gestured to the chair, and Kazim slowly settled onto it. Closer now, he saw that the images on the screen were of a building in New York City. "What has happened?" he asked, pointing.

"Atta," someone spoke.

Kazim was bewildered. "Atta?"

"Yes," the person next to him replied. "Mohamed Atta."

Kazim was startled and his eyes opened wide. "Mohamed Atta? From the classes?"

"Yes." The person next to him nodded enthusiastically. "From the classes you taught, right here at this mosque."

Kazim pointed to the screen. "He did this?"

"He and others who were with him," someone explained.

"Those friends of his who used to come to the classes," the first one reported excitedly. "They flew an airplane into that building."

"Atta hit the North Tower of the World Trade Center," someone added. "In New York City."

"Someone else flew a plane into the South Tower," another yelled.

Both buildings were on fire, but as they watched, the top of the North Tower seemed to descend straight down, and as Kazim stared at it he realized the building was collapsing. A cloud of dust rose in the air and in no time at all, the building was reduced to a giant pile of rubble.

Cheers went up around him, but Kazim sat motionless, his eyes glued to the screen. His mind, though, was far away, lost in the memory of the days he spent teaching at the Al-Qaeda camp high in the mountains of Afghanistan, planning with Khalid Sheikh Mohammed for just such a day as this.

Tears filled Kazim's eyes, then slowly streamed down both cheeks and as they did, he whispered to himself, "The planes."

Acknowledgments

My deepest gratitude and sincere thanks to my writing partner, Joe Hilley, and to my executive assistants, Lanelle Shaw-Young and Dillon Burroughs, who work diligently to turn my story ideas into great books. And to Arlen Young, Peter Glöege, and Janna Nysewander for making the finished product look and read its best. And always, to my wife, Carolyn, whose presence makes everything better.

BOOKS BY: MIKE EVANS

Presidents in Prophecy

Stand with Israel

Prayer, Power and Purpose

Turning Your Pain Into Gain

Christopher Columbus, Secret Jew

Living in the F.O.G.

Finding Favor with God

Finding Favor with Man

Unleashing God's Favor

The Jewish State: The Volunteers

See You in New York

Friends of Zion:Patterson & Wingate

The Columbus Code

The Temple

Satan, You Can't Have My Country!

Satan, You Can't Have Israel!

Lights in the Darkness

The Seven Feasts of Israel

Netanyahu (a novel)

Jew-Hatred and the Church

The Visionaries

Why Was I Born?

Son, I Love You

Jerusalem DC (David's Capital)

Israel Reborn

Prayer: A Conversation with God

Shimon Peres (a novel)

Pursuing God's Presence

Ho Feng Shan (a novel)

The Good Father

The Daniel Option (a novel)

Keep the Jews Out! (a novel)

Donald Trump and Israel

A Great Awakening Is Coming!

Finding God in the Plague

Hitler, The Muslim Brotherhood, and 9/11

TO PURCHASE, CONTACT: orders@TimeWorthyBooks.com
P. O. BOX 30000, PHOENIX, AZ 85046

MICHAEL DAVID EVANS, the #1 *New York Times* bestselling author, is an award-winning journalist/Middle East analyst. Dr. Evans has appeared on hundreds of network television and radio shows including *Good Morning America, Crossfire* and *Nightline,* and *The Rush Limbaugh Show,* and on Fox Network, *CNN World News,* NBC, ABC, and CBS. His articles have been published in the *Wall Street Journal, USA Today, Washington Times, Jerusalem Post* and newspapers worldwide. More than twenty-five million copies of his books are in print, and he is the award-winning producer of nine documentaries based on his books.

Dr. Evans is considered one of the world's leading experts on Israel and the Middle East, and is one of the most sought-after speakers on that subject. He is the chairman of the board of the ten Boom Holocaust Museum in Haarlem, Holland, and is the founder of Israel's first Christian museum located in the Friends of Zion Heritage Center in Jerusalem.

Dr. Evans has authored 106 books including: *History of Christian Zionism, Showdown with Nuclear Iran, Atomic Iran, The Next Move Beyond Iraq, The Final Move Beyond Iraq,* and *Countdown.* His body of work also includes the novels *Seven Days, GameChanger, The Samson Option, The Four Horsemen, The Locket, Born Again: 1967,* and *The Columbus Code.*

✦ ✦ ✦

Michael David Evans is available to speak or for interviews.

Contact: EVENTS@drmichaeldevans.com.